Remains of Innocence

Remains of Innocence

J. A. Jance

HARPER LUXE

An Imprint of HarperCollins*Publishers*

REMAINS OF INNOCENCE. Copyright © 2014 by J. A. Jance. All rights reserved. Printed in the United States of America. No part of this book may be used or reproduced in any manner whatsoever without written permission except in the case of brief quotations embodied in critical articles and reviews. For information address HarperCollins Publishers, 195 Broadway, New York, NY 10007.

HarperCollins books may be purchased for educational, business, or sales promotional use. For information, please e-mail the Special Markets Department at SPsales@harpercollins.com.

FIRST HARPERLUXE EDITION

HarperLuxe™ is a trademark of HarperCollins Publishers

Library of Congress Cataloging-in-Publication Data is available upon request.

ISBN: 978-0-06-232642-3

14 ID/RRD 10 9 8 7 6 5 4 3 2 1

In honor of the Hotshots, twenty good men and true,
and to Marty Gossenauer, because I felt like it

Remains of Innocence

Prologue

Liza Machett's heart was filled with equal parts dread and fury as she pulled her beater Nissan into the rutted driveway of her mother's place, stopped, and then stepped out to stare at the weedy wasteland surrounding the crumbling farmhouse. In the eleven years since Liza had left home, the place that had once been regarded as messy or junky had become a scene of utter desolation.

Spring had come early to western Massachusetts and to the small plot of land outside Great Barrington that had been in her father's family for generations. Liza had heard that in a much earlier time, while her great-grandparents had lived there, both the house and the yard had been immaculate. People said Great-Grandma Machett herself had tended the garden full of prize-winning roses that had surrounded the front porch. Shunning help from anyone, she had donned an old-fashioned homemade bonnet and spent hours toiling in the yard, mowing the grass with a push-powered mower.

Great-Grandma Machett had been gone for decades now, and so was all trace of her hard work and industry. Thickets of brambles and weeds had overrun the grass and choked out the roses. Long ago a swing had graced the front porch. Swinging on that with her much older brother, Guy, was one of Liza's few happy childhood memories. The swing was gone. All that remained of it were two rusty chains that dangled uselessly from eyebolts still screwed into the ceiling boards. As for the porch itself? It sagged in the middle, and the three wooden steps leading up to the front door were completely missing, making the door inaccessible.

As a consequence, Liza walked around the side of the house toward the back. On the way, she tried peering into the house through one of the grimy storm windows that had been left in place for years, but the interior view was obstructed by old-fashioned wooden window blinds that had been lowered to window-sill level and closed tight against the outside world. A shiver of understanding shot through Liza's body, even though the afternoon sun was warm on her skin. The blinds existed for two reasons: to keep prying eyes outside and to keep her mother's darkness inside. Liza was tempted to turn back, but she squared her shoulders and kept on walking.

In the backyard, the freestanding wood-framed one-car garage, set away from the house, had collapsed in on itself long ago, taking Selma's ancient Oldsmobile with it. That was the car Liza remembered riding in as a child—a late-1970s, two-toned cream-and-burgundy Cutlass that had once been her father's. Somewhere along the way, her mother had parked the Cutlass in the garage and told her children that the car quit working. Liza thought she had been in the third grade when her mother had announced that they no longer needed a car. From then on, Liza and Guy had been responsible for their own transportation needs—they could catch the bus, ride their bikes, or, worst case, walk. Now the vehicle was a rusted-out hulk with only a corner of the back bumper still visible through pieces of the splintered garage door. Looking at the wreckage, Liza wondered if her life would have been different had the car kept running. After all, that was about the same time her mother had turned into a recluse and stopped leaving the house.

The only outbuilding that seemed to be in any kind of reasonable repair was the outhouse. The well-trod footpath to it led through an otherwise impenetrable jungle of weeds and brambles. Liza had hated the outhouse growing up. The smell had been vile; the spiders that lurked in the corners and would swing down on cobwebs in front of her eyes had terrified her. The presence of the path told her that the anachronistic outhouse, probably one of the last ones in the county, was still in daily use. That made sense. The social worker had told her that Selma's electricity had been turned off months ago due to lack of payment. Without electricity to run the pump at the well, the house would no longer have any indoor plumbing, either.

Liza's father had left when she was a baby. She didn't remember ever having met him, but she had heard stories about how, decades earlier, he and his father, working together, had remodeled the place for his widowed grandmother, bringing the miracle of running water and indoor toilets into the house. Legend had it Great-Grandma Machett had stubbornly insisted on using the outhouse and on keeping the hand pump at the kitchen sink that drew water from a cistern near the house. If that hand pump was, through some miracle, still in operation, it was probably the only running water Liza's mother had.

"Stubborn old bat," Liza muttered under her breath.

She had never admitted to the kids at school that they used an outhouse at home. Guy hadn't told anyone about that, either. Once Great-Grandma Machett passed on, they had moved into her place, and after Liza's father left, the only bathroom in the house had become Selma's private domain. No one else was allowed to use it because, she had insisted, running all that water through the faucets and down the toilet was a waste of electricity and a waste of money.

"We're too poor to send money down the drain like that," her mother had insisted. "I'm not going to waste the pittance your no-good father left me on that."

That meant that the whole time Liza and Guy were in grade school, they had been forced to do their sponge-bath bathing at the kitchen sink. That was where they had hand-washed their clothing as well. All that had been doable until the hot water heater had given out, sometime during Liza's last year of elementary school. After that it had been cold water only, because heating water on top of the stove for baths or for washing clothes had been deemed another extravagant waste of electricity and money.

Liza remembered all too well the jeering boys on the grade-school playground who had bullied her, calling her "stinky" and "dirty." The stigma stayed with her. It was why, even now, she showered twice a day every day—once in the morning when she first got up, and again in the evening after she got home from work.

Gathering herself, Liza turned to face the back door of the house she hadn't stepped inside for more than a decade, even though the place where she lived now was, as the crow flies, less than five miles away. Looking up, she noticed that, in places, the moss-covered roof was completely devoid of shingles. Just last year, Olivia Dexter, her landlady in town, had replaced the roof over Liza's upstairs apartment in Great Barrington. That roof hadn't been nearly as bad as this one was, but Liza had seen firsthand the damage a leaky roof could do to ceilings and walls and insulation. How, she wondered, had her mother made it through the harsh New England winter weather with no electricity and barely any roof?

Liza's mission today was in her mother's kitchen, and that was where she would go. The disaster that inevitably awaited her in the rest of the house would have to be dealt with at a later time. She remembered all too well the narrow paths between towering stacks of newspapers and magazines that had filled the living room back when she was a girl. Maybe all those layers of paper had provided a modicum of insulation during the winters. Even so, Liza wasn't ready to deal with any of that now, not yet.

Liza made her way up the stairs and then stood for a moment with her hand on the doorknob, willing herself to find the courage to open it. She knew how bad the place had been eleven years earlier, on that distant morning when she had finally had enough and fled the house. Rather than facing it, she paused, unable to imagine how much worse it would be now and allowing a kaleidoscope of unwelcome recollections to flash in and out of focus.

The memory of leaving home that day was still vivid in her mind and heart, even all these years later. Her mother had stood on the front porch screaming taunts and insults at Liza as she had walked away, carrying all her worldly possessions in a single paper grocery bag. She had walked down the half-mile-long driveway with her eyes straight ahead and her back ramrod straight. There were still times, when she awakened in the middle of the night, that she could hear echoes of her mother's venomous shouts—*worthless slut, no-good liar, thief.* The ugly words had rained down steadily as she walked away until finally fading out of earshot.

Liza Machett had heard the old childhood rhyme often enough:

Sticks and stones may break my bones
But names will never hurt me.

That was a lie. Being called names did hurt, and the wounds left behind never really healed over. Liza's heart still bore the scars to prove it. She had learned through bitter experience that silence was the best way to deal with her mother's periodic outbursts. The problem was, silence went only so far in guaranteeing her safety. There were times when even maintaining a discreet silence hadn't been enough to protect Liza from her mother's seething anger.

Liza understood that, on that fateful day, a pummeling from her mother's fists would have come next had she not simply taken herself out of the equation. Their final confrontation had occurred just after sunrise on a warm day in May. It was the morning after Liza's high school graduation, an event that had gone totally unacknowledged as far as Selma Machett was concerned. Liza's mother, trapped in a debilitating web of ailments both real and imagined, hadn't bestirred herself to attend. When Liza had returned home late that night, dropped off by one of her classmates after attending a graduation party, Selma had been waiting up and had been beyond enraged when Liza came in a little after three. Selma had claimed that Liza had never told her about the party and that she'd been up all night frantic with worry and convinced that Liza had really been out "sleeping around."

For Liza, a girl who had never been out on a single date all through high school, that last insult had been the final straw. A few hours later, shortly after sunrise, Liza had quietly packed her bag to leave and had tiptoed to the door, hoping that her mother was still asleep. Unfortunately, Selma had been wide awake and still furious. She had hurled invectives after her departing daughter as Liza walked across the front porch and down the steps. The porch had still had steps back then.

Liza walked briskly away with her head unbowed beneath Selma's barrage of insults. At the time, Liza's only consolation was that there were no neighbors nearby to witness her mother's final tirade. Walking away from the house, Liza had realized that she was literally following in her older brother's footsteps and doing the same thing Guy had done five years earlier. He had walked away, taking only what he could carry, and he hadn't looked back.

Liza had been thirteen years old and in eighth grade on the day Guy left home for college. A friend had stopped by shortly after he graduated and given him a lift and a life. During the summer he had waited tables in the Poconos. Then, armed with a full-ride scholarship, he had enrolled at Harvard, which was only a little over a hundred miles away. As far as Liza was concerned, however, Harvard could just as well have been on another planet. Guy had never come back—not over

Christmas that first year nor for any of the Christmases that followed, and not for summer vacations, either. From Harvard he had gone on to Maryland for medical school at Johns Hopkins. Unlike Guy, all Liza had to show for enduring years of her mother's torment was a high school diploma and a severe case of low self-esteem.

Did Liza resent her brother's seemingly charmed existence? You bet! It was perfectly understandable that he had turned his back on their mother. Who wouldn't? Liza remembered all too well the blazing battles between the two of them in the months and weeks before Guy left home. She also recalled her brother's departing words, flung over his shoulder as he walked out the door. "You're not my real mother."

Those words had been true for him, and that was his out—Selma was Guy's stepmother. Unfortunately, she was Liza's "real" mother. Half brother or not, however, Guy had always been Liza's big brother. In walking away from Selma, he had also walked away from Liza. He had left her alone to cope with a mentally damaged, self-centered woman who was incapable of loving or caring for anyone, including herself.

All the while Liza had been growing up, there had been no accounting for Selma's many difficulties, both mental and physical, real and imagined. There had been wild mood swings that most likely indicated Selma was bipolar—not that she'd ever gone to a doctor or a counselor to be given an official diagnosis. There had been episodes of paranoia in which Selma had spent days convinced that people from the government were spying on her. There was the time she had taken a pair of pliers to her own mouth and removed all the filled teeth because she was convinced the fillings were poisoning her. It wasn't until long after Liza left home that there was a name for the most visible of Selma's mental difficulties. She was a hoarder. Liza found it disquieting that hoarding was now something that could be spoken of aloud in polite company and that, in fact, there was even a reality television show devoted to the problem.

Liza had watched the show occasionally, with a weird combination of horror and relief, but she had never found a way to say to any of the people who knew her now, "That was my life when I was growing up." Instead, like a voyeur driving past a terrible car wreck, she watched the various dysfunctional families on the small screen struggling with issues she knew intimately, from the inside out. In the well-ordered neatness of her own living room, she could compare what she remembered of her mother's house with the messes and horrors in other people's lives, all the while imagining what Selma's place must be like now after another decade of unchecked decline.

Sometimes what she saw on one of the shows moved her to tears. Occasionally the televised efforts of loved ones and therapists seemed to pay off and damaged people seemed to find ways to begin confronting what was wrong with their lives and perhaps make some necessary changes. With others, however, it was hopeless, and all the painful efforts came to naught. The people trying to help would throw things in the trash—broken toys, wrecked furniture, nonworking appliances—only to have the hoarder drag the garbage back into the house because it was too precious to be tossed out.

For her part, Liza suspected that Selma was one of the ones who wouldn't be helped or fixed. She doubted her mother would ever change, and Liza knew for a fact that she had neither the strength nor the will to force the issue. If Guy had offered to come home and help her? Maybe. But all on her own? No way.

As a teenager, Liza had dealt with the shame of how they lived—the grinding poverty and the utter filth of their existence—as best she could. She had put up with her mother's ever-declining health and occassional screaming rages. Liza's smallest efforts to clean anything up or throw away one of her mother's broken treasures had been met with increasingly violent outbursts on her mother's part. Liza understood now that she most likely wouldn't have survived high school had it not been for the timely intervention of first one and subsequently several of her teachers.

It had been at the end of phys ed during the first week of her freshman year. After class, some of the girls had been taunting Liza about being dirty when Miss Rose had come into the locker room unannounced and heard what they were saying. She had told Liza's tormentors to knock it off and had sent them packing. Ashamed to show her face, Liza had lingered behind, but when she came out of the locker room, Miss Rose had been waiting for her in the gym.

"How would you like a job?" she had asked.

"What do you mean, a job?" Liza had stammered.

"I need someone to come in after school each afternoon to wash and fold the towels," Miss Rose said. "I couldn't pay you much, say ten bucks a week or so, but you'd be able to shower by yourself and wash your own clothes along with the towels."

That was all Miss Rose ever said about it. Liza didn't know how Miss Rose had known so much about her situation. Maybe she had grown up in the same kind of squalor or with the same kind of mother. Not long after that, some of the coaches of the boys' sports teams had asked Liza to handle their team laundry needs as well.

Eventually she had been given her own key to both the gym and the laundry. She spent cold winter afternoons and hot spring days in the comforting damp warmth of the gym's laundry room, doing her homework, turning jumbles of dirty towels and uniforms into neat stacks and washing her own clothing at the same time. As for the money she earned? The collective fifty dollars a week she got for her efforts from various teachers and coaches, all of it paid in cash, was money that Liza's mother never knew about, and it made all the difference. It meant that Liza was able to eat breakfast and lunch in the school cafeteria rather than having to go hungry.

In the end, Liza had done the same thing her brother did—she left. But she didn't go nearly as far as her brother's hundred miles. Guy had been brilliant. Liza was not. Her mediocre grades weren't good enough for the kind of scholarship help that would have made college possible, but her work record with the coaches and teachers had counted as enough of a reference that she'd been able to land a job in Candy's, a local diner, the first week she was on her own. She had started out washing dishes and had worked her way up to waitress, hostess, and finally—for the last year—assistant manager. Candy had taught her enough about food handling that, in a pinch, she could serve as a passable short-order cook. She didn't earn a lot of money, but it was enough to make her self-supporting.

Liza's car was a ten-year-old rusted-out wreck of a Nissan, but it was paid for and it still ran. That was all she needed. Her home was a tiny upstairs apartment in an old house off Main Street in Great Barrington. It could be freezing cold in the winter and unbearably hot in the summer, as it was right now in this unseasonably late April heat wave, but the apartment was Liza's and Liza's alone, and she kept it immaculately clean.

She never left home in the morning without first washing and drying the dishes. Her bed was made as soon as she climbed out of it. Her dirty clothes went in a hamper, and when she came back from the Laundromat, her clean clothes went in dresser drawers or on hangers. Her floors were clean. Her trash always went out on time. There was never even so much as a hint of mouse droppings in the freshly laundered towels she took out of her tiny linen closet and held up to her face.

Driving out to her mother's place from the hospital that morning, Liza had measured the distance on the odometer. She had been surprised to realize that the hospital was a mere four miles and her apartment only another mile beyond that from her mother's squalid farmhouse. Somehow, in all the intervening years, she had imagined the distance to be much greater. She had always told herself that she would never go back, no matter what, and she hadn't—not until today. Not until a social worker had tracked her down at work and given her the bad news.

Selma had evidently fallen. Unable to get up, she hadn't been found for a number of days. A postman had finally notified someone that her mail was piling up in the mailbox at the end of the driveway, and a uniformed deputy had been dispatched to do a welfare check. Selma had been found unconscious on the floor of a room that bore no resemblance to a living room. Revived at the scene, she had been forcibly removed from her house and taken by ambulance to the hospital. Selma was currently in the ICU where doctors were doing their best to rehydrate her with IV fluids and nourishment. Liza had been told that Selma was in stable condition, but the social worker had made it plain that the outlook wasn't good. Despite her relatively young age—Selma was only fifty-seven—her emphysema was much worse, and her next stop would most likely be a bed in the hospice care unit of the Sunset Nursing Home. The end might come in as little as a few days or a few weeks at the most.

Hearing the news, Liza tried to feel sorry for her mother, but she could not. The woman had brought it on through years of chain-smoking and neglecting her health. Liza had always told herself that as far as her mother was concerned, she was done; that if Selma ever needed help, Liza wouldn't go—wouldn't cross the street or lift a finger to help her mother, but when push came to shove, Liza had caved.

The social worker had come by the diner to let Liza know. Before the social worker had finished telling her what had happened, Liza had her phone in hand and was dialing her boss's home number to let Candy know that she was going to need someone else to cover her shifts for the next few days. Within forty-five minutes, she had turned up at the ICU, as dutiful as any loving daughter. She rushed down the polished corridor to Selma's room as though there hadn't been a lifetime's worth of bad history and eleven years of total estrangement between them.

And what had Liza expected for her trouble? Maybe she hoped the long-delayed reunion with her mother would turn into one of those schmaltzy Hallmark moments, with Selma reaching out to embrace her daughter and saying how precious Liza was; how much she had missed her; how glad she was to see her; how sorry she was for all the awful things she had said those many years ago. Of course, that wasn't what happened—not at all.

Selma Machett's eyes had popped open when Liza warily approached her mother's bedside.

"Where've you been?" Selma demanded. "What took you so long? I told them not to do it, but those stupid jerks in the ambulance brought me here anyway. And when I told them I needed my cookbook, they couldn't be bothered. You know the one I mean—my old *Joy of Cooking*. I need it right now. I want you to go to the house and get it—you and nobody else."

No, not a Hallmark moment by any means. Liza understood full well that her mother simply issued orders rather than making requests. *Please* and *Thank you* weren't part of Selma's vocabulary. Liza also knew that her mother had a vast collection of cookbooks, moldering in her filthy kitchen. Not that she'd ever used any of them. In fact, Liza couldn't remember her mother ever cooking a single meal. All the while Liza was growing up, they'd survived on take-out food, burgers and pizza that her mother had somehow managed to pay for. Afterward, the wrappers and boxes, sometimes with stray pieces of pizza still inside, were left to rot where they fell.

Even though Liza knew it to be a futile exercise, she attempted to reason with her mother. "Look, Mom," she said placatingly. "They have a very good kitchen here at the hospital. You don't need a cookbook. When it's time for you to eat, they'll bring your food on a tray."

"I don't care about that," Selma snapped. "I want my cookbook, and I want it now. The key's still where it's always been, under the mat on the back porch. Go now. Be quick about it."

Which is exactly how Liza came to be here. When she lifted the mat, it disintegrated in her hands, falling in a brittle heap of disconnected rubbery links on the top step. After inserting the key and turning it in the lock, Liza stood on the far side of the door for the better part of five minutes, trying to summon the courage to venture inside.

Knowing that the power was off and that the inside of the house would be beyond filthy, Liza had done what she could to come prepared. She had stowed a small jar of Vicks in her purse. She had stopped at the drugstore and bought a package of face masks and a box of surgical gloves. Finally, after dabbing the eye-watering salve under her nostrils and donning both a mask and a pair of gloves, she opened the door.

No amount of advance warning could have prepared her. The stench was unimaginable. Covering her face with her hand, Liza fell backward and fought, unsuccessfully, to push down the bile that rose in her throat. Giving up, she clung to the crooked porch rail and heaved the hamburger she had eaten for lunch into a waist-high mound of moldering trash that had accumulated next to the steps.

At last, wiping her mouth on the tail of her blouse and steeling herself for another assault on her senses, Liza edged the door open again. To begin with, that was all she could do—crack it open. A heaping wall of rotting garbage, this one stacked almost ceiling high, kept the door from swinging open completely. As Liza sidled into the room, finger-sized roaches and fist-sized spiders scurried for cover.

Selma had always been a chain-smoker. Underlying everything else was the stench of decades' worth of unfiltered Camels, but that was only in the background. In the foreground were the unmistakable odors of rotting garbage and of death. Liza chalked up the latter to some dead varmint—a rat or mouse perhaps—or maybe a whole crew of them whose decaying corpses were buried somewhere under the mounds of trash.

Leaving the back door open, Liza stepped gingerly into the room, sticking to a narrow path that meandered through the almost unrecognizable kitchen between unstable cliffs of what looked to her like nothing but refuse. The mountains of garbage were tall enough that they obscured the windows, leaving the room in a hazy gloom. Although Liza knew this to be the kitchen, there was no longer any sign of either a stove or a sink. If her great-grandmother's hand pump still existed, it was invisible, completely buried under masses of debris. The refrigerator was hidden behind another evil-smelling mound. Standing on tiptoe, Liza saw that the door to the freezer compartment was propped open, revealing a collection of long-abandoned contents, their labels indecipherable behind a thick layer of mold. Next to the fridge was the tall stand-alone bookcase that held her mother's cookbooks. She could see the books, their titles completely obscured behind a thick curtain of undisturbed spiderwebs.

There were few things in life that Liza hated more than spiders and their sticky webs. These were clotted with the desiccated corpses of countless insects who had mistakenly ventured into the forest of silky threads and died for their trouble. Liza knew that hidden behind the layer of webs was the book she was charged with retrieving. If she squinted, she could almost make out the bright red letters of the title through the scrim of fibers.

Gritting her teeth, Liza pushed the webs aside far enough to reach the book. She had the cover in her hand when a spider glided down a web and landed on her arm. Screaming and leaping backward, Liza dropped the book and, with a desperate whack from the back of her hand, sent the startled spider sailing across the room. When Liza looked down, she saw that the book had landed spine up on the floor, sitting like a little tent pitched on the dirty floor among an accumulation of mouse turds. And scattered across the filthy floor around the half-opened book were what appeared to be five one-hundred-dollar bills.

For a moment, Liza could barely believe what she was seeing. Squatting down, she picked them up one at a time. The unaccustomed gloves on her hands made for clumsy fingers, and it didn't help that her hands were shaking. She examined the bills. They looked real enough, but where had they come from, and what were they doing in Selma's copy of *Joy of Cooking*?

Stuffing the bills in the pocket of her jeans, Liza picked up the book itself. Holding it by the spine, she flapped the pages in the air. As she did so, two more bills fluttered out from between the pages and drifted to the floor.

Liza was amazed. Seven hundred dollars had been hidden in one of her mother's cookbooks! Where had the money come from? How long had it been there? Had her mother kept the bills squirreled away the whole time Liza had been growing up—the whole time she was struggling to fit in at school while wearing thrift shop clothing and buying her school lunches with money she had earned by doing sports teams' laundry? Had there been money hiding in her mother's cookbook even then? And if there were seven hundred dollars in this one book, what about the others? Was money concealed in those as well?

Using the book in her hand, Liza swept away the remaining spiderwebs and reached for another book. The two mammoth volumes next to the empty spot left behind by the absent *Joy* turned out to be Julia Child's *Mastering the Art of French Cooking,* Volumes 1 and 2. A quick shuffle through the 652 pages of Volume 1 was good for five hundred bucks. Ditto for Volume 2. With close to two thousand dollars now crammed in her pocket, Liza reached for the next book on the shelf: *Betty Crocker's Quick and Easy.* A thorough examination of that one surfaced only three hundred dollars, but by the time Liza had worked her way through the entire collection, she had amassed close to thirty thousand dollars. It was more money in one place than Liza had ever seen in her life, more money than she had ever thought her mother had to her name.

At last the bookshelf was cleared. The cookbooks, plucked clean of their hidden treasure, lay in a careless heap on the floor. During the search, Liza had gone from first being surprised and amazed to being beyond furious. The more money she found, the more she wondered if the small fortune in hidden bills had been in Selma's possession the whole time. If so, why had Selma always pretended to be poor? Why had she denied her children and herself simple creature comforts like running water and hot baths that some of that money might have afforded all of them?

As a teenager, Liza had never thought to question the fact that they were poor. Their poverty was an all too demonstrable reality. She had listened in silence while her mother bewailed their fate, complaining about their lot and blaming the fact that Liza's father had run off—presumably with another woman—leaving them with barely a roof over their heads and not much else. Liza knew from something her brother had said that before Anson Machett bailed, he'd at least had the decency to quitclaim the family home—the farm and the run-down house that had belonged to his great-grandparents—to his soon-to-be-abandoned wife. Before Guy left home, Selma had told the kids that their father was dead, having died in a car wreck somewhere in California. Selma had offered no details about a memorial service or a funeral. First their father was gone and then he was dead.

Now, at age twenty-nine and standing in the desolation of Selma's filthy kitchen, Liza Machett found herself asking for the very first time if anything her mother had told them was true. If Selma had lied to them about being poor, maybe she had lied about everything else, too.

After gathering the last of the money from the books, Liza stayed in the kitchen for a long time, too stunned to know what to do next. Should she go to the hospital and confront her mother about all this? Should she demand to be told the truth, once and for all?

Ultimately Liza realized that a direct confrontation would never work. Instead, she reached down, pawed through the pile of books, and retrieved the one at the bottom of the heap—the *Joy of Cooking*. Pulling the thick wad of bills from her pocket, she extracted seven of them and placed them in various spots throughout the book. If Selma remembered the exact pages where she had stuck the money, then Liza was screwed. Otherwise, Liza could hand the book over to Selma and act as though she hadn't a clue that there was money hidden inside.

She hoped the trick would work. If Selma didn't realize Liza had discovered her secret, it would buy Liza time—time to look for answers on her own and to sift through the rest of the debris in the house. Liza knew that once she reached the living room, she would find stacks of back issues of *National Geographic*, *Life*, and *Reader's Digest* as well. What if those had all been seeded with money in the same way the cookbooks had? There was only one way to find out for sure, and Liza was determined to do so—she intended to search through every single one.

Back outside with the cookbook in hand, Liza stripped off her mask and gloves and drew in a deep breath of clean fresh air. Her Nissan, parked at the end of the driveway, sat unlocked and with the windows wide open. Leaving the windows open kept the interior from getting too hot. That was important especially during hot weather since the Nissan's AC had stopped working long ago.

Liza dropped the book on the passenger seat before going around to the other side to climb in. When she turned to fasten her seat belt, the tail end of her ponytail swished in front of her face. That's when she smelled it—the same pungent combination of foul odors that had plagued her as a girl and that had been the cause of so much painful bullying from the other kids. The odor of decay in her mother's home had somehow permeated Liza's hair and clothing. She could barely tolerate sitting in the car knowing that she was probably leaving the same stinky residue on the car seats and carpeting.

Hating the very idea, Liza headed for her apartment rather than for the hospital. She would go see her mother and deliver the book, but only after she had showered and washed her hair. Looking at the book, she realized it probably smelled the same way. Once she hit Great Barrington, she pulled in to the drive-in window of the local Dunkin' Donuts and ordered a bag of their Breakfast Blend coffee beans. She had heard that coffee beans helped get rid of bad smells. It seemed worth a try.

At home, Liza located a gallon-sized Ziploc bag. She placed the book inside that along with all the bills she had stuffed in her pockets. Then, having added the whole beans, she zipped the bag shut before going into the bathroom to shower.

She stood under the stream of hot water for the next fifteen minutes, trying to wash away the dirt and grit from her mother's house. With her eyes closed, she hoped she was washing off something else as well—the soul-destroying contamination of her mother's many betrayals.

She needed to send Selma Machett's perfidy circling down the drain every bit as much as she needed to rid herself of the odor of mouse droppings and rotting food that, despite all her scrubbing, still seemed to cling to her skin.

Chapter 1

The sun was just coming up over the distant Chiricahua Mountains to the east of High Lonesome Ranch when a rooster crowed at ten past five in the morning. At that hour of the day, it might have been one of the ranch's live resident roosters announcing the arrival of a new day, but it wasn't. This was the obnoxiously distinctive crowing of Sheriff Joanna Brady's cell phone.

Groping for the device in its charging stand on the bedside table, Joanna silenced the racket and glanced across the bed. Her husband, Butch, slept undisturbed with a pillow pulled over his head. Taking the phone in hand, Joanna scrambled out of bed. Now that Lady, her rescued Australian shepherd, had decamped to a spot next to Joanna's son's bed, she no longer had to deal with tripping over a dead-to-the-world dog when it came to late-night callouts, which usually meant there was serious trouble somewhere in Cochise County.

Hurrying into the bathroom and closing the door behind her, Joanna answered, "Sheriff Brady."

"Chief Bernard here," a male voice rumbled in her ear. "Sorry to wake you at this ungodly hour, but I could sure use your K-9 unit if you can spare them."

Alvin Bernard was the police chief in Bisbee, Arizona. Once known as a major copper-producing town, Bisbee's current claim to fame was its reputation as an arts colony. It was also the county seat. Alvin Bernard's departmental jurisdiction ended at Bisbee's city limits, the line where Joanna's countywide jurisdiction began.

Years earlier, Joanna had been elected to the office of sheriff in the aftermath of her first husband's death. Andy Brady had been running for the office when he died in a hail of bullets from a drug cartel's hit man. When Joanna was elected sheriff in her late husband's stead, members of the local law enforcement old boys' network had sneered at the outcome, regarding her election as a straight-up sympathy vote, and had expected Joanna to be sheriff in name only. She had surprised the naysayers by transforming herself into a professional police officer. As she developed a reputation for being a good cop, that initial distrust had melted away.

She now had a cordial working relationship with most of her fellow police administrators, including Bisbee's Chief Bernard.

"What's up?"

"Junior Dowdle's gone missing from his folks' house up the canyon. He left his room sometime overnight by climbing out through a bedroom window. His bed hasn't been slept in. Daisy's frantic. She and Moe have been up and down the canyon several times looking for him. So far there's no trace."

Junior, Moe and Daisy Maxwell's developmentally disabled foster son, had been found abandoned by his paid caregiver at a local arts fair several years earlier. Once his blood relatives were located, they had declined to take him back. That was when the Maxwells had stepped in. They had gone to court and been appointed his legal guardians. Since then they had cared for Junior as their own, giving him purpose in life by teaching him to work as a combination busboy and greeter in the local diner that bore Daisy's name.

In recent months, though, Junior's behavior had become increasingly erratic, both at home and in the restaurant. Only a few weeks earlier the family had been given the dreaded but not-so-surprising diagnosis— not so surprising because the doctor had warned the Maxwells a year earlier about the possibility. Now in his early sixties, Junior was suffering from a form of dementia, most likely Alzheimer's, an affliction that often preyed on the developmentally disabled. Under most circumstances, a missing person report of an adult wouldn't have merited an immediate all-out response. Because Junior was considered to be at risk, however, all bets were off.

"He's on foot then?" Joanna asked.

"Unless some Good Samaritan picked him up and gave him a ride," Alvin answered.

"Okay," Joanna said. "I'll give Terry a call and see what, if anything, he and Spike can do about this."

Terry Gregovich was the human half of Joanna's departmental K-9 unit. Spike, a seven-year-old German shepherd, was Terry's aging canine partner.

"You're sure Junior left through a window?"

"Daisy told me they've been concerned about Junior maybe wandering off, so they've gotten into the habit of keeping both the front and back doors to the house dead-bolted. It was warm overnight, so Daisy left the window cracked open when Junior went to bed. Had Daisy Maxwell ever raised a teenage son, she would have known she needed to lock the window as well."

"That's how he got out?"

"Yup, it looks like Junior raised the window the rest of the way, pushed open the screen, and climbed out."

"Do you want me to see if I have any additional patrol officers in the neighborhood who could assist with the search?"

"That would be a huge favor," Alvin said. "We'll be using the parking lot of St. Dominick's as a center of operations. Once the neighbors hear about this, there will be plenty of folks willing to help out. From my point of view, the more boots we have on the ground, the better. It'll make our lives easier if Terry and Spike can point the search crews in the right direction."

"I'll have Dispatch get back to you and let you know if anyone else is available."

She called Terry first, dragging him out of bed, then she called Dispatch to let Tica Romero, her overnight dispatcher, know what was going on. The City of Bisbee and Cochise County had a standing mutual aid agreement in place, but it was better to have everything officially documented in case something went haywire. Mutual aid in the course of a hot pursuit was one matter. For anything else, Joanna had to be sure all the necessary chain-of-command t's were crossed and i's were dotted.

Butch came and went through the bathroom while Joanna was in the shower. Once dried off, she got dressed, donning a neatly pressed everyday khaki uniform and a lightweight pair of lace-up hiking boots.

Early on in her career as sheriff, she had worn business-style clothing, most of which couldn't accommodate the Kevlar vest she wore each day right along with her other officers. Then there was the matter of footwear. After going through countless pairs of pantyhose and wrecked pairs of high heels, she had finally conceded defeat, putting practicality ahead of fashion.

Minutes later, with her bright red hair blown dry and her minimally applied makeup in place, she hurried out to the kitchen, where she found Butch brewing coffee and unloading the dishwasher.

"What's up?" he asked.

"I'm on my way to St. Dominick's," she explained. "Junior Dowdle took off sometime overnight. Alvin Bernard is using the parking lot at St. Dom's as a center of operations, and he's asked for help from my K-9 unit."

Joanna knew that her husband maintained a personal interest in Junior's life and welfare. She and Butch hadn't been married when Junior first came to Bisbee after being abandoned at the Arts and Crafts Fair in Saint David. Bringing him to Bisbee in her patrol car, Joanna had been stumped about where to take him. Her own home was out. The poor man wasn't a criminal and he wasn't ill. That meant that neither the jail nor the hospital were possibilities, either. In the end, she had taken him to Butch's house in Bisbee's Saginaw neighborhood, where Junior had stayed for several weeks. A restaurant Butch had owned previously, the Roundhouse in Peoria, Arizona, had once fielded a Special Olympics team, and Butch had been one of the team coaches. He had taken charge of Junior with practiced grace and had kept him until more suitable permanent arrangements could be made with the Maxwells.

"You're going to join the search?" Butch asked, handing Joanna a cup of coffee.

She nodded.

"All right," he said. "If they haven't found Junior by the time I drop the kids off at school, I'll stop by and help, too. Do you want breakfast before you head out? It won't take more than a couple of minutes to fry eggs and make toast."

That was one of the advantages of marrying a man who had started out in life as a short-order cook. Joanna didn't have to think long before making up her mind. Depending on how her day went, the next opportunity to eat might be hours away. Besides, this was Alvin's case. She and her people were there as backup only. In addition, Butch's over-easy eggs were always perfection itself.

"Sounds good," she said. "Do you want any help?"

"I'm a man on a mission," Butch told her with a grin. "Sit down, drink your coffee, and stay out of the way."

Doing as she'd been told, Joanna slipped into the breakfast nook. She'd taken only a single sip of coffee when Dennis, their early-bird three-year-old, wandered into the kitchen dragging along both his favorite blankie and his favorite book—*The Cat in the Hat*. There wasn't a person in the household who didn't know the story by heart, but Joanna pulled him into a cuddle and started reading aloud, letting him turn the pages.

They were halfway through the story when two dogs scrambled into the kitchen—Jenny's stone-deaf black lab, Lucky, and a relatively new addition to their family, a fourteen-week-old golden retriever puppy named Desi. The puppy carried the tattered remains of one of Jenny's tennis shoes in his mouth. Both dogs dove for cover under the table of the breakfast nook as an exasperated Jenny, wearing a bathrobe and with her wet hair wrapped in a towel, appeared in the doorway.

"I was only in the shower for five minutes," she fumed. "That's all it took for Desi to wreck my shoe."

"Wait until you have kids of your own," Butch warned her. "Desi will be over it a lot faster than a baby will. Besides, it could have been worse. It's only a tennis shoe. When Lucky was a pup, he always grabbed one of your boots."

Leveling a sour look in Butch's direction, Jenny knelt down by the table. Rather than verbally scolding the miscreant puppy, she glowered at him and gave him two thumbs-down—her improvised sign language equivalent of "bad dog." Next she motioned toward her body with one hand, which meant "come." Finally she held out one cupped hand and patted the cupped one with her other hand, the hand signal for "give it to me."

There was a momentary pause under the table before Desi squirmed out from under his temporary shelter and handed over the mangled shoe. In response, Jenny gave him a single thumb-up for "good dog." Two thumbs would have meant "very good dog," and currently, no matter what he did right, Desi didn't qualify. Once the puppy had been somewhat forgiven, Lucky dared venture out, too. He was rewarded with the two-thumb treatment before Jenny took her damaged shoe in hand and left the room with both dogs on her heels.

Joanna couldn't help but marvel at how the hand signals Jenny had devised to communicate with Lucky were now making it possible for her to train a service dog as part of a 4-H project. There was the expectation that, at some time in the future, Desi would make a difference in some person's life by serving as a hearing assistance dog.

"Your breakfast is on the table in five," Butch called after Jenny as she left the room. "Two eggs scrambled, whole wheat toast. Don't be late."

"I'm afraid training that dog is more work than Jenny anticipated," Joanna commented. "After losing Tigger the way we did, I'm worried about her ability to let Desi go when it's time for him to move on." Tigger, their previous dog, a half golden retriever, half pit bull mix, had succumbed within weeks of being diagnosed with Valley Fever, a fungal disorder commonly found in the desert Southwest that often proved fatal to dogs.

"Jenny and I have already discussed that," Butch said, "but you're right. Talking about letting go of a dog is one thing. Handing the leash over to someone else is another."

Joanna nodded in agreement. "We all know that when it comes to horses and dogs, Jennifer Ann Brady has a very soft heart."

"Better horses and dogs than boys," Butch observed with a grin. "Way better."

That was a point on which Joanna and Butch were in complete agreement.

"Speaking of horses, did she already feed them?"

For years the horse population on High Lonesome Ranch had been limited to one—Kiddo, Jenny's sorrel gelding, who was also her barrel-racing partner. Recently they had added a second horse to the mix, an aging, blind Appaloosa mare that had been found, starving and dehydrated, in the corral of a recently foreclosed ranchette near Arizona Sunsites. The previous owners had simply packed up and left town, abandoning the horse to fend for herself. When a neighbor reported the situation, Joanna had dispatched one of her Animal Control officers to retrieve the animal.

After a round of veterinary treatment at county expense, Butch and Jenny had trailered the mare home to High Lonesome, where she seemed to have settled into what were supposedly temporary digs in the barn and corral, taking cues on her new surroundings from Kiddo while she gained weight and recovered. Dennis, after taking one look at the horse, had promptly dubbed her Spot.

In Joanna's opinion, Spot was a far better name for a dog than it was for a horse, but Spot she was, and Spot she remained. Currently inquiries were being made to find Spot a permanent home, but Joanna suspected that she had already found one. When Butch teased Joanna by saying she had turned High Lonesome Ranch into an unofficial extension of Cochise County Animal Control, it was more true than not. Most of the dogs that had come through their lives had been rescues, along with any number of cast-off Easter bunnies and Easter chicks. Now, having taken in a hearing impaired dog and a visually impaired horse, they were evidently a haven for stray animals with disabilities as well.

"The horses are fed," Butch answered. "Jenny and the dogs went out to do that while I was starting the coffee and you were in the shower."

By the time Jenny and the now more subdued dogs returned to the kitchen, Joanna was ready to head out. After delivering quick good-bye kisses all around, she went to the laundry room to retrieve and don her weapons. For Mother's Day a few weeks earlier, Butch had installed a thumb recognition gun safe just inside the door. Located below a light switch, it was within easy reach for Joanna's vertically challenged five-foot-four frame. With her two Glocks safely stowed—one in a holster on her belt and the other, her backup weapon, in a bra-style holster—Sheriff Joanna Brady was ready to face her day.

It generally took the better part of ten minutes for Joanna to drive her county-owned Yukon the three miles of combination dirt and paved roads between High Lonesome Ranch at the base of the Mule Mountains and her office at the Cochise County Justice Center. In this instance she drove straight past her office on Highway 80 and headed into Bisbee proper. St. Dominick's Church, up the canyon in Old Bisbee, was another four miles beyond that.

The time Joanna spent in her car each day gave her a buffer between her job and her busy home life. On this late-spring day, she spent some of the trip gazing off across the wide expanse of the Sulphur Springs Valley, taking in the scenery—the alternating squares of cultivated fields and tracts of wild desert terrain punctuated with mesquite trees—that stretched from the nearby Mule Mountains to the Chiricahua Mountains in the distance, some thirty miles away. She loved the varying shades of green that springtime brought to the desert, and she loved the very real purple majesty of the mountains rising up in the distance to meet an azure sky. As much as she thought of this corner of the Arizona desert as being hers, it was always humbling to remember, as her history-loving father had loved pointing out to her, that much less than two hundred years ago everything she could see had been the undisputed domain of the Chiricahua Apaches.

Today, however, she didn't bother admiring the landscape. Her thoughts were focused on Junior Dowdle—a troubled individual with the body of a grown man, the ailments of an old one, and the heart and mind of a child. Knowing that Junior was out in the world somewhere—lost, alone, and unprotected— was heartbreaking, and she uttered a quiet prayer as she drove. "Please help us find him," she pleaded. "Please let him be okay."

Driving through the central business district of Old Bisbee on Tombstone Canyon Road, Joanna kept her

eyes peeled, watching for anything out of the ordinary
on side streets or on the steep scrub-oak-dotted hillsides
that loomed above the town. If Junior had wandered
outside in the dark, it wouldn't have taken him long to
cross that narrow strip of civilization and find himself
lost in a desert wilderness with neither food nor water.

Joanna had just passed Tombstone Canyon Methodist
Church when her radio crackled to life.

"Alvin Bernard just called. Terry and Spike have
arrived at the Maxwells' house. They're working on
finding a scent. Everyone else is at St. Dom's."

"Okay," Joanna told Tica. "I'm almost there, too."

When Joanna arrived at the parking lot for St.
Dominick's Catholic Church, she found Father
Matthew Rowan, one of St. Dom's two resident priests,
standing at the gate directing traffic. He pointed Joanna
toward a clutch of official-looking vehicles. Tucked in
among the collection of patrol cars sat a 1960s-era VW.
The chaplain sticker on the VW Bug's back bumper
explained its odd presence among the other official
vehicles. The vintage VW belonged to Joanna's friend
and pastor, the Reverend Marianne Maculyea, who in
the past month had been certified as a chaplain for the
local police and fire departments. It was no surprise
to Joanna that, if first responders were on the scene,
Marianne would be, too.

Pulling into the open spot next to the VW, Joanna stayed in the car for a moment, taking in the scene. The hustle and bustle might have been part of something as innocuous as a church bazaar. Cars came and went. The center of activity seemed to be a hastily erected eight-by-ten-foot canvas canopy. Some enterprising soul had used several matching sawhorses and a piece of plywood to create a massive makeshift table on which a six-foot-long paper map of the city had been tacked down. Surrounded by teams of officers and volunteers, Chief Bernard was bent over the map, assigning people to the streets and neighborhoods they were expected to search.

Twenty yards away from Chief Bernard's command center, a clutch of ladies from several nearby churches were setting up a refreshment buffet complete with a coffee urn, stacks of Styrofoam cups, and a surprising selection of store-bought and homemade baked goods and cookies. A blond teenage boy, someone Joanna didn't recognize, sprinted past her. Carrying a thermal coffee carafe in one hand, he waved in Joanna's direction with the other. Looking at her rather than at traffic, he came close to stepping into the path of another arriving vehicle.

"Look out!" Joanna called out, and he jumped back just in time.

Another stranger, a woman Joanna had never seen before, shouted after him, too. "For Pete's sake, Lucas! Watch what you're doing! Pay attention."

Joanna turned to the woman, a harried-looking thirty-something. Her long dirty-blond hair was pulled back in a scraggly ponytail. "He's yours?" Joanna asked.

When the woman nodded apologetically, a faint whiff of booze and an even stronger scent of cigarette smoke floated in Joanna's direction.

"My son," she answered, "fourteen years old and full of piss and vinegar. Once the coffee was ready, he wanted to be the one to take it to Chief Bernard." Then, glimpsing the badge and name tag on Joanna's uniform, the woman's eyes widened in recognition. "You're Sheriff Brady?"

Joanna nodded.

"I'm Rebecca Nolan. Lucas is my son. My daughter, Ruth, Lucas's twin sister, is over there."

The woman nodded toward the refreshment table. Following Rebecca's gaze, Joanna caught sight of a teenage girl who, with her mouth pursed in concentration, was laying out straight lines of treats in a carefully designed fashion. Rebecca had said the girl was Lucas's twin. True, they were about the same size— fair skinned and blue eyed—with features that were almost mirror images. They were also dressed in matching bright blue track suits. When it came to hair, though, the two kids weren't on the same page. Lucas's dark blond hair resembled his mother's. Ruth's, on the other hand, was mostly dyed deep purple, with a few natural blond strands showing through here and there. A glance at the girl's purple locks was enough to make Joanna grateful that her own daughter's hair didn't look like it came from a box of crayons.

"I hope you don't mind the kids being here," Rebecca added quickly. "I'm homeschooling them, and we've been doing a unit on community service. When I heard what happened, I told the kids to get their butts out of bed because we were coming down to help. I don't know Moe and Daisy well, but we live just up the street from them. It seemed like the right thing to do."

Marianne stepped into the conversation and handed Joanna a cup of coffee. "Good morning, Rebecca," she said cordially. "So glad you and the kids could make it."

Rebecca nodded. "I'd better go help," she said, backing away.

"You know her?" Joanna asked as Rebecca melted into the refreshment crowd.

"I met them at Safeway shortly after they arrived in town," Marianne said. "They've only been here a few months. Rebecca is divorced. Moved here from someplace in New Mexico with a boyfriend who disappeared almost as soon as they got to town."

"What does she do for a living?" Joanna asked.

Marianne shrugged. "I'm not sure, but she's home-schooling the two kids, which strikes me as a full-time job all its own. I know for a fact that I wouldn't be any good at homeschooling, and neither would Jeff." Jeff Daniels was Marianne's husband.

Joanna nodded. "The same goes for me," she agreed. "I've never been teacher material."

They stood for a moment, sipping their respective cups of coffee in the early morning cool and appreciating the quiet comfort of an enduring friendship that had started in junior high. Bisbee may not have boasted an official Welcome Wagon organization, but Reverend Maculyea filled the bill anyway. When it came to newcomers in town, you could count on Marianne to have a handle on them—where they came from, what they were about, and whether or not they needed any kind of assistance. Other people lived their lives by drawing circles in the sand designed to keep people out. Marianne's whole purpose in life was to draw circles that pulled people in.

"You got here fast," Joanna observed as another pair of cars nosed into the lot and parked where Father Rowan indicated. "I'm the sheriff. How come you got the call before I did?"

To anyone else, it might have sounded like a dig, but Marianne didn't take offense. "I wasn't called," she explained. "I heard it from Jeff. He went out for an early morning run up the canyon and came across Moe Maxwell, who was already out looking for Junior on his own. Jeff convinced Moe that he needed to call the cops, then came straight home and told me."

"You're the one who summoned all the ladies?" Joanna asked, nodding toward the gathering of women who were bustling around setting out tables and folding chairs.

Marianne grinned. "I didn't have to summon all of them," she replied. "All I had to do was call the first two people on my list. Each of those called two more. It's the first time we've used CCT," she added. "It worked like a charm."

For months, Marianne had been spearheading a team of local pastors and parishioners who had established something they called Christ's Crisis Tree, a phone tree organization that used a combination of text messages and landline calls to mobilize members of various churches to respond quickly to community emergencies, where they provided refreshments to all those involved, first responders and volunteers alike.

Marianne's grin faded as quickly as it had come. Joanna turned in time to see Daisy Maxwell, disheveled and distraught, coming toward them. Marianne hurried forward to embrace the woman.

"So sorry," Marianne said. "I'm sure they'll find him soon."

Daisy nodded numbly. "I hope so," she agreed. Then she turned to Joanna. "That guy from your department was up at the house, the one with the dog."

"Terry Gregovich," Joanna told her.

"Before I left, I gave him some of Junior's clothing so the dog would have his scent. I hope and pray it works. That's why Chief Bernard had everyone else, including these wonderful volunteers, meet here at the church instead of at our place. He didn't want people disrupting the scent and interfering with the dog."

"Spike's good at his job," Joanna said reassuringly. "Would you like some coffee, Daisy? Something to eat?"

That was what people did in difficult times—they offered food and drink. Daisy rejected both with a firm shake of her head, all the while gazing in wonder at the bustling parking lot.

"Where did all these people come from and how did they get here so fast?" she asked. "It's only a little past six. How did they even know what had happened?"

"They care about you," Marianne said, "and they care about Junior, too. Let's go sit down for a while."

Taking Daisy by the arm, Marianne led her to a nearby table. Meanwhile, Detective Matt Keller, a

Bisbee police officer and Alvin Bernard's lead investigator, wandered over to the refreshment area and collected a cup of coffee before joining Joanna.

"Making any progress?" she asked.

Matt shook his head. "Not much. I've talked to all the people who live on O'Hara, the Maxwells' street," he said. "Because it was so warm last night almost all the neighbors had their windows open, but nobody seems to have heard or seen anything out of line, including Jack and Lois Radner, who live right next door. I talked to both of them and to their son, Jason, whose bedroom faces Junior's. So far I've got nothing that would help with timing, not even so much as a barking dog."

Joanna looked away from the detective in time to see two sheriff's department patrol vehicles nose into the parking lot. As she walked over to confer with her deputies, her phone rang and Terry Gregovich's name appeared in her caller ID.

"I could use some help up here," he said.

"Where are you? Did you find a scent?"

"We found one, all right. The trail from the house led up to the highway above town at milepost 337," he said. "We're there now. Spike may be able to follow the trail on the pavement or across the pavement, whichever it turns out to be, but we won't be able to do either one until we have someone up here to direct traffic."

"Two patrol deputies just arrived," Joanna told him. "I'll send them right up. You said milepost 337?"

"That's right," Terry confirmed.

"If somebody up on the highway gave Junior a ride, he could be miles away by now."

"I know," Terry said. "If the trail ends in the middle of the pavement, we'll know that's probably what happened."

Joanna hustled over to the two cars just as Deputies Ruiz and Stock stepped out of their vehicles. Deputy Stock's usual patrol area was on Highway 80 between Tombstone and Benson, while Deputy Ruiz spent most of his time on the stretch of Highway 92, west of Don Luis and out as far as the base of the Huachuca Mountains.

Joanna turned to Deputy Stock. "Did you see anyone walking on the highway as you came over the Divide?" she asked.

Jeremy shook his head. "Not a soul," he said. "Do we have any idea how long Junior's been gone?"

"Less than ten hours," Joanna said. "He took off sometime during the night. Right now, I need both of you up on the highway at milepost 337 to assist the K-9 unit. Spike picked up Junior's scent and followed it there. Before they can venture onto the pavement, they need someone directing traffic."

"On our way," Jeremy said. He turned to head out, but Joanna stopped him.

"No lights or sirens until you get there," she cautioned. "I don't want a hundred civilians milling around on the highway. One of them might get killed."

As the deputies hurried to do her bidding, Joanna went in search of Alvin Bernard. She wanted to tell him she had just heard from Terry Gregovich. To do so, she had to get in line behind one of her least favorite people, Marliss Shackleford, the *Bisbee Bee*'s intrepid reporter. Marliss may have been Joanna's mother's closest chum, but she was also a gossipy busybody and the bane of Joanna's existence. Knowing that Marliss dished out the same kind of torment to Alvin Bernard made it only slightly less irksome to Joanna.

As soon as the reporter caught sight of Joanna, she registered her surprise. "How come you and your people are here, Sheriff Brady?" Marliss demanded abruptly. "My understanding is that Junior disappeared from the Maxwells' place on O'Hara. That's well inside the city limits and outside your jurisdiction. Isn't this whole circus a bit of an overreaction to someone simply wandering off?" She waved dismissively at the crowd of people milling in and out of the parking lot.

"Most of these folks are volunteers," Joanna told her. "My people are here because Chief Bernard requested my department's assistance, and we're happy to oblige. As for its being an overreaction? I doubt that's how Daisy Maxwell would characterize it. In fact, Daisy is right over there chatting with Marianne. Why don't you ask her?"

Marliss scurried off in search of Daisy Maxwell. "Thanks for getting rid of her," Alvin Bernard muttered once the reporter was safely out of earshot. "I was afraid she was going to be on my case all morning long."

Quickly Joanna briefed him on the situation with Terry and Spike.

"Should I call off the street search, then?" Chief Bernard asked.

"Not yet," Joanna replied. "Just because Junior wandered up to the highway doesn't mean he didn't come back down into town somewhere else. I sent a pair of uniformed deputies up there to direct traffic. What we don't need on the scene is a mob of civilians."

"You're right about that," Bernard agreed.

"Why don't I go see if I can assist my guys?" Joanna told him. "I'll call you directly if we find any sign of Junior."

When their conversation was interrupted by questions from someone else, Joanna took the opportunity to slip away. Once in her Yukon, she exited the parking lot, drove back down to Tombstone Canyon, and then headed north to the junction with Highway 80. Merging into the southbound lane, she turned on her light bar and flashers and drove slowly down the highway, scanning the shoulders on both sides of the road as she went. When she reached mileage marker 337, she pulled over to the side of the road and tucked in behind Deputy Stock's Ford Explorer.

"Where's Terry?" she asked.

"Up there," he said, pointing up the steep hillside above the highway. "He and Spike took off up that gully."

Years earlier, when the new highway bypass was built, the roadway had been carved out of the series of undulating limestone cliffs that covered the hillside. The mounds of cliffs were separated by steep gullies. During rainstorms those washes turned into cascades of fast-running water. Bone dry at the moment, they offered a natural but rough stairway leading up through otherwise impassable terrain. Pulling a pair of binoculars off her belt, Joanna scanned the mountainside.

When Anglos had first arrived in what was now southeastern Arizona, the Mule Mountains had been covered by a forest of scrub oak. The trees had been cut down to provide firewood for home use as well as for smelting the copper being mined underground. As a girl, Joanna had hiked these hills with her father.

Back then most of the scrub oak had been little more than overgrown bushes. Decades later those same slow-growing shrubs had matured into genuine trees, growing here and there in dense clusters.

Joanna was still scouring the hillside with her binoculars when Spike and Terry popped out from behind the cover of one of those groves of trees. They remained visible for only a matter of moments before resuming their climb and disappearing into another clump of scrub oak a few yards farther on. Even from this distance Joanna could see that Terry was struggling to keep up with his agile dog. Spike, nose to the ground and intent on his quarry, lunged forward with his brushy tail plumed out behind him.

Joanna knew that Terry Gregovich prided himself on being in top physical condition. If this was proving to be a tough climb for him, how had Junior managed it? The missing man was in his early sixties. He was naturally clumsy and anything but a natural athlete. Joanna was hard-pressed to imagine Junior making the same climb, especially alone and in the dark. Still, she also understood that the trail didn't lie. Junior's scent had to be there because that's what Spike was following.

"Did there happen to be a full moon last night?" Joanna asked.

"Yes, ma'am, there was," Deputy Stock answered. "Out between here and Tombstone it was almost as bright as day."

Just then Joanna heard the dog. Spike's excited, purposeful barks alerted everyone within earshot that he had located his target. Almost a minute later, Terry reappeared, popping out of the second grove of trees. As Deputy Gregovich came into view, Joanna's phone rang.

"I found him," Terry said urgently.

"Where?" Joanna asked. "Is he all right?"

"I can't tell if he's all right or not," Terry replied. "I can see him, but I can't reach him. I called to him, but he didn't respond. He doesn't appear to be breathing."

"Where is he?"

"At the bottom of a glory hole inside a cave of some kind. I always heard rumors about a series of limestone caverns under the mountain, but I never really believed it. The narrow opening that leads into it is hidden in the trees directly behind me."

Joanna knew that the Mule Mountains were riddled with natural caverns and man-made glory holes—small test holes that had been drilled into the earth by prospectors and left abandoned when no ore was found.

"Which is it?" Joanna asked, "a glory hole or a cave?"

"A little of both," Terry replied. "The cave itself is natural, but there's a small glory hole inside it that someone must have worked for a while. The tailings outside the entrance are hidden under the trees. If I'd been on my own, I would have missed the opening completely. Fortunately, Spike didn't. Someone put an iron grate across the entrance to keep people out. Junior evidently crawled under it. So did Spike and I. The glory hole is a few feet inside the cave, and it's a big drop-off. I can see Junior facedown at the bottom of that, lying on top of a layer of loose rock and boulders where it looks like the side of the hole collapsed. There's a cat or kitten stuck down there, too. It's on an outcropping halfway between where I was and where Junior is. I can't see it, but I can hear it crying. I'll bet that's what happened. Junior was following the kitten, and they both fell."

"Can you get to him?" Joanna asked.

"Not me, not without ropes and a winch."

"Okay," Joanna said. "I'm on it. Calling for help right now."

Chapter 2

Within seconds of Joanna's 911 call, Rescue numbers 5 and 6, along with an ambulance, were on their way. She warned the operator that the firefighters needed to arrive with whatever equipment was required to cut through the metal grate that blocked the way into the cavern. Junior, Terry, and Spike may all have been able to slither under the barricade to gain entrance, but if Junior was inside and injured, they'd need an opening wide enough for rescuers to carry him back out.

Joanna's second call, a terse one, was to Chief Bernard. "I think Terry and Spike found him," she said.

"Dead or alive?"

"Can't tell," Joanna said. "He's taken a bad fall in a cave up above the highway. Terry says that so far he's not responding. Until an EMT can reach him and check him out, we won't know if he's just unconscious or if it's something worse. The fire department is dispatching trucks, equipment, and an ambulance. Let's give them a chance to do their thing before you mention any of this to Moe and Daisy. There's no point in upsetting them any more than they already are until we know the real score. Besides, the fewer people we have to work around up here, the better."

"What about traffic?" Chief Bernard asked.

"I sent Jeremy Stock and Armando Ruiz out to shut down highway traffic in both directions and divert it through town. That's the only way to make it safe for emergency personnel to operate. You know as well as I do that there's no room to park on the shoulder without having vehicles obstruct the traffic lanes."

"Makes sense," Chief Bernard said gruffly. "Keep me informed."

By the time Joanna was off the phone, she heard the wail of approaching sirens echoing off the canyon walls. She waited for the crew to scramble out of their vehicles and begin assembling loads of equipment to pack up the mountain. The incident commander, a Bisbee Fire Department lieutenant named Adam Wilson, approached Joanna. "Morning, Sheriff Brady," he said. "Where's the problem?"

She pointed up the gully through the limestone cliffs toward the spot where Terry and Spike had disappeared into the dense grove of trees. "In a cave up there," she said. "I'll take you."

"Any word on the victim?"

"Unresponsive as far as I know," she said. "To get him out, you'll have to cut through a metal grate."

"Right," Wilson said. "Will do." He turned back to his crew. "I'll go up top with Sheriff Brady and bring the K12 saw with me. You guys bring the come-along, ropes, rappelling harnesses, chains, the Stokes basket, blankets, and medical supplies. Oh, and box lights, too. Move it."

It was a steep climb. Shimmying over rocks and dragging herself up the steep grade hand over hand, Joanna was grateful for the tough khaki of her pants as well as her sturdy hiking boots. There were spots where she worried that her scrabbling along would send a shower of loose rocks and boulders raining back down on Lieutenant Wilson, who was behind and beneath her.

When they finally reached the trees, Joanna was out of breath and panting with exertion. Beads of perspiration rolled down her face, stinging her eyes. It provoked her to realize that Lieutenant Wilson, despite carrying the thirty-pound gas-powered saw on his back, had barely broken a sweat. Then she remembered that he had won the Bisbee Hill Climb the previous two years. With that in mind, she decided she wasn't doing too badly after all.

"Where to now?" Wilson asked, looking around as he came into the shady gloom beneath the canopy of trees. The ground around them was littered with a layer of loose rock that she recognized as tailings from the glory hole. For a time Joanna had no answer, but then she caught sight of Terry and Spike as they came into view, slithering, one at a time, under a rusty iron grate that was virtually invisible in the muted sunlight.

She stepped up to the metal barrier made from iron rods that had been drilled into the limestone cliff face and then welded together to form what should have been an impenetrable barrier. Determined digging by some four-footed creature had created a cleft under the grate that granted entrance. No doubt that was how Junior had gotten inside as well.

"Still no response from Junior?" Joanna's question came out in a breathless gasp.

Standing up, Terry made a futile attempt to brush the coating of gray dust off his uniform and off the dog's burnished black-and-brown coat.

"Not so far," he replied. "At least not from him, but that poor cat is raising all kinds of hell. It must be hurt pretty bad." He looked at Joanna. "Are you going in?"

She nodded.

"If you've got some Vicks on you," Terry cautioned, "you'd better plan on using it."

A dot of Vicks VapoRub under the nostrils was a time-honored way for cops to deal with the foul odors often associated with homicide scenes. Considering Junior had been missing for only a matter of hours, Joanna was surprised that the smell could already be that bad, but she didn't argue. Instead, she reached into the pocket of her uniform and pulled out the tiny can marked Burt's Bees Lemon Butter Cuticle Cream.

For Christmas, Maggie Dixon, Joanna's clueless mother-in-law, had sent her a zipped plastic container full of Burt's Bees products. Maggie's presents were always a little off. The previous year she had sent a gift package of makeup that had clearly come with the purchase of some cosmetic or perfume item at an upscale shopping emporium. The pastel hues in the collection had clearly not been chosen to complement Joanna's complexion or her red hair and green eyes. She had donated the unopened package to the church rummage sale and forgotten about it.

This year's present, a Burt's Bees assortment of salves and ointments, was most likely a regifted item Maggie had picked up somewhere along the trail as she and Butch's father motored their hulking RV from one campground to the next. Maggie was prickly enough that Joanna and Butch spent as little time as possible in her company. Even with limited contact, however, Maggie had made it clear that she disapproved of Joanna's minimalist approach to cosmetics, which included short fingernails that were seldom, if ever, professionally manicured and polished.

Upon seeing this year's gift, Joanna had regarded it as yet another snide commentary on what Maggie considered to be Joanna's hopelessly inadequate beauty regime. Joanna's first instinct had been to toss the whole thing in the trash without even bothering to open it, but then she spied that small metal container of cuticle cream.

For a long time, Joanna had kept standard-sized jars of Vicks VapoRub in the glove compartments of her various vehicles, leaving the jars in the car because they were too bulky to carry on her person. The cuticle cream container was flat and no larger than a silver dollar. Once she got rid of the cream, she had refilled the tiny slender container with Vicks and carried it with her everywhere, slipped invisibly into the shirt pockets of her various uniforms.

"Step back now," Lieutenant Wilson warned as Joanna daubed some Vicks under her nostrils.

A moment later, the metal-slicing K12 saw howled to life. With a shower of sparks, it bit through the iron rods, slicing them as easily as if they had been made of butter. By the time the opening was large enough to allow upright passage in and out of the cavern, the remainder of the crew had arrived, bringing along the rest of their equipment.

Wilson shut off the saw and turned to Joanna. "Are you in or out?" he asked.

"In," she replied, passing him the Vicks. "Want some? Terry says we're going to need it."

"Thanks," he replied. Wilson applied some of the gel and then addressed his crew. "Okay, guys. Somebody give Sheriff Brady here a helmet. She'll need a head-lamp, too."

The guy who handed over his helmet was another six-foot bruiser. Once on Joanna's head, the thing was so big that it covered her eyes completely. While Joanna adjusted the helmet straps for a better fit, Wilson buckled on his rappelling harness and then helped her into one as well, giving both harnesses a final snap to be sure they were properly secured.

"You'll need these," he said, handing her a pair of leather rappelling gloves. Predictably, the gloves were too big, too.

"This way," Wilson explained. "If what Terry says is true and the rocks inside are unstable, the harnesses guarantee that we won't fall to the bottom the same way Junior did. Ready?"

Nodding in reply, Joanna followed Wilson through the opening and into the cavern. Despite the sharp odor of menthol under her nose, her unwilling nostrils filled with the ugly smell of death that was thick in the air. As a rule Joanna wasn't claustrophobic, but as the darkness closed round, she more than half expected that their sudden intrusion might send a colony of bats bursting into flight. The only sound that greeted her straining ears, however, was the plaintive yowling of what sounded like a badly injured kitten.

The LED lights on their helmets helped lighten the gloom. Even so, it took several moments for their eyes to adjust to the darkness. Once Joanna could see, she realized that she and Lieutenant Wilson were standing in a low earthen entryway that led back into what was probably a much larger cavern. The ceiling in the first room was tall enough that Joanna, at five foot four, was able to stand upright. Adam Wilson, who was well over six feet, had to stoop over in order to walk. In one corner of the room just inside the doorway, a slight depression in the earthen part of the floor and a scatter of small bones indicated that an animal of some kind—a coyote or maybe even a bobcat—occasionally used the place as a den.

Lieutenant Wilson moved forward a foot or two and then stopped abruptly. "Watch your step," he warned. "There's a long drop-off here."

Even with the sturdy harness, Joanna approached the edge warily and peered down into the hole some hopeful prospector had carved out of the earth probably more than a century earlier. About ten feet down, stranded on a narrow ledge, was the marooned kitten. Another twenty feet below that, Junior Dowdle lay, facedown and unmoving, on a boulder-littered floor.

"Looks like there's been at least one rockfall in here and maybe more," Wilson observed, "but there's no way to tell when the last one happened. Maybe that's what caused Junior to fall. You stay here. I'll rappel down and check things out."

Joanna had attended a mountain rescue workshop. Rappelling wasn't something she was good at, but she had done well enough to pass the course. If the situation called for rappelling, her technique wouldn't be pretty, but it would get the job done.

Wilson spoke into the radio on his shoulder. "Okay, guys," he said. "Bring in a crew to handle my rope. The cat's down about ten feet. At my signal, haul me back up. Once the cat's safely out of the way, I'll rappel down and assess the victim."

On his command, the rope-handling team edged into the cave, filling the cramped space and forcing Joanna up against the rough wall. Standing there, looking out across the void, she caught sight of a crystal winking back at her in the reflected lights of any number of headlamps. Her father, D. H. Lathrop, had once shown her a broken chunk of geode, its interior alive with lavender crystals. He claimed that someone had carried it out of another limestone cavern, a much larger one townspeople had always dubbed the Glory Hole, before the entrance to that had been walled off with tons of debris from construction of the Highway 80 bypass.

Joanna turned her attention back to the scene just as Lieutenant Wilson went over the edge and dropped out of sight. The crew manning his rope let it out slowly. Moments later, two sharp tugs on the rope indicated he was ready to return to the surface. When he reappeared, he was holding a bloody, struggling kitten by the nape of its neck.

Joanna edged her way over to the lieutenant to take charge of the injured animal. Once she had it in hand, she very nearly dropped it. Clearly terrified, the traumatized kitten fought for its freedom, biting and scratching anything that got near it. Needle-sharp claws penetrated Joanna's shirt, slicing through any skin not covered by either the leather gloves or her Kevlar vest.

Careful not to disrupt the crew, Joanna edged back out through the entrance. In the blinding sunlight her first real glimpse of the wounded animal sickened her. It was a gaunt and gangly tabby, a female, probably not more than three or four months old. Her face was a bloody mess. The ears had been sliced through over and over, most likely with a tool like a razor, leaving behind wreckage that was little more than an ear-shaped fringe. The kitten's entire body was covered with tiny round scabs where someone had burned her with lit cigarettes.

Absolute fury surged through Joanna's body like a bolt of electricity, and it took a moment for her to regain control. "I need water over here," she barked. "Now."

One of the firefighters, a guy whose name tag identified him as Corporal Arturo Fisher, sprang forward with a bottle of electrolyte-infused water in hand. Seeing the injured kitten, Arturo's face contorted in anger, but he immediately understood what was needed. Opening the bottle, he poured water into his cupped hand and offered it to the injured animal, who lapped up every drop. When the kitten finally had her fill, she looked up into the man's eyes as if to say thank you.

"If the bastard who did this isn't dead, he sure as hell should be," Fisher muttered.

Joanna found herself nodding in agreement. She was accustomed to dealing with the terrible things people did to other people. The damage that had been inflicted on this helpless animal made her blood boil.

The kitten heaved a plaintive sigh. As if aware that she had arrived in a safe haven, she closed her eyes and subsided limply against Joanna's chest, resting and relaxed this time rather than squirming and fighting. Just then another member of the fire crew walked up behind Joanna and tapped her on the shoulder.

"Excuse me," he said. "Lieutenant Wilson's calling for you. He says the victim is dead. He wants to know if you want to go down and do a survey."

At that point in the investigation, Joanna had no homicide detectives on the scene. Of all the people in her department, she was by far the smallest physically. If the firefighters were going to have to be raising and lowering people up and down with ropes, she was a better candidate than anyone else. She had some training in crime scene investigation. Armed with the camera on her phone, she knew she'd be able to record what was down there as well as any of her CSI folks could. Besides, before Joanna delivered the bad news from the scene to anyone else, including Moe and Daisy Maxwell, she wanted to verify that the dead man really was Junior.

"Okay," she said, nodding. "I'm ready, but what do I do with this?" she asked, glancing at the sleeping kitten.

"I'll take care of her," Corporal Fisher volunteered, stepping forward. "Give her to me while you go check things out. If the dead guy did this, the bastard got what he deserved."

Chapter 3

As the guys in the cave adjusted the rigging on her harness, Joanna looked down into the darkness and pondered what Corporal Fisher had just said. She had known for some time that Daisy and Moe had been having issues with Junior—that he'd been acting out and behaving in ways he never had before. Still, was it possible that he could have done something so appallingly evil to a defenseless kitten? In Joanna's previous dealings with him, the man had almost always been unfailingly kind—sweet, even. Up until only a matter of weeks ago, he had been at Daisy's every day, where he spent his shifts greeting customers with stacks of menus and a beaming smile.

Whenever Joanna had seen Junior around animals, he had been gentle and respectful. Only a week ago, when Jenny had taken Desi into the restaurant on a service dog training exercise, not only had Junior been there, he had also been absolutely delighted with the pup. Joanna couldn't make a connection between the Junior she recalled laughing at Desi's antics and the cold-blooded person who had mutilated a helpless animal. Was it possible that Alzheimer's could cause those kinds of personality changes and result in episodes where people would behave in ways that were entirely foreign to their previous natures? Try as she might, Joanna couldn't wrap her mind around the idea that Junior would do such a thing. She doubted Moe and Daisy would be able to, either.

As the team of rope handlers lowered Joanna into the hole, she was grateful for the light on her helmet and for Lieutenant Wilson's steadying hands on her shoulders as he caught her on the way down and guided her to a smooth landing. The rough surface at the bottom of the hole meant that every shifting rock underfoot was an invitation to a twisted ankle or a broken leg.

"This is a crime scene," she admonished. "Did you touch anything?"

Wilson shook his head. "All I did was check for a pulse; there wasn't one."

Joanna pulled out her iPhone and turned on the camera application. As she began snapping pictures, she used pages torn from a pocket notebook, folded and numbered, as makeshift evidence markers. Each time the flash went off, the contrast of the brilliant light followed by overwhelming darkness left Joanna momentarily blinded, but as near as she could tell, there were no footprints or marks of any kind visible on the rock-strewn surface that would indicate anyone other than the dead man had been here.

"Do you think he fell?" Joanna asked, pausing her photo shoot.

"I'm not so sure about his falling," Wilson waffled. "Maybe he jumped, or he could have been pushed. Come take a look at his face. I doubt a simple fall from that distance would have caused that much damage."

With Lieutenant Wilson's hand leading her forward, Joanna made her way closer to the fallen victim. The first thing she noticed about the man was that he was wearing a pair of blue-and-white-striped short-sleeved pajamas. One house slipper, a slip-on Romeo, was still on his right foot. Its mate lay ten feet or so away, toe up against the side of the rock wall.

As soon as Joanna got a clear look at the victim's face, she recognized Junior, despite the fact that only half his face was still intact. The other half, pancaked on top of a boulder, had crumpled in on itself like a squashed jack-o'-lantern. She didn't need a medical examiner to tell her that much of what she was seeing on the floor around the victim was the mixed splatter of gray matter and blood. Only a tiny amount of blood had dribbled out of the corner of the mouth of the disfigured face. That told her that Junior had most likely died instantly. For a moment she was struck by the unfairness of that. The kitten had suffered; he hadn't.

Steeling herself for the task at hand, Joanna resumed taking pictures. She stayed at it long enough to create a comprehensive photo and evidence marker log that contained fifty or more shots.

"What now?" Wilson asked as she finished and pocketed her phone.

"My next call is to the M.E.," she said. "In situations like this, do you bring the remains out or does the M.E.?"

"We do, although Dr. Machett sometimes has his own ideas about how things should be done," Wilson said. "I'm not sure his new helper, Ralph, is physically capable of coming down here, and I doubt Dr. Machett will want to do so, either. Might dirty one of the fancy suits he's always wearing. He strikes me as one of your basic prima donnas."

Dr. Guy Machett wasn't high on Joanna's list, either. The still relatively new M.E., who never let anyone forget that his medical degree came from Johns

Hopkins University, had been hired to take over as Cochise County medical examiner when Dr. George Winfield had retired. Doc Winfield, who happened to be Joanna's stepfather, had been a well-loved and much-respected colleague. The same could not be said of his successor.

Machett's whole way of doing business—including his high-handedness and lack of empathy—had put him at odds with many of the folks in law enforcement circles. It came as no surprise to Joanna that he had developed a less-than-stellar working relationship with local firefighting teams as well. Joanna didn't add chapter and verse to Lieutenant Wilson's derogatory comment. A simple nod of her head was agreement enough.

"Okay," she said. "I'll go back up and make some calls. Are you coming?"

"Not yet," Wilson said, shaking his head. "I'll stay with the remains until someone decides what's to be done. It's a matter of respect."

Joanna tugged on her rope. Moments later she rose through the cool dark air. As she neared the surface, her vision improved enough so she could just make out the legs of the rope handlers through the murky darkness on the surface. Moments later hands reached out to deposit her on firm ground.

"Thanks, guys," she said.

One of them laughed. "Better you than Ernie Carpenter," he told her. "If he'd been the one down there, we'd have needed another four guys just to handle the rope."

Outside the cave, Joanna found Corporal Fisher sitting in the shade, tucked up against the trunk of a scrub oak, tenderly cradling the sleeping kitten. She nestled comfortably against his chest as though she belonged there. One front leg draped down casually over the arm of the firefighter's protective gear.

"Mind if I share your tree trunk?" Joanna asked.

"Help yourself." Fisher paused and then added, "What's going to happen to this poor little thing?"

"First we'll get her some veterinary care," Joanna answered. "Then we'll try to find her owner."

When Joanna pulled her telephone out of her pocket, she was surprised to discover it was nearly eight o'clock. Close to two hours had passed since she had first arrived in the parking lot at St. Dominick's. With the victim found and identified, Joanna's first call was to Chief Bernard.

"I've seen him," she said. "It's Junior, all right."

"He's dead then?" Bernard asked.

"Yes."

"Figured as much," Bernard said. "Someone from the fire crew just called for Reverend Maculyea and she took off in a hell of a hurry. My guess is she's on her way to you right now." He paused then asked, "How did it happen?"

"He either fell or was pushed," Joanna answered. "In any case, I'd say he died on impact. That's not official, but it's what I saw."

"Have you called Dr. Machett?" Chief Bernard asked. "If the body's on the far side of the highway, it's not inside the city limits—your jurisdiction instead of mine."

"I haven't called him yet," Joanna answered, "but I will."

"Best of luck with that," the chief said. "So what's the deal? Are we dealing with an accident, a suicide, or a homicide?"

Joanna remembered what Lieutenant Wilson had said about the possibility that Junior might have jumped or been pushed. "Too soon to tell," she answered.

"He died on impact?"

"That's how it looks."

"Knowing he didn't suffer will be a comfort to Moe and Daisy."

Joanna thought about the horribly damaged kitten. Hearing about that wouldn't provide the Maxwells any comfort at all.

"There are some troubling details at the scene that will need to be investigated and could be difficult for

Moe and Daisy to handle," she told him. "Whatever you do, don't let them come here. For one thing, it's rough terrain. I doubt either one of them is in any condition to make the climb." She paused for a moment. "The Maxwells belong to St. Dom's, don't they?"

"That's my understanding," Chief Bernard said.

"Before you call off your search teams, have Father Rowan take Moe and Daisy into his office. Ask him to have them wait with him there until Marianne and I arrive."

"Does that mean you'll be doing the next-of-kin notification?" Chief Bernard asked. "What about Dr. Machett? Shouldn't he be there, too?"

"As I said, he's one of my next calls."

"Okay," Chief Bernard said with a sigh. "Better you than me on both counts—doing the notification and dealing with the M.E."

Joanna's first call was to Dispatch. Tica Romero was now off shift. Joanna's lead dispatcher, Larry Kendrick, had come on duty.

"I need a homicide detective and the CSI unit at a crime scene above the highway west of Old Bisbee," she told him. "I don't know which detective is up right now. I'm hoping for Deb Howell. I don't think Ernie Carpenter can handle the climb. Whichever it turns out to be, tell him or her to drive as far as milepost 337.

We're straight up the gully from where the emergency vehicles are parked. If they come that way, they'll walk right into the crime scene. Have them call my cell when they're close, and I'll direct them the rest of the way up the hill."

"Got it," Larry said. "Anything else?"

"Yes, I need to call the M.E. next, and after that Jeannine Phillips at Animal Control. I'll make those calls while you're summoning everybody else."

When Joanna dialed the M.E.'s office, the phone was answered by Machett's gravelly voiced receptionist and secretary, Madge Livingston. Madge had adored Guy Machett's predecessor and made no bones about despising her current boss. She was a pushy sixty-something who could have retired years earlier. Rumor had it that she was staying on now for no other purpose than to make Guy Machett's life miserable.

"Good morning," Joanna said when she answered. "Sheriff Brady here. Could you put me through to Dr. Machett?"

According to Guy Machett's playbook, the M.E. expected to be addressed as Dr. Machett no matter what. None of this informal Doc stuff for him. "Doc," he had informed Joanna snippily early on when she had erred in that regard, "is one of the seven dwarfs. Do I look short to you?"

You look like a jerk, she had thought, but she hadn't said so.

"Does this have anything to do with you guys having the highway shut down? What happened? Did a couple of drug dealers off each other?" Madge demanded. "Good riddance. Maybe it'll spare the taxpayers some expense."

"It's not a couple of drug dealers," Joanna said patiently. "Now could you please put me through to Dr. Machett?"

"I can't. He's on his way out of town and won't be back for two days. He just left."

"Call him back," Joanna said. "We need him."

"It'll be better for me if you call him," Madge said.

Joanna found the situation almost laughable. Chief Bernard didn't want to call Guy Machett and neither did the M.E.'s own secretary. No doubt Madge was right. Whoever had the misfortune of interrupting whatever was penciled into Dr. Guy Machett's day-planner was going to get an earful.

"Do you have his cell-phone number?" Madge asked.

It was Joanna's turn to sigh. "Yes," she said, scrolling through her contacts. "I've got it."

She punched in the number. "Sheriff Brady here," she said when Dr. Machett answered. "We've got a body for you."

"Crap," he grumbled. "Just what I wanted on a bright spring morning. Who and where?"

"It's a male named Junior Dowdle who took a bad fall."

"You've already identified him?"

"Junior is someone I know," Joanna explained. She wasn't surprised that the M.E. didn't recognize the name. Daisy's Café was far beneath Guy Machett's level of sophistication. "Junior was found at the bottom of a glory hole inside one of the limestone caves above Highway 80 in Old Bisbee. Outside Old Bisbee, actually," she corrected. "My jurisdiction rather than Alvin's."

"Did you say he's in a cave?" Machett asked.

"That's right. He went off a thirty-foot drop into an old mine shaft. The guys from the fire department can probably raise and lower you in and out on a rope."

"Me on a rope?" Machett said with a short laugh. "Are you kidding? Couldn't I just swing in on a vine?"

Cochise County—Joanna's jurisdiction as well as Dr. Machett's—included huge tracts of empty, mesquite-covered desert. Dr. Machett always seemed offended that the people who lived and died there often did their dying in inconvenient, out-of-the-way places.

"I've never been in a cave," Machett declared, "and I've never wanted to be, either. Just because some brain-dead spelunker decides to die in a hole in the ground doesn't mean I'm going to go up and down a rope ladder to examine the guy in situ. No way. They don't pay me enough money to go crawling around in snake-infested caves."

Joanna remembered what Adam Wilson had said about the M.E. not wanting to dirty one of his precious suits, which, Joanna had noticed, were almost always of the expensive Italian-made variety. Cochise County obviously paid him enough to make Dr. Machett's expensive wardrobe possible. As for snakes? Joanna had seen no sign of one of those anywhere inside the cave.

"Are you saying you want me to have the guys from the fire department retrieve the remains before you take a look at them?"

"By all means. Tell 'em to have at it!"

Joanna heard the genuine relief in Machett's voice. It occurred to her that maybe his reluctance wasn't just about the suit. Maybe the M.E. was actually afraid of cold dark places and of snakes, too.

"Once they get the dead guy out, have them call my new diener, Ralph Whetson, to come pick up the body."

The first time Machett had dropped the five-dollar word "diener" into casual conversation, Joanna had gone to the trouble of looking it up. She knew it was highbrow, in-crowd jargon that meant nothing more or less than "morgue assistant." She might have liked Dr. Machett more if he hadn't insisted on using it at every possible opportunity. She also noted that where the rescue crew on the mountain had spoken with unfailing respect about "the remains," Guy Machett felt free to refer to "the dead guy" with something verging on contempt.

"Any idea when you'll be able to do the autopsy?" Joanna asked.

"Not until Saturday sometime. I'm out of town today and tomorrow, getting back late in the evening, so probably not first thing in the morning, either. Maybe in the afternoon. I'll have to let you know. Do you want Ralph Whetson's number?"

"I can get it," Joanna said. "Thanks."

Ending the call, she went over to the group of men gathered near the entrance of the cave. "Dr. Machett isn't available. He says you should bring the remains up now," she told them. "I'll call Ralph Whetson and have him wait down on the highway for you to bring Junior there."

As the crew went into body-retrieval mode, Corporal Fisher stood up and handed the kitten to her. "Duty calls," he said.

Tucking the sleeping feline inside her shirt, Joanna dialed Animal Control. The woman in charge, Jeannine Phillips, was a longtime Cochise County Animal Control officer. Years earlier, when the unit had been moved over to the sheriff's department, supposedly on a temporary basis, Jeannine had been none too happy about the new chain of command. There had been a period of bad blood between her and Joanna. Then, just when their relationship was finally smoothing out, Jeannine had been severely wounded in an altercation with people running a dogfighting ring at the far north end of the county. When her injuries left Jeannine incapable of returning to active duty, Jeannine had accepted a desk job. With her in charge, Joanna's Animal Control unit had a reputation for being one of the best in the region.

"Sheriff Brady here. I'm up above Old Bisbee. Where's your closest ACO?" Joanna asked. "I need one."

"Natalie Wilson is somewhere out around Double Adobe," Jeannine answered. "She's coming to the shelter with a load of north county strays. Why? What's up?"

"I've got a badly injured kitten who needs some immediate attention from Dr. Ross."

Millicent Ross was the only vet in town these days. She was also Jenny's boss and Jeannine Phillips's longtime domestic partner.

"What happened?" Jeannine asked.

"She took a bad fall among other things," Joanna answered. "There may be some internal injuries, but she's also been severely traumatized. Somebody shredded her ears, most likely with a razor blade. They also covered her body with burns from lit cigarettes."

Joanna heard a sharp intake of breath over the phone.

"Okay," Jeannine said. "I'll put the phone on voice mail and come there myself. The last thing that poor kitten needs is to be stuck riding around in a truck full of barking dogs. Where are you?"

"A little north of the old Glory Hole," Joanna said. "Milepost 337. We're up the mountain right now. A dead man was found in a cave along with the kitten. The fire department is in the process of recovering the remains. When they bring him down to Dr. Machett's minivan, I'll bring the kitten down, too."

After calling Madge back and asking her to dispatch Ralph Whetson, Joanna stood up gingerly so as not to disturb the kitten. She walked over to the entrance of the cave in time to see a group of sweat-soaked men emerge, carrying Junior's blanket-swathed body in a basket.

Once outside, they paused long enough to remove their helmets and stand at attention, waiting. Terry

Gregovich and Spike joined them. Corporal Fisher did not. He was the only one of Wilson's crew who moved determinedly away from the quiet gathering, his helmet still firmly atop his head.

Lieutenant Wilson was the last to emerge. When he saw Fisher walking away and still wearing his helmet, the lieutenant called after him. "Get back here, Fisher," he ordered. "Helmet off. Show some respect."

"Respect?" Fisher repeated. He stopped moving but he didn't turn around, and he didn't remove the helmet, either. "Are you kidding me? Did you see what that monster did to that poor cat? He doesn't deserve any respect. If you think I'm going to be part of this . . ."

"If you want to have a job when this incident is over," Wilson growled, "then you will be part of it because I'm ordering you to be part of it. I don't care what you think Junior Dowdle did or didn't do. Now get back here and stand at attention with everybody else."

"But—" Fisher began.

"No buts," Wilson warned him.

Sighing, Corporal Fisher complied. He returned to the crew, removed his helmet, and came to attention. Once he was in place, Wilson assumed the same stance and bowed his head.

"Let us pray," he said quietly.

One by one the men clustered around the blanket-shrouded body bowed their heads, too, including Deputy Terry Gregovich and Sheriff Joanna Brady.

"Into thy hands, O Lord, we commend his spirit," Wilson intoned. "Amen."

"Amen," the others agreed.

"Amen," Joanna added.

It was a quiet moment—a simple moment. It was also, Joanna feared, the last vestige of real respect that would ever be paid to Junior Dowdle. If it turned out he was responsible for torturing the kitten, the good things the man had done before would soon be forgotten. She was sorry to have been there for the solemn ceremony and glad to have been there—sorry Junior was dead and glad to have witnessed the quiet decency of the group of hardworking men who were taking his remains back home to the people who would grieve over Junior's death no matter what he had done.

Some of the men made as if to gather up their equipment. Lieutenant Wilson forestalled that with a shake of his head. "Leave it for now," he said. "We'll get it later. Right now let's walk him down the hill."

One by one the other members of the crew fell into step behind the four guys charged with carrying Junior's body. The ungainly procession made its way back down the rugged pathway to the highway in complete silence.

Joanna, bringing up the rear, occasionally had to scoot along on her butt in order to keep from falling and jarring the sleeping kitten tucked inside her shirt.

Her descent was the exact opposite of dignified. When she finally reached the bottom, she scrambled to her feet and brushed off the coating of gray dust that covered her clothing. Looking around, she was grateful to find Marliss Shackleford had not yet arrived on the scene. The last thing the sheriff of Cochise County needed right then was to have her photo plastered on the front page of the next day's *Bisbee Bee* with a demeaning caption saying something to the effect of SHERIFF JOANNA BRADY FALLS ON BUTT WHILE RESCUING INJURED KITTEN.

With Moe's and Daisy's broken hearts hanging in the balance, Joanna thought the less said about that poor kitten, the better.

Chapter 4

By the time Joanna reached the highway, the basket laden with Junior Dowdle's earthly remains had already been loaded into the Dodge Caravan known around town as the M.E.'s "meat wagon." As the van pulled away, Lieutenant Wilson sidled up to Joanna. "A word, please?"

"Of course," Joanna said. "What's up?"

In answer, Wilson removed an iPhone from his pocket. After turning it on and locating a file, he handed it to Joanna. Squinting at the screen in the bright sunlight, all she could see was what looked like a pile of brown and white rags, lying on the rubble-strewn floor.

"What is it?" she asked.

"This mess was under Junior's body," Wilson said tersely. "I can't tell for certain, because they were all pretty well smashed together, but I think it's a bunny, a puppy, and at least one other kitten. They weren't visible until we moved the body."

Joanna swallowed hard. That was why the whole cavern had reeked of death. Junior Dowdle wasn't the only victim who had died there; so had several others.

"I guess I'll need to send one of my techs back down to take more photos and gather more evidence," Joanna said after collecting herself.

"I thought you would," Wilson agreed. "That's why I told the guys to leave our equipment in place."

Marianne's VW appeared on the scene. In her role as chaplain, she was there to offer support for the first responders as well as to comfort the other people affected by the incident. Joanna had finished briefing her when the folks from her department began showing up.

Jeannine Phillips had something of a reputation as a speed demon. This time, fueled by a case of severe moral outrage, she was the first of Joanna's officers to arrive. Jeannine came equipped with a tiny receiving-blanket-lined pet crate. When Joanna removed the sleeping animal from inside her shirt and placed her in the crate, the exhausted kitten didn't so much as stir.

"Poor little thing," Jeannine murmured, peering at the animal's visible injuries. "Who would do such a thing?"

"At first glance," Joanna replied, "it looks like the bad guy could be Junior Dowdle."

"Daisy Maxwell's Junior?" Jeannine asked in disbelief. "The guy who always hands out the menus?"

Joanna nodded.

"No way!" Jeannine exclaimed.

"As I said, that's how it looks," Joanna replied. "Junior was found dead on the floor of an old glory hole. We found the kitten in the glory hole too, and she's not the only animal victim. I've just been told the bodies of three other dead animals were found under Junior's body—another kitten, a rabbit, and a puppy, too."

"I can't believe Junior would be capable of a stunt like this," Jeannine declared. "I would have sworn the man didn't have a mean bone in his body."

"That's my thought, too," Joanna agreed. "My initial assumption was that he was responsible, but as I came down the mountain, I arrived at a different conclusion, and I believe the crime scene photos bear that out. Let's take a look."

Removing her iPhone from her pocket, Joanna turned it on, found the camera roll, and then scrolled through the set of photos she'd taken inside the cave. After studying several of them closely, she handed the phone over to Jeannine. "Here," she said. "Take a look at this one and the three that follow."

Frowning, Jeannine stared at the screen. "What am I looking for? What am I supposed to see?"

"I want you to notice what you're not seeing," Joanna said. "Junior is wearing short sleeves. Do you see any bite marks or scratches on either of his hands or forearms?"

Jeannine peered at the screen again. "Not really," she said with a frown.

"May I look, too?" Marianne asked.

Joanna nodded and Jeannine passed the phone to Marianne, who also stared at the photos for several long seconds.

"We know Junior died last night. It's safe to say the cat ended up in the glory hole about the same time. Believe me, when Lieutenant Wilson handed that kitten over to me a little while ago, she scratched the daylights out of me. If Junior was responsible for her injuries, she would have fought him, too, but there's not a single scratch or bite mark anywhere on his arms or hands."

"He might have had her in some kind of restraints," Jeannine suggested.

"True," Joanna agreed, "but I didn't see any evidence of that on the cat, either. If he'd used duct tape, for example, there'd still be adhesive clinging to her coat."

"You're saying that someone else besides Junior might be involved?" Marianne asked.

Knowing that anything said at the scene would be subject to Marianne's chaplaincy vow of silence, Joanna wasn't concerned about answering.

"We'll get Dave to use the photos to re-create some 3-D images. Lieutenant Wilson thought the spot where Junior landed was farther away from the side of the hole than a simple fall would suggest."

"Like maybe he was pushed?"

"Maybe," Joanna agreed. "And it's possible whoever tortured that kitten might have had something to do with it." Joanna turned to Jeannine. "Have there been any reported cases of missing kittens recently?"

The head of Animal Control nodded. "A couple," she answered. "And now that you mention it, we had a missing Easter bunny, too. In fact, the rabbit and at least one lost puppy were from houses up in the canyon, here. Most of the time when pets go missing like that, we chalk it up to coyotes."

"In this case, the coyotes may be getting a bum rap," Joanna observed, "and perhaps Junior Dowdle is, too."

"What do you want me to do?" Jeannine asked.

"Take the kitten to Dr. Ross. Tell her that there's a slim chance that a killer may have left trace evidence on the kitten's fur. We'll need her to take swabs of every speck of blood she finds, in case there's been some DNA transfer."

"Will do," Jeannine said.

"In the meantime," Joanna continued, "I'll dispatch a detective to Dr. Ross's clinic to stand by while the animal is being treated and the samples collected. If human DNA is present, we'll need to maintain the chain of evidence, the same way we do when Dr. Machett performs an autopsy."

Nodding, Jeannine strode off, cradling the injured kitten's crate in her arms as tenderly as if she were carrying a baby. She was driving away when a sheriff's department unmarked patrol car pulled up. Detective Deb Howell, one of Joanna's three homicide detectives, stepped out.

"What's going on?" she asked. "Dispatch told me somebody was dead. When I asked homicide, suicide, or accident, they had nothing to tell me."

Joanna responded to Deb's question with one of her own. "Who's back at the office, Ernie Carpenter or Jaime Carbajal?"

"Both," Deb answered. "They were there doing paperwork when I left. Why?"

"I have an assignment for one of them," Joanna said. "Whoever draws that short straw isn't going to thank me."

Over the years Joanna and her entire investigation team had stood in on their share of autopsies. Still, it was one thing to be in the morgue while an M.E. dissected a dead body. It was quite another to be in a treatment room with a veterinarian working on a living, breathing kitten. Joanna wasn't sure if she'd be able to handle a situation like that, and she wasn't sure how either one of the Double C's would respond, either. When her call was put through to the bullpen, Ernie Carpenter answered.

"We've got a chain-of-evidence problem," Joanna told him. "I need someone to go to Dr. Ross's office and stand by while she works on a badly injured kitten."

"As in a kitten that's still alive?" Ernie asked.

"Junior Dowdle was found dead, and the injured kitten was found nearby," Joanna explained. "There may be blood evidence on the kitten that will help us determine what happened to Junior."

"Sorry," Ernie said. "It sounds like Jaime's your man. I fainted dead away in the delivery room when my son was born. I caused such a fuss that Rose wouldn't let me anywhere near her when our daughter was born two years later. So, no. I can deal with autopsies on dead guys until hell freezes over, but I'm squeamish as all hell when it comes to living creatures."

Ernie Carpenter had a reputation for being tough as nails, but Joanna didn't even rib him about his admission.

"All right, then," Joanna replied. "Send Jaime to Dr. Ross's office. Since Deb's going to be making like a mountain goat and heading back to the crime scene, I'd like you to meet me at St. Dominick's. I want you there when it's time for me to give Moe and Daisy Maxwell the bad news."

"They don't know he's dead?" Ernie asked.

"Not yet," Joanna said. "At least I don't think they know."

"All right," Ernie said. "I'm on my way. I'll find out everything else there is to know when I get there."

By the time Joanna ended the call, her lead CSI tech, Dave Hollicker, had arrived and was awaiting orders. "What's the deal?" he asked.

"Junior Dowdle ran away from home last night," she explained. "He was found dead inside an old mine shaft halfway up the mountain. A crew from the Bisbee Fire Department was called in to retrieve the body and bring it back down here."

"I saw Ralph Whetson leaving in the minivan," Deb said, "but where's Dr. Machett? Shouldn't the M.E. be here in person? Isn't that his job?"

"Not today," Joanna replied. "The M.E. is currently out of town and out of the picture."

"What about the autopsy, then?" Deb asked. "When is it and who'll do it?"

"Dr. Machett will do it when he gets back," Joanna answered. "We don't have a firm schedule on that.

Most likely it won't happen before Saturday afternoon at the earliest."

"Where's the crime scene?" Dave asked.

Joanna pointed. "Up there. The shaft is a glory hole inside a limestone cavern. The entrance to that is hidden inside that second big grove of scrub oak halfway up the hill. If it hadn't been for Terry and Spike, we never would have found him. The scene's been pretty well disturbed because of all the comings and goings of the recovery crew. Some additional evidence was found once Junior's body was moved. Once you retrieve that, I want you to measure the distance from the rim of the glory hole to the point of impact so we can do a computerized simulation. We need to know if he simply fell, took a running jump, or was pushed."

"Did you take photos?" Dave asked.

"Some, but I want you to take a whole lot more." She paused and gave Dave a searching look. "How are you in caves?"

"Don't worry about me," he said with a grin. "I'm an old spelunker from way back."

"Good; go talk to Adam Wilson. Bisbee F.D. still has equipment up there to help you in and out. Once you're back on solid ground, I'd like you and Deb to cover the whole area, starting from the entrance to the cave and working your way down the trail Junior followed. From there go all the way back to his house. Terry and Spike can show you the route. Collect whatever you find along the way."

"Are we looking for anything in particular?" Dave asked.

"Anything that doesn't belong," Joanna said. "Somewhere between point A and point B, I'm hoping you'll find a mess of cigarette butts or chewing gum and maybe even some helpful DNA. I also want you to be on the lookout for any kind of blood spatter. Whatever you find, bag it, tag it, and bring it back."

"What about you?" Deb asked.

"Reverend Maculyea and I are going to meet up with Ernie Carpenter down at St. Dominick's, where the three of us will have the dubious honor of breaking a few hearts."

Chapter 5

As Joanna headed back down to St. Dominick's, twenty-five hundred miles away on a hillside outside Great Barrington, Massachusetts, Selma Machett's small, sad funeral was just getting under way.

Liza Machett had heard about Haven's Rest Cemetery from one of her customers at Candy's, and she was surprised to learn that was also the cemetery in which Selma herself had chosen and partially paid for a plot well in advance of her final illness. From its website Liza learned Haven's Rest offered a low-cost, all-inclusive service that came complete with a memorial service on the grounds, cremation, and burial in a two-foot-by-two-foot plot that was much smaller in both size and cost than a standard burial plot.

Each grave came with a flat granite marker that would cover half of the plot itself. The old cemetery in town featured a motley collection of moss-covered headstones in all sizes and shapes. Some had fallen over completely. Others stood canted at crazy angles. The carved inscriptions there, some of them barely visible, dated back for most of three centuries. Haven's Rest was different. One of the reasons it was so "affordable" was due to the fact that the uniformly flat headstones meant the whole thing could be mowed by one guy— the funeral director's brother-in-law—who could cover the entire cemetery on a riding mower in twenty minutes from beginning to end.

Even though Guy had been out of their lives for years, once Selma had gone into hospice, Liza had swallowed her pride and tracked her brother down at his new office somewhere in the wilds of Arizona. He had immediately made it clear that he had written Selma off years ago and that, for him, showing up at the funeral would be nothing short of hypocritical.

"So that's it, then?" Liza had demanded, her voice rising. "That's what you do, isn't it? You wash your hands of everything. You go off to live your perfect life and leave me stuck cleaning up the mess!"

Guy had hung up on her then, and that was the last time they spoke. When Selma died, Liza didn't bother calling. There was no point. That was why, on this rainy Thursday morning, there was only one folding chair reserved for grieving family members under the blue canvas canopy next to Selma Machett's tiny grave.

As Craig Masters, the funeral director, intoned his comforting words, Liza was struck by the fact that her mother had had no friends of her own. The people who had come today were Liza's friends, and most of those were people from work—her fellow employees at the diner and the customers from there as well, all of whom seemed like family but were far less trouble.

Studying those gathered there, Liza sorted the familiar faces in her customary fashion, by order rather than by name: two eggs over easy, hold the hash browns, with English muffin on the side; French toast, no cinnamon, crisp bacon; two eggs scrambled with sausage patty, cottage cheese instead of hash browns; short stack with scrambled eggs, sugar-free maple syrup. These were Candy's stock-in-trade—guys who worked hard, drove hefty pickup trucks, and brought their big appetites to the diner for breakfast almost every day. When the city had come through and tried to restripe the parking lot to make more spaces for compact cars, Clifford "Candy" Small had gone ballistic.

"These guys all work for a living," he had told the clipboard-wielding and very much cowed emissary from the City Planning Department. "They need someplace to eat where they can park their trucks without having to worry about scratching somebody's precious Prius. Now get the hell out of here and leave me alone."

The guy with the clipboard left. The faded parking lot striping big enough for pickups stayed put, at least for now, and so did the guys who drove them. Many of those same guys had come to the funeral today, along with the restaurant's full contingent of worker bees. Candy, Liza's boss, was there, as were her fellow waitresses—Sue Ellen, Honey, Jeanette, Frieda, and Lois. The funeral's attendees included all the busboys and dishwashers—Ricky, Salvatore, Xavier, and Tommy—and the other two cooks, Alfredo and Cosmo, had shown up as well. Liza was touched that they had all come to the funeral to show their support, and she was equally sure they'd all be coming back to the diner later where some of them would have to work. Candy's had been closed to the public for the day both so employees could attend the funeral itself, and also because it was the site of the postfuneral reception.

In the twenty-six years Candy had owned the place, he had shuttered his doors only twice before. Once he had been forced to close because the power had gone off for twelve hours and all the food in the coolers went bad. The second time had been in honor of his own mother's funeral. This was number three.

Someone pushed a button, and the earthenware urn began its slow descent into the ground as Liza, dry-eyed and stone-faced, watched it disappear. The top had just slipped out of sight when a beefy hand dropped heavily onto Liza's shoulder.

"Sorry," Candy Small muttered under his breath. "So sorry. Take as much time off as you need. Whenever you're ready to come back to work, you'll still have a job."

Liza looked up at him gratefully because she knew that that single word from him, "sorry," was meant to cover it all—not only for the fact that Selma Machett was dead, but also for everything that had gone before. He understood more than anyone else the tangled relationship she'd had with her mother because Candy was the only person in town to whom Liza had confided the gory details. Candy was her boss, her friend, and the closest thing to a father Liza Machett ever had.

When it came to stature, Candy Small didn't match his name—he wasn't in the least bit small. He had been born with the name of Clifford, although hardly anyone in town remembered his given name. As a child he had never gone anywhere without at least two jawbreakers in his possession—one tucked into his cheek and another held in reserve in the pocket of his jeans. By the time he graduated from eighth grade, the other kids and most of the teachers, too, had started calling him Candy. In high school a few of the older kids had tried making fun of him for having a girlish-sounding name. Back then, Candy had yet to grow to his full height of six foot four. Even so, once he had cleaned the clocks of all his would-be tormentors, no one ever made fun of his name again, at least not to his face.

Occasionally a new traveling salesman, making a cold call, would stop by Candy's Diner with the preconceived notion that the owner of the place would turn out to be some blue-haired lady in her sixties or seventies. That would have been true if Candy's widowed mother, Wanda, had still been at the helm. Instead, she had retired to Florida several years before her death, passing the family diner, previously named Wanda's, along to her oversize son. Employees always got a kick out of seeing the startled expressions on the hapless newcomers' faces when Candy, all three hundred pounds of him, emerged from the kitchen, wiping his huge hands on his apron and demanding to know what they wanted.

The newbies quickly learned that when it came to business, Candy Small drove a hard bargain. When it came to people, however, the man was a pushover. If a kids' sports team in town needed a sponsor, he was there. If the high school band was looking to raise money for new uniforms or a trip to the Rose Bowl, he was happy to oblige. And if someone was down on his or her luck, Candy would help out by having a load of groceries delivered to the home of a struggling single mother or sending one of his busboys out to shovel the sidewalks of elderly people who could no longer handle that task themselves. Candy's innate kindness was how he had come into Liza Machett's life in the first place.

He had heard about her situation from one of Liza's teachers at school. When she had fled home that morning with a high school diploma, no money, and no prospects, he had taken a chance on her. First he gave her a job in his restaurant and then he helped her find a place to live, advancing her enough money to cover the first and last month's rent on an apartment. Liza wasn't the first employee he had helped, and she wasn't the last, either, which partially explained the diner's stable of long-term and very loyal employees.

As Craig Masters closed out Selma's brief ceremony, he announced that everyone was welcome to come to the reception. Liza knew that she'd be given a ride to the restaurant in the funeral home limo, so she stayed where she was as the small crowd dispersed. Only when the others were gone did the single stranger in attendance—a stoop-shouldered, balding old man wearing a rain slicker and leaning on a cane—make his approach. When he arrived at Liza's chair, he spoke to her in a quiet voice as if concerned about being overheard.

"I knew your father," he said. "Back when he still drove a bread truck, back before he took off. I've been out of the game for a long time now, but I still hear things on occasion. I'd be careful if I was you, Miss Machett. Those guys don't never forgive, they don't forget, and they don't play around, neither."

Having delivered what sounded very much like a warning, he turned abruptly and limped away, threading a path between the granite markers and leaving behind a trail of footsteps in the damp grass. Watching him go, Liza was left with a hundred unasked questions. She wanted to chase after him and say, "You knew my father? Who are you? What bread truck? What can you tell me?" But she did not. Could not. It was almost as if she were bolted to that flimsy folding chair.

She was still watching him walk away when Mr. Masters appeared at her elbow, holding out a hand to assist her to her feet. "Ready?" he asked.

"That man," she said, pointing toward the figure disappearing in the distance. "Do you know who he is or where he's from?"

"Name's Jonathan Thurgard," Mr. Masters answered. "I believe he lives in Stockbridge, and he's a Korean War vet. At least, that's what I've heard, but I don't know it for sure because when he signs the guest book he never lists an address. He has a reputation for showing up at funerals all over western Massachusetts, usually when the deceased served as a member of the military. He stands on the sidelines and then plants a tiny American flag next to the flowers before he leaves. He didn't leave a flag, but was your mother a veteran by any chance?"

"Not that I know of," Liza said.

"Well then, perhaps he was one of your mother's friends."

Liza shook her head. She knew better than anyone that Selma Machett didn't have any friends. "He said he knew my father."

"There you go then," Mr. Masters said with a dismissive shrug that indicated the topic had been adequately covered. He held out his arm. "Shall we go?"

Taking Craig Masters's arm, Liza allowed herself to be led across the field of markers and deposited in the idling limo that had been waiting patiently on the shoulder of one of the many paved lanes that wandered through the cemetery. Liza knew Craig's brother-in-law, Lester Woundy, from the restaurant—three eggs, scrambled hard, a side of ham along with biscuits and gravy. When he came into Candy's for breakfast, he was usually dressed in his lawn-mowing/grave-digging overalls. Today, though, tapped as the on-call limo driver, he was dressed in a dark suit and a white shirt, with his bulging neck confined inside to a too-tight collar and a blue-and-gray-striped tie.

Once Liza was inside the limo, Craig leaned over and spoke to Les. "Drop her at Candy's," he directed. "You won't need to wait. Someone else will take her home after the reception."

"Nice turnout," Les said to Liza as he put the Town Car in gear and in motion.

While standing at the cash wrap either as hostess or cashier, Liza was often a party to the conversations of people sitting at the counter. She remembered hearing Les say once that he liked small funerals best because there weren't as many chairs to fold up and put away afterward. From those overheard conversations, she also knew what Les's game plan would be.

Once he dropped her off, he'd return to the cemetery and change out of his limo-driving duds and into work clothes. Then he'd retrieve the backhoe that was always kept discreetly out of sight in a garage during funerals. Armed with the backhoe, he'd push all the bouquets of flowers into the grave before adding in the dirt he'd dug up earlier and stored twenty yards or so away from the grave, decorously covered with a green tarp during the proceedings. Once any remaining flowers and the excavated dirt had been dumped back into the hole on top of the urn, Les would unroll and replace the turf he had carefully cut out earlier that morning. After that it would be time to return the backhoe to the garage and go out for a beer. Or two. Or maybe even three.

"Yes," Liza agreed. "It was a nice turnout."

Leaning back against the headrest, Liza allowed her eyes to close. She was exhausted. For the past month, she had worked harder than she had ever worked in her life, and that superhuman effort had exacted a terrible toll—physically, mentally, and emotionally. She had worked most of her shifts at the diner, she'd visited her mother at least once a day, and she'd used every other remaining moment to oversee the workmen rehabbing Selma's house.

It had taken almost as long for Selma to die as it had to fix the house. In the end, and with the help of Ted Jackson, the local We've Got Junk franchisee— pecan waffle, crisp bacon, iced tea—she'd had thirteen Dumpster loads of stuff hauled away from her mother's house. Liza had realized early on that she would have to tackle the enterprise in a systematic fashion.

When the rehab project started, there was no electricity in Selma's house and no sign of any kerosene lanterns, either. Selma Machett had evidently learned to live like the birds, rising with the sun and bedding down at sunset. Because Liza needed to work on the house around her shifts at the diner, there were times when she had to be at the house far into the night. That meant one of her first tasks was to bring her mother's utility bill situation up-to-date and get the power turned back on. She had also begun the process of reinstating her mother's home owner's insurance.

Once the power was back on, Al of Al's EZ Plumbing—whole wheat BLT with no T, french fries, and a Pepsi—came in and got the sewer pipe cleared and the septic system pumped. Although it was most likely not an entirely environmentally approved activity, Al had pumped out the outhouse as well, after which the hole had been filled, the outhouse demolished, and a sweet little some-assembly-required potting shed straight from Home Depot was erected where the outhouse had once stood.

"If you're trying to sell the place and some nosy home inspector comes looking for an outhouse," Al instructed her, "you look at him all innocent like and say, 'Outhouse? What outhouse? That's my mother's gardening shed.'"

Supplied with power and water, Liza went to work on the books and on the magazines, too, that had been stacked, row upon row, in Selma's house. It wasn't just the cookbooks that had money squirreled away inside them. Liza had to look through everything—through hundreds of dog-eared paperback mysteries and romance novels; through every single volume of the *Encyclopaedia Britannica* with corners of pages turned down where Selma had researched the symptoms of her many various and untreated maladies; through stacks and stacks of crumbling *National Geographic* and *Life* and *People* magazines to say nothing of countless *Reader's Digest*s. Early on, Liza managed to unearth the dining room table. That way she could sit under an overhead light and with a fan blowing cool air in her direction during the endless hours while she paged through book after book after book and magazine after magazine.

It was like a nightmare Easter egg hunt. Not every volume held a cache of cash, but enough did that it was worth Liza's while to do a complete job of it. By the time she finished, $147,000 had been filtered through her coffee bean decontamination process. She had also found a flock of canning jars filled with coins. Those amounted to around five hundred dollars and didn't stink the way the bills did.

Every hundred-dollar bill that surfaced added another brick to the wall of resentment Liza was building toward her mother. Had Selma had all this money in her possession the whole time Liza had been growing up? If so, why the hell had she pretended to be poor? Why had she forced her daughter to live as though they didn't have two pennies to rub together? Why?

For the first Dumpster load, Liza had hauled the crap out through the kitchen door, down the crooked back steps, and then up into the Dumpster. After that, Ted convinced her to let him install a chute from the dining room window down to the next waiting Dumpster. She got to the point that she could toss a book from across the room and hit the Dumpster chute window almost every time.

Liza handled the books and magazines herself. For the kitchen, she hired two of the busboys from the restaurant, brothers Salvatore and Xavier Macias. Hardworking immigrants from Ecuador who sent money to their family back home each week, Salvatore and Xavier were more than happy to tackle that ungodly mess during their off-hours. Once they started, Ted rigged up a second Dumpster chute from the kitchen to make their lives easier as well. When the kitchen had been cleared of garbage and dead appliances, Liza looked around and had them remove the kitchen cabinets and the ancient linoleum along with the damaged wallboard. Then they moved on to the bathroom and bedrooms and did the same, stripping everything down to the studs.

In Selma's bedroom and bathroom, Liza was appalled at how much of the trash was stuff that had been purchased and never even opened, much less used. Unfortunately, mouse droppings rendered the excess paper products as well as the new and used clothing, some with price tags still attached, unusable and unsalvageable. When they finally got down to the bare bones of furniture, Salvatore and Xavier were happy to take the chests of drawers and the tables and the plain wooden chairs. The putrid odor clinging to the cloth meant that all upholstered pieces went to the Dumpster.

By this time, the army of pickup-driving guys from Candy's was on full alert, and they were all more than happy to work for cash on the barrel. As long as the money was good, none of them asked where it came from, and because it was all in the Candy's Diner family, as it were, not one of them cut any corners when it came to his part of the job.

John, of Great Barrington Electric—two eggs over easy; bacon crisp; hash browns crisp; coffee, cream and sugar; and a coffee, cream and sugar, to go—redid the electrical service, bringing it into the twenty-first century. Ralph Boreson of Boreson Home Remodeling—OJ; oatmeal with raisins, brown sugar, and cream; whole wheat toast—handled all the permits in a timely fashion since his sister-in-law worked in the building department and was able to move things along. Ralph also managed to find the low-end cabinets and fixtures, which had been installed the previous week. This week he'd had a full crew on-site, installing and taping wallboard, painting walls, installing new flooring, and replacing single-pane windows with double panes.

"It's not all top of the line," Ralph told Liza, "but the house will look good enough that no one will be able to rip you off by claiming it's nothing but a teardown."

Seeing the results, Liza had to agree. The place looked clean and smelled clean. In fact, it was downright livable again, not that she ever intended to live there. Now, though, she'd be able to list it and sell it. In fact, she had made an appointment for early next week with Rose Kelly—egg salad sandwich, hold the bread, tomato slices on the side, and green tea. Rose was a local real estate agent whose bright red Kia was often the only small car tucked in among all those hulking pickups. Rose was eager to do the listing and already had a potential buyer in mind.

"Excuse me, miss," Les Woundy was saying. "We're here."

Liza roused herself out of her stupor and looked around. The limo had pulled up in front of Candy's, where a handwritten sign on the door said, SORRY! CLOSED FOR A PRIVATE FUNCTION.

After allowing Les to help her out of the limo, Liza shook off her lethargy and went inside. The counter by the cash wrap had been turned into a bar, with Honey Baxter pouring generous drinks into red paper cups. Honey was an energetic seventy-something with bright blue eye shadow and a beehive hairdo that was decades out-of-date. She still worked full-time and cared for an ailing husband even though she was almost twenty years older than Selma Machett had been when she died.

Honey looked up as Liza came in the door, and there was a tiny lull in the general conversation.

"Well, there she is!" Honey announced. "You come right on over here, sweetheart, and let me give you something that'll be good for what ails you. I make a mean sloe gin fizz."

"How about a glass of white wine?" Liza suggested. "I have a feeling one of your sloe gins would put me on my lips."

In a matter of seconds, conversations in the room resumed and the noise level amped up. The restaurant was full of people juggling loaded plates, napkins, silverware, and drinks. The long counter had been turned into a makeshift buffet, which meant that there was far less seating than people were used to, especially considering that customers who usually drifted in and out over the space of several hours had all arrived at once. Since none of these people knew Selma personally, the after-funeral gathering was a far more lighthearted party than one would have anticipated.

Candy sidled up beside her. "How are you holding up?" he asked.

"Okay," Liza said. "Better than expected. Thanks for doing this," she added.

"Least I could do," Candy replied. "The guys tell me that work on the house is pretty much finished."

Liza nodded. "Everybody really pitched in. They've done an amazing amount of work in an astonishingly short time."

"You have me to thank for that," Candy said with a self-satisfied grin. "I told some of those lazy bastards to get with the program, otherwise they'd have to deal with me!"

When someone came by to ask Candy a question, Liza wandered off through the crowd—mingling, talking to people, thanking them for coming, and thanking them for whatever role they had played in the home-rehab miracle. She had taken only a sip or two of wine and a single bite of an egg salad sandwich when a vehicle with flashing blue lights pulled up outside the restaurant's front door.

Moments later a beefy deputy—Leon Bufford—ham and cheese omelet, side of bacon, double hash browns, double white toast, coffee, and a large milk—barged into the room.

The crowd fell silent. Deputy Bufford stood in the door briefly, scanning the room. At last his eyes found their target. "Hey, Liza," he said. "You'd better come with me. Quick."

"Why?" she asked. "What's wrong?"

"Looks like somebody burned down that house of yours—all the way to the ground."

Chapter 6

B y the time Joanna returned to the parking lot at St. Dominick's, the place was deserted because Alvin had dismissed his entire crew of volunteers. The church ladies, along with their accompanying refreshment tables, chairs, and any remaining goodies, had also disappeared.

As Joanna and Marianne stepped out of the mid-morning sunlight and into the cool interior of the church, Joanna felt a sudden chill that had nothing to do with the building's stone-clad exterior and everything to do with the emotional burden of her job.

While serving as Cochise County sheriff, Joanna attended not one but two fallen officer memorials inside the hallowed halls of St. Dominick's Catholic Church. The first had been for a departmental jail matron,

Yolanda Ortiz Cañedo, who had succumbed to cervical cancer. The second had been for Deputy Dan Sloan, who had been gunned down by a fleeing homicide suspect. In fact, Joanna's first dealings with Father Rowan had been on the night Deputy Sloan had died, when she and the newly arrived Catholic priest had joined forces to do a next-of-kin notification to Deputy Sloan's widow. Sunny Sloan had been pregnant at the time. Now a single mother, she worked part-time as a clerk in the sheriff department's public office.

This time, as Joanna entered the church, she was carrying the burden of knowing she was the bearer of heartbreaking news. Turning to Marianne, she asked the question that was in her heart. "When bad things happen, why do we always end up at St. Dominick's?"

Marianne simply shook her head. It wasn't necessary for her to say anything aloud. She understood. Unspoken communication was one of the blessings of their longtime friendship.

They walked down the center aisle together. At the front of the church, they turned left into what they knew to be the study—a book-lined office Father Rowan shared with the parish's other priest, Father Patrick Morris, who was currently away on an extended sick leave. The room was dimly lit. In the artificial gloom, Father Rowan sat at a polished wood desk facing Moe and Daisy Maxwell. A few feet away, Ernie Carpenter stood at ease in front of a towering bookcase. As Joanna and Marianne entered, everyone in the room turned toward them expectantly. From the anguished look on Daisy's tear-streaked face, Joanna knew the woman already understood the new arrivals wouldn't be bringing good news.

"You found him?" Daisy asked in a hushed voice.

Joanna nodded. "I'm sorry," she said.

"He's dead then?"

Joanna nodded again.

"Where?" Daisy asked. "What happened to him?"

"He fell at least thirty feet into an old mine shaft inside a cave up above the highway."

"Junior in a cave?" Daisy asked. "That makes no sense. He was afraid of the dark. Terrified. That's why we always had to leave a lamp on in his room—in case he woke up at night."

"But that's where he was found," Joanna continued, "in a cave. I saw him myself. The M.E. has yet to confirm this, but I believe he died on impact. As I said, he fell about thirty feet. Is there a chance Junior would have taken his own life?"

"No," Daisy insisted at once. "That's simply not possible. Absolutely not. Suicide is a mortal sin. It must have been an accident."

"You said you thought he died on impact," Moe interjected softly. "Does that mean he didn't suffer?"

"I don't believe he did," Joanna replied, "but again, that's just my opinion. The real answer to that will have to come from the medical examiner."

"I'm glad he didn't suffer," Moe said resignedly, reaching out to take Daisy's hand. "As sick as he was and the way things were going, it's probably just as well."

Joanna understood the reasons behind Moe's quiet statement. Junior had been developmentally disabled. He suffered from a horribly debilitating illness that eventually would have left him lost and helpless. Had he somehow managed to outlive his foster parents, who would have cared for him? What would have become of him? Those may have been the tough realities behind Moe's comment, but Daisy definitely wasn't on the same page.

She snatched her hand away from her husband's in sudden fury. "It is *not* just as well!" Daisy hissed at him. "There's nothing about this that's 'just as well'! For one thing, we never got to say good-bye to him. Besides, what would Junior be doing outside by himself in the middle of the night? And why would he go near a cave? Remember what happened when we tried to take him to Kartchner Caverns? Once Junior realized we'd be going into a cave and that it would be dark, he absolutely refused to set foot inside, even though we'd already paid for the tickets."

"But the people were very nice about it," Moe reminded her. "They refunded the tickets, remember?"

Without acknowledging his comment, Daisy turned beseechingly to Joanna as if looking for answers. Unfortunately, all Sheriff Brady had to offer Junior's grieving foster parents were more questions, tougher ones at that.

"Did Junior have any pets?" she asked.

"Pets?" Daisy repeated. "You mean like a dog or a cat? We had a parakeet named Budgie once, back when Junior first came to live with us, but he died."

Joanna felt her heart rate quicken. "How did he die?" she asked.

Daisy shrugged. "Budgie? Who knows how come birds die? I came out to the living room one morning, uncovered his cage, and there was Budgie, lying dead on the floor of the cage with his feet sticking straight up in the air."

"Had he been harmed in any way?"

"Harmed?" Daisy asked. "How would I know? It's not like somebody did an autopsy. Budgie was a parakeet, for Pete's sake, and he died. We put him in a matchbox and buried it in the backyard. Why on earth are you asking me about Budgie? What does he have to do with what happened to Junior?"

"Did you ever observe Junior doing anything harmful to animals?"

Daisy's fury, once focused on Moe, was now fully trained on Joanna. "Never!" she exclaimed. "Not one single time. Junior loved animals, and he was as gentle as can be with them. You saw how he was when Jenny brought that new puppy of hers into the restaurant. He absolutely loved it. But you still haven't told me why you're asking these idiotic questions."

"Because Junior's body wasn't the only thing we found in the mine shaft," Joanna explained. "There were several animals in there with him. Three of them were dead. The fourth, a kitten, is severely injured but still alive."

Daisy seemed mystified "What kind of animals?"

"Pets, most likely," Joanna answered. "A small dog or else a puppy, a rabbit, and two cats. The one that's still alive shows signs of having been tortured. She's at Dr. Ross's office being treated."

"You're saying you think Junior had something to do with what happened to all those animals—the dead ones as well as a tortured kitten?" Daisy asked in disbelief. "Are you crazy?"

She stood up and made as if to leave. Until now Ernie had stood still and silent in the background.

Now he stepped forward, notebook in hand, and blocked Daisy's way. "Excuse me, Ms. Maxwell," he said. "If you don't mind, we still have a few more questions."

Moe took Daisy by the hand. "Wait," he urged. "We have to answer their questions. It's the only thing we can do to help. Please."

Reluctantly Daisy allowed herself to be guided back to her chair. Once there, she sat bolt upright, as if prepared to flee at a moment's notice.

"When's the last time you saw Junior?" Ernie asked.

Daisy closed her eyes before she answered. "About eight thirty, when we all went to bed. We have to get up early to open the restaurant. We're usually in bed before nine."

"Had you noticed anything out of the ordinary with Junior in the past few days?" Ernie asked. "Had he been out of sorts or upset about anything?"

Daisy leveled an icy glare in Ernie's direction. "What do you know about Alzheimer's patients?" she demanded.

Ernie shook his head. "Nothing," he admitted.

"Trust me, anything and everything can upset them," Daisy answered. "Even though Junior could no longer work, I took him to the restaurant with me anyway. He liked having a regular schedule. That way, even if I was in the kitchen and he was out front, I could keep an eye on him. His mood swings came and went, but they weren't any worse than usual."

"Was he aware of his condition?" Ernie asked. "Of his prognosis?"

"You mean since he already wasn't quite right in the head, was he aware he was losing even more of his marbles?" Daisy replied sarcastically. "No, Detective Carpenter, one of the few blessings of his being developmentally disabled meant that those kinds of abstract concepts were beyond him. Moe and I knew, of course. Even though we told him to begin with, I doubt Junior ever understood what was happening. I wanted him to have as much time as he could, and I wanted it to be as good as we could make it. The idea of taking his own life would never have occurred to him."

With that, Daisy lapsed into uncontrollable sobs. Moe absently patted her shoulder, but the woman was beyond comforting. Eventually Moe turned to Joanna. "What happens next?"

"There will have to be an autopsy, of course."

"When?"

"Not until Saturday. Dr. Machett is out of town."

"When will we be able to schedule the funeral mass?"

"Not until Dr. Machett releases the body. You can go ahead and talk to the people at the funeral home and do some tentative planning—maybe for sometime early next week—but you won't be able to finalize those plans until the M.E.'s office gives you the word."

Moe nodded.

"Did Junior have any particular friends?" Ernie asked. This time he addressed his question to Moe rather than Daisy.

"He knew lots of people in town from the restaurant. He sometimes played checkers and dominoes with the kid from next door, Jason Radner. Jason was always great with Junior. He never teased him or made fun of him, and he didn't let the other kids pick on him either."

"Detective Keller from Bisbee PD already talked with the Radners," Joanna told Ernie. "I believe he interviewed both parents early this morning and maybe Jason, too."

After jotting this down, Ernie turned again to Moe. "Is there anything you can add to what your wife already told us about Junior's situation in the days and weeks before this happened? She didn't notice anything out of the ordinary. Did you?"

"Not really," Moe said. "For months now we've been dealing with a new normal, which means everything was out of the ordinary. Junior would wake up in the morning talking about people being in his room during the night—people we never saw or heard. We often heard him pacing back and forth in his room overnight, awake and restless. That's why we had to start locking the doors with the dead bolt—to keep him inside. It never crossed my mind that he might crawl out a window. What was I supposed to do, put bars on it? Turn him into a prisoner in his own home?" With that, Moe Maxwell, too, dissolved into uncontrollable sobs.

In the interim, Daisy's tears had subsided. This time she was the one who reached out and offered a comforting hand to her husband. Joanna took heart from that small gesture. As waves of sorrow and blame ebbed and flowed around the couple, she hoped that Daisy and Moe would manage to form a united front in the face of their mutual tragedy—that Junior's death wouldn't become an insurmountable wedge that would drive them apart. Unfortunately Joanna knew that all too often the death of a loved one, especially the death of a child, could doom the marriage of the parents.

"Those people he talked about," Daisy offered, taking up where Moe had left off. "The nighttime visitors weren't real, you understand; they were more like hallucinations. Junior would tell us that his family had come to see him. He didn't have any birth sisters, but I understand there were girls in one of the foster families where he lived when he was younger.

"Not one of those people have ever visited here, at least not in real life, but that's what happens with Alzheimer's patients. Their minds slip back to some long-ago time in a way that turns the past into the present. And what Moe said is right. Junior wasn't upset about anything. Yes, he'd had occasional angry outbursts recently, but the last one of those was several weeks ago when he dropped a dish at the restaurant and it broke."

"Nothing since then?"

"No," Daisy said.

"Aside from Junior's mental deficiencies," Ernie continued, "did he have any physical ailments? Was he in pain, by any chance?"

"He was getting older," Daisy conceded. "He had some joint pain in his lower extremities and some difficulties walking. His doctor suggested we use over-the-counter medications. We were limited in what we could give him because the wrong combinations of drugs might have added to his confusion and made his Alzheimer's symptoms worse."

"Was he ever violent?" Joanna asked. She had seen Junior in full meltdown mode at the restaurant once. Daisy had ultimately been able to calm him down, but at the time Joanna had been startled by how angry he had been and how seemingly out of control.

"Do you mean, was he violent with us?" Daisy asked.

Joanna nodded.

"No," Daisy said firmly, shaking her head. "Not ever."

"How was he with other people?"

"He threw the checkers board at Jason once," Moe admitted. "Junior didn't like to lose."

Ernie made another notation in his notebook.

"He may have thrown the checkers, but he didn't hurt Jason," Daisy offered quickly as if attempting to minimize Moe's last comment. "Junior never hurt anybody, not ever."

Joanna's phone rang just then. Glancing at the caller ID and seeing Casey Ledford's name on the screen, Joanna walked out of Father Rowan's study to take the call.

For years the war on drugs had been the gift that kept on giving as far as high-tech budgetary items at the Cochise County Sheriff's Department were concerned. Before the well went dry, Joanna's department had been given a latent fingerprint setup that had lain fallow for months because she had no one trained to run it. Then Casey Ledford had come back home to Bisbee as a single mother with a relatively useless fine arts degree that offered few opportunities for supporting her daughter, Felicity. Joanna had been smart enough to hire her on the spot. In the years since, Casey's skill at drawing had made her a whiz at enhancing partial prints and uploading them into AFIS, the national Automated Fingerprint Identification System. Together Casey and Dave Hollicker made up Joanna's CSI unit.

"Hi," Casey said when Joanna came on the phone. "I just talked to Larry Kendrick and heard about Junior. I'll bet Moe and Daisy are wrecks."

That was one of the disadvantages about small-town law enforcement—everyone knew everyone else.

"They're taking it pretty hard," Joanna agreed.

"Sorry to be late to the party," Casey continued. "My dad had surgery at the VA hospital in Tucson early this morning, and I wanted to be there with my mom. Dad came through the surgery with flying colors, and I'm just now coming back into town. Is there anything you need?"

Joanna thought about that and about what she had heard from Moe and Daisy.

"Do you happen to have your equipment with you?"

"Yup," Casey said. "You know what they say—never leave home without it. I've got everything I need in the trunk of my car. Why?"

"Moe and Daisy are still at St. Dom's with Father Rowan right now," Joanna answered. "Junior evidently left the house in the middle of the night by climbing out a window. That's where Terry and Spike picked up his trail. Do you know where their house is?"

"Sure," Casey answered. "The Maxwells live just up the hill from my folks."

"There's an element of animal abuse in all of this, something that seems out of character for Junior," Joanna said. "Daisy says that since he was scared of the dark, his leaving the house on his own to take a hike in the middle of the night seems off. I'd like you to call Terry Gregovich and get a fix on which window Junior used to exit the house. Then I'd like you to go to the Maxwells' place and dust the windowsill, the screen, and whatever else you deem appropriate. I'm wondering if anyone else was involved in Junior's going AWOL."

"Got it," Casey said. "I'm on the far side of the Divide, but I'll get right on it."

As Joanna ended the call, Moe and Daisy emerged from the study with Marianne right behind them. Lost in their own world of hurt, the grieving couple walked past Joanna without even noticing her. Marianne stopped.

"They're on their way to the mortuary," she explained. "Father Rowan and I both offered to come along as backup, but they said they'd manage on their own. How are you doing?"

Joanna's phone rang again. This time Jenny's number appeared in the caller ID screen.

"It's not true, is it?" Jenny asked when her mother answered. She sounded close to tears.

"What's not true?"

"I just heard about Junior," Jenny said, "and I heard about that poor kitten, too. Someone said Junior is the one who hurt it, but I can't believe that, Mom. Junior wouldn't do something like that, would he?"

"How do you even know about all this?" Joanna asked. "Has word of what happened already spread to the school?"

"I'm not at school," Jenny corrected. "The teachers have an in-service meeting today. We got out early—at noon. Dad picked me up and took me to work so I could get in a few extra hours because we'll be gone this weekend. When I got here, Detective Carbajal's patrol car was parked outside, and Amy, the receptionist, told me what was going on."

One of the ways Joanna maintained her sanity was by trying to keep her work life and her home life completely separate. When she was at work, Butch kept the home fires burning. That meant he routinely handled most of the afterschool travel arrangements, including ferrying Jenny to and from her part-time job at Dr. Ross's office.

At the time Joanna had sent the injured kitten there and dispatched Detective Carbajal to keep watch, it never occurred to her that Jenny would be there, too. And Jenny's remark about the weekend was a reminder that Joanna had somehow forgotten that the whole family was scheduled to trek over to Silver City, New Mexico, that weekend, leaving on Friday. The three-day excursion to a rodeo would include Jenny and Kiddo's participation in a barrel-racing competition.

"Well?" Jenny asked impatiently. "Would he?"

Brought back to the present, Joanna answered. "I don't know for sure one way or the other. Maybe he did; maybe he didn't. That's what we're looking into right now."

"Junior never seemed like that kind of person," Jenny objected. "Anybody who would do horrible stuff like that to a helpless animal has to be really sick."

"Yes," Joanna agreed. "Whoever did it was sick, all right. The problem is, sometimes people you know—even people you think you know well—don't show their true colors in public. They present one face to the world while, underneath, they're somebody else entirely."

There was a brief silence after that. Finally Jenny said, "I still don't think Junior did it."

In that case, Joanna thought, *you and Daisy Maxwell are of one mind.*

Chapter 7

Liza Machett stood on the shoulder of the road, leaning against Candy Small's comforting bulk and staring at the clot of emergency vehicles blocking her mother's driveway. Beyond the vehicles was the still-smoldering heap of wreckage that had once been her mother's house. Liza's weeks of intensive labor, to say nothing of the thousands of dollars she had spent on cleanup and repair bills, had literally gone up in smoke. Firefighters were still on the scene, putting out hot spots, but Liza already knew the place was a total loss. Even the garage had caught fire and burned. All that remained standing was the newly installed garden shed.

While Liza watched, one of the vehicles in the drive, a bright red SUV, detached itself from the others, executed a U-turn, and then sped in their direction. It stopped next to where Liza and Candy stood. When the driver's door opened, Great Barrington's fire chief, Roland Blakely—ham and cheese omelet, cottage cheese, tomato slices, hold the toast—stepped out, doffing his hat to Liza.

"Someone told me you were here," he said. "Sorry about all this. It's a tough break. I know you've invested a whole lot of time and effort in this over the last few weeks. Unfortunately, both the house and garage were completely engulfed before the first units arrived on the scene. I knew you were at the funeral. Nobody else was in the house, were they? None of your coworkers?"

Liza shook her head. "They were all at the funeral," she answered. "Why do you ask?"

"Was anyone working here with equipment that might have caused a short or a spark or something like that? When you're dealing with a fire at a construction site, that's what we often find—that one of the workers screws up and does a faulty installation or some new piece of equipment suffers a case of infant mortality."

"No," Liza replied. "As far as I know, no one was working today, and I wasn't here, either. I went straight from my apartment to the funeral."

Chief Blakely nodded. "Let's say for argument's sake that it turns out the fire wasn't accidental."

"You're saying it might be arson?"

Blakely nodded. "Since both structures burned, that's a possibility. Do you know of anyone who bears a grudge against either you or your mother? Maybe there was a property dispute of some kind with one of the neighbors?"

Liza shook her head. "No," she said, "nothing like that, and I can't think of anybody who would wish us ill."

That wasn't true, of course. Even as she said the words, Liza was thinking about the warning she'd been given just that afternoon when Jonathan Thurgard had spoken to her in the cemetery. Was this what he had meant? Did the fire have something to do with the people he had mentioned, the ones her father had dealt with, the ones who didn't forgive or forget? Or—and this seemed far more likely—was it something to do with the money Selma had kept hidden away in the house? Liza had already suspected there had to be something wrong with the money. Otherwise, why would Selma have kept it hidden? Now whatever that was had come back to bite her in the butt—starting with burning down the house.

"Do you have home owner's insurance?" Blakely asked.

Liza nodded. She had renewed the policy only two weeks earlier. She'd had to wait until the cleanup was done and the remodel far enough along before an insurance underwriter could come through and assess the situation. He had checked on all the permits and had carefully inspected the new plumbing and electrical work. ·

"You'll need to call, report the loss, and get a claims adjuster out here," Chief Blakely said. "If you call my office in the morning, we can give you our file number as well as the one for the police report."

Since the policy had been reinstated so recently, Liza couldn't help but worry. What if the fire did turn out to be arson? Would the insurance company assume that Liza herself was behind it? Would they accuse her of burning down her own home in order to collect on the insurance? In that case, the insurance company might balk and refuse to pay the claim altogether.

Putting her roiling thoughts aside, Liza realized Chief Blakely was still talking. "Right now, the fire's still too hot and the structure too unstable for us to send anyone inside to look for the cause. I'm sure the sheriff's department will want to talk to you about this, and one of our fire inspectors will be reaching out to you as well. How should they get in touch?"

Liza reeled off her phone numbers—her cell and home numbers as well as the number at work.

"All right then," Blakely said when she finished. "Again, sorry about this, and sorry about your mother, too."

Liza nodded. "Thank you," she murmured.

Having been dismissed, Candy took hold of her arm and led her back to the car. "Come on," he said. "Let's get you home, unless you'd rather come back to the restaurant. I'm sure there are still people there."

Between the funeral and the fire, Liza was beyond crushed. Going back to the diner and having to break the bad news about the house to all the people who had invested so much time and effort in it was more than she could handle.

"Home would be better," she said. "What am I supposed to say to all the guys who helped me? How can I face them?"

"I'll tell them for you," Candy said grimly. "After all, you're not the one who burned the place down."

"Let's hope the insurance company believes that," Liza added.

Twilight was ending as Candy turned the corner onto Liza's tree-lined street. The neighborhood contained any number of older, larger homes, some of which had been converted into buildings with multiple-unit rentals. Liza was lucky in that her landlady, Olivia Dexter, a spinster who had inherited the family home, still occupied the two lower floors along with her two kitties and her extensive collection of hardback books. Olivia still had access to Liza's apartment from inside the house, but she had converted what had once been a fire escape into a separate entrance that allowed Liza to come and go from her attic apartment with as little disruption of Olivia's life as possible.

"You'll be all right, then?" Candy asked as he parked his Impala across the street from the house. "You don't want me to come up and stay with you for a while?"

"No," Liza said. "I'll be fine. Thanks for taking me out there. It would have been tough to do alone."

"You're welcome," he said.

She got out of the car and watched as he drove away. It was only after the car had turned the corner and disappeared from sight that she looked up at her apartment and noticed that the lights were on. That was odd. It had been almost noon when she left to go to the funeral home. Because she didn't have a separate meter on her apartment and because she knew Olivia was always struggling to make ends meet, Liza was conscientious about turning off the lights when she left for the day. As Selma Machett's daughter, she was incapable of doing anything else.

If the lights were on in her apartment and if someone had been inside, there was probably a simple explanation. Maybe there had been a problem at the house that day—a leak in the new flashing on the roof during the afternoon rainstorm or maybe a blocked pipe—that had resulted in Olivia's calling in a repairman of some kind. However, Liza was able to entertain that idea for only as long as it took her to walk up the driveway.

When she was even with the passenger door of her Nissan, she saw that the window had been broken. Even though the aging Nissan was unlocked, a brick had been thrown through the passenger-seat window. A layer of shattered glass covered the front seats. The paperwork from the glove box—her registration and insurance papers—was strewn on the floor. The mat on the floorboard, under which she kept a spare key to her apartment, had been lifted and pushed out of place. The spot where the key should have been was empty.

Shocked, Liza backed away from the car door without touching it while a wave of fear spread through her body. Someone had burned down her mother's house during the funeral. Now it looked as though someone had let themselves into Liza's apartment. For all she knew, they might have forced their way inside.

Liza studied the windows on the ground floor. Lights blazed throughout Olivia's portion of the house, too, but that didn't mean anything. Olivia spent most of her waking hours in a sitting room at the back of the house, reading or watching television. With her television set blaring, it was unlikely that she would have noticed the sound of breaking glass when the car window was smashed in the driveway out front.

Liza felt violated, so her first inclination was to charge up the stairs and order whoever had invaded her space to leave at once. After a moment, however, good sense prevailed. How many times had the unsuspecting heroine in a movie gone to the basement to check on something that wasn't quite right even though everyone in the audience was yelling, "Don't go in the basement"?

The women in the movies might not be smart enough to take the hint, but Liza was. She didn't climb the stairs, and she didn't step up on the front porch and ring Olivia's doorbell, either. Instead, on shaking knees, she backed all the way across the street and then sank down onto the curb with her silhouette hidden behind the shielding bulk of an out-of-control laurel hedge.

Her hands shook violently as she dug in her purse for her cell phone. Once she had the phone in hand, her trembling fingers were so clumsy that it was almost impossible to dial. Eventually, on the third try, she connected with the emergency operator.

"Nine one one. What are you reporting?"

"I just got home from a funeral," she said, whispering urgently into the phone. "Somebody broke into my car, and there are lights on in my apartment—lights I didn't leave on. There's a chance whoever did it may still be inside."

"What's your name, and what's the address?"

Struggling to speak normally, Liza gave the operator the required information.

"Where are you right now?" the operator asked.

"I'm across the street and out of sight. A friend just dropped me off."

"Stay right there," the operator cautioned. "I'm summoning units right now. If you see someone coming out of the house, do not engage them in any way. If they drive off in a vehicle, try to get the make, model, and license plate number, but that's it. Do not attempt to detain them, and do not try to follow them. Understand?"

"I understand," Liza repeated.

She didn't require much convincing. First her mother's house had been torched, and now this. Liza was petrified—beyond petrified, especially with James Thurgard's stern warning still ringing in her ears, the warning about the people who never forgot and never forgave. Apparently, they were now after her.

The operator came back on the line. "Are you still there, Liza?"

"Yes, I'm here."

"Any sign of movement inside the house?"

Liza had been keeping an eye on the windows in her apartment. "None," she said. "I haven't seen anybody."

"Stay put," the operator advised. "Officers are on their way."

Even as she spoke, Liza heard the sound of an approaching siren. Only after the patrol car stopped in front of the driveway and an officer stepped out did Liza emerge from her hiding place and hurry to meet him.

"Hi, Liza," Bruce Schindler said at once. "How's it going? You think someone's broken into your place? Which one is it?"

Liza recognized Officer Schindler, too—corned beef hash, two poached eggs, whole wheat toast, coffee, tomato juice.

"Up there," she said pointing. "When I left there this morning, none of those lights were on."

"That's Mrs. Dexter's house, right?" he said. "I grew up in this neighborhood. Have you talked to her?"

"I was afraid to ring the bell. If whoever did it is still upstairs, I didn't want to let them know that I was home."

A second patrol car pulled up and stopped, and an officer named Michael Lundgren stepped out. He was someone who came into the restaurant occasionally. Liza recognized his face, but he wasn't enough of a regular that she could recite his standard order.

"Okay," Officer Schindler said. "You stay right here, Liza. Mikey and I will go check things out. Where's the entrance?"

Liza pointed. "There's an outside entrance on the far side of the house."

As she said the words, Liza realized that if someone had come sneaking down the stairs and gone out the back way, she might not have seen them, even though she had been sitting right there. The house itself would have shielded them from view.

"Any other doors in or out?"

"There's another stairway inside the house, just to the right of the front door. The door at the top of that, the one that leads into my apartment, is usually left unlocked so Olivia or workmen can get inside as needed."

"All right then," Officer Lundgren said. "Let's go catch ourselves some bad guys. I'll go up the outside stairs; Bruce, you keep an eye on that front door."

The two of them set out at a trot while Liza melted back into the darkness to watch. Officer Lundgren made for the outside stairway. Bruce Schindler stationed himself just outside the front door in a spot where he'd be able to see into the vestibule through the sidelights. Behind her Liza heard doors opening and closing as curious neighbors up and down the street came out on their porches to see what was going on.

Eventually a shadow darted across one of the lit windows in her apartment. Sometime after that, Olivia's front door opened and Lundgren stepped out onto the porch. For several long moments the two cops conferred, then they both disappeared into the house. Again they were gone for some time before reappearing on the front porch. As they came down the walkway toward her, Liza stepped back into view.

"Did you find anyone?" she asked.

Bruce Schindler nodded grimly. "Someone had been there, all right, but by the time we arrived he was long gone. When's the last time you saw Olivia Dexter?" he asked.

"This morning," Liza said. "She was working out in her garden when I was waiting for the mortuary limo to show up. She came over and apologized to me for not coming to the funeral. She has a phobia about funerals."

"She won't have to worry about that anymore," Officer Lundgren observed.

"Why?" Liza asked. "What do you mean?"

"Because she's dead," he said. "Strangled, most likely. I found her at the top of the inside stairway leading to your apartment. She was right outside the door. She may have heard someone moving around up there and gone to investigate."

"She's dead?" Liza repeated numbly. "You're sure? I can't believe it. Someone murdered Olivia?"

As the world spun around her, Liza stumbled forward and leaned against the front fender of the nearest patrol car. Her legs gave way. If Bruce hadn't moved quickly enough to catch her, she would have fallen. He opened the door and eased her into the backseat of the patrol car, where Liza sat with her teeth chattering and with her breath coming in short hard gasps.

"Mike's calling for the homicide unit," Bruce said. "Are you going to be all right? Should I call an ambulance?"

"No," Liza managed at last. "Just let me sit here for a few minutes. I'll be okay."

Chapter 8

It was three o'clock in the afternoon before Joanna finally made it back to the Cochise County Justice Center. As she pulled into the parking lot, the presence of several media vans gave notice that her chief deputy, Tom Hadlock, was holding a press briefing.

Tom had once served as Joanna's jail commander. When her former chief deputy, Frank Montoya, had been hired away to become chief of police in Sierra Vista, Joanna had tapped Tom to be her new chief deputy. What she hadn't understood at the time was that although Tom was fine in one-on-one interactions, he was painfully shy when it came to any kind of public speaking. Since Joanna's chief deputy also functioned as her media relations officer, that had been a problem. However, a year's worth of Toastmasters training meant Tom was now in far better shape to field any and all media questions concerning Junior Dowdle's death.

Joanna herself was happy to avoid the press by driving around back, parking in her reserved shaded spot, and ducking into the building through the private door that led directly into her office.

Kristin Gregovich, Joanna's secretary, had placed the day's worth of correspondence in several neat stacks on Joanna's desk, organized in order of relative importance and urgency, with the topmost layer being the most critical. Joanna had spent most of the day riding herd on the Dowdle investigation. Now she had only a couple of hours in which to handle that day's mundane paperwork so she could leave things in good shape for Tom over the weekend. She felt guilty about leaving him with such a full plate. When she and Butch had made plans to be out of town for three days, it hadn't occurred to her that Tom would be in charge of an active investigation that might or might not turn out to be a homicide.

Joanna had barely started when Kristin poked her head in the door. "I thought I heard you come in," she said. "Detective Howell is on the phone."

Joanna picked up the handset. "Hey, Deb," she said. "Any luck?"

"We had some luck, all right," Deb Howell said, "all of it bad. Terry and Spike led Dave Hollicker and me all the way back to the Maxwells' place, following the same trail Junior took. We found nothing at all along the way—no blood, no cigarette butts, and no footprints, either. At the last minute when we were almost back at the house, Dave slipped on some loose gravel and took a tumble. He's either broken his ankle or sprained it. He's on his way to the hospital to have it x-rayed. Terry's driving. I've arranged for someone to come collect Dave's car and take it back down to the motor pool."

"Good thinking," Joanna said, trying not to sound as exasperated as she felt. It was bad enough that she was going out of town and leaving Tom Hadlock in charge of the Dowdle investigation. Now, with one member of her two-person CSI unit on the disabled list, he would be working with one hand tied behind his back. As for Dave's injured ankle? That meant her department was looking at a workman's comp claim that would most likely generate mountains of paperwork.

"What about Casey?" Joanna asked. "Did she have a chance to dust for prints?"

"She did, and she found some, both inside and outside Junior's room. When Dr. Machett finishes with the autopsy, we'll have Junior's prints. Casey will need to get elimination prints from both Daisy and Moe."

"Be sure she collects a set of prints from Jason Radner, too," Joanna suggested. "According to Moe, he sometimes palled around with Junior."

"Will do. That should be easy enough since all three Radners are due at the department any minute."

"They're coming here?" Joanna asked.

"For all I know, they're already there," Deb replied. "I believe Ernie is. Matt Keller told Ernie that when he was interviewing the Maxwells' neighbors first thing this morning, he got the feeling there was something slightly off about Jason, as though he knew more than he was saying. At the time Matt talked to him, it was early in the day, and he didn't know Junior was dead. Ernie went ahead and scheduled an additional interview. I'm coming, too, and I'm only minutes away."

"Are the Radners coming armed with an attorney?" Joanna asked.

"I can't speak to that," Deb replied, "but I wouldn't be surprised if they do. If a cop working a homicide invited my son to drop by for a little heart-to-heart, I'd see to it that an attorney was present, just to be on the safe side."

Joanna thought about Jenny. "I would, too."

"One more thing," Deb said. "What's going on with the autopsy?"

"Dr. Machett has a conflict," Joanna answered. "He's out of town today and tomorrow, too. He says the autopsy can't be done until sometime Saturday, but he didn't specify an exact time."

"We're pulling out all the stops to work this case," Deb muttered. "Wouldn't it be nice if Guy Machett had the same sense of urgency?"

"Yes," Joanna said. "It would indeed."

Once she was off the phone, Joanna headed for the interview room. The OCCUPIED sign had already been turned over. Rather than going inside and interrupting the process, Joanna went into an adjacent room and turned on the audio/video feed. Jack and Lois Radner sat perched nervously on two of the molded plastic chairs that surrounded a small Formica table while their son slumped dispiritedly in the far corner. Next to him and on full alert was Burton Kimball, Bisbee's leading criminal defense attorney. Ernie Carpenter, notebook open in front of him, sat diagonally across the table from Jason.

"You'd say that you and Junior were friends?" he asked.

"Sure," Jason answered. "We played checkers and sometimes dominoes."

"When's the last time you saw him?" Ernie asked.

"Yesterday," Jason replied with a shrug. "Yeah, last night when I took our garbage can out to the street. He was sitting on his porch."

"Did you say anything to him? Exchange words?"

"Just, 'Hey,' I guess. We didn't really talk. It was time for dinner. I had to get back inside."

"Have you noticed any changes in Junior's behavior recently?" Ernie asked.

"Look," Jason replied. "I knew he was sick, with that old-timer's disease."

"You mean Alzheimer's?"

"Yeah, that's the one. So he had been a little different lately, but nothing really bad. Sometimes he would get sort of upset."

"Like when he threw the checkers at you?" Ernie asked.

Jason shot a quick look in the detective's direction, as though surprised that Ernie already knew about the thrown checkerboard.

"Yeah," he said. "Like that."

"Did Junior have any other friends besides you?" Ernie asked.

"I don't know," Jason said. "Maybe. I mean he knew people from his mom's restaurant. They're all sort of friends of his, right?"

"But no other close friends?"

"No," Jason said, "not that I know of."

That was the moment when Joanna saw what Matt Keller had seen. Jason Radner was lying about something. Ernie must have seen it, too.

The door to the viewing room opened behind Joanna. Deb Howell stepped inside and sat down. "How's it going?" she asked.

Joanna put her finger to her lips.

"You never saw him hanging out with anyone else from the neighborhood?" Ernie continued. "It sounds like you were his only friend."

"I guess," Jason conceded.

"Were you ever inside Junior's room?" Ernie asked.

"Sure," Jason said, "lots of times. We went there to play with his Xbox."

"In that case, before you go home, we'll need a set of prints from you."

Jason's father, Jack, rose to his feet. "Fingerprints!" he roared. "You want to fingerprint my boy? Are you accusing him of murdering Junior? You told me we were coming in here for a routine interview, and now you want to take his prints?"

Burton Kimball held up a calming hand, and Jack Radner subsided back into his chair. "Is that really necessary, Detective Carpenter?"

"Yes, it is," Ernie answered. "Casey Ledford, our latent fingerprint tech, just finished dusting Junior's room. That means we'll need elimination prints from anyone who has been inside his room. That's the only way we'll be able to sort known visitors from unknown ones. We'll be taking Moe's and Daisy's prints as well."

"Asking for elimination prints isn't the same as making an accusation, Jack," Kimball assured Jason's parents. "It's standard procedure."

"Let's go back to last night for a moment," Ernie continued, turning back to Jason. "I understand your bedroom is directly opposite Junior's on the far side of a narrow passageway that runs between your house and his. Is that correct?"

Jason nodded.

"Is your bedroom window usually open or closed?"

"It was open last night," Jason volunteered. "It was hot. The window was open and the fan was on, so I wouldn't have heard anyone talking."

"Are you saying there were people talking?" Ernie asked.

"No," Jason said a bit too forcefully. "I said if there had been people talking, I wouldn't have been able to hear them."

"Look at his face," Deb observed. "He's lying about that or he's lying about something else. Maybe there were people outside, and he heard them. That might mean we have a witness who doesn't want to talk."

Joanna nodded. "Sounds like a possibility," she said.

"What time did you go to sleep?" Ernie asked.

Jason shrugged. "I don't know exactly. Sometime after Mom and Dad went to bed."

"We usually go to bed once the news is over," Lois Radner said, speaking for the first time. "So right around ten thirty or so."

"I'm assuming you and Mr. Radner didn't hear anything, either?" Ernie inquired.

"No, we didn't. Jason has a fan in his room, and we have one in ours. They're noisy, but they work. We have an AC unit up on the roof, but it's so expensive to operate that we don't use it unless we absolutely have to."

"You didn't participate in the search this morning?" Ernie asked.

"No, we commute together to Fort Huachuca," Jack said. "We both work on post and have to leave the house by seven."

"What happened to Junior?" Jason asked.

In Joanna's experience, guilty parties didn't have to ask about what happened to a homicide victim because they already knew. Jason Radner was lying about something, but the fact that he'd asked the question was a mark in his favor. On the other hand, there was a chance that Jason might be smarter than they thought.

"He fell," Ernie answered. "Fell far enough and hard enough that he died."

Jason swallowed hard and blinked as though trying to stem some tears. "I'm sorry," he mumbled. "I mean, I'm sorry for him and for Mr. and Mrs. Maxwell, too."

If Ernie read anything into Jason's sudden apology, he didn't let on. "Let me ask you this," Ernie said. "What was Junior like when it came to animals?"

"What do you mean?"

"I mean, did you ever see him doing anything inappropriate as far as animals are concerned?"

"You mean like messing with them or hurting them or something?"

"Exactly," Ernie said.

Jason shook his head, but he looked decidedly uncomfortable.

"See there?" Deb whispered excitedly. "He does know something."

That was Joanna's take, too.

"So you never saw him mistreating animals?"

"No," Jason said quickly. "I never saw anything like that."

The defense attorney suddenly seemed to have seen and heard enough. Burton Kimball held up his hand.

"I think that's about it, Detective Carpenter. If you have no intention of holding my client, I believe we'll be on our way."

"Of course," Ernie said agreeably. "But do remember to stop by the front desk on your way out. I still need those prints."

The Radners rose to leave. Ernie waited until they left the room before shutting off the recorder and joining Joanna and Detective Howell in the adjacent room.

"The kid is hiding something," Ernie said. "And we need to figure out a way to get him to tell us what it is."

When Joanna returned to her office, Detective Jaime Carbajal was in the lobby just outside her door. Seated on a chair near Kristin's desk, he was leaning back with his eyes closed and his head resting against the wall. He wasn't asleep, however, because he got to his feet as soon as Joanna walked by and followed her into his office.

"Sometimes I hate people," he said quietly.

"The vet's office was that bad?" she asked.

"It was bad."

"Is the kitten going to make it?"

"Dr. Ross thinks so. She has a couple of broken ribs along with everything else. The doc used Super Glue to try to put the poor thing's ears back together. If it doesn't take, the ears may have to be amputated. By the way, did you know that's why they invented Super Glue—to use in surgical procedures?"

"I had no idea," Joanna said, "but here's what I want to know—did Dr. Ross find anything we can use?"

"Maybe," Jaime said. "There were bloodstains all over the poor thing, but some of them look more promising than others because they don't appear to be connected to any of the existing wounds. Dr. Ross collected dozens of samples. I already handed the samples over to the evidence clerk and asked him to put them in the fridge. You want me to take them to the crime lab in Tucson in the morning?"

"Yes, please."

"You don't think Junior is responsible for what happened to the cat, do you?" Jaime asked.

"No, I don't," Joanna said, "and I'm beginning to think he didn't kill himself, either, accidentally or otherwise." She paused and then asked, "What kind of people start their journey to the dark side by torturing animals?"

"Serial killers," Jaime answered at once.

"Right."

"So maybe Junior was a serial-killer wannabe?"

"No," Joanna said. "I don't think so. For one thing, that kitten is tough. She didn't go down without a fight. I took the crime scene photos. There weren't any bite marks or scratches on Junior's arms and hands. In addition, Moe and Daisy claim Junior was scared of the dark, and he was especially scared of caves. I believe someone enticed him out of the house and into the cave. Think about it. What if the killer convinced Junior that the kitten was in trouble and needed his help? He would have gone there in an instant, middle of the night or not, no questions asked."

Even as she said the words, Joanna knew she was right, as a lightbulb switched on inside her brain. The injured kitten may not have been Junior's victim, but she could still be the reason he was dead.

"DNA testing on that much material is going to cost money," Jaime observed.

Joanna looked at him and nodded. "Yes, it is," she said, "and we're going to pay the piper, whatever the price may turn out to be. I believe we've got a budding serial killer on our hands, and I'm hoping Junior Dowdle was the first victim. We'll do whatever it takes to keep from having a second."

Jaime walked as far as the doorway, then he stopped and turned back. "By the way," he said. "I almost forgot. Dr. Ross makes sure that every animal that comes into her office gets chipped, whether the owners can afford it or not."

"Does our kitten have a chip?"

Jaime nodded. "Sure does. Her name's Star. She belonged to a family named Jalisco. They live in one of the apartment buildings up by the old high school."

"Belonged?" Joanna asked. "As in past tense?"

"Dr. Ross's secretary called to let them know Star had been injured and was undergoing treatment. The mother, Roseanne, is a clerk out at Safeway. She's also newly divorced. She said she already told her daughter that Star ran away and probably got run over. Roseanne says that at the time the kitten disappeared, she was wearing a pink ribbon and no tag. She also said that whatever the vet bill is, she can't afford it. Her suggestion was that Dr. Ross go ahead and put Star down."

"That's not going to happen," Joanna declared.

"No, it's not," Jaime agreed. "I told Dr. Ross that if nobody else will take Star, Delcia and I will, and that whatever the bill is, we're good for that, too."

"You don't have to do that," Joanna said. "That cat is evidence. The department will pay for her care."

"All right then," Jaime said, "but there's one more thing I should mention."

"What's that?"

"The next time you have a case like this, it's Ernie's turn to go to the vet's office."

"Fair enough," Joanna replied. "Are you going to interview Roseanne Jalisco directly?"

Jaime nodded. "Her kids are out of school this afternoon and tomorrow, too. I thought I'd track her down at work tomorrow, rather than questioning her at home in front of the little ones. She told Dr. Ross's receptionist that Star has been missing for about three days. Dr. Ross estimates that's how old some of the wounds are."

"Whoever did it is going to jail," Joanna declared forcefully.

"I know," Jaime replied with a grim nod. "That's what I told Star, too."

With that, Detective Carbajal walked out of Joanna's office. Watching him go, Sheriff Joanna Brady couldn't help but smile. On the surface Jaime was a big, tough guy. What Joanna had learned about him was that under that gruff, scary exterior lurked a real softie. Joanna liked him all the better for knowing that.

It was almost nine o'clock that night before she finished doing what needed to be done. She had written up an official report about the crime scene and printed out the collection of photos she had taken down in the mine shaft. She had pulled Tom Hadlock in and briefed him on everything that was going on. She had spoken to Dave Hollicker and confirmed that his ankle was badly sprained, but that he'd be in to work on crutches as long as someone would agree to drive him. She also had managed to reach Guy Machett, had a firm schedule for the Dowdle autopsy, and had notified Deb, the lead detective, of same. Joanna ended her long day by knocking off the remainder of her paperwork. Only when her desk was clear did she gather up her purse, turn off the lights, and head out the door.

Dennis was in bed and Jenny incommunicado in her room by the time Joanna got home. She reheated the plate of green chili casserole Butch had left for her in the fridge, slathered on some sour cream, and then went looking for him, taking her plate of food along with her. She found her husband in his office, hunched over his computer, working on his third book. He looked up at her when she came in and then glanced at his watch. "Another fifteen-hour day," he observed. "How are you doing?"

"Better than Moe and Daisy Maxwell," she said.

"Do you want to talk about it?" Butch asked.

Joanna had touched base with Butch earlier in the evening and briefed him on some of it, but after living the case all day, she was done. "Not really," she said. "What time do we need to leave in the morning?"

Butch seemed genuinely surprised. "You still want to go?"

A couple of years earlier, Joanna might have used the Dowdle investigation as an excuse for canceling the Silver City excursion, but she was older now, and, she hoped, a little wiser, too. Life had taught her a few lessons. For one, she now understood that her father wasn't nearly as perfect as she'd always thought him to be. Sheriff D. H. Lathrop had often used involvement in the job as a way to dodge his responsibilities as a husband and father. Joanna was determined that she wouldn't make the same mistake.

"Homicide investigation or no," she said, "I promised Jenny I was going, and I will. What time do we leave?"

Butch grinned at her. "Wonders will never cease," he said. "Let's say wheels up at ten. It's a four-hour drive, hauling that trailer, and I'd like to be there before everybody else gets off work. We can caravan over. Jenny and I will be in the truck pulling the horses; you and Denny can follow in my car. Jenny, Desi, and the horses will stay at Katy Beltran's place outside of town. There's a dance tomorrow night and Jenny and Katy plan on going to that together. You, Denny, and I have hotel reservations in town. The three of us will go someplace nice for dinner both nights."

Katy was someone Jenny had met on the rodeo circuit. The girls had become friends as well as friendly competitors. If the horses had been boarded at the rodeo grounds, Jenny would have had to stay there, too, sleeping in the camper shell on the truck. As far as Joanna was concerned, having everybody stay at the Beltrans' ranch was far preferable, as was having Jenny go to an out-of-town rodeo dance with a girlfriend rather than alone.

"You've got it all planned out, don't you," Joanna said.

Butch nodded and grinned. "I do my best," he said.

Chapter 9

Liza Machett stole a glance at her watch and rubbed her eyes. It was after midnight. She was alone in an interview room at the Great Barrington Police Department, where she had spent the better part of the last five hours. Some of the time she had been left alone, waiting, but most of the time Detective Amos Franklin, a homicide cop, had been with her, asking questions.

He had assured her that this was just a routine interview and that he was trying to get a handle on everything that had happened, but Liza wasn't convinced. He hadn't read her her rights, so she assumed that meant that she hadn't been declared a suspect, at least not so far. She also hadn't asked for an attorney, although she was beginning to wonder if she should have.

The door opened. Franklin came back into the room, carrying a cup of foul-smelling coffee—brackish, ugly stuff that had been at the bottom of a coffeepot and should have been thrown out hours ago.

Liza didn't want coffee. She wanted to go to bed, but she didn't know where. Her apartment was an active crime scene. Her landlady's home was an active crime scene. And whatever was left of her mother's house, the one she had labored so hard to make livable, was also an active crime scene. She didn't want to answer any more questions; she wanted to quit for the night—to tell the detective that she'd come back and tackle all this tomorrow. The problem was, she worried how Detective Franklin might interpret that. Would her pleading to be let out of the interview room cause him to assume she was a guilty party rather than an innocent one?

"Okay," Franklin said, resuming the chair opposite her that he had abandoned fifteen minutes earlier. "I know this has been a terribly difficult day for you, Ms. Machett, and I won't keep you much longer. Let's just go over a couple of things again to make sure I have it all down."

He made a show of opening a notebook and spreading it out in front of him. Then he took out a pen and sat with it poised over a perfectly clean page. Liza knew that was all for appearance's sake. She had already spotted the video camera in the far corner of the room, up near the ceiling. Each time the interview was interrupted or resumed, Detective Franklin made a production of turning his high-tech equipment off and on.

"What things?" Liza asked.

"We've already verified your alibi any number of times. You were at the funeral with at least forty people when the fire broke out at your mother's place. We don't have an official time of death on Ms. Dexter just yet, but unofficially it looks like you were either still at the reception or else at the arson scene when her homicide took place. The location of her body would suggest that she overheard something happening in your apartment and was murdered when she went to investigate. Although she was the homicide victim, her part of the house hadn't been disturbed in any way. Your apartment, on the other hand, was ransacked. Your car was broken into. That leads me to think that you're the real target here, and yet you sit here claiming to have no enemies and no idea why someone might have it in for you?"

"That's right," Liza said. "I don't."

"What about your brother—your half brother?"

"Guy? What about him? What does he have to do with this?"

"I was just on the phone to the attorney who's handling your mother's estate. He tells me that, according to the terms of Selma Machett's will, her home—or whatever is left of it—goes to you and you alone. Even though the property was originally owned by your father's family—Guy's father's family—your brother isn't named as a beneficiary under your mother's will."

That wasn't exactly news to Liza. Selma and Guy had been estranged for years. Liza said nothing.

"As to your mother's house—the house you've spent a small fortune on rehabbing during the last few weeks—it's been burned to the ground," Franklin continued. "Maybe your brother took exception to the will. It wouldn't be the first time a disgruntled heir who was written out of a will decided to go after the person who made out like a bandit."

"My brother wouldn't do this," Liza said. "Guy has his own life. He wrote us off a long time ago."

"He didn't come to the funeral?"

"He didn't have to. He was my mother's stepson."

"Where does he live these days?"

"In Bisbee, Arizona. I understand he's the M.E. there."

"Anyone else that you're aware of who might have a murderous grudge against you or your mother or Olivia Dexter? When stuff like this happens, there's usually a reason. I'd like to know if you have any idea about that—not only who but why."

Sitting alone in the little interview room while Franklin went to get his evil-smelling cup of coffee, Liza had concluded that this had to be about the money. Maybe the money belonged to the people Jonathan Thurgard had warned her about. Somehow they had determined that Liza had the cash, and now they wanted it back. That must have been what they were searching for in her apartment, and they had murdered Olivia when she interrupted them, all of which made Liza glad that she'd been smart enough not to store the money in her apartment.

The sensible thing would have been for Liza to come clean right then and tell Detective Franklin the whole story, but she didn't. She had grown up under Selma Machett's thumb and lived by her rules for too many years. Some of Selma's paranoid rants about the world being full of crooked cops had rubbed off on her daughter.

Liza had worked in the diner for almost a third of her life. When a jerk of a customer came in and hassled the waitresses, they always served him the worst possible coffee and then made fun of him behind his back when he wasn't smart enough to send the bad coffee back. As Detective Franklin sat there, drinking his cup of swill, Liza Machett made up her mind. Anyone so dim as to drink that appalling excuse for coffee didn't deserve to be trusted, not with Liza's money and certainly not with her life. As a consequence, the answer she gave him now was the same one she had given him hours earlier.

"I have no idea," she said.

"If you'll pardon my saying so, you're a very attractive young woman," he said, favoring her with a sly look. "Is it possible you have a disappointed boyfriend lurking in the background?"

Liza's difficult childhood and worse adolescence had left her in a social vacuum. She could handle the easy banter that was tossed back and forth in the restaurant, but she had trust deficits that made romantic entanglements prohibitive. At twenty-nine, she didn't like to think of herself as an old maid, but she suspected she was well on her way to that outcome.

"No boyfriends of any kind," she said.

"Girlfriends then?" Franklin persisted. She caught the small smirk at the corners of his lips and understood what it meant. If Liza didn't have boyfriends, he automatically assumed she was a lesbian.

"None of those, either," she told him.

"If you can't say who or why, how about what?" Franklin said. "They went through both your car and apartment in a way that indicates they were looking for something specific. Maybe they found it; maybe they didn't. We won't know for sure until you can get back inside to take an inventory of what's missing. What occurs to me is that often when we encounter these kinds of unexplained break-ins, there may be some other agenda involved, like illicit drugs, for example, or the presence of drug-making paraphernalia. Is that a possibility here, Ms. Machett? Are you involved in the drug trade, or is it possible someone mistakenly believes you to be?"

Liza's hackles came up. "I'm not involved with drugs. I don't use them; I don't sell them; I don't manufacture them. I'm a law-abiding citizen without so much as a speeding ticket on my record. I didn't burn down my house. I didn't murder Olivia Dexter. I didn't ransack my own apartment, so I'd like you to start treating me like a victim instead of a criminal. Now, if you're not going to arrest me, I'm going to leave."

She stood up, expecting Franklin to object and order her back in her chair. Instead, he didn't move. "Where exactly are you going?" he asked. "You won't be able to go home, at least not tonight, and probably not tomorrow, either."

"I'll figure it out."

"Would you like me to give you a lift?"

"No, thank you," she said. "Wherever I'm going, I'll get there on my own."

A telephone hung on the wall. Franklin reached over, lifted the receiver, and pressed in a code. After a moment, the lock on the door buzzed and the door itself swung open. Without another word, Liza stepped out into the hallway.

"Stay in touch," Detective Franklin called after her.

She walked away from him without looking back. Halfway down the hall, she realized she'd made a mistake. She was still dressed in the clothing she'd worn to the funeral, including a pair of heels—low heels, but heels nonetheless. It was the middle of the night, she had no idea where she was going, she had no car, and her feet were killing her.

Out in the lobby, she was astonished to see the familiar figure of Candy Small, slumped and dozing in a chair next to the door.

"What are you doing here?" she asked.

"Bruce Schindler called and told me what had happened. I came right down. Are you all right?" He glanced as his watch. "What the hell have you been doing in there all this time?"

"Being interviewed by Detective Franklin. I'm supposedly the victim here, but if you ask me, he's treating me more like a suspect."

Candy shook his head. "Amos Franklin was a jerk when we were in fifth grade. Nothing has changed. Come on."

"Where are we going?"

"Since your place is tagged as a crime scene, I guess you're coming home with me," Candy answered.

"I could always stay at the Holiday Inn," Liza suggested. It was only a halfhearted objection because she was too exhausted to make more of a fuss.

"No," Candy said. "You're staying in my spare room. You'll need some different clothing and shoes and whatever else, but we can get those later today after the stores open up. Right now I'm taking you home. No arguments."

His car was parked right outside in what, during the day, was a loading zone. Candy's collection of waitresses swore he was the model for the Norwegian bachelor farmers that peopled Lake Wobegon on NPR's *Prairie Home Companion.* Liza understood at once that he wasn't making a pass at her; this was an offer of a safe place to spend the night, no strings attached.

"Thank you," she murmured as he helped her into his car, a two-year-old Impala.

"You're welcome."

Candy climbed into the driver's seat and started the engine. "Is this about the money?" he asked.

"Is that what the bad guys were looking for in your apartment?"

She had told Candy about finding the money. He was, in fact, the only person she had told. It had come up in conversation when she had been trying to figure out how to organize repairing her mother's house. At Candy's suggestion, she had used one of the empty employee lockers off the restaurant's kitchen to store the bulk of her cash. Since the place was open round the clock, that had seemed like a wise idea. Now she hoped that whoever had broken into her apartment hadn't done the same thing at the restaurant.

"I think so," she said.

"Did you tell Amos about the money?"

"No, I was afraid he'd figure out some way to confiscate whatever I have left. He's already as good as accused me of committing fraud, suggesting that I burned down my own place just to collect the insurance money. Since I was at the funeral and couldn't possibly have started the fire, he must think I hired someone to do it."

"Why would you fix up the house and then burn it down?" Candy asked. "That makes no sense."

"Not to me, either," Liza said miserably.

They turned into the driveway of Candy's 1950s-era bungalow and pulled inside a surprisingly spacious two-car garage, with a door that closed behind them. The house was only a few blocks from the restaurant. When the weather was decent, Candy often walked back and forth to work. When the door finished closing, he came around to help Liza out of the passenger seat.

"Somebody I didn't know came to the funeral today," Liza said as they headed into the house. "His name is Jonathan Thurgard. He claimed that he knew my dad and he said something about watching out for people who never forgive and never forget. It sounded like he was trying to warn me about something or somebody."

"What did he say exactly?" Candy asked.

"That he had known my dad back in the old days when they both drove bread trucks."

Candy stopped in his tracks just inside the kitchen. "Your dad drove a bread truck?" he echoed.

"Evidently," Liza said.

"Holy crap! Why didn't I know about this before?" Candy demanded. "Why didn't you tell me?"

He sounded either surprisingly angry or surprisingly scared; Liza couldn't tell which.

"How could I tell you something I didn't know myself until this afternoon?"

"Come on," he said. "We've gotta go." Grabbing Liza's upper arm in a surprisingly painful grip, he spun her around and propelled her back into the garage and toward the car.

"Ouch," she whimpered. "That hurt. Let go of me."

"I meant it to hurt," he said.

"Why?" she demanded, more angry now than scared. "What do you think you're doing?"

"I gave you a set of bruises because you're going to need them. They're your ticket to ride."

"What on earth are you talking about?"

When they reached the car, instead of opening the front passenger door, he opened the rear one and shoved Liza inside.

"Lie down on the seat so no one can see you," he ordered, "and don't move."

"I'm not lying down until you tell me what's going on and where we're going."

"Don't you watch the news?" Candy demanded. "Haven't you been following that big racketeering trial going on in Boston?"

"Hello," Liza said. "Are you kidding? In case you haven't noticed, my mother just died. Between her being in the hospital and me rehabbing her house, I haven't exactly been sitting around eating bonbons and watching the evening news. I know there's been a big trial—some kind of old mobster guy—but I haven't been paying attention."

"It's not just some old mobster," Candy replied. "The mobster happens to be Johnny 'Half-Moon' Miller. His older brother, James, aka 'Big Jim' Miller was a stone-cold killer if ever there was one. Ditto for Half-Moon."

"But what does any of this have to do with me?"

"It has everything to do with you, because if the Millers are after you, sweetheart, you are in deep trouble."

"You're scaring me."

"And it's a good thing, too. Now give me your cell phone."

"Why? Don't you have yours?"

He stood there with his hand outstretched, not taking no for an answer. Finally, she dug her phone out of her purse and handed it over. He immediately turned it off and removed the battery.

"Hey," she objected. "What are you doing? I need that."

In response, he stuffed the now-dead phone into his shirt pocket. "No, you don't," he replied. "Now, are you going to lie down or not?"

"Do I have a choice?"

"Not if you want to live," he said grimly. "If somebody's watching my house, it's close enough to time for me to go to work that they won't think twice about my leaving for the restaurant at this hour."

"What about me?"

"As far as they're concerned, they'll think you're still here, which is exactly what we want."

With no further objections, Liza did as she was told and lay down in the backseat. Slamming the back door, Candy hustled around to the front seat. Once in the driver's seat, he opened the garage door, turned the key in the ignition, and then shifted into reverse. After waiting long enough for the garage door to close again, he tore out of his driveway and rocketed forward with the tires screeching on the pavement.

"So that's where we're going?" Liza asked. "The restaurant?"

"That's right. First we're going to collect your money, then we're going to see a friend of mine and figure out a way to get you the hell out of town."

"How come? What's wrong?"

"The Millers spent decades ruling the roost as far as the Massachusetts drug trade was concerned. In the seventies and eighties they were able to operate practically out in the open, because they paid off everybody who needed to be paid off."

"I still don't understand."

"That's because you're not paying attention," Candy said irritably. "How do you suppose the Millers transported their drugs out to their various suppliers and brought the money back to Boston? How did they deliver the bribes that made it possible for them to stay in business? I'll tell you how. They bought themselves a bakery, a working bakery, but the guys who drove bread trucks for them delivered a hell of a lot more than bread, and once Big Jim was gone, Half-Moon ran the business on his own."

"You're saying my dad was mixed up in all that?"

"Don't be naive," Candy admonished. "Of course he was mixed up in it. He took off, didn't he?"

"Yes, he did," Liza conceded, "when I was just a baby. He ran off with another woman—a blonde."

"I'm willing to bet that your father didn't take off with any blonde," Candy declared. "More likely, he took off with some of Big Jim's money, and now some of Half-Moon's associates are coming after you to get it back."

"You think they're watching us right now?" Liza asked.

"They'd be stupid not to. They'll have someone watching the house and someone watching me."

He pulled into what Liza guessed was his customary parking place behind the restaurant. Instead of getting out, however, he picked up Liza's cell phone. Without turning it on, he held it to his ear, pretending to be talking on it when he was really talking to Liza. Realizing Candy was that sure they had been followed from his house, Liza felt a shiver of real fear pass through her body.

"What happens next?"

"They used bread trucks, so we'll use a bread truck, too," Candy said. "I'll pull up next to the loading dock. Andrew McConnell should be here with the bread delivery in forty-five minutes. I'll get your money out of the locker. Once Andrew shows up, I'll give it to him. Then I'll create a diversion. When that happens, get out of the car, climb into the back of Andrew's truck, and stay there. He'll know where to drop you off. All you have to do is follow instructions. Got it?"

"It sounds like you and Andrew have done this before," Liza observed quietly.

"Yup," Candy said. "Many times. You ever hear of the Underground Railroad?"

"Sure," Liza said, "but that was back in the old days, during the Civil War, when they were smuggling slaves out of the South."

"That was Underground Railroad 1.0," Candy replied with a chuckle. "Welcome aboard 2.0. From now on, this is the story: you're on the run from your bad-guy husband—the one who put those ugly bruises on your arm. I'm putting you in the care of some good folks who would be a lot less likely to help if they knew that the people who are after you are some of Half-Moon Miller's old pals."

"That's how this works? I claim to be a victim of domestic violence?"

"That's right. Make up a good story and stick to it like glue. Whatever you do, don't get back in touch with me. Since you were with me earlier tonight, they'll probably be watching me, too, same as they are right now. Got it?"

"Got it," Liza replied, "but where do I go?"

"You must have someone. What about your brother? Where's he?"

"In Arizona."

"Go there, then," Candy advised. "As I recall, your brother was always a real smart guy. Have Guy help you figure out how to deal with this mess. Good luck, and for Pete's sake, keep your head down."

Pocketing her phone, Candy got out of the car and slammed the door behind him. For the next hour Liza stayed where she was, not daring to move and hardly daring to breathe. She heard the bread truck pull up beside her and then she waited some more, wondering what the diversion would be.

When it came, there was no mistaking it. Sirens sounded and lights flashed as a fire truck pulled up behind the Impala. Doors slammed open and shut as another emergency vehicle arrived on the scene. With amber and red lights pulsing behind her, Liza cautiously pushed open the door and scrambled outside. The bread truck was parked right next to her, and the driver's door was wide open. Holding her breath, she clambered into the vehicle, made her way into the back, and sank down onto the floor.

For a long time after that, nothing happened. Much later she heard the grumble of engines as the emergency vehicles departed. Soon after that, Andrew McConnell—two eggs over hard, whole wheat toast, hot cocoa—came out of the restaurant and loaded a dolly into the back of the truck. Next to the dolly he set Liza's roll-aboard suitcase, the one that held the money.

"Just settle in and stay put," Andrew warned her. "You don't get dropped off until close to the end of my route."

Chapter 10

On Saturday morning, when the parade of girls on horseback charged through the gate and surged into the dusty rodeo arena at a full gallop, Denny squealed with excitement. "There she is," he said, pointing. "There's Jenny."

Joanna saw at once that he was right—there was Jenny, bent low over Kiddo's back, holding aloft a huge American flag that streamed out behind both horse and rider. The troop of girls circled the arena at a gallop several times before coming to a stop before the judge's stand, where they stood stock-still while a recorded version of the "Star-Spangled Banner" blared over the loudspeakers.

Butch and Dennis immediately doffed their Stetsons. Standing next to them with her hand over her heart,

Joanna felt her eyes fill with tears of motherly pride. She knew that only the best riders were tapped for flag duty. Jenny's proficiency on horseback was a skill she had acquired all on her own. Jenny and Kiddo had won countless barrel-racing competitions, but the trophies and buckles they had accumulated had everything to do with Jenny's own pursuit of excellence and very little to do with parental guidance or insistence. Yes, Butch and Joanna made sure horse and rider made it to the various far-flung rodeo venues, but Jenny and Kiddo were the ones who put in the hours of practice, day after day and month after month.

An hour later, when Jenny and Kiddo placed second in the barrel-racing competition, there was no hiding Butch's disappointment. They cleared the three barrels flawlessly but had come up short in the speed depart-ment, well behind Katy Beltran on her dapple gray mare, LaLa.

"Kiddo's a great horse," Butch said, "but if Jenny's going to participate at collegiate levels of competition, she needs a mount that's younger and faster."

Joanna gazed at her husband in astonishment. "You're kidding, right?"

"Not at all," Butch replied. "If Jenny wanted to be a concert pianist, we'd be in the market for the best pos-sible piano. This is the same thing. We should be in the market for the best possible horse. Kiddo will be fine when comes time for Denny to learn to ride, but for right now I think the horse has earned the right to retire from competition. He can hang out at home with Spot instead of being dragged all over God's creation to rodeos."

"Do you understand how much good quarter horses go for?" Joanna asked.

"I've got a pretty good idea," Butch said with a cagey grin. "More than we paid for the pickup truck and trailer we bought to haul Jenny and all her gear from place to place."

"You've been looking into this, haven't you?" Joanna surmised, finally tumbling to the fact that she was late to this particular party. Evidently the Kiddo retirement conversation had been taking place for some time without Joanna's being privy to it.

Butch nodded, a little sheepishly.

"Have you already found a suitable candidate?"

"Katy's dad raises quarter horses. Yesterday when we got here, Jenny and I took a look at the horses he currently has available. None of them really grabbed her. She has her heart set on one that's about to go on the market north of Phoenix—a five-year-old mare that Dr. Ross heard about. She belongs to friends of a vet Dr. Ross knows up in Payson. They're willing to make us a good deal."

"It sounds like this is already a fait accompli."

"Pretty much," Butch admitted, "but remember, Joey, we're lucky. This is all about horses, not boys." He smiled at her, then said to their son, "Come on, Denny. Let's go get us some hot dogs."

Butch and Denny left Joanna sitting alone and stewing about having been left odd man out of the new horse discussion. Still, she had to acknowledge that Butch's final argument was a winning one. At Jenny's age, an abiding interest in horses was far preferable to an abiding interest in boys, especially considering the fact that at seventeen, the same age Jenny was now, Joanna was already pregnant without being married. Her wedding to Andy Brady had been somewhat tardy.

A few minutes later, when Butch and Dennis returned with hot dogs for everyone, Joanna stifled an urge to gripe about the mustard and ketchup smeared all over Denny's face and on his relatively clean clothes. This was a time to have fun, she reminded herself, not a time to be the mean mommy. Jenny showed up a few minutes later with Desi on a lead at her side. The dog, excited by all the commotion around him, was being a handful, not at all unlike an unruly toddler. As Jenny struggled to get him to behave, Joanna once again acknowledged the wisdom in Butch's approach—better horses and dogs than an unwed pregnancy and a baby.

"Sorry you didn't take first," Joanna said, handing over the hot dog Butch had brought for Jenny. If it had been up to Joanna, there would have been two hot dogs—a fully loaded one for Jenny and a plain one for Desi—but sharing people food wasn't an approved activity in the service dog training manual.

"We should have done better," Jenny said glumly, "but at least it was Katy and LaLa we lost to rather than Sonja from El Paso. I would have hated to lose to her. She's such a snob."

"Yes, you should have done better," Butch agreed. "Tough break, but there's always the next round."

"Maybe," Jenny agreed. "I hope so."

Having seen the error of her ways and been outvoted besides, Joanna decided now was as good a time as any to concede defeat. "I expect that your future barrel-racing events will be just fine," she said, "especially if the rumors I'm hearing are true."

"What rumors?" Jenny asked.

"That we're getting a new horse."

Jenny turned to her mother with her face suddenly alight. "Really? You mean it?" she asked. "We can do it?"

"Yes," Joanna said.

"Her name's Maggie," Jenny continued. "She's a palomino."

Joanna could see that since the new horse already had a name, she was indeed late to the party. On the other hand, she couldn't deny that the prospect of having a horse that shared the same name as her troublesome mother-in-law had a certain perverse appeal.

"I can hardly wait to meet her," Joanna said.

They sat in the grandstand with the late-spring afternoon sun beating down on their backs and with gritty rodeo action unfolding in front of them. Denny loved every bit of it. The first bronco-riding competitor landed facedown in the dirt. Standing up and brushing himself off, he exited the arena accompanied by the rodeo announcer's familiar but unwelcome words, "Nice try, but no time."

That was the moment Joanna's phone rang. When she went to answer, Deb Howell's number showed on the screen.

"I went to the morgue for Junior Dowdle's autopsy," Deb announced. "Dr. Machett didn't show. I've been here waiting for more than an hour. Ralph Whetson is here, too. He's tried calling the M.E.'s home as well as his cell. No answer. Rather than putting Chief Deputy Hadlock in Guy Machett's crosshairs, I thought I'd check with you first and get your read on the situation."

Over time Joanna had encountered plenty of difficulties in dealing with Guy Machett, but missing a scheduled autopsy had never been one of them. Scheduling was sometimes tough, but once something was on the calendar, the M.E. had always been reliable and punctual. He also demanded punctuality from any detectives who were supposed to be in attendance.

"Have you checked with Madge Livingston?" Joanna asked.

"Tried," Deb answered. "With her boss out of town, Madge and some of her fellow Harley riders are off on a weekend road trip to Lake Havasu. She isn't picking up, either."

"Maybe Dr. Machett had car trouble and is stranded somewhere," Joanna suggested. "Even so, just to be sure, you should probably do a welfare check at his house. You know where he lives, don't you?"

"Of course I know where he lives," Deb replied. "On the Vista. Where else?"

The Vista, in Bisbee's Warren neighborhood, was composed of two parallel streets that ran on opposite sides of a now mostly barren park. The Vista had long been home to members of Bisbee's upper crust, all the way back to the town's early mining days.

"Keep me posted," Joanna said as she rang off.

To derogatory hoots and hollers from the grandstand, another bronco-riding hopeful had just bitten the dust half a leap after his horse, War Paint, a comical-looking black-and-white paint, had cleared the chute.

"What's up?" Butch asked over Denny's head.

"Dr. Machett was due at an autopsy at two, but he's currently MIA," she said.

"It's the weekend," Butch said. "He's a bachelor. Maybe he got lucky."

The bull-riding event was just getting under way when Deb called back. "I hate to bother you again, Sheriff Brady, but I think you need to come home."

"Why?" Joanna asked. "What's wrong?"

"Dr. Machett is dead," Deb said.

The words took a while to sink in.

"Dead?" Joanna repeated. "How? What happened?"

"At first glance I'd say he was subjected to several different kinds of torture," Deb responded, sounding shaken. "It's bad—as bad as anything I've seen."

"Have you contacted Chief Bernard?" Joanna asked.

"Yes, ma'am. That was my first call," Deb said. "Detective Keller is on his way, but Chief Bernard said I should call you and see if you have any suggestions about what to do. He's asking that we make this a joint operation, but without an M.E. available, what the hell are we supposed to do about the crime scene?"

"Give me a few minutes," Joanna said. "Let me see what I can do."

Butch had heard enough of Joanna's side of the conversation to know something was terribly amiss. He reached into his pocket, pulled out his wallet, and handed a five to Jenny. "Why don't you take Dennis down to the snow cone booth?"

"What's up?" he asked once the kids were out of earshot.

"Guy Machett is dead," Joanna said. "Murdered. Deb just found his body. She's called Chief Bernard. He's asked for our help, but with no M.E. to do the preliminary crime scene analysis . . ."

Butch didn't let her finish the sentence. "Of course you have to go," he said. "Just put Denny's car seat in the truck. He can ride home with Jenny and me tomorrow."

"You're sure?"

"Of course I'm sure," Butch said. "We'll be fine. You go do your job."

Joanna left the grandstand at a run. Out in the parking lot, she jumped into Butch's Subaru. Once inside that, she drove through the part of the lot that was reserved for participants' horses and trailers. When she found their rig, Kiddo and Spot were tethered together near the back of the trailer, munching away on a pile of hay. Jenny had been unwilling to leave Spot to fend for herself alone in a relatively new corral over the weekend, so the blind horse had come along for the ride.

The two horses looked up with interest as Joanna raced past to put Dennis's car seat in the back of the truck. Headed back to the Subaru, she paused long enough to give both horses a quick scratch on their respective noses.

Then, leaving the horses to their hay, Joanna hurried back to the car, connecting her Bluetooth as she went. Before she got into the car, she pulled a set of bubble lights out of the glove box, attached them to the top of the Subaru, and turned them on. Heading out of town, she couldn't help noticing how much the landscape around Silver City and Tyrone, complete with miles of flat-topped rust-colored mine tailings dumps, reminded her of Bisbee.

Only when she was well under way did Joanna place her first phone call. That one was to Claire Newmark, a member on the Cochise County Board of Supervisors and one with whom Joanna had developed a reasonably cordial relationship. Claire answered on the third ring.

"Sheriff Brady here," Joanna said urgently. "Sorry to interrupt your Saturday afternoon, but we've got a problem."

"Sounds bad," Claire returned.

"It is," Joanna answered. "Someone has murdered Guy Machett."

"Our M.E.?" Claire was clearly shocked. "Are you serious?"

"Very. I've got an active homicide crime scene with investigators there or else en route, but until there's a medical examiner to perform a preliminary analysis, there's no way to process anything."

"A while ago, when Dr. Winfield was unavailable, didn't we bring in an M.E. from Pima County on a contract basis?" Claire asked.

"You're right. We did. The problem is, they would only send someone to us if there wasn't something urgent in their own jurisdiction. Even if their workload is clear, any sub they could send out instantly is still more than two hours away. And we're not just dealing with the Machett case, either," she added. "We discovered his homicide only after he failed to show up to perform a previously scheduled autopsy."

"The one on Junior Dowdle?" Claire inquired.

"Yes," Joanna agreed. "Junior's."

"Okay, we're talking two cases rather than one," Claire confirmed. "What are you suggesting?"

"My mother will probably give me all kinds of hell for this, especially since she and George are about to head out for their summer cabin in Minnesota. Even so,

I might be able to talk them into delaying their departure long enough for George to help us out. He's familiar. We know him, and we know his work. If we offered to take him on a contract basis with the same kind of pay we'd have to fork over for a sub from Pima County, George might be willing to help out for a time. The problem is, I don't want to raise the issue with George without first having some sort of go-ahead from the board. Before I broach the subject, I need to be able to say with some confidence that he'll be adequately paid for his trouble."

Claire thought about that for a moment. "Even if we offered him the same hourly rate, we'd still be getting a bargain because we wouldn't be having to pay travel time, too. Right?"

"That's how it looks to me. Assuming he agrees and is currently available, we could have someone at the crime scene at least two hours before anyone else could get there. Time counts in cases like this, Claire," Joanna added. "The sooner we process the crime scene, the sooner we can get to the bottom of whatever happened."

"Where are you right now?"

"I just left the rodeo grounds in Silver City. The GPS says I should be back in Bisbee in a little under three hours. With my blue lights flashing, I'll be able to shave some time off that. If you can get me some kind of quasi-official go-ahead, I'll call Doc Winfield and see if I can negotiate a peace treaty with him."

"With him or with your mother?" Claire asked.

That was one of the reasons Joanna and Claire got along so well. Claire's prickly relationship with her own mother was surprisingly similar to Joanna's relationship with Eleanor Lathrop Winfield. Claire may have been the person elected to the board of supervisors, but her mother, Winifred Holland, considered herself to be an ex officio member of that same body, complete with all the rights and responsibilities thereof.

"A little of both," Joanna agreed with a slight laugh. She was not looking forward to tackling Eleanor on the subject, but if it had to be done, she was the one to do it. Joanna doubted George Winfield would mind stepping up to the plate if the county needed him, but she knew her mother would be less than thrilled.

"Drive safely," Claire advised. "I'll be back in touch."

Joanna's phone rang before she had time to call anyone else. "Chief Bernard here," Alvin said. "You know what's happened?"

"Yes," Joanna answered. "Deb brought me up to speed."

"Is it okay with you for me to declare this a joint operation?"

"Whatever you need."

"Where are you now?" Chief Bernard asked.

"Coming back from Silver City as fast as I can," Joanna told him. "What's happening on your end?"

"For right now, we've got the crime scene secured. No one's to go back inside until we've got search warrants in place. Detective Keller is on his way to see Judge Moore with warrant requests for Guy Machett's home, his office, his Internet accounts and telephone lines, as well as his banking information."

"Sounds like a plan," Joanna said.

"Since no one's allowed at the crime scene right now, I'd like to draft Deb Howell to help my officers canvass the neighborhood."

"Done," Joanna said. "I'll call Dispatch to summon my troops and put them at your disposal."

"What about the M.E. situation?" Chief Bernard asked.

"I've got a phone call in to Claire Newmark on the board of supervisors. I'm waiting for a call back."

"How do we handle the crime scene?" Alvin asked. "When it comes to investigating homicides, Fred, my poor little CSI guy, is completely out of his depth."

Joanna knew that to be true. After the Bisbee Police Department's longtime evidence tech, Charles Reppe, had retired a year earlier, budgetary constraints had sent the city personnel department looking for the cheapest possible replacement. Joanna was familiar with the old saying "There's cheap, fast, and good. Pick any two." In that regard, Fred Harding was in a class by himself. With a diploma in crime scene investigation from a none-too-up-and-coming online school, he was cheap, all right, but he was also neither quick nor good.

"I know Dave Hollicker got hurt yesterday," Alvin continued, "but if your people could help us out here, I'd really appreciate it."

"Since Dave is on crutches, he won't be much use at a crime scene, but he's not bad when it comes to computers and data-mining searches. Let's use him to see if he can uncover what's behind this. I don't want to jump to conclusions here, but we both know that it's a good bet that Guy Machett was killed by someone he knew, or, rather, by someone who knew him."

"You're suggesting that we put Dave to work doing a background check on the victim?"

"Yes," Joanna answered.

"Good," Alvin Bernard said. "I'll direct that all the telecommunications info gleaned from the warrants should go to him."

"As for the crime scene itself," Joanna suggested, "Deb Howell may be a relatively new homicide detective, but she's also taken every crime scene investigation course the Arizona Department of Public Safety offers. Working together, Deb and Casey Ledford should be able to get the job done."

"Thank you." Alvin sounded relieved. "I owe you one. Maybe even two."

Joanna sped along for the next hour or so, alternately making and receiving phone calls. She summoned her folks to the crime scene, outlined what was expected of them, and let them know that until the M.E. situation had been clarified, there might be precious little for them to do.

As she traveled the almost empty highways, cruising around whatever traffic was out there, she had time to think. The murder of a medical examiner was bound to be big news. That meant there would be a media storm surrounding this case. In the process, whatever had happened to Junior Dowdle was likely to be pushed to a back burner no matter how determined Joanna was to prevent it. She had a limited number of assets at her disposal. With two homicides to solve in as many days, she would find her investigative resources stretched to the breaking point.

Deb's brief description of the scene made it sound as though Guy Machett's murder was anything but a random event. He'd been targeted by someone, but why? Was the cause to be found in his work life or in his personal life? Guy had always struck Joanna as an arrogant twit with a very high opinion of himself and his accomplishments and little regard for others. Joanna realized now that she had no idea who his friends or relations were. Was he married? Had he ever been married? He never failed to mention going to Harvard and getting his medical training at Johns Hopkins, but he'd made almost no mention of where he had grown up. In order to understand why the man was dead in the here and now, Joanna and her investigators would need an encyclopedic understanding of Guy Machett's past and present.

As Joanna approached the first Willcox exit, the Subaru's fuel gauge showed she had less than a quarter of a tank left. She pulled off and stopped at the first gas station. She was reaching for the hose when her phone rang again. This time Claire Newmark's name and number appeared on the screen.

"We won't be able to make this official until next week's meeting," Claire said, "but for right now, if you can talk Doc Winfield into coming back on a contract basis, you're authorized to do so."

"All right," Joanna said. "Thank you so much. George will be fine, but wish me luck with my mother."

"Always," Claire said with a laugh.

She was about to hang up when Joanna had a sudden stroke of inspiration. "Wait," she said. "There's one more thing."

"What?" Claire asked. The shortness of that clipped one-word question indicated that Claire Newmark felt she had already done more than her share of Cochise County business for a weekend afternoon.

"When the board of supervisors hired Guy Machett to be the new M.E., did you run a background check on the man?"

"Of course we did," Claire answered. "We wouldn't have been doing our due diligence if we hadn't."

"Do you still have it?"

"We must. In fact, I might even have a copy of it on my laptop. Why do you ask?"

"I've asked Dave Hollicker, one of my CSIs, to look into whatever there is to be found about Guy Machett. Having access to that background check would give us a huge leg up."

"But that was a confidential report," Claire said, hesitating. "I'm not sure I can release it to just anyone."

"This is a homicide investigation," Joanna reminded her. "Machett is dead, and I'm not asking you to release that report to just anyone. I want you to send it to Dave Hollicker, the criminalist I've assigned to look into Machett's past. Using that report as a jumping-off point will save huge amounts of wasted time and effort. If you're concerned about liability issues, check with the county attorney. Arlee Jones should be able to advise you on that."

"Okay," Claire agreed. "I was looking through my files. It turns out I do have it. I'll check with Arlee and then get back to you."

That was exactly how Joanna wanted it to work. In the complicated world of Cochise County bureaucracy, a request that came to Arlee Jones top down from a member of the board of supervisors was more likely to receive favorable treatment than one that came from Joanna. She was coming up on the end of her second term in office, and she had learned it was better to dodge certain obstacles than butt up against them.

Having put that request out into the universe, Joanna finished filling the tank and got back into the car before taking a deep breath and punching in the number for her mother's landline.

"Good afternoon," George Winfield boomed. "How are things in the world of barrel racing?"

Grateful to hear her stepfather's voice on the phone and not Eleanor's, Joanna knew she was in the clear, but only temporarily.

"We've got a homicide, George," she said. "Alvin Bernard and I need you."

"Excuse me," George said with a chuckle. "I believe you must have perfected the art of time travel. I'm not the medical examiner anymore. Guy Machett is."

"The problem is, Guy Machett is the victim," Joanna explained. "I'm calling on behalf of the board of supervisors to ask if you'd consider coming back on a contract basis for however long it takes to work out some other more viable plan."

When George spoke again, he was no longer joking. "Where and when did he die?" George asked seriously. "And where and when do you need me?"

"When is your call. As to where? The body was found at Machett's house on the Vista over an hour ago after he failed to show up for a scheduled autopsy. I took the time to check with the board of supervisors before I called you. Claire Newmark just now got back to me with the okay. They'll pay you the same rate they paid Pima County when they subbed for you a couple of years ago."

"How sure are you this is a murder?"

"Deb Howell says that's how it looks to her. I'm prepared to believe her, but I haven't arrived at the scene yet. I'm coming from Silver City. I'm on I-10 west of Willcox, but I'll be turning down 191 in a couple of minutes. Traffic is light. I'm making good progress."

For the longest time, there was dead silence on the phone. Joanna held her breath. If George turned her down, she was in trouble. She'd have to go crawling to Pima County. After already wasting an hour, she knew there was no telling how much longer it would take to get another medical examiner to the scene.

Finally George spoke again. "Ellie is not going to like this. You do know that we're supposed to leave for Minnesota next week?"

"I do," Joanna conceded, "and I didn't suggest this to make your life miserable. I'm asking because I'm desperate, because I've got two deaths that both need investigating."

"Junior's and this one?" George asked.

"Right."

"I've got no equipment."

Joanna had sold insurance long enough to understand this as a pro forma objection. George had already said yes. Now he was merely haggling over the details. She went for the assumed close.

"I'll have Ralph Whetson, Guy's assistant, meet you at the crime scene. He'll bring along everything you need. Do you want me to talk to Mom about this?"

"I'll tell her myself," George said, "but I expect you'll be hearing from her soon."

Joanna barely had time to give Ralph Whetson the lowdown before Eleanor's call came through.

"My husband is supposed to be retired." Eleanor launched into her tirade without bothering with the telephone nicety of saying hello. "You can't just disrupt our lives willy-nilly. I have some say in the matter, you know, and I won't stand still for this kind of treatment."

"We need him, Mom," Joanna said as soothingly as she could manage. "Desperately. Did he tell you what's happened?"

"He said Guy Machett is dead."

"That's true," Joanna agreed. "Who knows how long it will take the board of supervisors to find a permanent replacement? In the meantime, without an M.E. available, my people can't process the scene."

"Well, I guess you've got him," Eleanor returned ruefully. The speed of her concession was one for the record books. "He took off like he'd been shot out of a damned cannon. He hasn't moved that fast since last fall when he was chased by that swarm of yellow jackets, the ones that had taken up residence in his outdoor grill." Eleanor paused. "You said two cases?"

"Yes, Guy Machett's case and Junior Dowdle's."

"Well, then," Eleanor said with a sniff, "if that's the case, I suppose you really do need him, but I won't have him taken advantage of, either. You promised to pay him a fair wage, right?"

"Yes," Joanna said. "I've already verified that with the board of supervisors."

"I guess that means he won't be home for dinner."

"I don't suppose he will," Joanna agreed.

Joanna hung up the phone with the sad realization that she wouldn't be home for dinner, either.

Chapter 11

Liza lay in the upstairs bunk over the cab of a rumbling Peterbilt and watched as the ribbon of asphalt that was westbound I-90 unspooled in front of her. She had lain there, awake and watchful, for hours as the gigantic rig lumbered through the late afternoon and on into the night.

It turned out Candy Small's underground railroad wasn't a railroad at all. It was trucks, first the bread truck that was really nothing more than a delivery van and now this long-haul rig heading west. It had been a long day of riding and waiting. After exiting Candy's Impala, Liza had spent several uncomfortable hours being bounced around in the back of Andrew McConnell's van. He had finished his route in the early afternoon and immediately hustled Liza into his own car, a rusted-out Jeep.

"Where to now?" she asked.

"Next stop is Albany, New York," he told her. "We work with a women's shelter there. They're the ones who put together the rest of the transportation package."

"You've done this before?"

Andrew nodded. "More than once. Candy says most of the time cops can't do much to help in domestic violence situations. When the best thing for someone to do is get out of Dodge, that's when we step in."

Liza stole a self-conscious glance at the bruises Candy had deliberately planted on her upper arm. She could see now that his was an ingenious plan. Those telltale marks gave Liza a visible and perfectly understandable reason to be an anonymous woman fleeing for parts unknown. Those injuries apparently had also served to mobilize an invisible cadre of committed people who were willing to help domestic violence victims escape their tormentors and who would therefore respect Liza's need for secrecy. She would leave behind no trail of plane, rail, or bus reservations or even gas station receipts that would reveal where she had gone.

As far as her pursuers were concerned, it would seem she'd simply vanished into thin air. She couldn't help but wonder, though. What would happen if some of Half-Moon Miller's stray mobsters or even the cops caught wind of Andrew's involvement? How much would it take for him to blurt out everything he knew?

Andrew's Jeep was noisy and came with a nonexistent suspension system. Even so, riding in the passenger seat of that was far more comfortable than bouncing around on the floor of the delivery van. It was comfortable enough that Liza actually dozed off. When she awakened nearly an hour later, they were pulling into the underground parking garage of a low-rise mixed-use building.

"Take the elevator up to the first floor," Andrew directed. "You're looking for Aimee's House of Beauty. Ask for Doreen. They're expecting you."

"I thought you said you were taking me to a shelter," Liza objected. "You're dropping me off at a beauty shop?"

"Trust me," Andrew said. "If you want to disappear, this is the place to do it. Good luck."

Walking in the front door of the salon and dragging her precious roll-aboard behind her, Liza discovered that Aimee's looked like any other beauty shop on the planet. A row of shampoo basins lined the back wall. Along the other walls were six separate operator chairs, five of which were occupied with customers. Liza stopped at the front desk and asked for Doreen. That transaction caused an immediate but subtle shift in the atmosphere of the room as everyone—beauticians and customers alike—glanced in her direction, while the young woman at the reception desk came to attention.

"Of course," she said. "Right this way. Doreen's expecting you."

The receptionist hustled Liza past the other stations, through a curtained doorway, and into a back room, one that contained little else but another station complete with a chair and a shampoo bowl. A woman stepped forward to greet her, hand outstretched. "I'm Aimee," she said.

"What about Doreen?" Liza asked.

Aimee gave her a wink accompanied by a conspiratorial smile. "There is no Doreen," she explained. "It's a code. I take it you're Candy Small's friend?"

Liza nodded mutely.

Aimee gave Liza a critical up-and-down appraisal. "Did you bring along any other clothes?" she asked, nodding in the direction of the roll-aboard. "Maybe something a little more comfortable?"

Liza glanced down at the rumpled outfit she had worn to her mother's funeral. More than twenty-four hours later, it was much the worse for wear. Then she looked guiltily at the suitcase. She suspected that most women fleeing abusive spouses did so with a suitcase full of spare clothing rather than one full of money.

"Sorry," she said quickly, making up the story as it tumbled off her lips. "My mother just died. My husband forbade me to go to the funeral. One of Mother's friends brought some of her things to the funeral for me—photo albums and stuff. When I decided I was leaving, I couldn't just abandon it. It's all that's left of my mother's life."

It was a lie, of course, but it was also close enough to the truth to ring true.

"Don't worry," Aimee said soothingly. "You'd be surprised how many women in your situation show up with nothing but the clothes on their backs. Believe me, we're fully equipped. We've got a room down in the basement that's full of donated clothing and toiletries. You'll be able to find whatever you need there, including something suitable to wear and a bag to carry it in, too. Right now, let's work on your hair. You left home today as an abused wife. Right now you're a brunette with a long ponytail. I could probably turn you into a blonde, but there's another option I've found to be faster and more effective."

"What's that?"

"We'll turn you into a cancer patient."

"What do you mean?"

"People don't stare at cancer patients," Aimee said. "It's not polite. If we shave your head and give you a scarf to wear, I promise people will do their best not to look at you. That includes anyone who is actually looking for you. Of course, if you don't want to do something that drastic . . ."

Liza thought about Olivia lying dead on the stairway. The people who had murdered her landlady were also looking for her. In other words, drastic was exactly what was called for. "Shave away," she said.

Liza's transformation took less than an hour. Once her head was completely bald, Aimee spent the next twenty minutes demonstrating how to properly wrap her bare skull in a bright blue silk scarf. Looking at her unfamiliar reflection in the mirror, Liza was stunned by the difference.

"Amazing," she murmured.

"Wardrobe is next," Aimee announced. "Come on."

Liza followed her guide out into the corridor and down in the elevator to an underground storage area that had been cordoned off from the parking level. Inside was a room that looked like a department store's bargain basement. Racks of clothing filled the center of the space. Glass-topped counters along the sides of the room were stocked with everything from toothbrushes and dental floss to compacts and multiple shades of lipstick. Aimee stopped just inside the door and handed Liza an athletic bag she took down from a nearby shelf.

"You'll be able to carry this on top of your roll-aboard," she explained. "Fill it with what you need, but be sparing. In your situation, traveling light is better than being bogged down with too much luggage. As I said, don't take too much and don't take too long," she added, glancing at her watch. "This is a well-oiled machine. We're due to meet up with your ride at four o'clock. Do you have somewhere to go?"

"I have a brother in Arizona," Liza said.

"Okay, tell your drivers your general direction," Aimee advised. "Don't give them too many details. In fact, it might be better to say you're going to California. That way, if your ex does come looking for you, it'll be harder for him to pick up your trail. You'll start out on I-90. Go west on that until you want to turn south. This is a tag-team operation. The drivers of one truck will hook you up with the next one."

Liza was no stranger to thrift shop shopping. The process took her straight back to her childhood. She had spent most of her school years buying her clothing from other people's castoffs at the thrift stores both before and after Selma became a hermit. The differences between those trips and this one weren't lost on Liza. Then she had been resentful and angry. This time she was supremely grateful.

Liza spent the better part of an hour on her "shopping" spree. The racks and furnishings in the place looked as though they'd been liberated from a shut-down JCPenney store. Deep drawers that had once stocked lingerie for sale now stocked the same items for free. The selection of bras and panties came in a variety of sizes and, although donated, they were clearly new, most of them with price tags still attached. Liza had no problem finding some that fit. For clothing she settled on two pairs of worn jeans and several different T-shirts.

The far end of the room featured several racks of shoes. Liza looked through the section marked size eight and happily traded in her worse-for-wear heels for a pair of leather sandals. At the purse counter she emptied the contents of her own purse—a bargain base-ment last year's model from Marshall's—for a slightly used but still serviceable Coach bag. She had always longed for a Coach bag but had never imagined coming into possession of one, especially not under these cir-cumstances, as someone on the run.

On their way out of the dressing room, Aimee handed Liza two more silk scarves—one red and the other bright yellow. "Variety's the spice of life, you know," she said with a smile as Liza tucked the silk pieces into the top of her now bulging athletic bag.

As a last order of business, Aimee opened a file drawer, took out a black, no-frills cell phone, and handed it over.

"It's what they call a burner," she explained. "The minutes on it are already paid for, but it's recommended for emergency use only. If you call people you know, even people you think you can trust, they might inadvertently put your abuser on your trail. Understand?"

Nodding, Liza slipped the phone into the pocket of her jeans. There was no cash register at the door and clearly no expectation that she should pay for any of the goods.

At four o'clock that afternoon, dressed in brand-new used clothing, minus her ponytail, wearing the blue scarf, and armed with the roll-aboard, the bulging athletic bag, and a slightly used Coach purse containing a sack lunch, Liza arrived at Blackie's Truck Terminal in Albany in the passenger seat of Aimee's bright red Prius. After parking the car among a collection of towering semis, Aimee led Liza over to an orange-and-black moving van and introduced her to the two-man team of drivers lounging outside—Sam and Joe.

"This is Linda," Aimee said as the three of them shook hands. "She's on her way to L.A."

A few minutes later she handed Liza's luggage and purse first into the cab and then up into the overhead sleeping compartment. "Sam and Joe are only going as far as Chicago," she explained. "Because they'll take turns driving through the night, you can ride up here.

You should be somewhere close to Chicago by seven or so tomorrow morning."

"What then?"

"Don't worry. They'll hook you up with your next ride before they drop you off. They won't leave you stranded."

"You're sure?" Liza asked uncertainly.

"I'm sure. These are good guys."

"What do I owe you for all this?" Liza asked.

"Not a single thing," Aimee said. "Someone helped me years ago, and now I'm helping you. Maybe some-day, when you're in a better place, you can do the same."

"I hope so," Liza said.

The hours rolled by as the truck lumbered westward through the night. Liza could hear Joe and Sam chat-ting down in the cab, sometimes with each other and sometimes with other truckers over their CB radio. Above them there was nothing but silence and worry. It made Liza's heart ache to think that she was some-how responsible for Olivia Dexter's death. Her land-lady was dead for no other reason than that—she had been Liza's landlady. If Detective Franklin really did suspect Liza of being involved in Olivia's death, what did that make Liza now—a wanted fugitive? Then there was her brother. What about Guy? How would her brother react when she showed up unannounced on his doorstep after all these years? The problem was, Liza had nowhere else to go. Guy was it.

Hungry, Liza scrounged through the sack lunch Aimee had stuffed in her purse. Bologna had never been her first choice for sandwich makings, but in this case hunger was the best sauce. She devoured the sandwich, the chips, and the accompanying apple with a relish she wouldn't have thought possible. Somewhere along the way, several hours later, the truck pulled into a truck stop. While Sam and Joe stayed at the fuel island, Liza hurried inside to use the facilities.

She was still awake when Sam and Joe stopped for coffee and yet another pit stop. Again, Liza availed herself of the facilities but turned down the coffee. Going in and out of those places made her nervous. Security cameras seemed to be everywhere. She hurried past them, doing her best to avert her face, all the while praying that her scarf would stay where it belonged.

Back in the truck and back on the road for the second time, she pulled the scarf off, carefully folded it, and laid it aside. Then with the steady motion of the truck rocking her, she pulled a loose blanket over her body and finally fell asleep.

Chapter 12

The last thirty minutes of Joanna's two-and-a-half-hour drive were done in relative silence. She'd summoned everyone who needed summoning. Now she appreciated having some peace and quiet as well as time to think. Why was Guy Machett dead? Most of the time the basis for murder was either love or money. Which was this?

Had he been involved in some kind of illegal activity—drug dealing, maybe, or possibly money laundering? Or was his death related to his personal life? Was he involved in some kind of love triangle? Now that Joanna thought about it, she realized that she knew nothing about Guy Machett's love life. Did he have a steady girl stowed somewhere who would be devastated by his loss?

The one thing that raised any red flags was the fact that when the M.E. wasn't at work, he spent most of his time out of town. Maybe he had some kind of secret life going on. She thought about Dr. Machett's well-groomed appearance—his expensive taste in clothing, his perfectly coifed hair.

"What if he was gay?" Joanna said aloud, speaking only to herself. What if he spent time out of town in order to keep his love life away from the prying eyes of Bisbee's gossipmongers? If so, evidence of that kind of relationship was bound to surface in his phone or Internet records.

Joanna's phone rang again as she turned off Highway 80 and onto the Douglas Cutoff. A glance at the telephone screen revealed Madge Livingston's name.

"Deb Howell called me a while ago," Madge said in her gravelly voice. "She claims Dr. Machett is dead—that someone murdered him—but I'm having a hard time believing it. Is it true?"

"I'm not at the crime scene yet," Joanna answered, "but that's my understanding."

"What the hell happened?"

"Someone killed him. I don't know any of the details."

"It's a good thing I was out of town, otherwise I'd be at the top of your suspect list," Madge said. "I've been ready to throttle the man for months now."

The fact that Madge had despised Guy Machett was hardly news. Madge was a prickly, opinionated woman who had spent her entire career working in various departments of Cochise County government. Shipping her off to the M.E.'s office had effectively moved her out of the courthouse proper and out of everybody else's hair, as well. Over the years she had found all her bosses wanting. To hear Madge tell it, George Winfield had been the only exception to that rule, although Joanna seemed to remember there had been a few bumps in the road there, too.

"Do you know of anyone who wished him harm?"

"You should be asking if I know anyone who didn't wish him harm," Madge countered. "Guy Machett was a most unlikable young man."

"As far as you know, though, there've been no problems at the office? No threats of any kind?"

"None," Madge said. "At least none that I know of, but Dr. Machett wasn't the sort who took people into his confidence."

"He wasn't what you would call forthcoming?"

"No, he was not." Madge paused for a moment and then continued, "Deb asked me about his computer and phone. I told her if they weren't at the house, he might have left them in the office. I believe she's sending someone uptown to check."

"Good," Joanna said.

"Do you know how he died?"

"No," Joanna answered. "As I said, I'm not there yet. By now Doc Winfield may have established an approximate time of death, but I'm not aware—"

"Wait," Madge interrupted. "Is Doc Winfield coming back?"

"Just temporarily," Joanna began. "We needed an M.E. on the scene and—"

Madge didn't wait for Joanna to finish. "You tell Doc Winfield that I'm leaving Lake Havasu within the hour. I'll be home to help out just as soon as I can get there."

The phone call with Madge ended as Joanna turned right onto Cole Avenue. A few blocks later, she paused at the top of the Vista. The cluster of flashing lights breaching the twilight told her that the crime scene was a few blocks south and to the left, across from the tennis courts.

Due to the crush of vehicles, emergency and otherwise, Joanna was forced to park a block and a half from the crime scene and walk the rest of the way. She had shaved half an hour off the expected travel time from Silver City to Bisbee. Even so, the time lag had given media types from all over southern Arizona time to gather at the scene. As predicted, the murder of the medical examiner was big news.

Joanna was still dressed in what she'd worn to the rodeo—jeans, a western shirt, and a pair of outgrown cowboy boots she had inherited from her daughter. Out of uniform and without her badge, she found it easy to slip unnoticed through the crowd of mostly out-of-town reporters. An old-fashioned wrought-iron fence surrounded Guy Machett's front yard. Joanna was almost to the gate when her luck ran out. Marliss Shackleford spotted her.

"Yoo-hoo," she called. "Sheriff Brady, have you got a minute?"

Marliss trotted forward with a young purple-haired girl following at her elbow. Joanna recognized the young woman at once, but it took a moment to remember her name. Ruth. She and her brother had been among the volunteers who had gathered in the parking lot at St. Dominick's during Thursday's early morning search for Junior Dowdle.

Joanna stopped short. "Sorry, Marliss. I don't have a minute," she said. "And in case you haven't noticed, this is a crime scene. It's no place for children."

"I'm not a child," Ruth objected. "I'm fourteen years old, and I'm a blogger. Ms. Shackleford is letting me shadow her for the day. I was hoping I could interview you."

Joanna favored Marliss with what she hoped was a sufficiently withering glare before turning back to

Ruth."If you want to interview me, you'll need to make arrangements by contacting my office, not by showing up at a crime scene. Right now I have a job to do. I'm surprised Ms. Shackleford didn't inform you of that."

The girl looked disappointed. Marliss Shackleford simply shrugged off Joanna's implied criticism.

"Still," Marliss insisted, "as long as you're here, if you could just shed a little light . . ."

"As you can see, I've only just arrived," Joanna answered brusquely. "That means I don't know any-thing, and I can't tell you anything, either. Now, if you'll excuse me. I need to get inside."

"But—"

A bright light went on and Joanna realized that Ruth was using a cell-phone camera to record every-thing that was being said. As a result, some of the other media types started paying attention.

"Turn that thing off," Joanna ordered.

"Sorry," Ruth replied, quickly stowing the offend-ing machine.

It occurred to Joanna that she was dealing with a kid and perhaps her response had been more forceful than necessary. The truth was, Marliss Shackleford had an unerring ability to bring out the very worst in her.

"Call my office next week sometime," Joanna told the girl. "We'll set up a time for an interview."

With that, Joanna donned a pair of gloves, shoved open the gate, and made for Guy Machett's low porch, where the front door stood wide open. Through that Joanna glimpsed lights and movement inside the house, but no glimmer of light showed through any of the windows. Once she was on the porch, Joanna saw that the blinds on all the windows were closed and most likely covered with an inside layer of pulled drapes or curtains as well.

A uniformed Bisbee police officer stood next to the door. "Evening, Sheriff Brady," he said as she paused long enough to slip on a pair of paper crime scene booties.

"Is Chief Bernard here?" she asked.

"No, he and Detective Keller just left to join Detective Carbajal at the second crime scene."

"What second crime scene?"

"Up the canyon, at the morgue," the cop said. "Dr. Machett's office up there has been ransacked, too."

"When did that happen?"

"Probably sometime last night, the same as everything else. But they just found out about the problem uptown a little while ago when Jaime went up to Old Bisbee to check out the office."

Attempting to step inside, Joanna almost collided with George Winfield. Their momentary do-si-do might have been comical but neither of them was in any mood for joking around.

"You're done already?"

"With as much as I can do here," George replied with a nod toward the back of the house. "Ralph Whetson will be back to pick up the body once Detective Howell finishes taking the crime scene photos. I told him that when he comes back to the morgue, he should bring a detective with him so we can go ahead and do the Dowdle autopsy."

"Tonight?" Joanna asked. "How can you? I was just told that the morgue is under investigation as a possible crime scene."

"That's right," George answered. "As a matter of fact I just finished having a telephone conversation with Alvin Bernard on that very topic. He's still up at the morgue with Matt Keller and Jaime Carbajal. According to the chief, damage at the morgue is limited to Dr. Machett's private office. There's no sign that anyone entered or disturbed the lab area. Chief Bernard said he's designating the office area as off-limits, but we're free to work in the lab. Junior's autopsy has already been postponed for two days. I'm sure Moe and Daisy are anxious to move forward with funeral arrangements. This will allow them to do so. As for my performing an autopsy tonight? Your mother's already mad enough to spit nails, so there's not much point in my hurrying home. I could just as well get as much done as possible while the getting is good."

Joanna had plenty of firsthand experience with her mother's moodiness, but she doubted that she would prefer performing or observing an autopsy to doing battle with Eleanor Lathrop Winfield.

"Anything you can tell me on a preliminary basis?"

"Not much. Tentative time of death is overnight sometime, probably in the early morning hours. I'll know more about that later. There was a struggle. Guy's watch got broken and stopped at 11:46 P.M., but I'm estimating that the time of death is several hours later than that. From the number of visible cuts and contusions, he put up a hell of a fight. He had burns on his chest and groin that would be consistent with being repeatedly hit by a stun gun."

"Any idea about cause of death?"

George shrugged. "Unofficially, I'd say this was a case of waterboarding gone bad. Some of the bruising on his chest would be consistent with a failed attempt to revive him. What that says to me is that the assailants were trying to get him to tell them something, but he died before they got it out of him."

"He drowned?"

"I suppose it could have been something else," George said. "We'll have to wait and see. More on that later—probably tomorrow sometime."

With that, George continued on his way. Once Joanna was inside, her immediate impression was that the living room resembled a war zone. The remains of a shattered coffee table lay in front of a sofa. A plasma TV had been knocked from its supports over the mantel of the fireplace, and the hearth and a good part of the living room carpet were covered with a debris field of splintered glass from the broken screen. Off to one side of the room, an easy chair that matched the sofa lay tipped on its side. A scatter of mail covered the floor. Looking at it, Joanna imagined Guy coming into the house with an armload of mail only to be attacked from behind with so much force that the mail had been propelled into the air and across the room.

The plush beige carpet was dotted with spatters of blood and a dusting of microdots from a deployed Taser cartridge. A long archway marked the line of demarcation between the living room and the dining room. Several antique dining room chairs lay in broken heaps of wood next to a matching table, the polished top of which was marred by spatters of blood. Each piece of debris and blood spatter was accompanied by a numbered crime scene marker. The thin layer of black dust that covered every available surface indicated that Casey Ledford had already been here checking for prints.

"Deb?" Joanna called.

"Come on through," Detective Howell replied. "I'm in the kitchen bagging up the victim's clothes. Casey's working in his home office. Welcome to the party."

"Some party," Joanna said, pausing in the doorway of the kitchen.

The room was a scene out of a 1950s horror flick. The familiar gray Formica table and matching chairs were the same ones Joanna's former in-laws still used, but the chair sitting in the middle of the room also sat in the middle of a spray of blood spatter that covered the floor. Deb stood in front of the kitchen sink carefully removing an item of discarded clothing from a heap on the floor and preparing to slip it into an evidence bag. Joanna thought she recognized the item in Deb's gloved hand. It looked very much like the jacket to one of Guy Machett's expensive Italian suits.

Joanna knew that in the aftermath of serious assaults, perpetrators shed DNA along with their victims. She also understood that in some situations it was possible to retrieve DNA and even fingerprints from items made of cloth. The hope of finding usable evidence accounted for Detective Howell's careful handling of the clothing, and it was something Joanna applauded. She waited quietly until Deb finished.

"Can you tell how this went down?" Joanna asked. "From the looks of the living room, I'd say it started in there."

"Yup," Deb agreed. "No obvious broken windows, so no breaking and entering. I'd say someone picked the lock on the back door. They let themselves in and then sat around and waited for Machett to show up."

"No alarm?"

"He has one," Deb said. "It may have been turned on, too, but with the access code posted on the wall right next to the keypad, it didn't do a whole lot of good."

"Why put the access code there?"

"For a cleaning lady maybe, so she could let herself in and out without triggering the alarm?" Deb suggested. "Machett wouldn't have needed to write it down for his own use because the code was nothing but his birthday—month, date, and year. He probably used the same code for the alarm at his office, which means that once the bad guys had one code, they had them all. It also explains how they were able to access his office at the morgue without triggering an alarm there, either."

"If Guy Machett was that lax about security," Joanna mused, "he must not have thought he was in any danger. What about his neighbors? Did anyone see or hear anything out of the ordinary?"

"Nope," Deb said, "not a peep, but that's mostly because no one was home. Mr. Roland, the guy next door, moved into an assisted-living facility a month ago. Mrs. Holland, the neighbor on the other side, is off on a two-week cruise down the Danube."

"Excuse me," Ralph Whetson said, coming in through the back door, pushing a gurney loaded with a body bag in front of him. "Are you ready for me?"

"Not quite yet," Joanna said. "Let me finish taking a look around first." She turned back to Deb. "Walk me through it."

"From what I can see, I'm assuming the initial attack occurred in the living room and that there was more than one assailant. The scene suggests they tasered him there. Casey's already swept up enough of the microdots that she'll be able to ID the weapon," Deb said, gesturing in that direction. "He must have come around sooner than they expected and then he put up a hell of a fight. When they finally subdued him, they dragged him into the kitchen. You can see the marks the heels of his shoes left on the hardwood floor."

Joanna went back to the dining room and studied the floor where two matching heel marks were clearly visible.

"After that, they spent a considerable length of time here in the kitchen," Deb said.

"They took off his clothes?"

"All of them," Deb agreed, nodding at the stack of evidence bags that now contained the pile of clothing. "They duct-taped him buck naked to this chair. Look at this." She pointed to the single chair that had been placed in the middle of the room. "There's duct tape residue on the front legs of the chair and on the back uprights, too. They must have taped both his arms and legs to the chair and then ripped off the tape when they moved him into the bathroom. There's hair stuck to both the chair legs and the uprights."

In order for Joanna to see the residue, she would have had to step into the spatter of dried blood. She chose not to. "For right now, I'll take your word about that," Joanna said. "Doc Winfield was on his way out when I came in. He mentioned something about a stun gun. Is this where they used that?"

"That's my guess," Deb answered. "Once the initial Taser had been deployed, they could still use the weapon's stun-gun capabilities. That part of the program most likely happened here, and they used it over and over. When the Taser ran out of gas, they moved the operation into the bathroom."

"You keep saying 'they,'" Joanna observed. "Are you sure there was more than one perpetrator?"

Deb nodded. "Machett was a fit kind of guy who was into tae kwon do. The level of destruction present tells us that he fought back. If you look at the shoe prints here in the kitchen, you'll notice there are two different sets. One looks to be a size twelve or thirteen. The other one is smaller, maybe a size ten. So, yes, definitely more than one person involved in the attack."

The bit about Machett's martial arts proficiency surprised Joanna. It was something Deb knew about Guy Machett that Joanna Brady didn't. "How do you know he was into tae kwon do?" she asked.

"Trophies," Deb answered dismissively. "He must have had at least five or six trophies on the shelf in his office and a collection of belts hanging on the wall behind his desk. Haven't you ever noticed them?"

"Not really," Joanna said. The truth was, since Guy Machett came to town, she had never once set foot inside his office. She had been to the morgue on occasion, of course, but not into his private office. As far as she was concerned, that spot still had George Winfield's name on it. In her dealings with Guy Machett, avoiding his office had been Joanna's one small protest rite, and a secret one at that.

Leaving Deb in the kitchen, Joanna made her way down the hall and into the bathroom on her own. Like the rest of the house, it had escaped any kind of updating. The room was nowhere near what would nowadays be considered a suitable "master bath." The stains on the black-and-white tile indicated that the original toilet had probably been replaced at some point in the past, but everything else—the tile, the washbasin with its two separate spigots, and the oversize claw-foot tub—were most likely as-built equipment.

Guy Machett lay faceup on the tile. His naked body took up most of the available floor space in the small room. The cuts and bruises George had mentioned were readily apparent on his arms, legs, and face. Bare strips on his arms and legs indicated where duct tape had been brutally yanked away, taking a layer of skin and hair with it. The used duct tape had been left behind in a ball that had rolled under the sink. Machett's chest and groin were covered with the distinctive tracks left behind by the stun gun. Those burns were all too visible on the pale dead flesh, and so was everything else. Joanna was tempted to drop a discreet washcloth over the part of Guy Machett that should have been covered, but she didn't. This was a crime scene, after all.

Turning around, Joanna found both Deb and Casey standing behind her in the narrow hallway.

"Any idea what the attackers were looking for?"

"None," Deb said, shaking her head. "His phone and laptop are both missing. When we couldn't find any trace of them here at the house, Detective Keller and Jaime Carbajal took a search warrant and went to check out Guy's office. That's when they discovered that someone had broken in there as well."

"But nothing else is missing?"

"Not that we can tell, but there's a lot that isn't missing. Some high-end sound equipment, a second plasma TV, and several reasonably expensive pieces of jewelry—including a Patek Philippe watch—are all still here."

Joanna chewed on that for a moment. If Guy could afford that kind of watch, why hadn't he bothered to update the house?

"So this definitely wasn't a robbery," Joanna concluded. She turned to Casey, who was nodding her agreement. "What about the print situation? Find anything?"

"There are two distinct sets of prints that you see throughout the house. I'm pretty sure one set belongs to Guy Machett. Since the other set also shows up on the handle of the vacuum cleaner and on a broom handle and a mop, too, the second set probably belongs to a cleaning lady. In other words, unless the cleaning lady is also the bad guy, I'm saying the perpetrators wore gloves."

"Do we have any idea who the cleaning lady might be?"

"Not so far," Casey said.

"Hey," Ralph Weston called from the far end of the hall. "I'm still here. Are you ready for me now?"

"Sure," Joanna said. "Will you need a hand?"

"Nah," Ralph said. "I can manage it myself."

His use of that particular pronoun—it—really struck Joanna. The dead man who had always insisted on being "Dr. Machett" suddenly had been demoted to the lowly status of "it." As far as Ralph was concerned, his former boss was now nothing more or less than a job to be done and a body to be handled. Joanna couldn't help but remember how, just two days earlier, Guy Machett's whole manner of dealing with Junior Dowdle's death had been somewhat less than respectful.

Now his former helper was treating him in exactly the same way.

Just deserts, Joanna thought to herself. *What goes around comes around.*

Chapter 13

Joanna, Detective Howell, and Casey were standing in the living room when Joanna's phone rang. Dave Hollicker's name and number appeared on the screen. "Hey," she said. "Are you making any progress on that background check?"

"Not really," Dave admitted. "Claire Newmark just sent me something that's going to help with that, but I'm caught up in something else at the moment. I'm about to send it to you."

In Joanna's opinion, the background check on Guy Machett should have been Dave's top priority, but she stopped herself from delivering a reprimand. "What?" she asked.

"Detective Carbajal called me from Dr. Machett's office," Dave said. "He asked me to come out to the department and check out last night's security tape feeds. I thought that was more important, so that's what I'm doing. I just sent it to you, and I'm copying Chief Bernard."

"Good," Joanna found herself saying, despite her earlier misgivings. "Excellent!"

Joanna felt a sudden stirring of excitement. In recent years, Cochise County had, at great expense, installed top-of-the-line security cameras at the entrances to all county facilities. The base station was located inside the sheriff's department. That way, if an alarm was triggered at one of the sites, Dispatch could check on the situation before sending officers to the scene. Since the bad guys had evidently used Guy Machett's access code to let themselves into the M.E.'s office, no alarms had sounded, and no one had been alerted. Even so, there was now a good chance Guy Machett's killers had been caught on tape.

Moments later, Joanna's phone dinged an alarm announcing the arrival of new mail. When she opened the message from Dave, it was empty except for a single attachment that took its own sweet time to load.

"Tell me," she urged. "Does it show anything or not?"

"It shows something, all right," Dave told her, "but it's not going to help much."

At last the document opened. After another long wait, it began to play. The video came with a time stamp that read 3:26:42 AM. For a long time, nothing showed but a view of the tiny empty parking lot behind the morgue, then two figures appeared. When they came close enough, Joanna saw Dave's assessment was correct. The film established when the bad guys had entered Guy Machett's office, but that was all. Both of their faces were completely obscured by ski masks, and both were wearing gloves.

"Crap," she said. "You're right, Dave. It gives us a time and that's about it."

"Not quite," Dave said. "I think it tells us something more. I suspect we're dealing with some genuine bad guys. They're no doubt in the system; hence the gloves. That means someone took their fingerprints somewhere along the way, and they'll turn up in AFIS. They're also wearing masks. That means their mug shots are on somebody's facial recognition program as well. Now that we know that, I'll go back to working on the background check and see if it'll tell me where Guy Machett's life intersected with these thugs."

"You do that."

As Joanna ended the call, another one came in. Chief Bernard's name showed on the caller-ID screen.

"Jaime and Dave made a hell of a catch on that video feed," he said. "You can tell them I said so."

"I will," Joanna said.

"What about that pack of reporters? Are they still milling around outside?"

Joanna walked as far as the front door and peered outside. "Affirmative," she said. "They're all lying in wait and most likely won't leave until somebody talks to them. Are you coming back?"

Alvin sighed. "I guess I'd better come face the music. Doing a press conference with no next-of-kin information isn't my idea of a picnic. Any progress on that?"

"Dave didn't mention it, so I guess the answer is no. He'll be in a better position to tell us about Guy's friends and relations once he can lay his hands on Guy's phone and social media records. In the meantime, that's what we should turn our people loose on, too—finding out who his pals are. We also need to know the name of his housecleaner."

"Why's that?"

"The killers most likely wore gloves," Joanna explained, "but Casey Ledford says she found two sets of fingerprints all over the house. The location of some of them suggests they belong to a cleaning lady, most likely. Once we find her, she might be able to tell us if anything important is missing from the house."

"Okay," he agreed. "I'm on my way back. I'll be there soon."

For the next fifteen minutes or so, Joanna waited while Deb and Casey finished gathering their equipment and packing up. When Joanna led them out onto the porch, she found that the collection of media vans had expanded. Upon seeing them, the crowd of reporters fell silent. Then, as if on cue, Marliss shouted, "Sheriff Brady, are you going to give us a briefing now?"

"No," Chief Bernard said, striding into view. "This crime scene is in my jurisdiction, and I'll be doing the briefing. The sheriff's department is working this case jointly, however, and Sheriff Brady is welcome to join me."

For the next interminable half hour Joanna stood next to Alvin Bernard on Guy Machett's front porch while the reporters lobbed one question after another in their direction. Despite the lights from the various cameras, Joanna was able to see some of the folks assembled outside the fence. She was disappointed but not surprised that Ruth Nolan was among them. Joanna had hoped that Marliss would have had enough sense to take the girl home. Naturally she had not.

Things were starting to wind down when Joanna's phone rang in her shirt pocket. Excusing herself, she hurried inside. "Okay," Dave Hollicker said. "The background check Claire Newmark sent has been a great help. I have the names of Guy Machett's next of kin. His mother, Selma, and sister, Liza, both live in Great Barrington, Massachusetts. I can't find a phone listing for the mother, but I'm texting you one for the sister along with the nonemergency phone number for the Great Barrington Police Department."

"Thanks, Dave," Joanna said. "That's a huge help. I'll give the information to Chief Bernard as soon as he finishes the briefing."

"What information?" Chief Bernard asked, following Joanna into the house.

Joanna opened the text application and handed him the phone. He looked at his phone and then at his watch. "It's midnight on the East Coast," he said. "Since it's a joint operation and I just did the briefing, how about if you handle next of kin?"

Which is how, a few minutes later, Joanna found herself speaking to the clerk who answered the phone at the Great Barrington Police Department. Once she explained that she needed someone to do a next-of-kin notification to either Selma Machett or her daughter, Liza, Joanna wasn't the least bit surprised to be put on hold. She also wasn't surprised by the extended delay before someone else picked up the phone, but she was surprised by the way he answered the phone.

"Homicide, Detective Franklin."

"I'm sorry," Joanna said quickly, switching the phone to speaker. "I'm afraid there's been a slight misunderstanding. I'm Sheriff Joanna Brady, calling from Bisbee, Arizona. I didn't want to speak to a homicide detective. The homicide is here on my end. I'm looking for someone to do a next-of-kin notification."

"They said you were looking for Selma Machett," Detective Franklin said. "You missed her. She's deceased. Her funeral was Thursday. You're saying someone else is dead?"

"Her son, Guy Machett," Joanna answered. "He was found murdered in his home here in Bisbee, Arizona, earlier today. Perhaps you could put me in touch with his sister, then. I believe her name is Liza."

"No can do," Detective Franklin said.

"Why not?"

"Her boss reported her as a missing person when she didn't show up for work yesterday. That's bogus, of course. There's a big difference between going missing and being on the lam. As far as Liza Machett is concerned, I'm pretty sure it's the latter."

"What do you mean?"

"Miss Machett's mother's house burned down Thursday afternoon either during or after the funeral. Miss Machett's landlady, Olivia Dexter, was found murdered later that same evening. I brought Liza in for questioning because I think there's a good chance she was responsible for both—for the landlady's murder and for the house fire as well, which, by the way, we know for sure was arson. I knew Liza was lying when I talked to her, but I had no way to prove it. I had to let her go. However, when a person of interest in a homicide investigation goes missing the moment she's let loose, it doesn't take a Philadelphia lawyer to figure out what's really going on."

"Do you have any idea where she went?" Joanna asked.

"None at all," Franklin answered, "and believe me, we've been looking. She's not driving. She left her car behind. We've checked car rental agencies, airports, train stations, and bus terminals. I'm guessing she's holed up here in town somewhere."

"Is there a chance she might be responsible for her mother's death as well?"

Detective Franklin laughed heartily. "I like the way you think, Sheriff Brady. Since Liza was Selma's sole beneficiary, I wondered the same thing. I went so far as to check with Selma's doc. He told me Selma had been in hospice for two weeks before she passed and that she definitely died of natural causes. Anything else I can do for you?"

The conversation had taken such a turn that for a moment Joanna had no idea what to say next.

"Are there any other relatives, then?" she asked at last. "Anyone else we should know about?"

"Not around here, certainly," Detective Franklin answered. "I've been asking questions, of course. It turns out Liza's father took off years ago, when she was little. My understanding is that he ran off with another woman. As far as I know, no one's heard a word from him since, but he could still be alive. Do you have a cause of death on your victim?"

"We're not sure at this point. He may have drowned, but he was tortured extensively before he died. Was there any evidence of something like that in the land-lady's death?"

"Nope, that was a straight-out strangulation. She was found on the stairway leading to Liza's upstairs apart-ment. She may have stuck her nose into something Liza was trying to keep quiet and, as a consequence, poor Olivia had to go. That's one theory anyway. We're still referring to Liza as a person of interest in the Dexter homicide, but between you and me, I think she's a lot more than that."

"Is there a chance that Liza's involved in what hap-pened here?" Joanna asked.

"When did your guy die?" Franklin asked.

"Sometime Friday night or early Saturday morning. He was supposed to perform an autopsy on Saturday afternoon. When he didn't show up for that, someone went looking for him and found his body."

"Much as I'd like to say otherwise, I don't see how it's possible for Liza to be involved in what happened on your end. I'd be willing to bet dollars to doughnuts that she's still somewhere right here in Great Barrington. The last time I saw her was early Friday morning. I suppose she could have flown out in time to get to your side of the country and off her brother that night, but like I told you, we've been checking with all the airlines. I can tell you for sure that no one using her ID flew on any commercial flight on Friday. I suppose she could have used fake ID or else have flown private, but that's highly unlikely for someone who earned her living as a waitress in a diner."

When the call ended, Joanna turned to Alvin Bernard.

"That was unexpected," she said.

He nodded. "Sounds like that next-of-kin notification is going to be a problem."

"I'll say," Joanna agreed. "In more ways than one."

Chapter 14

"Up and at 'em, Linda," Sam called into the berth above the Peterbilt's cab. "This is the end of the road for you as far as we're concerned, because we've found you another ride. Want me to give you a hand with your stuff?"

It took a moment for Liza to realize first where she was, who she was, and that the truck was no longer moving. Sitting up and throwing off the blanket, she wondered how long she'd slept.

"Coming," she called. It took several long fumbling minutes before she managed to get the scarf on right. Finally finished, she passed down her luggage and purse.

"Sorry I took so long," she said, stepping out of the truck and into what turned out to be haze-covered early morning sunlight. "Where are we?"

"Welcome to Truck City in beautiful Gary, Indiana," Sam told her. "We were planning on taking you all the way into Chicago, but the guy we were supposed to hand you off to there had trouble with his rig on the far side of Detroit. Overnight we hooked you up with a buddy of ours, Howard Prince. Everybody calls him Bruiser. Aimee said you were headed for L.A., and Bruiser is going to Kansas City by way of Des Moines. That'll put you on Interstate 80. The good thing about ol' Bruiser is that he drives weekends. A lot of the guys don't, but Bruiser says he makes better time on Saturday and Sunday than he does during the week."

"Is he here?" Liza asked.

"Nope," Sam answered, picking up Liza's luggage and heading into the building. "He's still about an hour out."

Joe, who had already been inside, hurried out to meet them. "I talked to Bertha, and we're good," he said.

"Who's Bertha?" Liza asked.

"As far as Truck City is concerned"—Joe grinned—"you should call her Your Royal Highness. She's the old broad who owns the place. She says you're welcome to come on into the truckers' lounge. You can freshen up there and take a shower if you want. There are phones if you need one and some computers, too. You do whatever you need to do. When you finish, go out into the restaurant to wait. Bruiser's gonna have to gas up, but he'll come looking for you when he's ready to rumble."

Sam and Joe escorted Liza into a lounge area that came complete with worn but comfortable leather lounge chairs, several television sets, and a pair of what turned out to be pristinely clean restrooms. Sam set her luggage down outside a door marked HERS.

"You take care now," he said, reaching out and pulling her into a strong-armed hug. "You're doing the right thing getting away from a scumbag like that. A man who would hurt his woman when she's busy fighting cancer . . ." He stopped and shook his head. "There's words for low-down curs like that, but I can't say none of 'em in front of a lady. Best of luck to you."

When Sam let Liza loose, Joe gave her a hug and an encouraging pat on the shoulder. "If anybody gives you any guff about being here, just tell 'em to talk to Bertha."

Liza nodded. She was worried about being passed off from one set of strangers to another, and some of that discomfort must have showed.

"Don't you worry none about Bruiser," Sam added consolingly. "He talks way too much, which is one of the reasons he drives solo, but the man's a gentleman from the top of his head to the tips of his shoes."

"Boots," Joe interjected. "Bruiser wears boots, not shoes."

"Thank you," Liza said. "Thank you both for everything."

A few minutes after they left, Liza stood in a steaming shower with a powerful stream of water raining down on her naked body. It was odd to feel the water pounding directly on her tender bare scalp and even odder to shower without needing to use shampoo or conditioner.

After the shower she dried off and changed into clean underwear. She still had the small makeup kit that she had kept in her old purse. Once she had fixed her face and rewound the scarf she was ready to face the world again. Or at least the truck stop.

Out in the lounge, she tentatively approached the table where two aging desktop PCs sat side by side. One was taken by a beefy guy who was so completely engrossed in what he was watching that he didn't bother glancing in Liza's direction as she slid onto the chair beside him. What showed on his screen was something a very long way on the wrong side of R-rated, and it made the note taped to the bottom of the PC monitor self-explanatory: CLEAR YOUR HISTORY WHEN YOU

LEAVE. WE DON'T WANT TO SEE WHAT YOU'VE BEEN WATCHING.

Using Safari, Liza typed in the words: *Great Barrington Herald*. The *Herald* was the local newspaper, print copies of which were often left behind by customers who breakfasted at Candy's. Until the site came up on the screen, Liza wasn't even sure there was an online edition. What she saw took her breath away. Staring back at her was her own image—a copy of her senior photo taken from Great Barrington High's yearbook, the *Crusader*. According to the caption, Liza Elaine Machett was being sought as a person of interest in the Thursday-night homicide of longtime Great Barrington resident Olivia Octavia Dexter.

With her heart hammering in her chest, Liza quickly closed the page and shut down the search engine. She sidled a glance toward the man beside her. He was too engrossed in the naked images on his screen to pay the slightest attention to hers. She didn't need the reminder from the hand-printed sign to erase her search history before she grabbed her luggage and purse and fled the lounge.

Inside the restaurant, a large woman with a bright red bouffant hairdo and a beaming smile stood at the hostess counter. "I'm Bertha," she announced as she led

Liza to a booth near the window. "Hope you enjoyed your shower."

"I did, thank you," Liza said.

"Have yourself some breakfast now," Bertha added kindly, handing over a menu. "Order whatever you want. It's on the house. Someone in your condition needs to keep up her strength. I didn't have cancer at the time, but I had me a husband just like yours once. He's dead and gone now and good riddance. I know, it hurts like hell to leave, but sometimes it's the only thing to do. When Bruiser gets here, I'll let him know where you are."

With that Bertha flounced back to the hostess station, leaving Liza flushed with a combination of embarrassment and guilt. Between them, Candy and Aimee had provided Liza Machett with the perfect disguise. Everybody felt sorry for battered women and for cancer patients, too, and they all wanted to help. It filled Liza with shame to realize she was misleading these wonderful strangers by playing on their pity and their generosity.

How was it possible that she was here, fleeing everything familiar and throwing herself on the mercy of people she didn't even know rather than staying put and taking her chances with Amos Franklin? After all, he wouldn't be able to find any proof that she had done anything wrong because she hadn't. The detective scared her, but what scared her even more was whoever had burned down the house and murdered Olivia. Those people were after her, and they were deadly. Liza had no faith whatsoever that Amos Franklin and the Great Barrington Police Department would be able to offer her enough protection. In fact, given Amos's surly attitude, he was more likely to throw her to the wolves.

"Excuse me, would you be Miss Linda?" someone asked in a distinctly southern drawl.

Finished with her breakfast, Liza had been staring off into space and thinking about her photo on the *Herald* website. Startled out of her reverie, Liza found a tall man standing next to her booth. He was dressed in jeans, a faded flannel shirt, worn black cowboy boots, and an equally worn Stetson. He looked to be somewhere north of sixty. He had piercing blue eyes, and a network of smile lines crisscrossed his weathered cheeks.

Caught unawares, Liza almost blurted out her real name. Instead she managed to stifle the urge and simply nodded her reply.

"I'm Howard," he said. "Are you ready?"

When Liza started to rise, he offered an arm to help her up out of the booth. "My friends all call me Bruiser, my lady. Your coach awaits."

He led her out to the parking area. The coach in question was a sleek red Kenworth hauling a silver trailer. Black letters on the end of the trailer and penciled onto the doors on the cab read PRINCE AND SON TRANSPORT SERVICES, LEXINGTON, KENTUCKY.

"Prince would be my stepdaddy, and I'm the son," Bruiser explained as he stowed Liza's two pieces of luggage in an outside compartment. "He's eighty-seven and doesn't drive anymore, but I'm too damned cheap to change the name. I'd have to paint the whole truck. Besides, I sorta like it. You can ride up above if you want, or down here with me, whichever you prefer."

After spending most of the previous night lying down, Liza was ready to sit up for a while. She almost changed her mind when she climbed into the passenger seat and caught sight of the half-smoked cigar resting in the ashtray. Bruiser bounded into the driver's seat and caught her looking at the cigar. "Hope you don't mind," he said. "The little woman won't let me smoke at home, so I do it on the road."

"I don't mind," Liza said, thinking to herself, *Beggars can't be choosers.*

Sam was right. Bruiser talked. Steadily. He explained that the trip to KC, as he called it, would take eight hours, give or take.

"Assuming the guy's there at the warehouse with his forklift the way he's supposed to be, it'll take us forty-five or so to drop off the load in Des Moines. That'll put us into KC about six o'clock or so. Where you headed next?"

"West," Liza said. "L.A. eventually."

"Let me see what I can do, then. Lots of folks drive back and forth on I-80. I'll see if I can't fix you up with one of them. Not as many on weekends as during the week, but I'm sure we'll find you someone."

Liza settled back in the seat and simply let him talk. And smoke. He spent more than an hour talking into his Bluetooth before he had what he told her was a satisfactory set of drivers for the next leg.

"They'll be great. Kimi Sue and Oxman are a husband and wife team with a cute little dog name Major. They drive for Yellow Freight. We can meet up with them at Turk's in KC and they'll have you in Denver by morning. They'll be going on west from there, to Salt Lake and then south to their home base. They're willing to take you on as far as Salt Lake or else send you south to Albuquerque. It's up to you."

Liza closed her eyes and tried to visualize a map of the United States. She had been as far as New York City a couple of times, and her senior class had taken a trip to D.C. She'd already traveled farther into the interior of the country than she had ever expected to venture. Where was Albuquerque in relation to Bisbee? She was pretty sure Arizona and New Mexico were next door to each other. In Albuquerque maybe she'd only be an hour or so from where Guy lived.

"I'm not sure."

Bruiser laughed. "Well," he said. "You've got yourself plenty of time to think about it, little lady. You just settle back and relax."

With that, he punched in the lighter and pulled out another cigar.

Chapter 15

It was almost midnight when Joanna finally pulled into the garage at High Lonesome Ranch. She stopped long enough to key in the alarm code and lock her weapons away in the laundry room safe.

It was strange to come into a house that was dead quiet and empty. No Butch; no Jenny; no Dennis; no dogs running over one another as they raced to greet her. She couldn't remember when that had happened any time in recent history. Lucky and Lady were spending the weekend at Carol's house just up the road, and Desi, as part of his service dog training experience, was in Silver City with Jenny attending his first-ever rodeo.

Having spent a very long day in a pair of unfamiliar boots, Joanna's feet were killing her. The first thing she did upon entering the kitchen was drop into the breakfast nook and strip off the offending footwear. Then, in her stocking feet, she went looking for food. That was something else about being home alone. No Butch meant foraging for herself.

She had made a peanut butter and jelly sandwich and was about to take the first bite when the landline phone rang.

"You're home," Butch said, sounding relieved.

"Just got in," she replied.

"I know. I've been calling every fifteen minutes."

"Why didn't you call my cell?"

"Because I knew you were dealing with a homicide," Butch said. "I figured you had your hands full and thought it would be better if I talked to you after you got home. You were gone a long time. How are things?"

Joanna had taken a bite out of her sandwich and had to finish chewing and swallowing before she could answer. She gave him a shorthand version of Guy Machett's death, ending with the waterboarding followed by the failed attempt at resuscitation.

"In other words, he didn't tell them what they wanted to hear or give them what they came to get," Butch replied.

Joanna had come to rely on bouncing ideas off Butch. Now was no exception.

After pouring herself a glass of milk, she told him about the problem with Guy's next-of-kin notification.

"Calling her a person of interest is bogus," Butch observed. "You know as well as I do that's just a way of splitting legal hairs to keep Franklin from having to give her the Miranda warning the moment he lays eyes on her. And if Guy's sister has gone underground, how do you handle the press when you can't do a next-of-kin notification?"

"That's one of the things Alvin and I were huddling about. Everyone who lives on the Vista already knows who died. We can't very well hold up releasing Machett's name until Liza Machett is found. According to the people in Great Barrington, she's Guy's only living relative. We talked to Madge Livingston. She says she remembers the sister calling sometime in the last month. She said it wasn't a terribly long conversation and that it ended with Guy raising his voice. Madge claims that after that one call, Guy told her that if Liza ever phoned again, she should take a message rather than putting the call through."

"Sounds like there's some bad blood there," Butch suggested. "Is there any chance the sister is responsible for what happened to Guy?"

"That's what we're trying to figure out. If she is, she would have had to hire local talent for the hit. That's not easy to do when you're on one end of the country and your target is on the other."

"Maybe she's in Arizona, too."

"Detective Franklin says not. He claims to have had people checking to see if she purchased an airline ticket. So far no luck on that score. He thinks she's holed up somewhere right there in town with someone helping her stay out of sight."

"There are plenty of airports to choose from back east," Butch said. "I can't see how Franklin could have checked all of them. How's your mother taking to the idea that you pulled George back into your orbit?" he added, changing the subject.

"How do you think?" Joanna replied. "With two cases pending, we needed an M.E., and we needed one fast. Mother was on the phone to ream me out about it before George made it to the stop sign on Arizona Street. Since he was already in trouble tonight, he went ahead and did Junior's autopsy."

"And?"

"Junior Dowdle died of blunt force trauma from hitting his head on a rock when he fell. He also broke his neck. Either injury would have been fatal, so take your pick. George also found bruising on the small of Junior's back that could be consistent with his being pushed."

"So that's a homicide, too?"

"Looks like," Joanna agreed. "Now that the autopsy's done, George was able to release the body to the mortuary. Junior's funeral is scheduled for late Tuesday morning. That's all the news on my end. How about yours?"

"I called Dr. Ross and told her it's a go on buying Maggie," Butch answered. "I'm hoping Jenny and I can drive up to Payson next weekend to pick her up. Jenny is over the moon. Dennis is pissed. He wants to know when he's getting a horse."

Joanna laughed. "I think he's still a little young."

"That's what I told him." Butch chuckled. "He's a stubborn little guy. Takes after his mom on that score. He was still giving me the cold shoulder when I put him to bed."

"About Maggie," Joanna began. "Don't you think we should try to convince Jenny to change Maggie's name? I mean, what's going to happen when your mother finds out that she shares her name with our new horse?"

"She'll be fit to be tied," Butch said, laughing aloud. "I hope I'm there to see it."

"Yes," Joanna said, "and you know who she'll blame. It won't be her precious son!"

"I'm not worried at all," Butch replied. "If anyone knows how to handle my mother, you do. Now go to bed and go to sleep. I'm glad you're home safe."

Joanna went to bed, but she didn't go to sleep, not for a long time. For one thing, her conscience was bothering her. She hadn't liked Guy Machett. In fact, she had been less than kind to him on occasion, but she certainly hadn't wished him ill. And no one, arrogant asshole or not, deserved the kind of treatment that had been visited on him. The level of violence involved in Guy's death indicated the existence of some kind of secret life. The search warrant requests for phone, Internet, and bank records were being processed, but Dave Hollicker said it was unlikely that he'll have any results to work with on that score before Monday.

Then there was Junior. Poor Junior had been anything but arrogant. In fact, he appeared to be innocence personified, but he was dead, too. Was he also involved in some kind of secret life that Moe and Daisy Maxwell knew nothing about? Now that George Winfield had found the bruising and declared Junior's death a homicide, it was time to take a closer look at that crime scene. Someone must have been in the cave with Junior when he died, someone who had gone in and out of the cave by slithering under the grate the same way Junior had.

Joanna remembered that after Adam Wilson had used his saw to cut through the grating, he had wrenched it open wide enough for people to pass through, but the metal bars themselves were still sitting there, cemented into the limestone. Joanna sat up in bed and used her iPhone to write herself a note: *Find out if Casey dusted the grating for prints.*

Feeling she had finally done something constructive, Joanna put down the phone and tried to sleep. Then, just as she was about to drift off, she remembered little purple-haired Ruth Nolan trotting along at Marliss Shackleford's side. Ruth had used her self-proclaimed status as a blogger to justify her presence at the Machett crime scene. If she was pals with Marliss Shackleford, the girl probably also viewed herself as something of an intrepid reporter.

The thing that made Joanna's eyes pop back open was the realization that Ruth's family lived just up the street from Moe and Daisy's house. Ernie had questioned the next-door neighbors, the Radners and their son, Jason. They had claimed no knowledge about what had happened. Now Joanna found herself wondering if anyone had bothered to interview Ruth or Lucas Nolan. They were kids who lived on the same street. They were also kids who didn't seem to have the same kind of parental supervision as some of the other kids in town. If the mother had a reputation for staying out until all hours, maybe the kids came and went at odd hours, too.

Back at the Machett crime scene Ruth Nolan had asked Joanna for an interview. That was a request Joanna was now prepared to grant at the first possible opportunity. Before she did so, though, Joanna planned to take a look at Ruth's blog and see what kind of stuff was posted there.

With that much resolved in her head, Joanna was finally able to fall asleep.

Chapter 16

Bruiser handed Liza off to Kimi Sue and Jonathan "Oxman" Warner in the coffee shop at All Truck Travel outside of Kansas City. Based on size alone, it was clear why Howard Prince had earned the moniker Bruiser. It wasn't at all clear how Jonathan had become Oxman, but no one bothered explaining the origin of the nickname to Liza, and she didn't ask. Once turned loose, however, her new drivers told her everything else.

Kimi Sue and Oxman were a cheerful couple in their late forties. Onetime banking executives from Columbus, Ohio, they had been forced out of their former careers by a series of bank consolidations that had occurred in the late nineties. Lucky enough to come away with generous severance packages, they had pooled their resources, bought a truck, gotten their CDLs, and taken their show on the road. Fifteen years later they were still traveling together, and, to all appearances, enjoying it immensely. They now owned a home in Barstow, California, the home base of the trucking firm they worked for, but they generally spent very little time there. Instead, they traveled the country eighteen-wheeler style with Major, their tiny goateed Yorkie, along for the ride. Kimi Sue estimated that they listened to at least two hundred books a year as their truck rolled back and forth across the country.

Even though Bruiser had long since taken his leave, Kimi Sue and Oxman were content to hang around the truck stop, chewing the fat with friends, until well after dark. "Driving directly into the sun is a killer," Kimi Sue explained. "We usually take an afternoon break until after the sun goes down and then we drive through the night. At least that's what we do when we're heading west."

While the driving team was taking a break, Liza took one, too. Leaving Kimi Sue and Oxman in the truckers' lounge, she went into the restaurant and took a seat at the counter, where it felt odd to be on the customer side of things. Ready for a hot meal, she ordered the daily special—fried pork chops, mashed potatoes, and green beans. The pork chops were fine, the mash was instant. The green beans were canned and would never have made the cut at Candy's. At the end of her meal, when the waitress brought Liza a final coffee refill, she told Liza about her mother who had just been diagnosed with breast cancer and who would be having a lumpectomy the following week.

That was something Liza had learned. The scarf that worked so effectively as a disguise was also a license for strangers to strike up unwelcome conversations about their own or their friends' or relatives' battles or near misses with cancer. When the waitress walked away, the man seated next to Liza picked up the cancer thread and ran with it.

"A lot of people from around here head down to MD Anderson for cancer treatment," he said. "They're supposed to be good."

Liza had noticed the man when he came in. Wearing a sports jacket, white shirt, and tie, he was better dressed than most of the people in the restaurant. She had him pegged as a salesman of some kind. His next words threw her.

"So what part of Massachusetts are you from?" he asked.

Liza almost choked on her coffee. How did he know that's where she was from? Was he one of the people following her? If so, how could they possibly know she was here? What were his intentions? Would he try to snag her outside in the parking lot and keep her from making it back to the truck?

Feeling as though she had been stripped of all her supposedly effective disguises, Liza looked around desperately for help. The waitress, coffeepot in hand, was at the far end of the counter. Kimi Sue and Oxman had come into the restaurant, but they were seated in the section reserved for professional drivers.

The man next to her glanced in her direction, as if waiting for an answer. Had he seen her picture in the news and was he mentally comparing that high school photograph from the *Herald* with the features of the woman next to him?

"Boston," she murmured. It was the best she could do and as far away from Great Barrington as she could manage.

"Thought so," he said with a grin. "I can tell a Boston accent a mile away."

So that was it—her accent! On the one hand, she was relieved. On the other hand, it was a blow to her confidence. What good were disguises if someone could suss out where she was from the moment she opened her mouth? The less she spoke to anyone, the better.

"Is that where you're headed?" he asked.

"My aunt lives in Dallas," she said. "I'm going to visit her."

When Kimi Sue stood up to leave, Liza happily followed suit. "Nice talking to you," she said to the man, whose dinner order had just arrived. After paying her tab, she headed for her eighteen-wheeled moving refuge. Crossing the parking lot, she had to force herself to walk rather than run.

Once at the rig, Kimi Sue gave Liza the option of riding up front with whoever was doing the driving at the time or using the sleeping compartment upstairs, which she would most likely have to share with its usual occupant, Major.

Having spent ten of the previous twelve hours with Bruiser, a regular fire hose of conversation, Liza didn't have a problem making the choice. "I'll take the bunk," she said. "But are you sure you don't mind? If one of you needs to sleep, I'll be glad to come back down."

"Don't you worry about us, honey," Kimi Sue said. "It's Oxman's turn to drive. After all these years, I can sleep damned near anywhere. I'll grab some shut-eye between now and the next fuel stop. If his back is bothering him by then, he might want to go upstairs. If not, we'll leave you be. And don't mind Major. His bark is worse than his bite."

Clearly, Major was not fond of having strangers invade his space. When Liza first came up into the bunk, he barked nonstop for the next half hour. By then Liza was seriously questioning her decision. At last, though, with one final grumbling bark, Major turned tail and retreated to the far end of the bunk, where he curled up on one of the two pillows, daring Liza to even try appropriating one of those. For a long time, she simply sat on the edge of the bed, safe in her traveling cocoon, sensing the passage of miles and marveling at how much bigger this long swath of country was—bigger than she had ever imagined. When it finally came time to sleep, she curled up across the foot of the bed, careful to keep from coming into too close contact with the dog's declared territory.

They stopped for fuel at a place called Hank's, a truck stop on the far side of Topeka, a place so deep in the middle of nowhere that no other lights were visible in any direction. During Bruiser's interminable conversation, he had explained how some male truck drivers used empty milk or juice jars to relieve themselves along the road without having to make numerous stops. The bottle routine evidently didn't work for Kimi Sue, and Liza knew it wouldn't work for her, either.

While waiting for Kimi Sue to exit the restroom, Liza stood in front of the cashier staring up at a huge framed map of the United States that served as a wall decoration. The map depicted the country's system of interstates with references to major cities rather than small ones.

Studying it, Liza retraced her travels, remembering how long it had taken to get from place to place. Now, staring at New Mexico and the distance from Albuquerque to where she knew Bisbee must be, she realized that she had been sadly mistaken about how long it would take her to get from one to the other. Still, going south from Denver seemed like a good bet.

"Planning your route?" Kimi Sue asked.

Liza nodded.

"Where do you want to end up?"

"L.A."

"You could stick with us," Kimi Sue suggested. "We'll be back in Barstow by the end of next week. But you'll get there faster if you head down to I-10. Lots of long-haul guys there. Someone in the UR will find a good one for you."

"The UR?" Liza asked.

"The Underground Railroad. I thought you knew," Kimi Sue said. "That's what we call it. With me it was growing up with a father who beat my mother. With Oxman it was the other way around—his mother was the violent one. But we both grew up living that nightmare. It's one of the reasons we never had kids. We didn't want to put anyone else through that kind of living hell."

When Liza climbed back up into the upper berth, Major glowered at her, but he was now resigned enough to her presence that he didn't bother barking this time. She remembered what Bertha had said to her in the restaurant where Joe and Sam had dropped her off—that she'd once had a husband she'd had to put in her rearview mirror. Sam had hinted about some kind of violence in his past, and so had Bruiser. His truck driving company partnership had been in conjunction with a stepfather rather than a father.

And what did that say about Candy Small? When he had put those telltale bruises on her arm, he had known exactly what he was doing. Was it something he had seen as a kid with his father taking his frustrations out on his mother? Or perhaps it was the other way around. Maybe Candy was a confirmed bachelor for the same reason Kimi Sue and Oxman didn't have kids—because he didn't trust himself to be any better at marriage than his parents had been. And what about Aimee and the women who worked in that salon that was really a front for a mostly invisible women's shelter? Were they all victims, too? If so, Liza realized, the numbers were staggering. She had grown up trapped in her own particular brand of misery. She had always known that her own life was bad, but it had somehow escaped her understanding that other people's lives might have been just as bad if not worse.

Now, here she was benefiting from all those other people's experiences and from their misery as well. The UR, as Kimi Sue called it, was a loose-knit but effective army dedicated to rescuing domestic violence victims, one battered spouse at a time. It occurred to Liza then that perhaps she did belong here. The obvious bruises Candy had placed on her arm were phony, but the physical abuse she had suffered as a child at her mother's hands had been real enough. It turned out her mother's violence was the price of admission for this journey and for what she had originally considered to be undeserved assistance from this cadre of kind and motivated folks.

Traveling through the night, Liza no longer felt undeserving. With that thought in mind, she took off her scarf and folded the long strip of material into a small silk square. Holding it close to her breast, she closed her eyes and fell asleep.

Chapter 17

In the dream Joanna was running desperately after Dennis, who flew down High Lonesome Road, riding bareback on Spot. The horse was racing at a full gallop. Joanna chased after them, barefoot, screaming at Dennis that he needed to stop—that the horse couldn't see where she was going. All he did was turn back, look at her, laugh, wave, and keep right on going.

It was a relief when her rooster-crowing telephone awakened her out of the nightmare. "Good morning," George Winfield said. "Just like old times. I'm on my way to do the Machett autopsy. When I came through Bakerville, Daisy's was open, so I decided to stop in for breakfast. Care to join me?"

"I'm surprised they're open," Joanna said.

"So am I," George agreed, "but since they are, I wanted to give them my business—as a show of solidarity if nothing else."

"Where's Mom?" Joanna asked.

"Ellie was asleep when I got home last night, or at least she pretended to be, and she was still asleep just now when I left. If I can finish the autopsy in time to make it to church, I might start to worm my way back into her good graces. She has dinner plans scheduled for this evening. If I know what's good for me, I won't be late or absent."

"I'll come to breakfast," Joanna agreed, "but I have to shower and dress first."

"Take your time," George said. "I'll sit here, look at the paper, and drink coffee. Matt Keller is meeting me at the morgue at nine, so there's no rush."

"Since this is a joint case, do you want one of my people there?" Joanna asked.

"Up to you," George said. "It's Sunday. With two separate cases to solve, you've got to be chewing up overtime like crazy."

That was true. When Joanna had handed out work assignments for today, she had hoped that Guy Machett's autopsy wouldn't happen until Monday. Doing it on Sunday would increase the cost if she had to pay for one of her detectives to be on hand to witness the procedure. With Matt there, it wasn't as vital to have one of her people present, but still . . .

"You could do it," George pointed out, interrupting her thought process. "You're on salary. You get paid the same no matter how many hours you work. As you said, it's a joint operation. I know things are all hunky-dory with Alvin Bernard right now, but if that goes south, you're going to want your department to have its own record of what went on during the autopsy."

"I've witnessed some autopsies," Joanna cautioned, "but not that many."

"Neither has Matt Keller," George advised. "That's one of the reasons I think you should be there."

Joanna liked the fact that George was a straight shooter. When he passed out unsolicited advice, she tended to pay attention.

"Fair enough," she said. "I'm on my way."

With no kids to juggle, no animals to feed, no pets to dodge, and no breakfast to eat, Joanna was showered, dressed, and in the car in record time. She paused at the stop sign on High Lonesome Road long enough to send a text to Casey asking if she had dusted the metal grate for fingerprints.

Inside Daisy's, Joanna was surprised to find Moe Maxwell stationed at the front door with a stack of menus in hand. She was dismayed not only at finding

Moe filling in at Junior's usual station but at his being there at all. Her thoughts must have been written on her features because Moe's face darkened.

"I told Daisy we had to open," he explained. "All we were doing was sitting at home, crying, and driving each other nuts. Besides, you can't leave a restaurant inventory of food sitting around forever—use it or lose it."

George waved to her from the far corner of the room. "Don't bother with a menu," Joanna told Moe. "I know what I want, and you don't need to lead me to the table, either. I can find my way."

"Coffee?" Moe asked.

"Please."

While he went off to fetch it, George looked at her over the top of his reading glasses as well as over the top of the print edition of the *Arizona Daily Sun.* "Hope you didn't make the mistake of suggesting that it was too early for Moe and Daisy to be back at work. I did, and he nearly bit my head off."

Moe arrived at their booth with coffeepot in hand. He filled Joanna's mug. Then, without a word, he slopped enough coffee into George's mug to top it off before stomping away.

"Fortunately I was smart enough to keep my mouth shut," Joanna said. Then, after pausing long enough to take a sip of coffee, she added, "I'm glad to have you back."

George frowned. "That's the same thing Madge said last night when she called—that she was glad I'm back. I'm not, really. I told you I'd help you with these two cases, but that's it. Your mother and I have plans to leave town next week, and we're going. In the unlikely event that you make a quick arrest and the case goes to trial before we get back in October, then I'll have to fly in to testify if need be, but this isn't a permanent arrangement."

Moe came over to take their order. The retired letter carrier wasn't especially good when it came to taking orders or waiting tables, so it took some time. Once Moe walked away, George apologized to Joanna. "I didn't mean to growl at you, but I spent too many of the years with my first wife working too hard and not paying attention to the relationship. I'm not making the same mistake with Ellie. I said as much to Claire Newmark, too."

"Got it," Joanna said. "I won't ask again. Now, what else can you tell me about Junior's autopsy?"

"He died sometime around midnight," George answered. "The bruising on his back would be consistent with his being shoved from behind and propelled forward with considerable force, most likely by a blunt object of some kind—a round blunt object, the business end of a baseball bat perhaps. I was surprised by the amount of animal hair I found on his clothing—make that on the front of his clothing. Do Moe and Daisy have a number of pets?"

"The animals didn't belong to Moe and Daisy," Joanna answered grimly. "They were victims, too. They were dropped off the ledge alive and left to die. There were four animals in all. Three of them were already dead when Junior landed on top of them. The fourth, a kitten, is still alive—mutilated and badly injured but still alive. Millicent Ross is working to save it. We've also sent evidence from both the living kitten and the dead animals to the State Patrol crime lab in Tucson in hopes of locating human DNA."

George sipped his coffee reflectively. "It sounds to me as though you're dealing with a serial killer's starter kit and a starter victim, too."

"That thought crossed my mind," Joanna agreed. "Is there any chance Guy's murder and Junior's are related?"

George shook his head. "I don't think so. The two incidents are very different. What happened to Junior is consistent with an unprovoked attack. His back was turned. No defensive wounds at all. I'd say he was taken completely by surprise."

"Do you think his killer might have been someone he knew?" Joanna asked.

"Possibly," George agreed. "Guy Machett, on the other hand, tried to fight off his attackers. He had a number of visible defensive wounds, and I should be able to get scrapings from under his fingernails."

"What about the burns?" Joanna asked. "If we locate the weapon, do you think you'll be able to match his wounds to that?"

"Possibly," George said, "although I'm not sure. If you locate the weapon, however, there may be DNA evidence on it as well as on the duct tape that was used to secure him to the chair. Did you find any rolls of tape at the scene?"

"Only remnants," Joanna answered. "There weren't any rolls in Guy's garage, either. I don't think Dr. Machett was a DIY kind of person."

"So we're operating on the assumption that the killers came prepared with both the tape and the stun gun."

Joanna nodded. "We're also hoping that some of the perpetrators' DNA will show up on the tape, too. After all, that's what duct tape does—it sticks to things."

"Since Guy is mentioned by name in the article in the *Sun*, I assume that means you've located his next of kin?"

"No such luck." Joanna went on to explain everything Amos Franklin had told her about Guy's family and about the sister who had mysteriously disappeared.

"In other words, after the autopsy, I won't be releasing the body to a mortuary?"

"Not for the time being," Joanna said. "Not until we find some kind of family connection."

Their food came. Moe had mixed up the orders. Joanna waited until his back was turned before she traded her platter of over-easy eggs for George's over-hard. Considering what was coming, Joanna surprised herself by falling on her food as though she was starving—because she was. The paltry nourishment from last night's peanut butter sandwich had long since disappeared. When the bill came, George grabbed it first and insisted on paying. Ten minutes later, they pulled their respective vehicles into the parking lot at the M.E.'s office. They found Detective Keller, already green around the gills, pacing nervously back and forth in front of the office door.

"You took long enough," he grumbled.

Matt made it through the cataloguing of the visible wounds and the fingernail scraping, but once the first major incision was made, the detective bailed. "I told you he was a newbie," George said under his breath over the sound of Matt's retching from the lab's restroom. Gritting her teeth to choke back her own nausea, Joanna nodded and held her ground.

Sometime later George finally nodded more to himself than to anyone else. "Just as I suspected. Guy Machett drowned. The bruising on the back of his neck suggests that he drowned because someone bodily held his head under water."

By then Matt had eased his way back into the room and stood warily on the perimeter. "It's homicide, then?" he asked.

"Yes," George told him, snapping off his gloves. "Definitely a homicide."

Joanna let herself out the back door. She stood next to her Yukon in the parking lot behind the morgue, grateful for the blue sky arching overhead and for the heat of the late morning sun shining down on her body.

"Sorry about that," Matt Keller said, coming out to join her. His color was somewhat better, but she could tell he was embarrassed by his squeamishness. "Chief Bernard asked me to come give him a verbal briefing on the autopsy before we meet up with you and your people at one. I'd better get going, unless there's something else you want me to do here."

Down the canyon and just visible on the flank of the hill, Joanna caught a glimpse of St. Dominick's where

Mass had most likely just ended. Moe and Daisy's place was just up the hill from the church. Beyond that was the house Ruth and Lucas Nolan shared with their mother. Joanna had meant to ask either Marliss or Ruth for the name of Ruth's blog so she could glance at it before the interview. Now, though, on the off chance that the budding reporter might be able to shed some light on Junior Dowdle's killer, Joanna wanted that interview to happen sooner than later. Reading the blog entries could wait.

"Go brief your chief," Joanna said, "but just out of curiosity, did you do in-depth interviews with either Lucas or Ruth Nolan?" Joanna asked.

"Since they live just up the street from Moe and Daisy, I talked to both of them," Matt said. "Didn't get much."

"Ruth showed up at the crime scene with Marliss last night and asked to do an interview with me. I gave her the bum's rush, but maybe doing the interview would be a good idea. It might give me a chance to ask her some questions as well."

Once Matt left, Joanna did the same. Driving past St. Dom's, she noticed that the parking lot was empty. Rebecca Nolan's house on O'Hara, a small wooden rental with a tin roof, was perched on the hillside ten steps down from street level. When Joanna knocked on the wobbly screen door, Rebecca herself, barefoot and wearing a bathrobe, came to the door.

"Sheriff Brady," she exclaimed in surprise, peering around the door inside the screen. "What are you doing here?"

"I was hoping to talk to Ruth," Joanna said.

"What about?"

"She requested an interview last night," Joanna said, "for her blog. I was too busy then, but I have some time this morning. Is she available?"

"Oh, my," Rebecca said with a harsh laugh that sent a fog of boozy breath out through the screen. "Not that blog nonsense again. I'm afraid I've unleashed a monster on the world. It was an English writing assignment I gave her and Lucas several months ago. Now she's gone nuts. I keep telling her that the world isn't ready for a fourteen-year-old blogger."

"Who is it, Mom?" Ruth asked from somewhere behind her mother.

Rebecca spun around. "It's Sheriff Brady," she grumbled. "I keep telling you that you shouldn't be bothering important people with requests for interviews."

"It's no bother," Joanna replied, making sure that her voice carried through the open doorway to the ears of the purple-haired girl, standing listening but invisible behind her mother's back. "I was in the neighborhood and thought, if Ruth was home, perhaps we could do it now."

"I have time," Ruth interjected quickly. "Please, Mom. It's a chance to interview a real sheriff."

"Oh, I suppose it's all right," Rebecca conceded, "but don't make a pest of yourself. You're just a kid. There's no reason Sheriff Brady should bother giving you the time of day."

With that, Rebecca Nolan disappeared into the house. As soon as she was out of the way, Ruth's eager face appeared around the edge of the door. Unlike her mother, Ruth was fully dressed in a T-shirt and a pair of shorts.

"Let me go get my phone," she said. "I'll be right back."

Joanna waited for a few moments on the tiny landing that constituted the house's front porch. Glancing up at the mountain from where she stood, she could barely see the sharp edges in the rocks that marked the old Glory Hole. When Ruth reappeared, she had put on a pair of flip-flops and was carrying an old-style flip-top cell phone. An orange stripe had been added to her otherwise mostly purple hair, which was pulled back in a multicolored ponytail.

"You really don't mind?" Ruth asked eagerly.

"No, I don't," Joanna said. "Where would you like to do the interview? There's really no place to sit here. My car is up on the street. Is that all right?"

"The car is fine," Ruth said.

Joanna led the way back to the Yukon. When she opened the rear passenger door, the girl stopped and stared. The SUV had been rigged out as a patrol vehicle, complete with a protective screen between the front and back seats and again between the backseat and the luggage compartment. That way prisoners and suspects could be transported safely in the backseat without endangering whoever was at the wheel. The vehicle came complete with a full complement of radio transmission gear and an onboard computer. On the passenger side of the drive shaft sat Joanna's holstered shotgun.

"Can you really shoot that thing?" Ruth asked, pointing at the weapon.

"Can and do," Joanna replied. "I also have one of these." She patted the holstered Glock on her hip. "I can shoot this as well. I'm expected to maintain the same kind of shooting proficiency as the rest of my officers."

"I have to sit in the back, like a prisoner or something?" Ruth asked.

"That's right," Joanna replied with a smile. "As long as the shotgun is up front, you have to be in the back."

"And there really aren't any door handles back here?"

"That's right," Joanna said. "Nobody in back gets out until I let them out." Closing the door, she walked around to the driver's door and climbed in. "Now tell me, what did you want to ask?"

When she looked back at Ruth, the girl had her phone out and was using her thumbs to type in a message at what, to Joanna, appeared to be lightning speed. Joanna's texting skills weren't up to recording an entire interview.

"Did you always want to be sheriff?" Ruth asked.

"Not really," Joanna answered. "My husband wanted to be sheriff. He died in a line-of-duty shooting and the people elected me in his place. In other words, my becoming sheriff was more or less an accident. That was seven years ago now, though, and it turns out I love it."

"What's the worst thing about being sheriff?"

"Having to tell someone their loved one is dead."

"Like Mr. and Mrs. Maxwell with Junior?"

"That's right."

"What's the best thing?"

"Locking up a serious criminal and knowing that society is protected from additional harm from that individual for a very long time."

"Like lock them up and throw away the key?"

Joanna laughed. "Exactly."

"Were you an only child?"

The unexpected question wasn't an easy one to answer. Joanna's older brother had been born before her parents married and had been given up for adoption. She hadn't met him until long after her father was dead and she herself was an adult.

"Yes," she said after a moment's pause. "I was raised as an only child."

"I wish I was," Ruth said pensively. "Lucas is the perfect one. I'm not. He's way smarter than I am, especially at math. I'm better at English, though, and I read more than he does."

"We can't all be good at all things," Joanna said. "For instance, I'm not nearly as good at texting as you are."

Ruth shrugged. "Maybe I just practice more." She paused for a moment as if thinking about the next question. "Do you think you'll be able to find out what happened to Junior?"

"You need to understand that even the sheriff isn't allowed to comment on an active investigation. I guess I have to say, 'No comment' to that one."

Ruth's face broke into a grin. "I heard you say that to Marliss last night, but I've never had anyone say it to me before. It almost feels like I'm a real reporter or something."

"Aren't you?" Joanna asked.

"I guess."

"But you asked about Junior like you knew him. Did you?"

"I felt sorry for him," Ruth said. "When we first moved here, I'd see him out walking sometimes, but then his parents started locking him in at night. I think they were afraid that he'd get lost or something. At night, when the windows were open, I could hear him crying sometimes. A couple of times, when it was really bad, I went over and sang to him to help settle him down."

Joanna was stunned. "You sang to him?"

Ruth nodded. "I sang some of the songs we learned in Sunday school before Mom made us stop going. You know the ones I mean, 'Jesus Loves Me' and 'This Little Light of Mine.' He really liked those."

Joanna felt a shock of recognition. She remembered Moe and Daisy saying something about Junior claiming he'd sometimes had nighttime visitors. Daisy had insisted the phantom visitors were hallucinations, but now Joanna knew that wasn't true. Junior had had at least one nocturnal visitor. Joanna wondered if there were others.

"Did you go there often?" Joanna asked. "To sing to him, I mean."

"Not often," Ruth answered, "just a couple of times."

"Did you ever see Junior hanging out with anyone?" Joanna asked.

"Jason," Ruth said at once. "Jason Radner."

Noticing movement at the corner of her eye, Joanna saw a towheaded boy, Ruth's brother, Lucas, bound up the stairs. He came over to the Yukon and pressed his face against the rear passenger window.

"Mom says you should come inside," he said to Ruth. "Now," he added. "She says you should stop wasting the sheriff's time."

Joanna climbed out of the Yukon, came around the vehicle, and opened the back door so Ruth could exit.

"Thank you," Ruth said. "Should I send you what I write about you?"

"Please," Joanna answered, "or you could just send me the link to your blog. You can find my work e-mail address on the sheriff's department website."

Ruth nodded. "Okay," she said. "I'll do that."

By then Lucas had already disappeared down the stairs with Ruth trailing behind. Joanna remembered how she had trotted up the stairs, eager to be out of the house. She didn't seem nearly as happy to be going back inside.

Watching her go, Joanna felt a certain sadness. She hoped that neither Jenny nor Dennis would ever feel that way about her—that one of them was wanted and the other was not.

It was clear to her that Ruth Nolan was at war with her mother. Joanna had considerable experience in that kind of intergenerational conflict. In Ruth's case, dyeing her hair purple and singing "Jesus Loves Me" were both acts of rebellion, ones that most likely carried about the same weight in terms of motherly disapproval.

Shaking her head, Joanna put the Yukon in gear and headed out. It was almost time for the meeting she had called, and she didn't want to be late.

Chapter 18

It was just after sunrise when Kimi Sue and Oxman's rig pulled into the Trux-Travel truck stop outside Denver. Overnight the immense flatness of the Great Plains had been replaced by the soaring Rockies. When Liza climbed down from her overhead berth into the mountainous chill, she felt stiff and sore as her body protested the long hours of confinement. Kimi Sue had shown Liza how to exercise her ankles to keep them from swelling, and that seemed to be working.

"You might want to bring your stuff inside," Kimi Sue suggested. "William is your next ride, but he won't be here for another hour and a half. Grab a shower and some breakfast. William drives a tanker truck. We told him he should look for the lady with the bright blue head scarf."

After bidding Kimi Sue good-bye, Liza immediately took a shower. Because she didn't have to shampoo or rinse her hair, showering was a surprisingly fast process. Dressed in a change of clothing, she ventured out into the truckers' lounge. Once again, there was a bank of computers—three of them this time—situated along one wall. Since most of the truckers seemed to be focused on their own laptops, iPads, or iPhones, the idle PCs sat there in lonely, unused splendor.

Availing herself of one of those, Liza did a preliminary search for used car dealerships in Albuquerque. Kimi Sue had told her that the next driver would be going all the way to I-10, but Liza had already decided that she'd cut herself loose from the Underground Railway in Albuquerque and find her own transportation from there to Bisbee.

After locating several possible dealerships and jotting down the addresses, she gave herself permission to check out the news from Great Barrington. The headline on the *Herald*'s website took Liza's breath away: BELOVED RESTAURATEUR, CLIFFORD SMALL, DEAD AT AGE 53.

> Local restaurant icon, Clifford (Candy) Small, age 53, was found dead in the burned-out ruins of his house just after 7 AM today. The Great

Barrington Fire Department has labeled the fire suspicious. The incident is being investigated by both local fire and police departments.

This is breaking news. No further details are available at this time.

Astonished and horrified, Liza read through the brief piece again. Then, before anyone could read the story over her shoulder, she closed the website, erased her history, and fled the room. Outside, she paced back and forth in the chill air. Candy was dead, too? Why, because he had helped her? What other reason could there be? That made his death Liza's fault, too. Awash in guilt, she realized that if she was a person of interest in Olivia's case, she would most likely be one in this case as well. That meant the authorities would ramp up their search for her, and so would whoever else was after her. Liza had no doubt that those people were behind this new fire, the one in which Candy had perished.

Then another thought crossed her mind. What if the people who were chasing Liza had somehow forced Candy to divulge where she was, how she was traveling, and who was helping her? Did that mean that now all those Underground Railroad people were also in danger—Aimee, Sam and Joe, and Bruiser as well as

Kimi Sue and Oxman? Standing shivering and with her teeth chattering, she stared back at the building—at the people coming and going, at the trucks and cars pulling in and out. Her pursuers could be any of those passing people. By now, despite all the Underground Railroad's careful precautions, the bad guys might already know exactly where she was.

It took all of Liza's willpower to stay where she was and not go racing for the nearest hiding place, wherever that might be.

She had no idea how long she stood there, shivering in the frigid wind blowing down from the snowcapped peaks. At last the cold forced her inside. She slunk into the truck stop's restaurant and collapsed in the booth farthest from the front door that still offered a clear view of the entrance. Not that seeing the people coming and going would do her any good. Liza didn't know the faces of the people who were chasing her; she wouldn't have recognized them if they showed up at the same booth and sat down directly across the table from her.

A waitress arrived to take Liza's order. She wore her hair in an old-fashioned beehive that reminded Liza of Honey's back home. Thinking about Honey reminded her of Candy, and thinking about Candy caused unbidden tears to spring to her eyes before she could blurt out her order.

"Sweetie pie," the waitress said consolingly, "you just sit here and take a deep breath. Things may be bad right now, but they're bound to get better. What you need is something to eat. How about some bacon and eggs?"

Liza nodded. "Over easy, please, and some coffee, too," she managed. "Black coffee."

The coffee came. Liza dried her tears with some of the extra napkins the waitress had thoughtfully delivered along with the coffee. She sat with her hands wrapped around the cheap china mug hoping that the heat from the cup would leach into her chilled body.

When breakfast came, Liza tried to eat it. She downed one of the slices of bacon and nibbled at the toast, but that was all. She understood that what should she do now was walk as far as the nearest police station and turn herself in. If she didn't, other people might die, and if she did? That left the very real possibility that *she* might die, too. Just because she was in a jail somewhere wouldn't necessarily mean she was safe. The people who were after her were obviously ruthless and would stop at nothing.

No, she decided, turning herself in wasn't the answer, at least not yet. She'd go to Bisbee, talk with Guy, see if he had any ideas about what this was about—about who was after her and why. She'd ask his advice. After all, he was her big brother. With Candy gone, Guy was the only one left to ask. If he said Liza should turn herself in, she would.

She looked at her luggage. The roll-aboard, still full of the money, was stowed on the bench seat next to her. If whoever was trying to kill her had simply asked her to return the money, she would have done so, no questions asked. After all, it wasn't really hers in the first place. Whatever was left of it—a little under a hundred grand—was blood money now. People had died because of it—her friends had died because of it. Liza didn't know if she'd ever be able to bring herself to touch one of those bills again, much less spend it.

"Excuse me, ma'am," a deep voice asked. "Would you happen to be Linda?"

Liza looked up. The man standing in front of her was tall and muscular, with biceps the size of tree trunks. He was also a walking gallery of tattoos. The tops of some of the designs peeked out past the open collar of his denim shirt. Every inch of bare skin on his arms— from the bottom of his shirtsleeves to his wrists—was covered with an uninterrupted layer of colorful inks, everything from birds to butterflies, American flags to golden eagles. His nose had been broken, most likely more than once. He was completely bald—almost as bald as Liza herself. Clutched in one hand was a John Deere baseball cap.

Liza's first instinct was to blow him off and pretend she wasn't his intended passenger, but at last she managed a brief nod.

"I'm William, ma'am," he said, grinning and clapping the cap back on his head. The grin revealed several missing front teeth. "William Gray. I'm fueled up and ready to go anytime you are."

If anyone should have been called Bruiser or Oxman, this guy was him. The somewhat dignified name of William didn't suit him at all. He was fierce-looking. Liza should have been terrified of him. She should have stayed where she was and hitched a ride with someone else. The problem was, she was even more terrified of the people who were looking for her—the people who had killed Candy. No matter how scary this guy might appear, he couldn't possibly be that bad.

Liza reached for her bags. "I'm ready," she said. "As soon as I pay the bill, we can be on our way."

Outside William led her to a semi with two shiny tankers hooked on behind it. He didn't volunteer what was in the tanks, and Liza didn't ask. For the first time there was no overhead berth. That meant Liza rode in the cab with William, who chatted away in an amiable fashion. Liza was so upset over the news of Candy's death that she had a hard time listening or responding.

Before, she had ridden along in the series of rumbling trucks with some confidence that she was doing so under everyone's radar—that the people who were after her would never be able to pick up her trail. All that had changed. She had told Candy she was going to Arizona. What if he had told someone else?

Thinking about Candy led Liza to thinking about the restaurant. What would happen to the business? With Candy gone, who would take over and run it? And what about all the people who worked there? They would most likely be thrown out of work as well, all because of Liza.

As the tanker truck sped down the road, rather than watching the pavement ahead, Liza kept her eyes glued to the rearview mirror, keeping track of each vehicle that came speeding up behind them. Each time one came a little too close or stayed too long, Liza found herself holding her breath and letting it out only when the worrisome car or truck merged into the other lane and surged past.

"You can stop worrying," William said at last, penetrating her cloud of silence. "There's nobody out there, you know. I've been watching, too, and I ain't seen anybody suspicious."

"Sorry," she said. "I guess I'm just paranoid."

"From the looks of that arm, I'd say you've got good reason. What kind of cancer?" he added. Now that he had her attention, he seemed determined to engage her in conversation, choosing the most obvious option—cancer.

"Breast," she said, "lumpectomy and chemo." The lie came all too easily, without her even having to think about it.

William nodded. "My mom had that," he said. "Seven years ago. They caught it early. Now she does that Susan Komen race thing every year. What's amazing is that she was never a great one for exercising before she got sick. Now she's doing cancer walks and cancer bicycle rides all over the country, which, considering her age, is pretty impressive."

"How old is she?" Liza asked, more courtesy than due to any real interest.

"Seventy-one," William answered. "Other than having that one bout with cancer, the woman's ornery as all get-out and has never been sick a day in her life."

William's cheery answer sent Liza's mind down yet another dark channel. Candy Small hadn't made it to seventy-one, and right that minute, it seemed unlikely that Liza would make it that far, either.

Back in the truck stop in Denver, Liza had already decided that she'd only stick with the next ride as far as Albuquerque, but she didn't mention that to William Gray. As far as he was concerned, she was going all the way to Las Cruces. It wasn't until two in the afternoon when they pulled into the Albuquerque Truck Terminal that she told him she was bailing.

"You're sure?" William asked with a frown. "I've already lined up someone who can meet us in Las Cruces and take you as far as Phoenix."

She didn't want to admit that she was opting out of the Underground Railroad because she was afraid it had been compromised.

"No, thank you," she responded quickly. "I appreciate all your help and concern, but I'm sure. I have friends in here in Albuquerque," she added, hoping the lie didn't show. "I'll spend a few days with them."

"Give me the address," William said. "I can drop you off."

"No," she insisted. "I already called them. They'll come pick me up."

William wasn't thrilled with the arrangement, but he went along with it. Liza sat in the restaurant and pretended to be texting her friends on the burner phone while she waited for him to refuel and leave. Sitting with the phone in her hand, she wished she could call Guy. She'd had his number once, of course, but that had been in her own phone, the one Candy had taken away from her. The only way to reach Guy now would be to get the number from information, and she didn't want to do that. Instead, she'd wait until she got to Bisbee. She'd go to his office and talk to him face-to-face. Together they'd figure out what to do.

Once William's tanker eased back out onto the roadway, Liza found a pay phone and called a cab. Before it arrived, she went into the restroom with her luggage. Inside the stall, far away from prying eyes, she opened the roll-aboard and let the all-pervading scent of coffee beans overwhelm the restroom's industrial-grade room deodorizer. When this was over, Liza wondered if she'd ever feel the same way about coffee beans.

One by one she counted out fifty of her remaining and still astonishingly fragrant one-hundred-dollar bills and stashed them in the side pocket of her worn Coach purse. Five thousand was the top dollar she was prepared to pay for a vehicle. If she couldn't find a ride for less than that, she was either taking the bus or walking.

Chapter 19

Joanna was still in Old Bisbee and on her way to the Justice Center when Butch called. "Jenny's just now loading the horses," he said, "then we'll be heading out."

"You're not staying for the afternoon events?" Joanna asked.

"Jenny's call," Butch said. "For some reason she's ready to go home now. Surprised me, too. It's never happened before. She usually wants to stay until the bitter end. Not today, though, and it's just as well. I'm tired of eating dust, and Denny is cranky, too. He misses his mommy, and I miss my wife. What's happening on your end?"

"I started my day by witnessing Guy Machett's autopsy."

"Great," Butch groaned. "How did he die?"

"Just what I told you last night—he drowned. I've had people out combing the streets all morning, trying to see if anyone on the Vista saw or heard anything unusual. Dave Hollicker should be off work with a sprained ankle but came in anyway. He's at the department sorting through the information that's coming in from the search warrants. In the meantime, Casey Ledford has driven another load of crime scene evidence up to the Department of Public Safety crime lab in Tucson."

Call waiting buzzed with a blocked number on the screen. With as much as she had going on, Joanna decided she'd better take it. "Another call," she told Butch. "Sorry." She switched over to the incoming call.

"Sheriff Brady?"

The voice was familiar, but Joanna couldn't place it instantly. "Yes."

"Detective Amos Franklin here. Sorry to interrupt your Sunday. I called your department looking for you, and whoever answered the phone there gave me this number. I hope you don't mind. I never let anyone give out my home number."

"It's my cell," Joanna said impatiently, "and no, I don't mind. What's up?"

"We've got a new wrinkle on our end. A man by the name of Clifford Small was found dead in the burned-out wreckage of his home here in Great Barrington early this morning. I waited until our M.E. did the autopsy before I ran up the flag to you. He was Liza Machett's boss."

"Her boss?" Joanna repeated. "Wasn't he the guy who gave Liza Machett a ride home the other night after you interviewed her?"

"A ride to *his* home," Franklin corrected.

"Were he and Liza in a relationship of some kind?"

"Not that I know of," Franklin replied. "Liza Machett worked for him for years—ever since she graduated high school—but everyone I've talked to says it was strictly that—an employee/employer relationship, nothing more."

"No friends with benefits?"

"If it was, nobody's saying," Franklin replied, "but we're beginning to get a better idea of what we've got here. The autopsy clearly shows that Candy was tortured before he was stabbed, and he was dead before the fire started. The M.E. found no sign of smoke inhalation."

"Candy?" Joanna asked. "I thought you just said his name was Clifford. And you're saying he was tortured?"

"Candy's what everyone in town called him, ever since we were kids, and yes, he was tortured—badly."

"Are you thinking Liza is responsible for what happened to him?"

"I can't see how that's possible unless she had plenty of help. Candy weighed a good three hundred pounds. Liza couldn't be more than a third of that. Besides, call me sexist if you want, but I can't see a woman involved in something where torture is such a big part of it."

"What kind of torture?"

"His fingers and toes were systematically whacked off over a period of time, probably several hours. When the fun and games were over, he was killed with a single stab wound to the heart. That took some physical strength. Again, I don't think a woman could or would have done it."

Joanna thought about the footprints in the blood around the chair in Guy Machett's kitchen, a larger set and a smaller one. A man and a woman together? It was a possibility, and just because the search hadn't shown anyone traveling with Liza Machett's ID didn't rule out the idea of her traveling with fake ID of some kind. Joanna knew there were plenty of places where fake IDs were bought and sold on the open market, even in her small-town corner of the world.

"After Liza disappeared," Detective Franklin continued, "I started looking into a few things, because there were some rumors floating around. Several people suggested that Liza must have come into a substantial sum of money fairly recently. Before the house burned down last week, she'd spent a small fortune cleaning out and redoing her mother's place.

"Once I started asking questions, I learned that she'd been paying her workers mostly in cash. On a hunch, I called Craig Masters, the guy who runs the local funeral home. Sure enough, part of Selma Machett's final expenses had been paid in advance by Selma herself, but the remainder was paid in cash— thirty one-hundred-dollar bills that Liza handed over the morning of the funeral. According to Craig, that wad of money stunk to high heavens of coffee.

"Then I called another old friend of mine, Nancy Haller, who manages First National Bank and Trust here in Great Barrington. She says that she and her staff have been seeing an influx of what they call 'coffee money' for some time now, for at least the past month or so.

"She says it usually comes into the bank in hundred-dollar denominations. When the first batch showed up, one of the tellers brought it to Nancy's attention. The serial numbers on the bills were so old that most of their contemporaries have been taken out of circulation. It turns out that, other than the smell, these bills were in good shape. Since then Nancy's had her people keep track of the serial numbers, but she also put in a call to someone at the Treasury Department early on because she was afraid they might be dealing with some kind of counterfeit. Treasury sent out an investigator who determined that the bills were real enough. He said not to worry—that it was probably money someone, Selma Machett most likely, had been hoarding for a very long time—the old money-in-the-mattress kind of savings account."

By then, Joanna had pulled the Yukon into the private parking place behind her office at the Justice Center. "How old are these bills exactly?" she asked.

"Most of them date back to the late seventies. Some are a little earlier."

"The money may be what this is all about, then, or it could be something else," Joanna commented. "Whatever the killers are looking for, they're prepared to do whatever's necessary to lay hands on it. Do we have any idea how much money is involved?"

"Not exactly," Detective Franklin replied. "I've spent the morning tracking down everybody who did rehab work on Selma Machett's house. Nobody's willing to give me a straight answer. They're all claiming that it was a volunteer project organized by Candy Small. That's probably because they were paid in cash, and nobody's bothered to declare it as income. When I struck out with them, I checked with several local building supply places and lumberyards.

"It turns out Liza had recently become a very steady customer at more than one of those. Since she paid cash there, too, the stores don't have exact records of what she purchased, but they acknowledge her having ponied up money for a substantial amount of building material—plumbing fixtures, new kitchen appliances, flooring. Based on what I can verify and estimating the rest, I'd say she must have spent at least forty grand just on fixing up the house."

"The same house that burned down the other night," Joanna concluded.

"Correct," Franklin agreed, "all of which leads me to believe that we're talking about a fairly large sum of money since there's still enough of it out there to make it worthwhile to commit three separate murders."

"You've got the drop on us by a few days in all of this," Joanna observed. "We have yet to get responses on our requests for phone and e-mail information. Have you been able to uncover any kind of pattern of communication between Liza and her brother? Are there any records of phone calls or e-mails back and forth between them?"

"Everyone here is saying the same thing—that she and Guy were estranged. We did find a single call placed from Liza Machett's cell phone to a number in Bisbee that we've just now verified as the number for Guy Machett's office. That call was placed after Selma Machett was moved to hospice care and before she died. There's no sign that Liza made any effort to contact him by phone after Selma's death, at least not from her home or cell-phone numbers and not from any of the numbers associated with the restaurant where she worked, including the pay phone there."

"If she has a cell phone, have you tried locating her with that?"

"Yes, we did and came up empty. The last ping from her cell came through the cell tower closest to Candy's house. That was early Friday morning. Since then it's gone dead silent."

"What about e-mail?" Joanna asked.

"If Liza had a computer at home, we didn't find it," Detective Franklin answered. "It could be that it was taken during the break-in at her apartment. Without the computer, we don't know her search engine history, but she did have an e-mail account that we've been able to access. There's a lot of spam on it, mostly shopping sites, but most of her online correspondence was chatting back and forth with friends and some of the other waitresses at work. In other words, Liza Machett wasn't much of a social butterfly."

"No mention of the money or where it came from?"

"Not a peep. Not a single mention to anyone."

"Given all this," Joanna said, "what's your best guess about what's going on?"

There was a small pause before Franklin answered. "As I said before, one way or another, Liza came into a sizable sum of money, most likely money her mother had in her possession for some time. Other people may have become aware of that money, especially her contractors. It occurred to me that maybe one of them got greedy and thought Liza would be an easy target. I was in the process of looking into the whereabouts of all those guys last night when you called to tell me Liza's brother had been murdered. By the way, so far all the workers are present and accounted for."

"What happened the other night when you brought Liza in for questioning?" Joanna asked.

"I asked all the usual questions. Did she know who might have a grudge against her mother or her or her landlady? She claimed she had no idea, which, I'm now sure, was a straight-out lie. By then she must have figured out that whoever broke into her apartment was really after the money. If she'd had a brain, she would have come clean and given me a chance to help her. Instead, she chose to go into hiding. Given what happened to Olivia Dexter and now Candy Small, whoever is sheltering her isn't likely to come forward."

"You think she's still there?"

"That's what I think," he said.

"But this sounds as though you no longer consider her a suspect."

Amos Franklin sighed. "Unfortunately not. I thought for sure that she was behind the first fire, the one at her mother's house. She couldn't have set it herself, but she could have hired it out and walked away with the insurance proceeds. The fire investigators tell me that both of these fires—the one at Selma Machett's house and the one at Candy Small's place—were set by the same arsonist. I can't find any reason why Liza would have turned against Candy, so now I'm forced to admit that Liza has most likely been targeted, too, the same as her brother was. In fact, there's another possibility. Maybe Liza isn't in hiding at all. Maybe she's already dead, and we just haven't located her body."

"As far as we know, then, what your banker friend calls 'coffee money' is still the only motivating factor," Joanna theorized. "Will she let you know if any more of it surfaces?"

"Yes, and so will any of the other bank branches in town," Franklin replied. "I'm in the process of alerting all of them, but I wish I knew more about what the deal was between Guy Machett and his sister. Obviously something was out of kilter. Knowing what it was might help us. Did he ever confide anything to you about his family background?"

"Guy Machett and I worked together, but we were hardly pals," Joanna responded. "Our relationship never developed to the point of sharing confidences. He kept his distance. The people who worked most closely with him are Madge Livingston, the woman who was his secretary, and Ralph Whetson, his assistant up at the morgue. My people have already spoken to both those individuals. In the light of what you've just told me, we'll talk to them again. If you'd like to speak to them directly, I'll be happy to send along their contact information."

"Please," Detective Franklin said.

"I'm outside my office right now and late going into a meeting," Joanna said. "Either I'll e-mail you what you need once the meeting is over, or one of my people will be in touch."

"Fair enough," Franklin said.

Feeling that news about Candy Small's murder signaled a sea change in the investigation, Joanna hurried inside, where she found her investigations people assembled in the conference room along with Alvin Bernard and his detective, Matt Keller. Chief Deputy Hadlock was there as well, taking copious notes and preparing for the next journalistic assault. Having seen the collection of media vans in the parking lot as she passed, Joanna suspected that he had called another press conference, which was due to happen soon.

"Sorry I'm late," she apologized as she hurried to the empty chair at the head of the conference table next to Chief Bernard's.

"We figured you'd turn up sooner or later," Alvin observed with a grin. "You look like someone with something important to say. Care to share?"

Joanna nodded. "I just got off the phone with Detective Franklin back in Great Barrington. Clifford Small, also known as Candy—the guy who used to be Liza Machett's boss and the one who took her into his home early Friday morning after she was questioned by the police—was found dead this morning in the burned-out wreckage of his house. He had been tortured and murdered."

"Liza's mother's house was burned down," Deb Howell said. "This is a second case of arson?"

Joanna nodded. "According to Detective Franklin, both fires were likely set by the same arsonist.

Presumably whoever set the fire also murdered Mr. Small. According to the autopsy, the victim was dead before the fire started."

"What about the torture?" Ernie Carpenter asked. "Same M.O. as what we've got here?"

"No," Joanna answered. "For one thing, no stun gun was involved. Instead, the victim's fingers and toes were cut off over an extended period of time. Whether or not the bad guys got what they wanted, when it was over, they stabbed the victim to death and then burned down his house with his body inside. So we've got two questions for you to consider: Did Mr. Small tell them what they wanted to know? If so, what was it?

"According to Detective Franklin, Liza Machett has been handing out loads of cash for the past month or so in amounts that don't seem to jibe with her hand-to-mouth waitress existence. A local banker became suspicious about the money because the serial numbers were so old."

"How old?"

"Most of it came from the late seventies; some earlier. Oh, and it all smells of coffee."

"Coffee?" Ernie asked, as if not quite trusting his ears.

"Coffee," Joanna verified.

"How much money?" Jaime Carbajal asked.

"No way to tell," Joanna said, "but it's enough to cause a three-time killer to come calling." Turning her attention to Dave Hollicker, she continued. "Detective Franklin says Liza and Guy were estranged. Has your background check given you any clues about the Machett family dynamics?"

Dave opened his computer and stared at the screen. "As far as I can tell, he was an outstanding citizen. The only thing on his record was a speeding citation when he was eighteen. He owned his own home and carried very little debt. His car was paid for. In contrast, his sister works for minimum wage and just barely makes ends meet."

"In other words, you've been doing background checks on both of them."

"Pretty much," Dave agreed. "Guy's mother died when he was young. His father, Anson, remarried a few years later. Selma, Liza's mother, was Anson Machett's second wife. From what I've been able to learn, Anson deserted the family when Liza was a baby. Guy was your basic overachiever—smart, voted most likely to succeed, class valedictorian. He attended Harvard on a full-ride scholarship. On his college applications, he listed his father as deceased, but so far I'm unable find any verification that Anson Machett is dead.

"It looks like Liza never measured up to her older brother scholastically. She made it through school with only average grades and went to work in Clifford Small's restaurant shortly after high school graduation. There's no indication of any schooling beyond high school."

"It sounds like we have a golden boy on the one hand and an overshadowed sibling on the other," Joanna observed. "That could make for a dicey family dynamic."

"Yeah," Dave continued. "I don't think they're especially close. Guy's phone records came in this morning, a day earlier than I expected them. I found only one call from Massachusetts to him in the six months preceding his death. That one was placed to his office and came from what I've determined to be Liza's cell phone. That call was made about the middle of last month."

"According to Detective Franklin, that's also about the time Selma was moved into hospice care," Joanna supplied. "But that's all? No other telephone backing and forthing between them?"

Dave shook his head. "None, and that seems odd. When someone's dying, that's usually when the relatives—even feuding relatives who hate each other's guts—bury the hatchet temporarily, rally round, and burn up the phone lines. I suppose there could have been e-mail correspondence between them, but so far I haven't been able to get information from Doc Machett's Internet provider. That should come tomorrow."

Joanna noticed that without Guy being there to object, he had been summarily demoted from Dr. Machett to Doc Machett by Dave, and most likely by everyone else in the room as well. He would not have been pleased.

"Anything else interesting?" Joanna asked. "Since Liza came into some money, did he come into a windfall as well?"

Dave clicked over to still another screen. "Not that I can see. His bank records showed up last night. I've been going over them, but there's no sign of any irregular deposits. We did learn a few interesting things, however. For example, we were able to establish the names of both his former cleaning lady, Carmelita Ortiz, and his new one, Carmelita's granddaughter, Josie. Carmelita is having some health issues. Doc Machett left a check for Josie on the kitchen table, which she cashed on Saturday morning. This was only Josie's first week, and she came on Friday. Jaime's going to talk to both Carmelita and Josie later today."

"A new cleaning lady would help explain why the alarm access code was there on the wall," Deb offered. "It was posted so Josie could let herself in."

"The bank records do reveal that our upstanding Doc Machett did have one dirty little secret," Dave added with a mischievous grin.

"Enough of a secret to get him killed?" Alvin Bernard asked.

"I doubt that," Dave said. "Turns out the M.E. was a nudist who visited nudist colonies all over the Southwest. His favorite is one called the Whetstone Mountain Retreat. According to his credit card records, he spent a lot of his spare time and a good deal of his money there."

"A nudist colony in the Whetstones?" Alvin Bernard repeated. "Are you kidding? I didn't know we had any of those around here."

The Whetstone Mountains, one of the smaller mountain ranges in the area, lay between Sierra Vista and Tucson. Joanna didn't know the Whetstones boasted a nudist colony, either.

"Turns out there's more than just one nudist facility," Dave continued, "and Doc Machett seems to have visited them all. There's one on the outskirts of Tucson, up near Saddlebrooke, and another near the Boulders north of Phoenix, but the one on the Whetstones, north of Huachuca City, is where he evidently spent the bulk of his time."

Despite the seriousness of the situation, the people seated around the table couldn't quite contain their mirth or their grins. The idea of Guy Machett strutting around in the great outdoors and doing whatever nudists do without benefit of his upscale suits seemed to have tickled everyone's funny bones. Joanna felt obliged to bring her people up short.

"What is said inside this room is entirely confidential," she warned them. "If I hear of any leaks about the victim's having visited nudist colonies, there will be serious consequences. Understood?"

The grins disappeared. Everyone nodded in turn. "Yes, ma'am," Dave said, "and that's about all I have."

"All right," Joanna said. "After the meeting, I want you to get back to Detective Franklin in Great Barrington. Give him whatever he needs."

"Will do," Dave said.

Joanna glanced around the table. "Anyone else?"

Deb Howell raised her hand. "Doc Machett had a girlfriend. Her name's Amber Sutcliff, and she called me earlier. She told me the two of them were together at the Whetstone Mountain Retreat on Thursday and Friday. When she said that, I had no idea it was a nudist colony, but she's probably a nudist, too. She said she'd been trying to reach Doc Machett all day yesterday by phone and by texts. She was worried when he didn't respond, but she had no idea what had happened until she saw the story on the news this morning. She called in immediately, and Dispatch put her through to me. I asked her to come down here to do a formal interview. She's due any minute. I also told her we'd need a DNA sample. She said that would be no problem."

"How did she strike you on the phone?" Joanna asked.

"Very upset but also very cooperative."

"Was Guy out of sorts or worried about anything the last time she saw him?"

"She said he had mentioned earlier this month that his stepmother was sick and most likely dying, but he also said they were estranged and that showing up for her funeral would be hypocritical."

"Did Amber have any knowledge of Machett's family situation?"

"She mentioned there was a dying stepmother and a half sister named Liza. That's about all she knew—the half sister's name and the fact that Doc Machett and the sister weren't close."

Joanna turned her attention to Casey. "Other than driving two hundred miles this morning, what do you have to say for yourself?"

"When I showed up this morning with another load of evidence, the people at the crime lab in Tucson weren't exactly happy to see me. They asked if I had to pick one case over another, which one should take priority, I said this one. I hope that's all right." Casey looked at Joanna questioningly.

As far as Joanna was concerned, it wasn't all right. She didn't want Junior's case to get lost in the shuffle, but she also didn't want to contradict Casey with the whole investigation crew gathered in the conference room. "That's fine," Joanna said.

"I also heard back from Taser International," Casey continued. "The microdots I swept up in Doc Machett's living room lead back to a Taser that was reported stolen in a residential burglary in Tucson two months ago. I have a call in to the detectives on that case. So far I haven't heard back from them."

Joanna said, "At this point we believe we have three linked homicides—two in Massachusetts and one here. Since time and distance make it unlikely that one person is responsible, we're apparently dealing with two separate killers or teams of killers. That also means there's probably one individual behind all of it. He's the one standing offscreen and pulling the strings. The Taser connection may be our best lead to whatever local talent was used in the homicide here. Jaime, how about if you follow up on that? Property crimes don't get a lot of attention, but we might get lucky. Maybe we'll stumble into evidence that will lead us back to a known criminal operating in this area."

"I keep wondering about the money situation," Alvin Bernard said thoughtfully. "Shouldn't we be checking with banks around here for more of that coffee money?"

"I'll do that," Dave Hollicker volunteered. "I'm not much good right now when it comes to limping around talking to witnesses, but I can work on the phone and on the computer."

"Fair enough," Detective Keller said. "And I'll keep after Machett's neighbors. This is a small town. Someone must have seen something."

Deb's phone rang. She listened, hung up, and turned to Joanna. "Amber Sutcliff is here," she said. "Are we done?"

"As far as I'm concerned."

Deb stood up and then tapped Casey on the shoulder. "Could you come do the swab?"

Casey Ledford and Deb Howell left the room together.

Jaime stood up, too. "On my way to see Carmelita and Josie," he said and sauntered out of the room.

As the meeting disbanded and people filed out, Joanna counted them off in her head. Seven of the people in attendance, including Chief Deputy Hadlock, were totally preoccupied with Guy Machett's homicide. That left Joanna alone focused on Junior Dowdle, and she knew she needed help. Ernie Carpenter, who had paused long enough to hold the door while Dave maneuvered through it on his crutches, was the last to leave.

"Wait, please, Ernie," Joanna called after him. "I wanted to talk to you about your interview with Jason Radner."

Ernie came back into the room. "It's in the report," he said. "I didn't make much progress. The kid was lying about something, but Burton Kimball stepped in just when I was starting to get somewhere."

"I know," Joanna said. "I was watching, and that was my impression, too—that the kid was lying. Do you think he's responsible for what happened?"

"Are you asking if I think Jason killed Junior?" Ernie said. "No, I don't, but I do believe he knows something that he hasn't seen fit to tell us."

"So he's not a suspect?"

"No," Ernie said. "Not as far as I'm concerned."

"Then why don't we go see him?" Joanna suggested. "Just the two of us, you and I."

"Right now?" Ernie glanced at his watch and grimaced.

"Why not?" Joanna asked.

"Because today is Tina's birthday," Ernie said. "Rose is having a party for her, and I told her I'd be home by three. I could call her, but . . ."

Christina Aguilar was Ernie's granddaughter and the apple of his eye. She was also about to turn five. With two homicides on the table, Joanna needed all hands on deck. Still, a grandchild's fifth birthday party was something that happened only once in a lifetime. As Joanna struggled to balance work and family in her own life, she wanted her people to achieve the same thing.

"Don't worry about it," she said. "Go to the party. We can talk to Jason later."

"What about his parents?" Ernie asked. "After what happened the other evening, I don't think the Radners will let us anywhere near their son. What if it turns out we're both wrong about his being involved? Supposing we talk to him without having an attorney present. If he breaks down and admits to killing Junior, we'll never be able to use his confession in court because anything we take away from that interview won't be admissible."

Joanna considered Ernie's on-point objections for a moment before she replied. She had observed the changing expressions on Jason's face. He had been genuinely grief-stricken about Junior's death, but, like

Ernie, she remained convinced that the boy had been lying about something. There was some bit of knowledge Jason wasn't willing to share. Whatever that was might well be the key to what had happened.

"I guess," Joanna said finally, "the possibility of not being able to use a confession in court is a risk I'm willing to take."

Chapter 20

On the ride from Denver to Albuquerque, Liza had rethought her original idea of going to a car dealership in search of transportation. Buying a car privately was probably her best option. She had friends who had bought cars and furniture and plenty of other things through Craigslist and eBay and even from newspaper want ads. To do any of those things, however, she needed to be online. Once she exited the cab, she strolled into the Alvarado Transportation Center and deposited her luggage in a locker. After getting directions to the main library, she set out walking.

It was windy and cold. A surprisingly strong gust whipped off her scarf and sent it skittering down the sidewalk. Shocked by how cold the wind felt on her bare head, Liza raced after the scarf for the better part of a block before she finally managed to snag it. She paused at the entrance of the library and used her reflection in the plateglass doors to tug the scarf back into place. A man who was exiting waited patiently inside the lobby until she finished adjusting her head covering, then he pulled the door open and held it for her.

"Good luck," he told her, smiling as she passed.

Knowing he was referring to her phantom cancer diagnosis, Liza blushed furiously as she walked away, but she also understood that she needed the stranger's good luck wishes far more than he could possibly know.

Once William had finally given up on talking and had turned on whatever audiobook he was listening to as he drove, Liza had spent several hours mulling over her situation. Gradually the shock of learning about Candy's death had worn off. What hadn't worn off was her sense of culpability. She remembered Candy's reaction when she had told him about her father and the bread truck—the tiny snippet of information that had been passed along to her by Jonathan Thurgard. That was what had pushed Candy over the edge and caused him to launch Liza off on this cross-country trek. With Candy dead, Liza wanted to know—needed to know— what else Jonathan could tell her. She was convinced he was the key to all this.

Intent on finding a car, she made her way to the rows of computer terminals. Since all the computers were currently occupied, she wandered over to the periodicals section and searched out the Sunday edition of the *Albuquerque News*. After locating the want ads, she combed through the autos-for-sale section. Sitting in the library on the far side of the country from where Aimee had given her the cell phone, Liza finally dared use it for the first time and for several times after that as well. She went down the list of ads one at a time and hit pay dirt on her fifth try.

"I'm calling about your ad in the paper," Liza said tentatively, because all the vehicles in the previous listings had already been sold by the time she dialed the numbers. "Is the car still available?"

The woman who answered the phone sighed. "Yes, it is," she said. "It belongs to my mother. I had to take away her car keys this week when I checked her into an assisted-living facility. She just can't see well enough to drive. As a consequence, I'm afraid her Camry has more than a few bumps and bruises on it. It's fifteen years old, but it's very low mileage—only about sixty thousand miles—and it's in good shape mechanically. She's had it in for all the scheduled maintenance, and there's a book in the glove compartment to prove it."

"How much do you want for it?" Liza asked.

"I'd like to get about thirty-five hundred," the woman answered. "I was asking four thousand, but I'm willing to lower the price because I'm almost through cleaning out her house. We had the garage sale yesterday, and the junk people are coming to pick up everything else tomorrow morning. I've been using the car while I was here, but I'd really like to have it out of my hair before I fly home later this week."

Liza felt a jolt of empathy. She understood what this woman was going through. She had been through a similar nightmare with her own mother.

"Where are you? Can I come look at it this afternoon?" Liza asked.

"Of course," the woman said. "If you want to buy it, though, we'll probably have to finalize the deal tomorrow. I couldn't let you take it without my having a cashier's check."

"We'll sort it out," Liza said. "The car sounds like just what I'm looking for—old but reliable—and I may be able to lay hands on that much cash."

"Good," the woman said. As she reeled off an address, Liza heard the relief in the woman's voice. "When do you think you'll be here?"

"As soon as I can," Liza said.

Twenty minutes later a second cab deposited Liza outside a small apartment building on Mesa Street

SE on the far side of I-25. The car, complete with a hand-painted FOR SALE sign on it, was parked on the street outside a small, run-down apartment building. Calling the damage to the car "bumps and bruises" was understating the case. Liza remembered hearing that Camrys were the most stolen vehicle in the country. Obviously this one—dented or scraped on almost every panel and with one primer-covered door that didn't match the rest of the color scheme—was considered beneath contempt by even the least ambitious of car thieves. It also explained why no one had taken it off the seller's hands at the optimistic asking price of four thousand dollars.

Liza was prepared to bargain beneath the thirty-five-hundred-dollar mark. What she wasn't prepared for was the woman's very understandable questions about why Liza so desperately needed a car and why she was walking around with a purse full of cash. Liza was forced to spin a series of lies about being ditched by an abusive boyfriend and having to drive back home rather than fly because the boyfriend had stolen her ID. As she told that series of whoppers, Liza was embarrassed by how lame they sounded although the woman appeared to accept them without question.

Forty-five minutes later, after getting the paperwork done and listening to another daughter's woes about having to clean up her mother's messes, Liza drove away in the scuzzy Camry for thirty-two hundred cash on the barrel. She went back down the hill, parking as close as she could to the bus depot, where she retrieved her two bags. With them safely stowed in the trunk, she headed for the freeway. Knowing that William was headed south on I-25, she went back north to the junction with westbound I-40. She didn't need a map to look at to know that I-40 would carry her west and into Arizona.

Despite its ratty appearance, the Camry seemed to be in good working order. After adjusting the seat, the first thing Liza noticed was that the gas gauge was riding on empty. In the past few days, she had come to value the pleasant anonymity of truck stops. At Candy's, everyone had known everyone else. At truck stops, people came and went. Regulars were sometimes recognized and acknowledged, but no one tried to remember their individual orders the way the waitresses at Candy's had remembered their cadre of customers. At Candy's, the appearance of a hundred-dollar bill to pay a fifteen-dollar breakfast tab was a rarity and would have caused a stir. Liza had noticed that at truck stops, no one batted an eyelash when she dragged out one of her fragrant hundreds and handed it over to the cashier at a dining room cash wrap or at a travel shop counter, either. She guessed the same would be true at truck stop gas pumps.

She pulled into the next advertised truck stop, Poncho's. After filling the tank, she bought a pair of maps, one for Arizona and another for New Mexico, then she settled into a booth in the restaurant, ordered lunch, and studied the maps, planning her route. She could see that taking I-25 to I-10 would have been a more direct route to Bisbee, but she was still concerned about possibly running into William along the way or else into someone who knew William and who might have heard about the scarf-wearing cancer patient passenger who had bolted from his truck in Albuquerque. No, even though this might be the long way around, she marked off a route that led her through Flagstaff and then south on I-17 through Phoenix and eventually to Tucson, from which she'd head southeast to Bisbee.

Her food came—surprisingly good meatloaf with an equally tasty side of mac and cheese. While she ate, she thought about Jonathan Thurgard and wondered how much more he knew about her father and how much he would tell her. All she had to do was pick up the phone and ask. Finally, that's what she did. Still using her burner, Liza dialed information and asked for Stockbridge, Massachusetts. She had a pen ready so that when the operator gave her the number, she was able to write it down.

Moments later a distant phone rang in her ear. "Hello."

Liza had expected a man to pick up the phone. Having a woman answer took Liza by surprise. "Is Jonathan there?" she mumbled.

"Who's this?" the woman asked.

"A friend of his," Liza managed feebly.

"What friend?" the woman demanded. "What's your name?"

Not wanting to reveal her name, Liza made up one on the spot. "Mary," she said. "Mary Frost. Could I please speak to Jonathan?"

"You can't talk to him," the woman responded brusquely, "and I'm guessing you must not be much of a friend. If you were, you'd already know he's dead."

"Dead?" Liza echoed faintly, not having to fake her dismay. "When? How?"

"Last Thursday night," the woman answered. "Hit-and-run. Funeral's tomorrow. The obituary is available online. I have to go now. There's another call. The phone keeps ringing off the hook."

The woman hung up, leaving Liza to stare in disbelief at the disconnected cell phone in her hand. Jonathan Thurgard was dead, too, along with Candy

Small and Olivia Dexter? Who else? Liza wondered. And for the first time ever, she wondered about her mother's death. The doctor claimed that Selma had died of natural causes. She had been in hospice, after all, and under a doctor's care. When she had turned up dead, how carefully had anyone checked? There had been no autopsy. The body had been released to the funeral home immediately, and the remains had been cremated well in advance of the funeral. If Selma had been murdered, it was unlikely anyone would ever be held accountable.

Scarcely daring to look around, Liza left enough money on the table to cover her check and a generous tip. Then, gathering her purse and phone, she fled the restaurant. The people responsible for all those deaths were the ones who were looking for her. Liza was convinced that Jonathan Thurgard's death wasn't a random hit-and-run. It was a "hit" in the worst sense of the word. Just by speaking to Liza for those few seconds at Selma's funeral, Jonathan Thurgard had signed his own death warrant. Clearly, anyone connected to Liza or who attempted to help her was in mortal danger.

As Liza sped westward on the freeway, her head was a jumble of questions. Why was all this happening? Was it just about the money? How could it be? After all, there was far less money in the roll-aboard

now than there had been when she first began finding the squirreled-away bills in her mother's moldering
house, and yet people were still dying. Liza's friends
and acquaintances were still dying.

She glanced at the phone lying on the passenger
seat beside her. She desperately wanted to talk to her
brother. Maybe Guy would be able to answer some of
her questions. Liza had put off calling him. She had
wanted to show up unannounced so she could ask her
questions without him having any advance warning
that she was coming. Guy was five years older than she
was. If he knew something about their father and those
damned bread trucks, Liza Machett was determined
that he was going to share that knowledge with her.

Chapter 21

Leaving the conference room, Joanna stopped in the break room long enough to collect a cup of coffee before going to her office. By now Butch and the kids would be well on their way home from Silver City. She felt a little guilty about that, but she couldn't be in more than one place at a time.

She was in her office and still puzzling over what to do about Jason Radner when there was a timid knock on the door. "Come in."

When Joanna looked up, she was surprised to see Sunny Sloan step through the door. Sunny had been working in the sheriff's department's public office for the better part of six months. Even so, each time Joanna encountered Dan Sloan's widow, there was that awful instant of remembrance that took Joanna back to the night she and Father Rowan had come calling at Sunny's door, waking the poor woman with the appalling news that her husband was dead. Looking up from her desk, Joanna wondered if the reverse wasn't also true for Sunny—if seeing Joanna always took Sunny back to that terrible night as well.

"Someone's out in the lobby asking to see you," Sunny said.

"If it's a reporter, send them to Chief Deputy Hadlock," Joanna said.

"He claims he isn't a reporter," Sunny replied. "I already asked. His name's Lyle Morton, and you're the only one he's willing to talk to."

"Okay," Joanna said. "Bring him back."

Sunny nodded and disappeared. When she returned a few minutes later, she was followed by an elderly man riding a scooter. His craggy face, tanned and weathered, was topped by a headful of thinning white hair. The twisted knuckles on his hands went a long way to explain why he might have resorted to using a scooter.

Joanna stood and walked around to the front of her desk to greet him. "I'm Sheriff Joanna Brady, Mr. Morton," she said. "I understand you want to speak to me?"

"I'm Lyle," he said. "Nobody calls me Mr. Morton."

"What can I do for you?"

"I own the Whetstone Mountain Retreat," he said. "Guy Machett was a friend of mine."

"I'm so sorry for your loss," Joanna said at once, but in the momentary pause that followed, Joanna was dismayed to find herself imagining this angular old man riding a scooter in the nude.

Although she tried to suppress her consternation, Lyle seemingly read her mind and called her on it. He grinned at her. "I guess you know what kind of a retreat it is."

She nodded.

"When people come to the retreat the first time, my scooter makes a bit of a stir, but they adjust. There aren't many wheelchair-accessible nudist facilities on the planet, but ours is." He gave the handle of his scooter a fond pat. "Living in the nude may seem a bit far-fetched to begin with," he continued, "and being old and living in the nude even more so, but after a while what's odd is having to put on clothes and come into town like I've done today."

Joanna said nothing. Blushing, she simply nodded.

"I knew your dad, by the way," Lyle added, surprising Joanna for a second time.

"You did?"

"Yup. When I first got here, the property was caught up in a family feud, and I was able to get it for a bargain basement price. Everything was hunky-dory until I started pulling permits to go from running a ranch to running a retreat. Some of my cattle-raising neighbors took exception to that idea. There were several instances of fences being cut and livestock being allowed to roam onto my land and cause trouble. There was even one occasion when the pump on one of my wells was damaged. Your dad was sheriff back then. I called him, and he took care of it. He came by in person and gave the miscreants—a couple of teenagers at the time—a lesson in the realities of owning private property. Nobody went to jail, but D. H. Lathrop put the issue to bed once and for all.

"I'm still not best of friends with those neighbors," Lyle continued, "but we've learned to get along—live and let live. Last year, when we were all looking down the barrel at a forest fire, those same guys—all grown up now—came over to my place and helped build the fire line. The firefighters were there, dolled up in all their gear. The cowboys were there in their jeans and boots and hats, and my people were there in boots and hats and nothing else. You should have seen it. It was quite a sight!"

Lyle laughed heartily. Picturing the scene, Joanna chuckled, too.

"Please sit," Lyle added. "Makes me uncomfortable when folks end up standing when I can't do the same."

Instead of returning to the far side of the desk, Joanna sank down on one of the captain's chairs in front of it. "What can I do for you, Lyle?"

In a sudden transformation, all trace of laughter left the man's face. "Like I said, Guy Machett was a friend of mine—a friend as well as a client. The report on the news said he was killed sometime Friday evening. Since he left the retreat late Friday afternoon, I may have been one of the last people to see him alive. I came to see if I could be of any assistance."

Joanna sobered, too. "The homicide happened inside the city limits, but both the Bisbee PD and the sheriff's department are involved in the case. The lead investigators are Bisbee's Detective Matt Keller and one of my homicide detectives, Deb Howell. Detective Keller left a few minutes ago. Detective Howell is here, and she'll be glad to take your statement, but she's currently interviewing someone else, a woman named Amber Sutcliff."

"I know Amber," Lyle said. "Not well, but I've met her. She was Guy's girlfriend—a relatively new girlfriend. She's only been at the Whetstone a few times. They met at another colony closer to Phoenix. Guy enjoyed mixing it up now and then. He didn't just come to my place. He went to others, too."

Joanna recalled being shocked at seeing Guy Machett's naked body lying supine on the floor. The idea of his willingly trotting around wearing shoes and socks while otherwise in the buff was something she couldn't quite grasp. She preferred picturing the man properly attired in his expensive and carefully pressed suits. As for being in the nude with other people, to say nothing of with someone he was just starting to date? That didn't work for her either.

"How did he appear to you when you saw him last?" Joanna asked. "Was he upset or worried about anything?"

"Upset, yes," Lyle said. "Inconvenienced more than worried. He and Amber had planned to stay at the retreat for the entire weekend, but he had to cancel part of it—something about having to work on Saturday."

Junior Dowdle's autopsy, Joanna thought, *but how did the killers know about that?*

"Do you know anything about Dr. Machett's family situation?" Joanna asked.

Lyle frowned. "His father's evidently been out of the picture for a long time. I know his stepmother had been very ill. His half sister called to let Guy know that she was moving the mother . . ."

"Selma," Joanna said, supplying the name.

"The sister said she was moving Selma into hospice care. I asked Guy if he planned on going home for the funeral. He told me he had no intention of doing so. He and his stepmother had been estranged for some time—a number of years—and he felt there was no reason for him to make the trip."

Joanna's phone rang. Matt Keller's name appeared in the caller window. Excusing herself, Joanna went out into the reception area and sat down at Kristin's desk to take the call.

"Hey, Matt," she said. "What's up?"

"I just got off the phone with Sandy Henning," Detective Keller said.

Through a process of mergers and attrition, there was only a single bank left in town—a single bank with several branches. Sandy Henning was the manager in charge of the whole shebang.

"I know Sandy," Joanna said.

"Me, too," Matt said. "We were sort of an item back in the day, and we're still friends. Rather than wait until tomorrow to ask her to be on the lookout for that coffee money, I gave her a call at home just now. Turns out she's already been notified about that. She was told to have her people watch their transactions for any hundred-dollar bills reeking of coffee, especially ones with out-of-date serial numbers."

"Who notified her?" Joanna asked. "And how did they contact her?"

"The notice came through by e-mail on Friday afternoon. I'll forward a copy of it to you."

"Okay," Joanna said. "I'll get back to you."

She waited long enough for the e-mail to arrive and then read it through. The sender was listed as Cesar Flores, Special Agent, U.S. Treasury.

U.S. TREASURY ALERT

You are advised to be on the lookout for currency, specifically one-hundred-dollar bills, containing out-of-date serial numbers. Some or all of the bills may be readily recognizable due to the distinct odor of coffee. If any of the bills in question arrive in your banking establishment, please call the following number immediately.

The alert looked genuine enough; what bothered Joanna about it was the timing. According to Detective Franklin, the banker in Great Barrington had raised the coffee money issue weeks earlier. At the time, the banker had been told that the bills, although old, were still good. If he'd had some kind of reservations about them, why hadn't a notice been sent out then? Instead, this one had appeared weeks later, on the day before Guy Machett had been murdered and before Liza had been reported missing. Maybe Guy wasn't the only target. Maybe his sister was, too. If Liza was on the lam and using her so-called coffee money to cover expenses, maybe someone was using the power of the Treasury Department—most likely someone inside the Treasury Department—to cast a net wide enough to track her down.

Making up her mind and leaving Lyle cooling his heels in her office a while longer, Joanna called Matt back. "I need Sandy's number," Joanna said. "I'd like to talk to her."

A moment later, Sandy Henning was on the line. "Sheriff Brady here," Joanna told her. "I'm calling about that coffee money alert. Do you have a minute?"

"Sure," Sandy said. "What do you need?"

"Do you get alerts like this often?"

"Sure, they come in all the time, usually when there have been incidences of counterfeiting in the area. They send out lists of bogus serial numbers. I print up copies and pass them along to my tellers. That's what I did with this one. I sent e-mail copies to everyone on Saturday morning."

"Is there anything off about this one?" Joanna asked.

"What do you mean, off?"

"Out of the ordinary," Joanna answered. "For instance, who usually sends out these kinds of notices?"

"A guy in D.C., a Treasury agent named Cesar Flores. I doubt he sends them out personally. Cesar's department is the one in charge of communications with banks, so I'm sure they have a massive database. Still, his name is always the one on the send line. What's this all about, Sheriff Brady?"

"The currency we're all calling 'coffee money' has now been linked to three separate homicides," Joanna answered, "and the timing on this seems strange. Would you mind taking another look at it?"

"I just sent it to Matt. Give me a minute, and I'll look at the e-mail."

"You're right," Sandy said when she came back on the line. "I never noticed it until you asked, but the phone number is wrong. It's not a D.C. area code. I thought maybe Treasury had parceled weekend responses to a call center operating somewhere else, but I just tried calling it. After three rings, it came up as a disconnect. That's weird. Why would they send out an alert and then cancel the number before people have a chance to call in a report? It doesn't make sense."

It would if whoever sent the message already figured out what they need to know, Joanna thought.

"Is there anything else?"

"Yes," Joanna said. "If you happen to have it handy, I'd like Agent Flores's number."

"Of course," Sandy said. "I'm sure it's in my contact list." She found the number and read it off.

"Thanks," Joanna said after jotting the number down.

Joanna was about to hang up, but Sandy stopped her. "Matt hinted that this might have something to do with Guy Machett's homicide," Sandy said. "Is that true?"

"I can't answer that directly," Joanna said, "but I will say this. If anyone shows up in one of your branches this week and passes along any coffee money, have your tellers dial 911, because their lives may be in danger. Is that clear enough?"

"Absolutely," Sandra Henning breathed.

Joanna ended the call and then dialed Cesar's number. An answering machine clicked on after only one ring. "Special Agent Cesar Flores," a deep voice said. "I am currently out of the office. If this is a banking emergency, please wait for the tone and then press one to be connected directly to my cell phone."

In other words, Cesar Flores was important enough to be on call 24/7. Joanna waited for the tone and then pressed one.

"Agent Flores speaking."

"My name is Sheriff Joanna Brady," she said. "I'm calling about the alert you sent out on Friday warning banks to be on the lookout for certain kinds of currency."

"What alert? I wasn't even in the office on Friday. I was in New York City at a meeting. Notices like that don't go out without my personal stamp of approval. Who is this again?"

"Sorry," Joanna said quickly. "I'm sure there's been some kind of mistake."

There's a mistake here, all right, she thought, hanging up, *and the killers just made it.*

With the phone still in her hand, she consulted her contact list, settling at last on the name Frank Montoya. For years Frank had been her chief deputy and right-hand man, until he had been lured away from her department by a lucrative offer to take over as chief of police in the neighboring city of Sierra Vista. Joanna and Frank were still friends and colleagues, but she sorely missed having Frank's technical savvy at her disposal.

Cueing up the e-mail that Cesar Flores had categorically denied sending, Joanna turned it into a forward. She typed in both Frank's and Alvin Bernard's e-mail addresses along with the following message:

Alvin and I are working the Machett homicide, and we could use your help. Cesar Flores denies having sent this notice. Either he is lying about not sending

it or the person who sent it was pretending to be
him. Is it possible to verify that one way or the
other?

Also could you see about tracking down the con-
tact telephone number listed at the end of the
notice? It's now been disconnected, but I need to
know who owned it and where it was located.

Thanks, and boy, do I miss you.

J.B.

After that she scrolled through her incoming calls.
Once she located the one from Detective Franklin in
Great Barrington, she hit the call button.

"Franklin here," he said.

"This is Sheriff Brady. Did your M.E. list a time of
death for Clifford Small?"

A distant sound of papers being shuffled preceded
Detective Franklin's answer. "Between one and two
this morning. Why?"

"When was the fire first reported?"

"The 911 call came in shortly after three AM. The
fire was extinguished about half an hour later. The
body was found around five, but why all the questions?" Amos asked.

"I'm looking for a pattern here," Joanna said. "If
something comes of it, I'll get back to you."

Joanna was about to go back into her office when Deb Howell came past Kristin's desk. "I just finished interviewing the girlfriend and sent her on her way."

"Do any good?"

"Not much, but I'll go write it up."

"Before you do that, there's one more interviewee waiting in my office," Joanna told her. "His name's Lyle Morton. He's the owner of the Whetstone Mountain Retreat. He claims to be a friend of Guy's and says he last saw Guy on Friday afternoon when he and Amber left the retreat. It sounds like Lyle and Amber may have been the last people to see Guy alive."

"Is Mr. Morton dressed?" Deb asked.

Joanna smiled. "Yes."

"I'd better go talk to him then."

"A word of caution," Joanna said. "Lyle seems to know quite a bit about Guy's family background. I'd like to know what he knows without telling him everything we know, so please hold back the information that Guy's mother is dead and that his younger sister, his half sister, has gone missing. The last Lyle knew, Liza Machett was in Great Barrington and Selma was in hospice."

Deb nodded. "You've got it," she said. "My lips are sealed."

Detective Howell detoured into Joanna's office, collected Lyle Morton, and headed back to the interview room. Lyle trailed behind with the rubber tires of his cart whispering on the hallway's polished concrete floor.

Joanna sat for a while longer, lost in thought, after Deb and Lyle Morton disappeared. She was still sitting there when her new e-mail alert sounded. She wasn't surprised to see it was from Frank:

Looks interesting. I'll see what I can do.

F.

Relieved as she was to have Frank onboard with the problem, she still felt like a Ping-Pong ball being batted back and forth between the two opposing cases. Once again all her assets seemed to be focused on Guy Machett's murder while no one was working Junior's. Maybe it was time to change that dynamic. The other night, Ernie Carpenter had been the only officer in the interview room when Jason Radner's parents had put a stop to the questioning. She had been outside the room rather than in it. Matt Keller had been absent as well, and right now she was counting on his having been too busy to view the tape. She would leave Ernie to enjoy Tina's birthday party and use Matt Keller to do her dirty work.

She picked up the phone and dialed Matt. "Bringing Sandy Henning into the picture was definitely the right move," she told him. "Good work."

"Thanks," he said.

Joanna felt a momentary qualm of conscience. For days now, Matt Keller had been working his heart out. He didn't deserve to be thrown under the bus. Approaching Jason Radner behind his parents' backs wasn't fair to Jason, either, but right at that moment Joanna couldn't afford the luxury of being fair, especially since she knew the answer to her next question before she even asked it.

"You don't happen to know Jason Radner, do you?"

"Sure," Matt said. "He was on the JV football team last year when I was a volunteer coach. He and Curt, my son, hang out together occasionally. Why?"

"Jason's parents brought him in for an interview with Ernie Carpenter the evening we found Junior Dowdle's body. There are a couple more things that I'd like him to clarify, but I don't want to put his parents into a state of panic. Is there any way you could spirit him away from the house so I could ask him a few questions?"

"Jason's a good kid," Matt declared. "In fact, I'd say he's a great kid. I hope you're not thinking he had something to do with what happened to Junior. He wouldn't!"

"I agree completely," Joanna responded truthfully. "I don't think he's in any way responsible for Junior's death, but I do believe he knows more than he's letting on. He was in an interview room with a homicide cop asking him questions. He was probably scared to death. If we approach him again with more questions, we run the risk of making it look like he's ratting someone out even if he doesn't say another word. That's why I want to keep this informal and off the record. If we need what he says to be on the record later, we'll cross that bridge when we come to it."

"What if he says something self-incriminating?" Matt asked.

"Then I won't be able to use it."

There was a long pause after that while Matt Keller struggled with his own conscience. "Okay," he said finally. "What do you need?"

"See if you can spirit him out of the house long enough for me to have a private word with him."

"I'll see what I can do," Matt said.

Hanging up, Joanna left Kristin's desk behind, returned to her own office, and pulled four sheets of paper out of the printer behind her desk. Using a pencil she labeled them with the names of the four victims— Olivia Dexter, Guy Machett, Clifford Small, and Junior Dowdle. Since Junior was the first, she wrote down as much as she knew—time and manner of death, animal torture, interviews conducted, questions remaining, and finally a personal to-do list: talk to Jason; move the crime lab forward on the DNA issue; check on the injured kitten.

Setting Junior's sheet aside, she went to work on the Great Barrington cases, jotting down everything she could recall on each of those from her conversations with Detective Franklin. Olivia had been murdered on Thursday. Clifford Small had died in the wee hours of Sunday morning. The same arsonist who burned down Clifford's house on Sunday had burned down Liza Machett's mother's house on Thursday afternoon. In the meantime, Liza had disappeared into thin air. Joanna pulled out another piece of paper and labeled that one with Liza's name. She had to be the heart of the matter. After all, she had connections to the two victims in Massachusetts and to Guy as well. Unfortunately, she was the one about whom Joanna knew the least.

As she drew out the diagrams, an ominous pattern began to emerge. With crimes and crime scenes washing back and forth across the country, Joanna could see they were dealing with a collection of perpetrators: at least two in Bisbee and maybe more than one in Great Barrington as well.

Guy's killers had made mistakes. They had failed to contain Guy when they first encountered him. The damage from the fight in the living room testified to that. Then there was the bruising that suggested a futile attempt to revive their victim when the waterboarding went too far. It was easy to mark these guys off as less-than-adequate guns for hire, but it was inarguable that they had come to their mission in possession of first-rate intel.

They must have known in advance that Guy would be out of town, since they had used his absence to conceal themselves inside their victim's house. They must also have known when he was expected to return. That probably meant they had kept Guy under some kind of surveillance. Since it was unlikely that a pair of murderous thugs would risk turning up and showing their faces at a nudist colony, Joanna discounted the possibility that there had been any physical surveillance. It was more likely that they had somehow hacked into his phone or Internet communications.

Pushing Guy's paper to one side, she laid the one for Clifford Small next to it. Clifford "Candy" Small had been tortured, too, but in a way that differed from what had been done to Guy. Besides, bouncing back and forth across the country to commit three murders a day or so apart made no sense. So what had Clifford's tormentors wanted from him? If Liza Machett was the real target, maybe they suspected him of helping her and wanted him to tell them where she was. Had he capitulated? Had he given up Liza's whereabouts? There was no way to tell.

Gradually, though, pieces began to shift into focus, and you didn't have to be a conspiracy nut to see it. There were the bad guys who had been hired to do the actual work, but Joanna remained more interested in the guy behind the scenes—the one issuing the orders while staying safely out of sight. It had to be someone with money, power, and, without a doubt, connections to banking and/or the U.S. Treasury Department. As for Cesar Flores himself? Possibly. He had denied any knowledge of the coffee money alert, but he could have been lying.

Joanna's phone rang, startling her. Frank Montoya's name and number showed up on the screen.

"I found your phone," he said when she answered. "It's a burner, bought at a drugstore in Boston, Massachusetts, on Friday afternoon and activated that same day within ten minutes of the time stamp on the Treasury Department alert. One incoming call was placed to it. That number leads back to a bank in Gary, Indiana. At the time of the incoming call, the phone pinged off a cell tower in a town called Stockbridge, Massachusetts. Does that have anything to do with your case?"

"Not that I know of," Joanna answered.

"What about Great Barrington?" Frank asked.

Joanna felt her heart speed up. "What about Great Barrington?" she asked.

"That's the last place it pinged before it went dark. Cell tower 672. Downtown Great Barrington."

"What time was that last ping?"

"Two thirty-five this morning," Frank said. "It went off then and hasn't come back on since. Someone probably pulled the battery."

Joanna looked at the Clifford Small sheet. That was just after Clifford's time of death and just before the 911 call came in, reporting the fire. As far as she could tell there were two possibilities: (1) the killers got what they wanted from Clifford and wouldn't need to use the coffee money trail in their pursuit of Liza or (2) they had dropped the phone accidentally and the remains would be found in the ashes of Clifford Small's burned-out house.

"Thanks, Frank," she said. "Thank you more than you know. Send Dave Hollicker everything you can on that burner—where it was purchased, when, all of it. I'll have Dave forward the information along to Amos Franklin, the homicide cop in Great Barrington. What about the e-mail?"

"That's a little harder, but it's also more interesting. I can tell you that it didn't come from where it says it did, because the last IP address it bounced from is located somewhere in Poland."

Chapter 22

As Joanna made her way down the corridor, intent on seeing Dave Hollicker, Deb and Lyle Morton exited the interview room in front of her and turned in the opposite direction to return to the lobby. Lyle was busy regaling Detective Howell with a story about how people never believed him when he told them his tan line started at the tops of his boots.

"There were rattlesnakes all over the place when I bought the Whetstone twenty-five years ago, and they haven't exactly moved on. So we always tell first-time arriving guests, they don't have to go completely nude if they're not comfortable that way, but everybody wears boots, no exceptions."

That odd snippet of conversation gave Joanna pause. It sounded like a well-practiced comedy routine, and not something a grieving friend would say to a homicide cop investigating a good pal's murder. Curious, Joanna went into the viewing room and reviewed the digital recording. She listened through the first several minutes of the tape that featured the usual kinds of questions: How long had Lyle known Guy? Lyle estimated that Guy had been visiting the Whetstone Mountain Retreat for eleven or twelve years. Joanna found that bit of information surprising. It meant that Guy had been coming to Cochise County since long before he came here to work as the M.E.

The whole time Joanna had known the man, Guy had complained about being stuck in the wilds of Arizona. She had assumed that meant he had arrived in Bisbee as a newcomer to the desert. Now she knew he wasn't, and she wondered if Bisbee's proximity to the Whetstone Retreat was one of the reasons he had accepted the M.E. job in the first place.

Doing some math in her head, she realized that he would have started visiting the nudist colony while he was still in medical school. She remembered that Dave had told her Guy had gone to school on a scholarship, so how could a poor scholarship student afford to take vacations at a pricey nudist colony on the far side of the country? Up to now, this whole thing seemed to be about money that had mysteriously turned up in the hands of Liza Machett. Now it occurred to Joanna that perhaps a similar sum of money had found its way into Guy's hands as well.

Clearing the computer screen, Joanna went to the lab space at the far end of the corridor where her CSI unit held sway. With his crutches leaning against his desk, Dave Hollicker, alone in the office, was hunched over a desktop computer. He looked up at Joanna as she entered.

"Thanks for coming in when you could be out on the injured list," she said. "How's it going?"

"Plugging away," Dave said. "Much to my surprise Guy's e-mail records just came in. So far nothing jumps out at me. Can I help you with something?"

"Several somethings. Didn't you tell me Guy went to both Harvard and medical school on full-ride scholarships?"

"He did his first year," Dave said. "Strangely enough, I never saw a record of any additional scholarships being awarded to him, but I checked his credit report. Unlike most people, he graduated from Harvard and later from Johns Hopkins without a dime's worth of tuition debt. The money must have come from somewhere."

"Do me a favor and google Whetstone Mountain Retreat. I want to know how much it costs to stay there."

She waited while Dave tapped away at the computer keys and then read through whatever material appeared on his screen. He had to scan several pages before he found what he wanted.

"Here it is. Depending on the season, packages range from one to two grand a week. Off-season daily rate is a hundred thirty-five bucks. So it's not too pricey. Others are a lot more expensive. Here all meals are included. Horseback riding is extra."

"Naked horseback riding?" Joanna asked. "Not a pretty picture, and also staying there isn't cheap."

"Hardly," Dave agreed, "but then I could have told you that from just looking at Guy's credit card receipts."

"When did Guy finish up at Johns Hopkins?"

"He graduated from there five years ago and finished his residency a little over two years ago."

"So shortly before he came here?"

Dave nodded. "According to the background check."

"Lyle Morton, the owner of the Whetstone Retreat, claims Guy Machett has been a regular guest there for the past eleven or twelve years."

Dave nodded. "I can see where you're going with this. How could he afford to go there while he was still in school?"

"Maybe he had a benefactor," Joanna suggested, "an unknown benefactor."

"Maybe even the same one who gave Liza Machett her so-called coffee money?" Dave asked. Joanna liked the fact that Dave had immediately drawn the same conclusion she had.

Joanna nodded. "You mentioned that their father is supposedly deceased. What do we know about him?"

Dave clicked through several files. "Not much, but here it is. First name is Anson—Anson Jerome Machett. Born in Great Barrington, Massachusetts."

"Find out everything you can about him."

"Will do."

"Any minute now you should be getting an e-mail from Frank Montoya with some information on the phone number that was listed on the coffee money alert."

"Since when is Frank Montoya working this case?"

"Since I asked him," Joanna replied. "The phone's a burner. I want you to pass everything Frank sends along to Detective Franklin so it goes to him from us, rather than from Frank. Frank can tell us where the phone was bought and when. Detective Franklin will need to go for surveillance tapes. Frank is also sending along the ID number of a cell-phone tower where the phone last pinged. We need to know its proximity to Clifford Small's house."

Dave was still scribbling notes when Joanna's cell-phone rooster crowed at her. Matt Keller's name appeared in the caller window. "Let me know what you find," Joanna said to Dave as she walked away.

"I'm feeling a little underhanded about all this," Matt said, "but we've got a window of opportunity that gives us a clear shot at Jason. His folks have an event of some kind out on post this afternoon, so Curt and I invited him to come down to the park and shoot some hoops. We should be there in about fifteen. Does that work for you?"

"Perfectly," Joanna said. "I'll come by ostensibly to talk to you and then just happen to have a word with Jason. It'll be my Columbo moment."

For some strange reason, Butch and Jenny had both taken a shine to Peter Falk's television depiction of the bumbling detective. Compliments of Netflix, the two of them were gradually working their way through the Columbo canon. Joanna wasn't nearly as charmed as they were, but she had come to appreciate Columbo's seemingly throwaway comments upon which the solutions often hinged.

"Right," Matt said. "Copy that."

On her return trip down the corridor, Joanna again stopped off in the viewing room. This time she cued up Ernie's interview with Jason. She watched it again, paying particular attention to the questions that had elicited the boy's most visible responses. He had reacted strongly to the mention of Junior's hearing people talking through his open window and again to questions about Junior's involvement in any kind of animal abuse.

Armed with that much knowledge, Joanna headed out. Butch called as she pulled out of the Justice Center parking lot. "We just got home," he said. "We stopped for a late lunch in Willcox, so I'm serving notice that the cook is taking the evening off. Either grab something before you come home or plan on raiding the fridge after you get here. What's up with you?"

"I'm working," she said. "On my way uptown to talk to a potential witness."

Butch was using the speakerphone, and Joanna didn't want to advertise her intentions to her daughter. After all, Curt Keller and Jason Radner were younger than Jenny, but they all attended the same school.

"Okay," Butch said. "Do what you have to. Be safe."

It was midafternoon by the time Joanna reached the park that had once served as the playground for a now repurposed school building. The play area was at the far end of Tombstone Canyon, and Joanna parked on the street near the entrance. When she stepped out of the Yukon, she noticed at once that although it might be late spring down at the Justice Center, up here, where the sun had already disappeared behind the canyon walls, it was far cooler. She strode across the park and made her way to the basketball court where Jason Radner and Curt Keller were playing a fast-paced game of one-on-one with Matt watching from the sidelines.

Approaching Matt, Joanna made a show of carrying on an urgent discussion. "Hey, Curt," Matt called to his son when she finished, "come on. I need to run by the office for a minute. Sheriff Brady says she'll be glad to give Jason a ride back home."

Curt caught the ball and then looked questioningly at Jason. "Is that okay?"

Jason shrugged. "I guess," he said.

"How are you doing?" Joanna asked the boy as Matt collected his son and their gear and walked with Curt toward his car.

"Okay," Jason mumbled with a shrug.

It was important to establish some common ground. "Losing a friend like that is tough," Joanna said, walking Jason over to a bench in the far corner of the park. Taking a seat, she patted the spot next to her, inviting him to sit. With a reluctant sigh, Jason joined her.

"Will you be going to Junior's funeral?" she asked.

"I dunno," Jason answered. "It depends on if my mom can get off work. She doesn't want me to go alone."

"I don't blame her. That's what parents do when they see that their kids are in over their heads or having to deal with something difficult," Joanna explained. "They want to protect them."

"I don't need protecting," Jason insisted. "Why should I? I didn't do anything wrong."

"Maybe not," Joanna said, edging into the heart of the matter. "But you know something, don't you?"

She tossed the words into the air and then waited in silence to see what he would do. For a time the only sounds in the empty park came from birds chattering up and down the canyon and from the occasional vehicle driving past on the street. Eventually Jason spoke.

"I saw a dead cat," he said finally, speaking so quietly that Joanna had to strain to hear him.

A dead cat? The hair rose on the back of Joanna's neck. She had called that shot. Jason did indeed know something.

"Where did you see it?" she asked. "When?"

"At the end of the walkway between our house and Junior's. It was really messed up." Jason shuddered at the memory. "I remembered it as soon as Mr. Carpenter asked me about Junior messing with animals."

"Why didn't you mention it then?"

"Because I couldn't believe Junior would do such a thing."

"I don't think he did, either," Joanna said quietly.

Jason looked at her questioningly. "You don't? Really?"

Wanting him to feel free to talk to her, Joanna primed the pump with a little more information.

"No, I don't," she said. "There were dead and injured animals in the hole where we found Junior's body. One of those, a kitten, was still alive, but it had been horribly mutilated."

"Were the ears cut up?" Jason asked.

Joanna nodded.

"The cat I saw was like that, too," Jason said.

"I was one of the people who went down into the hole where Junior was found," Joanna continued. "I saw his arms and hands. He was wearing short-sleeved pajamas. If he had done something like that to a cat, he would have had scratches and bite marks showing, but he didn't have any—not a single one."

Another long silence followed. When Jason said nothing, Joanna spoke instead. "How long ago did this happen, Jason, and what did you do with the cat you found?"

"It was a month or so ago," Jason answered. "And I buried it."

"Where?"

"In the vacant lot between our house and the road. I can show you if you want me to. Are you going to dig it up?"

"We may need to," Joanna told him. "If we do, I'll have someone from my office be in touch with you. You're sure you'll be able to find it again?"

Jason nodded. "I put up a marker. I made a little cross out of sticks and twine."

"Did you tell your parents about this?"

Jason shook his head.

"What made you think Junior did it?"

"The walkway is between our house and the Maxwells'. Junior is the only other person I ever saw hanging out there."

"Did you tell Junior's parents about it at the time?"

"No," Jason said. "Not mine either, and I still haven't. I figured the Maxwells knew. They must have. It was right after that when they started locking Junior in at night. He hated that. I could hear him in his room sometimes, crying and begging them to let him out. Other times he spent the whole night pacing back and forth. I could see him through the window."

"Did you tell anyone else about the cat or about your suspicions about Junior?"

"Only Ruth."

"Ruth Nolan?" Joanna asked.

Jason nodded. "We're friends. Not boyfriend and girlfriend or anything, just friends. The Nolans live up the street. I told Ruth about the cat, and I told her about Junior, too—about what I suspected he had done to the cat and about his parents keeping him locked in his room. She felt sorry for him, too. She said that even if he did it, someone like that couldn't be held responsible for his actions. She came over to keep him company sometimes. She'd talk to him through the window; sing to him even."

Joanna already knew about the singing. Ruth had told her about that, but she had made no mention of the mutilated cat.

"This singing would happen when, in the middle of the night?"

"Yes."

"What did Ruth's mother think about her doing that?"

Jason shrugged. "She probably didn't even know," Jason said. "Ruth and Lucas aren't like other kids. They don't have a curfew. Their mother stays out until all hours, and they do, too. I heard my parents talking about Mrs. Nolan once. Mom said she should spend more time looking after her kids and less time hanging out at Grady's."

Grady's Irish Pub, a full-service bar, had once been one of several watering holes located in Bisbee's notorious Brewery Gulch. The bar's owner, Timothy Grady, had proven to be such a troublesome neighbor that other nearby clubs and eateries had finally prevailed on his landlord not to renew the bar's lease. Timothy had taken his bad attitude and equally bad clientele and moved a mile or so up the canyon to the site of a long-abandoned fast-food restaurant.

"You're saying their mother drinks?" Joanna asked. "And leaves her kids alone while she's out partying?"

Jason nodded. "Ruth says her mom goes to Grady's because it's close enough to walk. Mrs. Nolan got a DUI once. They took away her license, so she can't drive anymore; at least she's not supposed to, although I think she still does sometimes."

Having caught a couple of whiffs of Rebecca Nolan's early morning beer breath, Joanna had already decided that the woman wasn't a likely candidate for mother of the year, and it seemed as though Jason's parents shared that opinion. Ruth and Lucas as recent arrivals and homeschooled kids were already considered to be outsiders in town. Having a mother with a reputation as a barfly would make their social standing even less tenable. The tidbits Jason had provided made Joanna wonder if the situation was worse than she had originally thought. If Rebecca was a neglectful mother, how was she at homeschooling? The woman was probably a neglectful teacher as well. If so, her kids were being shortchanged in every way imaginable.

"How much do you know about Ruth's family?" Joanna asked.

"Not a lot," Jason answered with a shrug. "Her parents are divorced. They moved here from somewhere in New Mexico. Her father is a missionary or something on an Indian reservation."

"Where in New Mexico?" Joanna asked.

Jason frowned. "Some little town. I think it has something to do with cowboys."

For a moment, Joanna was stumped—Indians, cowboys, horses. Then it came to her. "Gallup, maybe?"

"Right," Jason said. "That's it—Gallup."

It didn't surprise Joanna to hear that Lucas and Ruth came from a fractured family, but it did surprise her to learn that they were left to their own devices much of the time while their mother was hanging out in bars. They lived just up the street from Moe and Daisy Maxwell. Was there a chance one of them had been out and about the night Junior died? If so, they might have spotted something out of the ordinary.

Eager to ask the Nolan twins about that very thing, Joanna stood up. "Thanks so much for your help, Jason. How about I take you home?"

Jason shook his head. "Thanks," he said, "but I'd rather walk. There's a shortcut from here. I go that way all the time."

He jerked his head in the direction of a series of steep stairs that zigzagged between houses perched on the side of the canyon. Joanna didn't envy Jason the climb. She also understood the real reason he was refusing her offer of a ride. He didn't want to run the risk of having friends and neighbors seeing him climb out of a vehicle with a Sheriff's Department logo on the side. After thinking about it for a moment, Joanna concluded that maybe he was right. With a possible wannabe serial killer loose in the neighborhood, being branded as a potential snitch was a bad idea. It might, in fact, be downright dangerous.

"Sure thing," Joanna said, stepping away from the bench. "Suit yourself."

"Sheriff Brady?" Jason called after her.

Joanna turned to look back at him. "What?"

"Thank you for telling me that you don't think Junior hurt that cat. When I thought he had done it, I was almost glad he was dead. Now I can be sorry. He's still dead, but it makes me feel better somehow."

"I understand," Joanna said, and she did. Jason was still sitting alone on the bench, staring at the ground and wrestling with a storm of conflicting emotions as Joanna drove away.

Half a mile down Tombstone Canyon she turned right past St. Dominick's and drove up the hill to Rebecca Nolan's place. Joanna wanted a chance to talk to Ruth again and to speak to Lucas as well, but when she knocked on the door of the little tin-roofed house, no one answered. Joanna stood on the small porch for several minutes in hopes someone would come back home. When they didn't, she got back into the car, drove straight to Grady's, and parked in a lot crammed with close to a dozen motorcycles.

For the better part of forty years the worn clap-board building had functioned as a hamburger joint that catered mostly to generations of teenagers dancing to a blaring jukebox. Now the hamburgers, fries, and milk shakes were long gone. Even though it was broad daylight, a red neon cocktail glass complete with a green neon olive glowed brightly in the window facing the street. Beyond the sign hung a blackout curtain designed to keep any outside light from entering the building.

Joanna was a small-town sheriff—a female small-town sheriff at that. Even in the twenty-first century, her walking into a bar alone during daytime hours would be sufficient to set local tongues wagging. As she entered the artificially darkened room, Joanna more than half expected to find her nemesis, Marliss Shackleford, lurking at the bar.

Once Joanna's eyes adjusted to the light, she was relieved to see that Marliss wasn't there, but Rebecca Nolan was, slouched on a wooden-backed barstool with a mostly empty pitcher of beer parked on the counter in front of her. Next to the pitcher sat an ashtray with a half-smoked cigarette resting in one of the slots. Bright red lipstick that resembled the faded shade on Rebecca's lips had left a stain on the cigarette's filter. Joanna guessed that Rebecca had most likely gone outside to smoke and then returned to the bar with the remainder of the half-smoked cigarette on hold for later.

Timothy Grady himself stood behind a grungy homemade counter, one that still hinted at its humble fast-food origins. The wooden surface was scarred with hundreds of carved initials. As Joanna entered the joint, both Timothy and Rebecca were staring up at a major-league baseball game playing silently on a flat-screen TV fastened to the faded wooden paneling on the wall above the bar. Joanna noticed that the other customers, most of them clad in leather motorcycle riding gear, were seated in booths around the perimeter of the room. Rebecca was the only person seated at the bar itself.

Timothy Grady initially glanced at Joanna with a welcoming grin as she slid onto the stool next to Rebecca's. Then, recognizing her or perhaps registering the significance of her uniform, his grin faded abruptly.

"Great," he muttered. "To what do we owe the honor of a visit from one of our local gendarmes? I assume you've dropped by to hassle me for some phony reason or other?"

"If you don't mind, I came here to talk to Mrs. Nolan," Joanna said pleasantly. "I'll have a cup of coffee if you have it, a Coke if you don't."

Hunching closer to the glass and staring into her beer, Rebecca sat with her arms resting on the edge of the bar. "Never did like cops much," she muttered under her breath.

The woman's mumbled delivery told Joanna that Rebecca Nolan was probably already over the limit. If she tried driving back home rather than walking, she would be ripe for adding another DUI to her collection, not to mention driving without a license. Joanna knew better than most that drunk drivers didn't lose their driver's licenses over one measly DUI conviction.

"You were a lot more friendly up in the parking lot the other morning when we were searching for Junior Dowdle," Joanna observed.

"Why wouldn't I be?" Rebecca shot back. "I was out there with my kids doing our civic duty. This is me on my free time. What I do on my free time is no business of yours."

"Speaking of your kids," Joanna said, "where are they?"

"At home most likely," Rebecca answered glumly. "Why do you want to know?"

"They're at home alone?"

"That's where I left them," Rebecca replied. "Hey, they're fourteen. That's a little too old to need a baby-sitter, especially in broad daylight. Come to think of it, why were you there talking to Ruthie this morning? What's that all about? I didn't think cops could talk to minors without their parents present?"

"Usually," Joanna agreed. "As for talking to Ruth earlier? Our getting together was her idea. As I told you earlier, she wanted to interview me for her blog. She said it was a homework assignment."

"Was a homework assignment," Rebecca muttered. "I already told you, that was months ago. She wrote that one essay and then that geeky Radner kid—what's his name?"

"Jason."

"Yeah, right. That's the one. He told her that if she wanted him to, he could put it up on the Internet for her and turn it into a blog. So, yes, the first one was a homework assignment, but it sort of got out of hand. To begin with, she wrote the entries and Jason posted them. Now Ruth has learned to post them herself. She calls it 'Roxie's Place,'" Rebecca added, drawing a pair of sarcastic airborne quotation marks around the last two words. "God, how I hated that yappy little mutt!"

Timothy came back and slammed a mug of coffee on the bar in front of Joanna, slopping some of the coffee in the process.

"That'll be five bucks," he announced. Joanna suspected he had doubled the usual price on her account. That's how much lattes went for downtown. He stood there staring at her belligerently. Joanna couldn't tell if he expected her to argue about the price or if he was simply waiting for his money. Either way, he made no move to offer her a coaster or a napkin. Reaching into her purse, Joanna pulled out five one-dollar bills. She carefully counted them out and then slapped them onto the bar in the middle of the puddle of spilled coffee.

Coffee money, Joanna thought, half smiling to herself and wondering if any of Sandy Henning's bank tellers would notice and sound an alarm.

Glowering at her, Timothy picked up the sodden bills. "What about the tip?" he demanded.

"What tip?" she replied. "You spilled a third of my coffee."

He stalked off, and Joanna turned back to Rebecca. "Who's Roxie?" she asked.

"You mean, who *was* Roxie," Rebecca replied. "I never wanted a dog to begin with, but my ex dragged that nasty little dog home from the pound. She peed and crapped all over the place. One day she disappeared.

Slipped out of the house somehow. Lots of coyotes where we used to live. One of them probably got her. Good riddance. That's all I've got to say about that. Ruth acted like losing that damn dog broke her heart. It sure as hell didn't break mine."

A shiver went up and down Joanna's spine. A pet goes missing for some unexplained reason, a loss that pushes a troubled young girl closer to the edge. Was it possible that months later, that same girl might turn Sunday school songs into a siren call and lure a mentally impaired man to his death? And what were the chances that the same girl would find a way to insert herself into the framework of the investigation into a murder she herself had committed?

How many times had Joanna heard of instances of serial killers insinuating themselves into criminal investigations? They did it to find out whether the cops were onto them, true, but there was often another reason as well—they truly believed they were better than everybody else and that no one would ever be smart enough to figure it out.

Ruth Nolan had come to Joanna, in all her blue-eyed, purple-haired innocence, asking to do an interview. She hadn't mentioned the Junior Dowdle situation in the beginning, but the interview had certainly led there. The possibility that Junior's killer had been right under Joanna's nose shocked her to the core, and it galled her to think that Ruth might have played her for a sucker.

Joanna took a tiny sip of Timothy's bitter, hours-old coffee while she assessed the situation. Rebecca was already drunk—enough so that not only was her speech slurred but her tongue was loosened as well. It was in Joanna's best interests and in Junior Dowdle's, too, that Joanna keep the woman talking as long as possible.

"Sounds tough," she said, feigning a sympathy she didn't feel. "When did all this happen?"

"When did Roxie disappear?" Rebecca's reply included a careless shrug. "Long time ago, before the divorce. When we came here, I put my foot down. I told Ruth that we were not getting another dog. Period!"

"Perfectly understandable. Losing a pet is hard on everybody, especially kids. Speaking of kids," Joanna added. "Did any of the detectives ever get around to talking to Ruth or Lucas?"

"About Junior Dowdle, you mean? Maybe they did or maybe they didn't. I'm not sure. Why would they?"

"For one thing, you live just up the street. Ruth and Lucas strike me as smart kids. They might have been outside the evening Junior died. Perhaps they noticed something unusual. Maybe they saw a stranger of some kind hanging around the neighborhood."

"I don't think so," Rebecca said. "They were home all day and for most of that they were inside. Lucas was on the computer working on an online algebra program. Algebra's beyond me. I can do arithmetic out the yin-yang, but since algebra is way over my head, I signed him up for an online tutorial. As for Ruth? She was out of it completely—never left her room all day except to go to the bathroom a couple of times."

"What do you mean, 'out of it'?"

Rebecca poured more beer, emptying the remains of the pitcher into her glass. "She got her period. Had the cramps. She was crying and bellyaching and wanting me to take her to the doctor. My ex still has the kids on his health insurance, but it only covers major medical. Doesn't cover doctor's visits or prescriptions, so I gave her one of my muscle relaxers. Put her out like a light. No more complaining."

Rebecca's casual admission of having given her daughter an illegal dose of prescription medication was enough to take Joanna's breath away. There was nothing warm and fuzzy about this woman; nothing maternal or loving, either. Here was a textbook case of a dysfunctional family breeding a dysfunctional child. How many defense attorneys had used that as an excuse to ask for leniency for their clients' murderous actions? If Ruth ended up on trial for Junior's murder, would

Burton Kimball point at Rebecca Nolan and attempt to use the same defense in Ruth's favor?

Suddenly Joanna's focus narrowed. She stared hard at Rebecca's ashtray and the lipstick-stained cigarette hanging off it. What she had just learned about Ruth Nolan put Rebecca's DNA-drenched cigarette filter in a whole new light. After a moment of consideration, Joanna picked her purse up off the back of her stool. Standing up, she swung the purse in a seemingly careless fashion, managing to crash it into Rebecca's still half-full glass of beer and into the empty pitcher as well. Spilled beer poured off the counter and onto Rebecca while the pitcher crashed to the floor on the far side of the bar, shattering into a thousand pieces.

"You stupid broad!" Timothy roared as he raced toward the mess. "What the hell do you think you're doing?"

While Rebecca gazed down in despair at her suddenly sodden tank top, Joanna plucked the cigarette out of the ashtray. Avoiding touching the filter, she slipped the cigarette into her purse. Pulling a twenty out of her purse, she slapped it down on the bar.

"Sorry about that pitcher," she said. "I'm pretty sure this will cover the damage."

With that she turned on her heel and walked away in an exit that was, in its own way, worthy of Columbo.

Chapter 23

Driving west on I-40 at 75 mph through the wide open landscape of northern New Mexico, Liza Machett found herself speeding around the semis lumbering along at much lower speeds and sticking mostly to the right-hand lane of the freeway. Alone and vulnerable in her little Camry, she was the hare to their slow-moving tortoise. She had felt safe and protected tucked away in the upper berths of those immense long-haul vehicles. Now, out in the open, she couldn't help wondering what secrets the trucks she passed were carrying along with their stated and advertised loads.

Her want-ad Camry had a radio. At least there was a device with knobs and buttons on it occupying that part of the cracked and sun-faded dash that was designated for a sound system. Unfortunately no sounds came out of it, so Liza traveled along in silence with nothing to divert her or keep her mind from straying back to the people who had already died because of her.

Other than the drivers' lounges in the various truck stops along the way where flat-screen TVs ran nonstop programming from Fox News, her traveling cocoon had been almost completely devoid of news coverage. Had it not been for the computers reserved for truckers to use, she wouldn't have known about Candy's death. When she made a pit stop just outside Gallup, she looked longingly at the lounge reserved for professional drivers, wishing she could go inside and glean more details about what progress, if any, was being made in the murders back home in Great Barrington and the one in Stockbridge, too. It sickened her to think that three people were dead for no other reason than having known and/or tried to help her. This was all her fault. Their blood was on her hands as surely as if she herself had murdered them.

Tonight was Sunday. By the time she stopped for the night, the public libraries would all be closed. She had heard that some of the more upscale hotels had business centers where she might be able to go online. If she could manage that, maybe she'd be able to learn more. If that proved impossible, however, she would show up in Bisbee on Monday morning without any more details than she already had. Guy was enough older than she was that Liza hoped he'd be able to supply some of the missing threads about their father's involvement with the mysterious bread trucks. That's where this all led— back to those damnable bread trucks.

Whatever the outcome of her conversation with Guy, however, Liza was determined that once it was over, she would go to law enforcement. She would go to the cops with him or without him. She was the one person who could tie together the two homicide cases back home in Massachusetts. She alone had the power to put the cops on the right trail and bring the murderer or murderers to justice. If she had to relinquish what money remained in her roll-aboard to make that happen, then so be it. The money had never been hers to begin with.

When she crossed the border into Arizona, she was surprised and disappointed that there were no saguaros anywhere in sight. Where had they gone? After all, didn't Arizona and saguaros go together like bread and butter or peanut butter and jelly? Instead, the long straight road rose gradually through a vast wasteland toward a line of blue-tinged mountains that had suddenly appeared on the far horizon. By the time she neared Flagstaff, she was amazed to realize that she had gone from empty desert into a forest of stately pines. Arizona was supposed to be a desert. Why were there so many trees?

Liza had expected to find some place to stay the night in Flagstaff, but as she drove through town, she realized it was too early to stop. Flagstaff was still a long way from Bisbee. Liza wanted to show up at Guy's office bright and early in the morning. Besides, if her pursuers had somehow stumbled on her connection with Candy's Underground Railroad, Liza wanted to put as much distance as possible between her present location and that of William, her most recent driver. She kept right on driving.

Heading south on I-17, she was amazed to see signs warning her of elk crossing the freeway. Elk? On a long downhill grade, she drove past the exit to Sedona. It was a place Liza had always wanted to visit. She remembered seeing photos of Sedona while she was still in school. The red cliffs had been hauntingly beautiful, but just now she felt no temptation to turn off and go exploring. Focused on her mission, she refused to be sidetracked.

After crossing a long, grassy plateau, she hit another steep downhill grade and there, unexpectedly, were the saguaros she had been missing earlier. They stood in tall ungainly poses, casting long shadows in the setting sun. As darkness fell, a huge metropolis of lights fanned out across the valley in front of her.

Phoenix was immense—too immense. Instead of turning off at one of the Phoenix-area exits, Liza kept right on going on I-17 until it intersected with I-10. Some two hours later she finally pulled off onto a front-age road in Tucson. It was after nine before she found a seedy enough hotel where the desk clerk accepted cash without requiring her to show any ID, which she claimed had been stolen. Naturally, the hotel in question wasn't upscale enough to include a business center.

Once in her room, Liza ate the hamburger she had picked up at a fast-food joint across the parking lot from the hotel. Her room boasted a bed with a dingy flowered spread, an equally forlorn sofa, and worst of all, a grimy carpet. Liza didn't care. Stripping out of her clothing, she showered. The tub was cracked and smelled faintly of mold. The torn shower curtain drooped because several of the hooks were either broken or missing. The tiny sliver of soap melted away just as the water went from hot to tepid. After drying herself with a threadbare towel, she fell into bed wearing only the oversize Trux-Travel T-shirt she'd bought in Denver.

The mattress was lumpy. The sheets felt like paper. The pillows were rock hard. The feeble air-conditioning unit under the window barely cooled the room, but none of that mattered. Oblivious to the freeway traffic roaring past outside her window and grateful to be stretched out on a bed that wasn't moving, Liza Machett closed her eyes. Thinking about finally seeing her brother again after all these years, she fell fast asleep.

Chapter 24

Once outside Grady's, Joanna used a pair of latex gloves to retrieve Rebecca's half-smoked cigarette from her purse. After dropping it into an evidence bag and labeling same, she called Dispatch.

"I need a deputy up in Old Bisbee on the double," she told Tica Romero. "I've got something that needs to go to the crime lab in Tucson ASAP."

"Deputy Stock is closest," Tica answered. "He just hauled in a DUI and is getting him booked."

"Good," Joanna said. "Send him along. I'm up the canyon in the parking lot at Grady's."

"Grady's Irish Pub?" Joanna heard the surprise in Tica's voice.

"Don't ask," Joanna said. "Just tell him to get here on the double. Is Detective Howell still there?"

"She went home."

"Too bad," Joanna said. "Have her come meet me, too. Same place. Tell her to wear her vest. We might be paying a visit to a homicide suspect."

Off the phone, Joanna scrolled through her contacts list until she found the crime lab number in Tucson. Her CSIs—Casey Ledford and Dave Hollicker—as well as her detectives were the people from Joanna's department who usually interacted with the DPS crime lab folks. Without specific contacts, all Joanna could do was call the main number. Early on a Sunday evening, it took time to get someone to pick up the phone and even more time to be put through to someone working DNA issues. The guy who finally took her call was a criminalist named Calvin Lee.

"Sheriff Brady," she told him. "From Cochise County."

"Oh, right," he said. "You're the lady who has us working overtime this weekend due to your having two homicides in as many days. If you've got somebody running Murder Incorporated down there, shouldn't you have your own designated crime lab?"

"Sorry about that," Joanna said.

"Don't be," Lee assured her with a chuckle. "Turns out I can use the extra hours. Besides, my wife's an animal lover. If I can help lock up whoever tortured that poor cat, I'll earn big points with her. What's up now?"

"Are you making any progress?"

"Some," he answered. "We've determined that some of the hair samples from your injured kitty contain both human and animal blood, feline presumably. That's easy enough. Despite what you see on TV, getting a DNA profile is not something we can wave a magic wand and have sorted before the ten o'clock news comes on. Once we have a profile, we'll still need something to compare it to. I was also told that you want us to check the clothing of your other homicide victim, and we will. We've had some success doing touch DNA, but that process takes longer than your basic cheek swab."

"This is about the case with the injured cat," Joanna said, "and that's what I have for you now—a possible comparison sample," Joanna told him. "Deputy Jeremy Stock is just now leaving my office east of Bisbee. He'll be bringing along a cigarette with lipstick on the filter."

"You want me to collect DNA from a cigarette filter?" Calvin asked disparagingly. "Couldn't you give me a straight-up cheek swab for a change?"

"The woman who smoked the cigarette isn't my suspect," Joanna explained. "Her fourteen-year-old daughter is a potential serial killer who may have murdered one person and might also be responsible for torturing the cat. At least that's my thinking at this time."

Calvin Lee took that in. "Only fourteen?" he asked. "That sucks. Okay, I can see how getting a cheek swab under those circumstances might be problematic. When's your deputy gonna get here?"

"An hour and a half to two hours," Joanna said. "I'll tell him to put the pedal to the metal."

"Did you say Deputy Stock?" Lee asked. "That's what his name is?"

"Yes," Joanna confirmed. "Jeremy."

"Okay, I'll send his name down to reception so they'll know he's coming and send him right up. I'm going to go on my dinner break before he gets here, because I probably won't have time to eat later. On the off chance that we're able to make this happen in a timely fashion, do you want it to go through regular channels?"

"No," Joanna said. "This is urgent. Call me directly."

She had just finished giving Calvin the number and hung up when Deputy Stock pulled into the lot behind her with his red lights flashing. "You have something for me?" he asked, leaning down to speak to Joanna as she opened her window.

Wordlessly Joanna handed him the see-through bag holding the half-smoked cigarette.

"That's it?" he asked, holding it up to the light. "All this fuss over a damned cigarette?"

"If it does what I think it will, it may help us take down a killer."

"All right, then," Jeremy said, slipping the bag into his shirt pocket and heading back to his Explorer. He had barely driven away when Deb Howell pulled up behind Joanna's Yukon. She came around to the side and slipped into the passenger seat.

"Tica said you may have found a killer. Which one?"

"Junior's," Joanna answered.

"Who is it?"

"I think it may be Ruth Nolan."

"You're kidding—that skinny little girl with the purple hair?"

"That's the one. I'd give you more details, but right now Ruth's mother is planted inside that bar. I want to have a chat with Ruth before we have to actively declare her a suspect, and I don't want to go see her alone."

"I don't blame you," Deb said. "I'll follow you there."

After parking Joanna's Yukon and Deb's Explorer on O'Hara Street, Joanna led the way to the Nolans' front door. As soon as she stepped onto the porch, she heard the unmistakable sounds of a video game shoot-out coming from inside. Joanna rang the bell. The front door had been left ajar. She heard the doorbell buzzing inside, but no one responded. Next she rapped sharply on the frame of the screen door. Still no answer. Finally she opened the screen door and let herself into the house with Deb on her heels. Inside the room, the noise from the video game was overpowering. Lucas Nolan sat on a shabby couch, totally engrossed in whatever was happening on his computer screen.

"Hey," Joanna shouted, trying to be heard over the racket. "Anybody home?"

Startled, the boy looked up and then immediately closed his computer. From the guilty expression on his face, Joanna suspected that playing computer games wasn't one of the things on his mother's list of approved activities.

"Sheriff Brady," he said. "Sorry, I didn't hear you. My mom's not here."

"I know," Joanna said. "I just saw her. I was hoping to talk to you or your sister."

"Ruth's not here, either," he said. "She went out early this afternoon, right after you left, and she still isn't back."

"Did she say where she was going?"

"Are you kidding?" Lucas asked with a grimace. "I'm her brother. Why would she bother telling me anything?"

"So then I guess we'll have to settle for talking with you," Joanna said. Not waiting for an invitation, she moved the computer aside and sat down on the couch. Deb chose a nearby chair. "Did any of the detectives interview you or Ruth about what happened last week?"

"About what happened to Junior, you mean?" Lucas asked.

Joanna nodded.

"Detective Keller asked us a few questions," Lucas replied. "At least he asked me a few questions. I talked to him that morning in the parking lot at St. Dominick's. I don't know if he talked to Ruth at the same time, but most likely he did."

"We've been too busy to get all the reports passed back and forth," Joanna said. "I'm sorry to have to go back over the same questions, but can you tell us what you told Detective Keller?"

"He asked about what happened the day before and did I see anything. I told him I was here at home, working on the computer."

"All day?" Joanna asked.

Lucas nodded.

"What about that night?"

"Same thing."

"What about your sister?"

"She was here, too. We both were. She was sick that day. I don't think she even got dressed."

Joanna wondered if Lucas had any idea that Ruth had slept through the day because her mother had slipped her a high-powered pill. "What about your mom?" Joanna asked. "Was she here?"

"She was here most of the day."

"What about that night?"

A cloud passed over Lucas's face. He didn't answer immediately.

"I take that to mean that she wasn't here," Joanna suggested. "I understand your mother spends a good deal of time at Grady's up the canyon. Is that that where she was that night?"

Lucas bit his lip and nodded. "Probably," he said.

"Did you go outside at all that night?" Joanna asked.

"No, I already told you. I was here the whole night. Most of that time I was here in the living room."

"What about Ruth?"

"She was here, too."

"Could she have slipped out without your knowing she was gone?"

"Maybe," he allowed. "The only time I get to play my games is when Mom isn't here. She's always complaining that I play them too loud and that they're going to damage my ears. Ruth might have left and I didn't notice, but I doubt it."

"Had there been anything out of line in the neighborhood that day or in the preceding days—strangers or vehicles that you didn't recognize or ones that shouldn't have been there?"

"Not that I remember," Lucas answered. "I went to bed before Mom got home. The next thing I knew it was morning. Mom was shaking me awake and telling me that Junior had gone missing. She said everyone in the neighborhood was going down to the church to help look for him, and we needed to go, too."

"You knew Junior?"

Lucas nodded. "He was a little weird. You know, different. He was like a grown man and a little kid, all at the same time. Ruth felt sorry for him, but she's like that about everything. She once found a grasshopper with a broken leg, and she wanted to take it to the vet."

"What happened to it?" Joanna asked.

"To the grasshopper? Mom stepped on it."

Joanna's opinion of Rebecca Nolan's mothering skills dropped several more notches.

"What about Roxie?" Joanna asked. "What happened to her?"

"You mean Ruth's dog?"

Joanna nodded.

Lucas shrugged. "She ran off, I guess. She got out of the house and disappeared. We looked everywhere for her for days, but we never found her. She was tiny. I think maybe an eagle got her or else a coyote."

With serial killers, there was often some traumatic event or a series of events in their past that set them off. From what little Joanna knew of Ruth's life, there seemed to be plenty of possible triggers: she had lost her dog; her parents had divorced; she had moved to a new town where she was a perpetual outsider due to being homeschooled. Added together, Joanna could see how all those separate events could take a serious emotional toll. Maybe it was unfair to focus so completely on Ruth, but right now that purple-haired girl was Joanna's primary target.

"Do you miss your old home?" Joanna asked, turning her attention back to Lucas.

"Are you kidding?" he asked derisively. "How could anybody ever miss Gallup? I hated it. I liked where we lived before—that was back in Missouri while Dad was going to seminary. When he graduated, we got shipped off to Gallup. That's what they do—they ship the new guys off to the worst places."

"What about Ruth?" Joanna asked. "Did she hate Gallup, too?"

"She didn't mind it as much as Mom and I did," Lucas said. "Especially after Dad gave her that dog. He got the dog for both of us, really—for our birthday. People do that with twins. They think one birthday present is enough for two people. Dad said we were supposed to share, but Roxie was Ruth's dog. She didn't want to have anything to do with me."

"Do you like being homeschooled?" Deb asked. "It must be tough to meet other kids."

"Not really," Lucas said with a shrug. "I go down to the Boys and Girls Club. And there's a new gym in town where some of my friends and I go to lift weights. Then there's a different bunch of us who play video games and keep score in a chat room."

"What about Ruth? Does she have any friends?"

Lucas sniffed. "Not many. She mostly hangs out with Jason Radner, and sometimes Junior."

Joanna was under the impression that Ruth's interactions with Junior were limited to midnight serenades. "She hung out with Junior Dowdle?" Joanna asked.

"Sure, he lived just down the street. Everybody knew him. Mom says Ruth thinks it's her job to fix every broken bird. She and Jason spent time with Junior. I didn't."

"Did Ruth ever say anything to you about finding a cat?" Joanna asked. "A dead cat?"

Lucas frowned and then nodded.

"When did that happen?"

"I don't know. A while ago. Jason found it and then told Ruth about it."

"Did Ruth ever say anything to you about how the cat died?"

Lucas shrugged. "Not to me."

Joanna was running out of questions. Worried that Rebecca might come home and find them there, Joanna decided it was time to leave. The last thing she needed was to end up in a confrontation with a pissed-off drunk.

She stood up, and so did Deb. "We'd better be going and let you get back to your game. Are you winning?"

"I was a little while ago," Lucas said. "Before I closed the computer." He added, "I'm real good at games, though. I'll be able to catch up."

Joanna pulled a business card out of her pocket. "My numbers are all there," she said. "When Ruth comes home, tell her I'd like to talk to her. Have her give me a call."

"Will do," Lucas said.

Back outside, it was full dark with only a few sparse streetlights to illuminate the way as Deb's and Joanna's shoes crunched on the gravel. Between the sides of the narrow canyon a tiny sliver of moon was rising on the far horizon.

"If Ruth really is our doer," Deb said, "where is she? It's past suppertime. Shouldn't she be home by now?"

"I don't think Rebecca Nolan is big on family dinners," Joanna said, "and that means I have no idea where Ruth might be."

As Joanna said the words, an eerie chill washed over her, one she couldn't shake. The neighborhood seemed peaceful enough, but she had a feeling that something evil was out there, prowling the darkening streets and hunting for another victim.

Chapter 25

Joanna was in the Yukon and slipping the key into the ignition when her phone rang. "Where are you?" Dave Hollicker demanded.

She heard the excitement and urgency in his voice. "Up in Old Bisbee and on my way home. Why?"

"I've found something interesting, and I want to show it to you."

"What is it? Can't you just tell me?"

"No, that would be like trying to give someone a haircut over the phone. Maybe I'm wrong. I want you and Deb to see it together so I can tell if the two of you have the same reaction I did."

Obviously, as far as Dave was concerned, his discovery couldn't wait until morning. "Okay," Joanna agreed reluctantly. "I'm coming, and I'll call Deb next."

After letting Deb know, Joanna drove through Bisbee's quiet streets. On Fridays and Saturdays the town filled up with out-of-town tourists. The motorcycle riders partying in Grady's were typical weekend visitors, but by Sunday evening, most of the out-of-towners went back home, leaving Bisbee's winding thoroughfares and steep streets to the locals.

As Joanna drove, she worried. If Ruth Nolan wasn't home, where was she? Would Joanna awaken tomorrow morning to discover that someone else had been murdered overnight? Should she call Alvin Bernard and Matt Keller and put them into the picture, or should she sit on her suspicions for the time being? Because that's all she had right now—suspicions. Tomorrow she'd contact Rebecca Nolan and ask her to bring Ruth into the department so they could take a set of elimination prints to match against the prints Casey Ledford had lifted from the window surround outside Junior's bedroom or maybe from the grate at the glory hole.

She wouldn't mention to Rebecca that the prints might not be exculpatory at all. It was more likely they'd be evidence of guilt. The problem was, Joanna knew from both Jason and Lucas that Ruth had been one of the nighttime visitors outside Junior's room. So even if her prints were found there, a good defense attorney would be able to convince a jury to discount them. There would have to be evidence over and above the prints. The best thing they had going for them might turn out to be the human DNA from the injured kitten. It would be ironic if evidence from the cat was what ended up bringing Junior's killer to justice.

Joanna and Deb caravanned back to the Justice Center together and parked side by side at the back of the building, Joanna in her reserved spot and Deb claiming squatters' rights to Chief Deputy Hadlock's currently unoccupied space.

"What's Dave up to?" Deb asked as Joanna punched the door code on the private entrance into her office.

"No idea," Joanna said, "but it better be good."

She switched on the overhead light. The moment it came on, the door into Kristin's office opened. Dave limped through it on his crutches. Held between his teeth was a single piece of copy paper. He had evidently overheard at least part of their conversation.

He stopped, removed the paper from his mouth, and laid it on Joanna's desk. "It is good," he said. "Take a look."

Together, Joanna and Deb peered down at the paper. It was a photograph of an old man and a tow-headed boy, both of them grinning proudly. They were standing side by side on what looked like a wharf of some kind. The boy was holding a fish that was a foot or so long. The caption under the photo said, "This year's Fourth of July Fishing Derby winner is ten-year-old Guy Machett, pictured here with his grandfather, Jerome Machett." The photo's credit line read "Photo courtesy of the *Great Barrington Herald*."

The photo was old and blurry—made with some old-fashioned technology that resulted in visible dots of ink on paper. Wanting a closer look, Joanna picked up the photo to study it. When she realized what she was seeing and recognized the craggy face and thinning white hair, her jaw dropped.

"That's Lyle Morton!" she exclaimed. "He was here just this afternoon."

Joanna passed the picture to Deb Howell. After studying it for a moment, Deb nodded in agreement. "It's got to be him," she said.

"But it isn't," Dave said triumphantly. "That's Jerome Machett—Guy's grandfather. I was out in the hallway when Deb was taking Lyle Morton into the interview room. The resemblance is so striking that I'm sure Lyle must be Guy's father and Jerome's son."

Contemplating that turn of events, Joanna went around the desk and sank down in her chair. "Sit," she ordered. Deb and Dave sat. Joanna turned on Dave. "How did you ever manage to sort this out?"

"The *Great Barrington Herald* was established in 1860 and has been continuously in print ever since," Dave replied."The town has a very active historical society. A number of years ago, they began digitizing back issues of the local paper. Their website is amazing. You asked me to see what I could find out about Guy Machett. I went to their website and typed in his name and hit a gold mine.

"There were articles about Guy being valedictorian of his class, leading the debate team that took a statewide title, winning a scholarship to Harvard, and graduating from med school. This photo was the next-to-last item I found. When I looked at it, I thought the old man looked familiar, but it took me a while to make the connection. As soon as I did, first I checked out Deb's interview with Lyle Morton, and then I returned to checking my databases. I found Jerome's date of death with no difficulty, but there's no sign at all of Anson's. I did notice, however, that shortly after he disappeared into the ether, a guy named Lyle Morton turned up owning a ranch in southern Arizona."

Dave paused long enough to give them a grin along with a dramatic wave of his hand. "Ladies," he announced, feigning a bow, "I believe that we have stumbled upon an early and rather successful member of the witness protection program."

For a time the room was quiet. "When I was interviewing Lyle, he never gave anything away," Deb said at last. "He acted like Guy was a friend and a client, nothing more."

"*Acting* is the operant word," Dave said. "The man's been doing nothing but acting for a very long time."

"Wait," Joanna said. "Think about this. All this time we've been thinking Guy's killers were after the coffee money, and maybe they are, but what if they were also looking for his father? What if Lyle is the real target? Do we know anything about what Anson did for a living?"

"No idea," Dave said, "but I'll try to find out."

"People don't go into witness protection for no reason. Once they do, they're supposed to cut all ties to the past. We know from the Morton interview that Guy had been visiting the Whetstone Retreat for years—starting while he was still in med school. That means Lyle broke with the WITSEC protocol early on, at least as far as his son was concerned. Guy was tortured before he died. The attempts to revive him suggest that he didn't give the killers what they wanted."

"You mean they were really looking for Lyle?" Dave asked.

Joanna nodded. "But that doesn't mean someone else wouldn't give up Lyle Morton's ID and location."

Joanna turned to Deb. "Did you tell him about Liza's going missing?"

Deb shook her head. "You asked me not to, so I didn't."

Joanna stood up hard enough to send her desk chair thumping into the wall behind her. She reached for her purse. "Let's go," she said. "Deb, you're with me. Dave, you're to get in touch with the U.S. Marshals Service and let them know that Lyle Morton's cover has been blown and that we suspect there may be people after him who are willing to commit wholesale murder in order to find him."

"Where are we going?" Deb asked.

"We're going to drive out to the Whetstone Retreat and give Lyle Morton the news that if bad guys are after him, they've not only murdered his son, but they may also have kidnapped his daughter. If we have to, we'll take the man into protective custody."

"We can't go there," Deb objected. "The Whetstone is a nudist colony."

"When the retreat had a forest fire emergency last year, I have it on good authority that the firefighters got to wear their firefighting gear. We're claiming the same first responder privilege."

Grabbing his crutches, Dave headed back to his lab. Once Joanna and Deb stepped outside, Joanna stopped on the sidewalk and stared at the two vehicles parked side by side. As the department's newest detective, Deb Howell's ride was a much-used Explorer. Joanna's, on the other hand, was an almost new Yukon.

"Get your weapons out of your car," Joanna directed. "We'll take my vehicle. It's in better shape—more power and way better springs. And here," she added, tossing her car keys in Deb's direction. "You're driving. You'll be Captain Kirk to my Lieutenant Uhura. I've got at least a dozen phone calls to make, starting with one to my long-suffering husband."

"Do you want me to light 'em up?" Deb asked after she clambered into the driver's seat and was buckling her belt.

"No," Joanna said after a moment's consideration. "No lights and stick to the speed limit. The less attention we call to this operation, the better. Do we even know for sure that Lyle was heading back home when he left the department after the interview?"

"That's what he said," Deb replied.

"It turns out Lyle Morton said a lot of things," Joanna said grimly, "and most of them weren't true. We'll go to the retreat first. If he's somewhere else, we'll have to figure out how to find him."

One at a time, Joanna punched her way through the necessary calls. She let Butch know what was up; ditto for Deb's sister, who was babysitting Deb's son. Next up was Alvin Bernard. These were joint cases and joint operations, Joanna decided, and keeping what she now suspected about Ruth Nolan or the Lyle Morton revelations to herself would not qualify as playing well with others.

The call to Alvin lasted almost half an hour. Joanna told him about what Frank had discovered and passed along the information that had been forwarded to Detective Franklin back in Great Barrington. She told him about the Lyle Morton/Anson Machett situation. Finally she got around to her suspicions and concerns about Ruth Nolan. After a long time spent talking back and forth about that thorny problem, Alvin and Joanna together decided that with everything going on with the Guy Machett case, they should focus on that and leave the Ruth Nolan situation alone for the time being. Joanna was relieved to have that decision be a joint one. If Ruth was out on the hunt tonight—if one night's delay in taking the girl into custody meant that someone else died—at least the responsibility wouldn't be Joanna's alone. At the end of the conversation, they agreed to a nine o'clock briefing at the Justice Center the next morning for all personnel involved in either or both investigations.

By the time that call was over, Joanna's iPhone was hot enough to burn her ear. Reluctant to use the police radio in case someone was following their movements on a scanner, Joanna called Tica Romero and asked her to station deputies on either side of the Whetstone Retreat on Highway 90, one patrol car north of Huachuca City and the other at the junction of Highway 90 and I-10. That way, if all hell did break loose at the retreat, they'd still have some chance of netting the bad guys.

The call after that was to Amos Franklin in Great Barrington. "Hey," he said, sounding downright cordial despite the lateness of the hour. "You and your people have done some great work out there, Sheriff Brady. Guess what? Cell tower 672 is less than one hundred yards from Candy Small's house. Arson investigators will be combing through the wreckage tomorrow. I've told them to be on the lookout for a cell phone, and I've got a ten o'clock appointment at the drugstore to come by and pick up their surveillance tape."

"No court order necessary?"

"Surprised me, too. Who woulda thought we'd find a drugstore owner who's willing to cooperate with the cops without having a gun held to his head?"

"Who would?" Joanna agreed.

"And I got back to Nancy, my friend from the bank. She went through her e-mails and located her correspondence about the coffee money. She found the response from Agent Flores at Treasury and forwarded it to me. Do you want me to send you a copy?"

"My phone's almost out of power. Can you text it to Detective Howell's phone?"

"Sure."

By the time Joanna finished relaying the phone number, they had just passed through the border check station on Highway 90. Lyle had told Deb in the interview that the turnoff to the retreat was the first left north of that. Deb had slowed and was looking for the intersection when call waiting buzzed in Joanna's ear. Holding the phone away from her ear, she saw "Blocked Call" on the screen.

"Sorry, Detective Franklin," she said. "I have to take this."

"Sheriff Brady?" a clipped male voice asked. This one wasn't nearly as cordial.

"Yes."

"I'm Roger Stephens with the U.S. Marshals Service. You are not to approach Mr. Morton in any way. He is to be left alone! That's an order."

"Excuse me, Mr. Stephens," Joanna returned mildly. "This is my jurisdiction, and you're not authorized to give me orders. We're investigating a homicide that occurred on my turf, and Mr. Morton is a critical witness."

"I'm aware of your homicide," Stephens replied. His exasperated tone reminded Joanna of Butch on those rare occasions when Denny's litany of why questions went one "Why?" too far.

"However," Stephens continued, "Mr. Morton's safety is our problem, and we will handle it our way."

Deb swung the steering wheel to the left onto a dirt road, and the SUV bounced noisily over the rails of a metal cattle guard.

Stephens was still talking when Joanna covered the phone's microphone with her hand. "How far?" she asked.

"Google says it's five miles to the next turnoff," Deb answered. "Two more miles after that."

Wishing she knew the man's rank, Joanna uncovered the phone. "Sorry," she said, "you were breaking up. I'm afraid I didn't get all that."

"I said," Stephens said, raising his voice considerably, "any effort on your part to approach Lyle will put him in grave danger."

"In case you haven't figured this out," Joanna said, "Mr. Morton is already in grave danger. So is Anson Machett, by the way. His son, Guy, has been murdered. His daughter, Liza, is missing. The daughter's boss was murdered and so was her landlady. If your job is to protect Anson Machett and his family, Mr. Stephens, allow me to say that you're doing a piss-poor job of it."

Joanna heard the man's sharp intake of breath. The long period of silence that followed indicated Stephens wasn't accustomed to being addressed in that fashion. Joanna suspected he was usually the one dishing out criticism and issuing orders rather than being on the receiving end of either.

"Where are you right now?" Joanna asked.

"At my office in Washington, D.C." he answered. "I came here to deal with this situation. I've put in a call to my agent in charge in Phoenix. He should be able to have someone at Mr. Morton's location shortly."

"How shortly?" Joanna asked.

"I'm not sure exactly, but probably within an hour or two."

"Not a good answer," Joanna said. "Too little too late. I have an armed response team on its way to his residence right now. The GPS gives us an ETA of a little over twenty minutes."

"An armed response team? You need to tell them to stand down."

"That's not going to happen."

"What exactly are your intentions, Sheriff Brady?"

"I intend to keep the man safe!" Joanna replied. "I believe some people—seriously dangerous people—are trying to kill him. I suspect you already know who those people are, or at least who's behind them. If you were any kind of a team player, you'd tell us what you know so we'd have some idea of what we're up against."

"I can't possibly divulge the nature of Mr. Morton's situation."

"Of course you can't," she said, "so I'm hanging up now."

"But—"

"No buts. You can stick your cover-your-ass excuses where the sun don't shine, Mr. Stephens. Feel free to have your agent in charge contact me at his convenience tomorrow. In the meantime, don't bother calling me back. I'm busy, and my phone's battery is at seven percent."

Joanna ended the call. Then, holding the power button down, she switched it off completely.

"Whoa," Deb said. "Why didn't you tell him how you really felt?"

They both broke into a fit of giggles. It was a natural enough reaction, just as Joanna's angry outburst had been. They were preparing to go into battle. They had no idea what would await them at the next turn in the road.

"I'll need to use your phone," Joanna said to Deb, holding out her hand. "That bastard won't have your number."

Without a word, Deb Howell pulled the phone out of her pocket and handed it over.

Chapter 26

What they encountered at the end of the road was the entrance to Whetstone Mountain Retreat and a formidable iron gate complete with a guard shack. An armed guard stepped up to the driver window when Deb stopped the SUV. The retreat may have been a nudist colony, but the guard was fully clothed. His khaki uniform, the businesslike semiautomatic pistol on his hip, and his Kevlar vest indicated that Lyle Morton was serious about security.

"We're closed," he said when Deb buzzed down the window. "Check-in is from ten AM to six PM daily. No exceptions. You'll have to come back tomorrow."

"We're not here to check in," Deb told him, flashing her ID. "We're here to see Mr. Morton."

"Names?" he asked, peering in the window.

"Detective Deb Howell and Sheriff Joanna Brady."

"One moment."

He returned to the guard shack and picked up the receiver on an old-fashioned telephone handset. After speaking into it briefly, he returned to the Yukon. There, using a cell phone, he snapped a photo of each of them and e-mailed them to someone else. Returning to the guard shack again, he picked up the telephone receiver. After a minute or so of waiting, the gate swung open. Before they could pass, he motioned for Deb to roll down the window again. "Do you know where you're going?"

"No idea," Deb told him.

"The first building, the one on your right, is the changing facility. You can put your clothes in an empty locker and take the key with you. Then follow the road all the way to the big house at the end. You'll go past several casitas, the dining hall, and the recreation building."

"This is official business," Deb said. "We won't be changing."

The guard shrugged. "Suit yourself, and watch out for golf carts," he added. "They have the right of way."

The dirt road ended just inside the gate. From there on, it was paved. They saw a building marked Changing Facility and drove straight past it. The guard's warning about golf carts having the right of way proved to be correct. They met three of them on the way and had to pull over on the shoulder to let them pass. Each cart carried two passengers. As they drove past, illuminated in the Yukon's headlights, it was clear that all the passengers were stark naked— except for the boots.

"Yikes," Deb said. "When they say nude, I guess they mean it."

The road wound past any number of casitas, small stucco-covered cabins that looked like they might have wandered over the state line from New Mexico. Some of the casitas had lights on inside. Others were dark and unoccupied. There was no mistaking the big house at the end of the road. Long and low and constructed of river rocks, it had probably started out as an ordinary ranch house built from whatever materials came most easily to hand. Lights glowed from every window. As they approached, a massive front door swung open. Lyle Morton, naked except for his pair of boots, rolled out onto the porch in his cart and then sat there waiting for them, backlit in the doorway.

Deb gaped at him for a moment and then turned uncertainly to Joanna. "Are you sure about this, boss?" she asked.

"I'm sure," Joanna said. "Let's do it."

When they stepped out of the vehicle, Joanna led the way.

"Good evening, officers," their host said cordially as they made their way up the winding wheelchair ramp that led to the porch. "It's rather late. What seems to be the problem?"

"We're here about your son, Mr. Machett," Joanna said.

Momentary shock registered on his face followed by resignation. "I see," he said. "Come in. I was just having a sip of cognac. Care to join me?"

"No, thank you," Joanna said. "We're on duty."

He rolled his cart into the house and then waited by the door until they both walked past. After closing it and turning the dead bolt, he directed them into a large living room, where several well-worn leather chairs were grouped around a coffee table in front of a river rock fireplace. On this late-spring evening it was laid with an unlit fire.

The coffee table was made from a single slice of polished wood that must have been cut from an ancient tree trunk. From the way the chairs were arranged, it was clear that one spot at the table—the one closest to the fireplace—had no chair. Lyle rolled past them and stopped his cart in the empty space, where a bottle of Courvoisier and a single snifter with a layer of amber liquid awaited his attentions. Beside the snifter sat a marble ashtray. An empty pipe lay inside the ashtray with a packet of tobacco and a book of matches positioned nearby.

"I'm afraid I wasn't entirely honest with you when I came to see you this afternoon," he admitted.

"We noticed," Joanna said. "It turns out we weren't entirely honest, either. That's why we're here."

Lyle picked up the pipe and proceeded to load and light it. Watching him, Joanna was struck by how thin he was. Dressed in clothing in her office he had seemed much larger. Now she saw him for what he was—a painfully thin, scrawny old man.

With the pipe successfully lit, he picked up the snifter and leaned back in the cart. "All right," he said, "who goes first?"

"Let's start with why you came to see us today," Joanna said.

"That's easy—because I wanted to find out as much as I could about what happened to Guy," he said. "There are some bad people in my past that I need to avoid. I wanted to know if they were behind what happened. You and Detective Howell here were very coy and didn't give anything away. I didn't learn a thing."

"It's an active investigation," Joanna said. "We're not supposed to discuss it."

"Fair enough," Lyle said. "Your turn."

Joanna decided to go for the gold. "We're prepared to discuss it now," she said. "We changed our minds because we believe you to be in danger. We know, for instance, that you're in the witness protection program. It seems likely that Guy's death has something to do with that."

Lyle nodded. "Can you tell me exactly how my son died?" During his visit to the Justice Center he had managed to make them believe his interest in Guy was that of a friend or acquaintance. That was no longer true. The grief on Lyle's face was as naked as the rest of him.

Joanna took a deep breath. "Guy was tortured before he was murdered. Someone used a stun gun on him over and over. When that didn't give them what they wanted, they tried waterboarding and apparently went too far. The M.E. found bruises on his body that suggest they tried to revive him at some point. Which also suggests that, even with the waterboarding, they didn't find what they were looking for."

A pained expression crossed Lyle's face. "You're saying Guy didn't give me up?"

"We don't believe he did."

Now Lyle's face contorted in anguish. There was a basket on the front of the cart with a small leather packet in it. When he regained his composure, he opened the packet, pulled out a hankie, and blew his nose. When he finished, he shook his head.

"I've been in witness protection for close to thirty years," he said, "living here most of that time. In all those years, nobody's called me Mr. Machett until just now when you showed up. How did you figure it out? Guy and I went to great pains to cover our tracks."

"Not great enough," Joanna observed. "One of my investigators happened across a photo of both your father and your son. At the time Guy was a boy and your father must have been about the age you are now. The resemblance between you and your father is remarkable. But what really set everyone looking for you is your daughter," Joanna said quietly.

Lyle's face fell. "My daughter?" he repeated. "I've done everything in my power to keep Selma and Liza out of it."

"Are you aware that Liza's mother is dead?"

"Was she murdered, too?"

"As far as I know she died of natural causes."

"Guy told me Selma was in hospice. I'm surprised he didn't let me know she was gone."

"He may not have known," Joanna said. "The phone records we've found show only a single call between Liza and Guy. That call was placed to him at his office several weeks ago. By that time, someone may have been monitoring Liza's phone calls."

"Monitoring her phone calls? Spying on her? After all these years, why would they do that now?"

"We believe it's about the money," Joanna said.

"What money?"

"In the past month or so, a large number of very old one-hundred-dollar bills were put back into circulation in and around Great Barrington. The bills were far enough out-of-date that a local banker asked the Treasury Department about them. Eventually those bills were traced back to your daughter."

"Crap!" Lyle exclaimed. "I gave Selma that money to help her take care of the kids. It wasn't meant to put anyone in danger."

"I take it you know about the money?"

Lyle ran a hand over his eyes as if trying to block out a memory. "Of course I do. It's money I stole from people I worked for years ago—mob-related people. They were moving drugs and money up and down the East Coast. They bought a bakery to use as a front for their business and used the bread trucks for cover. I drove one of those trucks. The amount of money involved was astonishing. Since there was so much going back and forth, I decided no one would be the wiser if some of it disappeared."

"You stole from the mob?" Deb asked.

Lyle nodded. "It didn't seem like a big deal at the time. I'd skim only one or two bills out of packages full of hundreds. Most of the people on both ends of the deals weren't that bright. They were generally also greedy and in a hurry, which meant they'd end up counting the packages but not the bills."

"How long did this go on?"

"A long time, and I wasn't the only one doing it, either. The drivers were the chumps running all the risks. We were the ones out on the highways with loads of illegal drugs and money, and we thought we deserved a little extra compensation. That worked fine until one of the drivers got too greedy. Once they figured out he was skimming, the guy was history."

"They murdered him?"

Lyle nodded. "No one ever found his body, but they located the car. It was full of bullet holes and spattered with blood. That sent a message to everybody involved. Since I had been in on the ground floor of the skimming, I had amassed a fair amount of cash. Instead of waiting around for the hit men to come after me, I went to the feds with what I knew on one particular crook and asked for a deal. They offered me witness protection."

"You, but not your family?"

Lyle bit his lip. "I had a girlfriend," he said. "I could take one but not both."

"In other words, you chose the girlfriend?"

Lyle sighed and nodded. "I had to. Trying to take the kids along would have been too complicated, although I hated leaving Guy behind."

"You hated to leave Guy," Joanna said, "but what about Liza?"

"Hell, she wasn't even mine. Selma put the screws to me. She was pregnant and claimed I was the father. I shaped up and married her, but as soon as I saw the baby—eight pounds two ounces and supposedly two months premature—I knew she had lied to me. I wasn't about to go off into my new life dragging along a wife who was a liar and a kid who wasn't even mine. I told Selma I had a girlfriend and I was leaving her, but it's not like I left them penniless. I deeded over the house so they'd have a place to live, and then I gave Selma a crapload of money. I told her I was paying my child support in advance."

A hard lump of anger formed in Joanna's gut. She disapproved of fathers who abandoned their families.

"Did Selma even know about the witness protection program?"

Lyle shot Joanna an appraising look before he answered. "No," he said finally. "She did not."

"What happened to the guy you testified against?"

"I never did—testify, that is. The guy died, supposedly of natural causes, before the case ever came to trial. I never had to go to court, but by then a couple of the other drivers had bitten the dust, too. I didn't dare go back."

"Probably a good decision," Joanna observed drily.

Lyle seemed to sense her change in attitude. "I didn't leave her broke," he said as if that should exonerate him. "Selma was supposed to use the money. I never expected she'd just hang on to it. Do you have any idea how much was left?"

"It must have been a fair amount. The detective I talked to from Great Barrington estimates Liza spent at least forty thousand in cash fixing up Selma's house. We initially thought the people targeting Liza and her friends were looking for the money. After talking to you, I'm convinced that's wrong. When the money started surfacing, whoever is behind all this must have thought you were the source of it. I believe you're the one they're really after, and they're killing people along the way, including Liza's landlady, her boss, and your son—all in hopes of finding you. For all we know, Liza may be dead by now, too, or she may just be on the move. She vanished the day after Selma's funeral and hasn't been seen since, but the last time some of her coffee money was reported, it surfaced in Gary, Indiana."

"Coffee money?" Lyle asked. "What's that?"

"The bills may have gotten moldy at some point. Coffee beans are what paper restorers use to get rid of the smell of mold. As recently as Friday, alerts purportedly from the Treasury Department went out to banks all over the country asking them to report the appearance of either old and/or coffee-smelling bills."

"Purportedly?"

"We've learned that Friday's alert didn't come from anyone in D.C.; it was routed through a server in Poland."

"So the alert was bogus?"

Joanna nodded. "Even though it didn't come from the Treasury, that doesn't mean we can rule out Treasury Department involvement. When the questionable bills first surfaced in Great Barrington, a concerned banker reported them to a Treasury agent named Cesar Flores. I asked Amos Franklin, the detective back there, to get me a copy of the banker's correspondence on the topic. He just sent it to me. I'd like you to take a look."

Joanna pulled out Deb's phone and turned it on. After locating Amos Franklin's text, she passed the phone to Lyle. He squinted at it and had to enlarge the image several times before resorting to a pair of reading glasses. Joanna watched the movement of his eyes as he scrolled through the document. When his eyes stopped moving, she noticed an unmistakable twitch in his jawline.

"Did you recognize someone there?" she asked.

"No," he said too quickly. "Not at all."

Joanna had learned to play poker at an early age. Her father, D. H. Lathrop, had taught her the ropes. He had also tutored her in the art of recognizing a tell, and this was clearly one of those. Three people were dead, including Lyle's own son. The young woman who considered herself to be his daughter was, if not already dead, then certainly in danger. Yet, instead of helping them, Lyle Morton sat there, looked Joanna in the eye, and lied about it.

Joanna took the phone back and reread the message herself, paying close attention to the names listed on the cc lines at the bottom. Finally she pocketed the phone.

"You referred to the people you worked for as 'bad people.' We need names, Lyle. I tried asking the guy from the Marshals Service about them, but his lips are sealed."

Lyle didn't answer immediately. Joanna waited him out.

"I'm not supposed to talk about them," Lyle said at last. "There were two brothers—the Millers. The older one—the one I worked for—was called Big Jim. His much younger brother had a birthmark shaped like a moon on his face. His name was Johnny, but every-body called him Half-Moon."

Deb, who had been busily taking notes, came to attention. "You mean Half-Moon Miller, the mobster guy who's currently on trial in Boston?"

Lyle nodded. "That's the one."

"Have you been asked to testify against him?"

"No, I've been out of the loop for too long. I wouldn't have anything useful to add."

"Maybe they were worried that you might," Deb suggested. "The appearance of that money right around the time the trial was starting might have sent ripples in every direction. It could have been reason enough for someone to want to take you off the board."

"Are you sure none of the names in that letter rang a bell?" Joanna asked.

"No," Lyle insisted, shaking his head. "There was no one there I knew."

"Have it your way, Mr. Morton," Joanna said abruptly, then she stood up. "Come on, Detective Howell. Since Lyle here isn't going to help us, we're done. No need to show us to the door," she added when Lyle made as if to accompany then. "We know the way."

Deb didn't speak until they were back outside "What just happened? I thought we were going to take him into protective custody."

"Screw protective custody," Joanna muttered. "Lyle Morton may be in witness protection, but he's also a lying piece of crap."

"He lied?" Deb asked. "About what?"

"About recognizing one of the names on that correspondence," Joanna said. "If we can figure out which one, we'll be a whole lot closer to figuring out what's going on."

"How do you propose to do that?"

"I'm going to call the U.S. Marshals and locate Mr. Stephens. He may not have a line on everything there is to know about the Miller operation, but he's on the right side of the country and has better sources than we do. One of the names in that banker's letter hit Lyle Morton where he lives, and we need to know which one it is."

Chapter 27

B ack in the Yukon, Joanna used Deb's phone to work her way through the U.S. Marshals Service until she finally found a duty officer who knew the score. Once Joanna explained the situation, he put the call through to Agent Stephens.

"I thought you said your phone was dead."

"It is. This one belongs to someone else. Now, do you want to continue to argue or are you interested in knowing why I called?"

"Why did you? I've already sent agents to look in on Mr. Morton."

"Is this a cell phone or a landline?" Joanna asked.

"Cell."

"Give me the number. I need to text you something. Once you read it, you can call me back."

"Okay," Stephens said grudgingly when he called back a few minutes later. "I've seen the letter. What about it?"

"I showed it to Lyle Morton," Joanna explained. "One of the names on the cc list got his attention, but when I asked him if he recognized anyone, he lied about it."

"So?" Stephens said. "Lots of people lie. Is that any reason to wake me up in the middle of the night?"

"It is when the guy who's lying happens to be in your witness protection program. It is when people are dying because your precious Lyle Morton poses a threat to someone. My first choice is an unknown someone who is hooked in with Big Jim and Half-Moon Miller, the guys Anson Machett used to work for back in the day. My best guess is that it's also someone who went under everybody's radar back then and is still under the radar now. I need to know who that person is, and so do you."

Knowing he was making up his mind, Joanna waited through the long silence that followed. "Okay," Stephens conceded finally. "I'll look into it. Should I call you back at this number?"

"No," Joanna said, "use mine. This phone belongs to one of my detectives. I'll be home in about an hour and I'll be able to charge mine then."

Joanna handed Deb her phone. "Thanks," she said. "I believe I'm over my temper tantrum now."

Almost two hours after leaving the Whetstone Retreat, Joanna was back home at High Lonesome Ranch. After locking away her weapons and plugging in her discharged phone, Joanna made herself a peanut butter and jelly sandwich, poured a glass of milk, and settled down in the breakfast nook for a solitary late-night meal that certainly didn't qualify as dinner. With Jenny's dogs locked in her room, only Lady padded into the kitchen from Denny's room to keep her company.

Half an hour later, when Joanna tiptoed into the bedroom, she transferred the phone over to her bed-side charger. Sunday was supposedly a day of rest, but it hadn't worked out that way. Once undressed and in bed, she was still too wound up to sleep. Unable to the switch off her brain, she tossed and turned as her thoughts bounced back and forth from case to case and problem to problem.

She couldn't quite wrap her mind around the idea that her hometown might also be an incubator for a fourteen-year-old wannabe serial killer. And how was it that a Boston mob case that had been making nationwide news for months had now inserted itself into Joanna's relatively mob-free Cochise County? Bringing someone like Roger Stephens into the equation was a gamble, but if someone in the upper echelons of the Treasury Department was involved in Guy Machett's horrific murder, Joanna's small-town police agency would be at a distinct disadvantage in dealing with them. She understood that people sometimes used fire to fight fire, so didn't it make sense to use feds to fight feds?

The last time Joanna looked at the clock it was twenty minutes to one. Her cell phone crowed her awake four and a half hours later at ten past five. Bleary-eyed and still half asleep, she was surprised when Alvin Bernard's name appeared on the screen.

"What's up?" she asked, heading for the bathroom with the phone and quietly closing the door behind her.

"We've got another situation up here in Old Bisbee," Alvin told her. "Ruth Nolan has gone missing."

Ruth? Joanna was instantly on full alert.

"On the surface it looks like an instant replay of the Junior Dowdle case," Alvin continued. "Her bed hasn't been slept in. The window is wide open; the window screen is unlatched and open. No sign of a struggle. Looks like she let herself out the window and walked away. She's a teenager; she's got purple hair. Maybe it's just what it looks like—a runaway and nothing more."

"When did this happen?"

"We're not sure. Ruth's mother was evidently out for most of the evening. She came home about an hour or so ago and went to the kids' rooms to check on them. Lucas was in bed fast asleep. Ruth was nowhere to be found.

"The mother's a mess," Alvin went on, "drunk and hysterical rather than drunk and disorderly. I was afraid for a while we were going to have to cuff her and lock her in a patrol car to cool off. She's raising hell and expecting the same kind of all-out response we did for Junior. I tried to explain that Junior's situation was different, but Mrs. Nolan told me that if we don't work just as hard to find her Ruth, she intends to file suit. She's right, of course. We do need to find the girl. My biggest concern is that she's dead, too."

"How can I help?" Joanna asked. "Do you need my K-9 unit?"

"Yes," Alvin answered without hesitation. "Absolutely, and any officers you can spare. If you could come uptown in the next little while, I'd appreciate your having a word with Mrs. Nolan while I'm organizing the search. You might have better luck reasoning with her than I did."

"I doubt that," Joanna said, "but I'll try. See you soon."

Once the call with Alvin was over, Joanna dialed Dispatch and told Larry Kendrick what was needed. Then, putting the phone down on the bathroom counter, she turned on the shower. By the time she stepped out from under the water, she could smell coffee brewing. Once she was dressed, she could tell that Butch was frying bacon and eggs.

"A peanut butter and jelly sandwich in the middle of the night does not constitute good nutrition," Butch scolded as he handed over a freshly poured mug of coffee.

Joanna gave him a quick good-morning peck on the cheek. "You sound like my mother," she said. "That's what she always said when Dad came in late and had a PB&J for dinner."

"It's one of those times when your mother was right," Butch said. "By the way, I tried calling you after I put Denny to bed. Your phone went straight to voice mail."

"The battery ran down," Joanna said. "I had to turn it off."

There were times she couldn't tell Butch everything, and this was one of them. She didn't mention that she had turned off her phone in order to dodge calls from Mr. Stephens of the U.S. Marshals Service. Had she told Butch about that, she would have had to tell him about Lyle Morton being Guy Machett's father and about Anson Machett being in the witness protection program. Since she couldn't talk about any of that, she couldn't mention Mr. Stephens, either.

"I gave you a new car charger for Christmas," Butch commented. "What happened to that?"

"When I came back from Silver City, I must have left it in your car."

"Figures," he grumbled, shaking his head. "I guess we need spare chargers in every car." Without another word, he brought a plate of bacon and eggs from the stove to the table and set the food down in front of her. "Eat," he ordered. "And while you're at it, tell me who called and woke us up bright and early this morning, and what's the current emergency?"

Between bites, Joanna filled Butch in on the situation with the Nolan family—the partying mother; the disaffected kids; the girl with the purple hair; Roxie, the dog that had gone missing.

"Sounds like things are tough for them all the way around," Butch commented. "If Ruth already interviewed you for her blog, have you looked at what she wrote?"

"Not yet. I've been a little busy."

"What's her website called again?"

"Roxie's Place. Before the interview, I meant to scan some of the entries, but I ran out of time."

"If you'd like, I can try taking a look at the blog a little later," Butch offered. "In the meantime, what do you think happened to her?"

Joanna thought about that for a moment before she answered. "My first choice would be that Ruth ran away. In that case, we find her and bring her home. My second choice would be, she ran into the same unknown bad guy who killed Junior Dowdle and who has now killed her, too. If that's what happened, we need to find her body."

When Joanna didn't continue, Butch looked at her questioningly over his raised coffee cup. "Is there a third choice?"

"Unfortunately," Joanna replied, "that's the worst one of the bunch. It would mean that Ruth Nolan turns out to be the person who killed Junior. If she left the house because she had personal issues that were escalating out of control, then it's likely we'll end up finding another body."

"I believe I'll stick with number one," Butch said gravely.

Joanna nodded. "My sentiments exactly."

It was ten past six when Joanna pulled into the parking lot at St. Dominick's. Father Rowan was there prepared to direct traffic. So far that didn't appear to be necessary.

"Not quite as big a turnout as for Junior," the priest observed. "The thing is, everybody in town knows the Maxwells. The Nolans are relative newcomers."

Father Rowan wasn't the only one to note the diminished response. As Joanna parked her car, an angry Rebecca Nolan turned up with Lucas in tow.

"So where is everybody?" she demanded when Joanna rolled down her window. "Last week the whole town went nuts when that dim-witted Junior went missing. Now that it's my little girl who's gone, where are all those goody-goody church ladies with their coffee urns and trays of cookies?"

Rebecca still wore the same grungy tank top she had been wearing in the bar the day before. She reeked of beer and cigarette smoke. Joanna noticed that Lucas, too, was still in the same blue track suit she'd seen him in on several previous occasions. Whatever the family income was, apparently not much of their budget was spent on wardrobe purchases.

Joanna was tempted to point out that it wasn't exactly in anyone's best interest, most especially Ruth's, for Rebecca to spout off about Junior Dowdle's diminished mental capacity. Considering the woman's current state, Joanna didn't bother. "Tell me what happened," she said.

"What do you think happened?" Rebecca shot back. "Ruth wasn't home when I got there! Aren't you a cop? I should think someone might have mentioned that to you by now."

Joanna ignored the barb. "What time did you get home?" she asked.

"I don't remember exactly," Rebecca said. "Sometime after the bars closed, I guess. Maybe two o'clock or so. When Ruth wasn't there, I woke Lucas up and asked him where she'd gone. He said she'd been out most of the afternoon. After that, I walked around the neighborhood looking for her. Finally I called 911."

By then it was also four o'clock in the morning, Joanna thought.

She turned to Lucas. "Did she ever come home after I talked to you?"

Lucas shook his head.

Rebecca rounded on Joanna. "Wait just a minute. You talked to Lucas? When? I never gave you permission to talk to him!"

"Please, Mrs. Nolan, could we just focus here? What's important is finding Ruth. What time did Ruth leave the house?"

Lucas looked first at his mother and then back to Joanna before he answered. "Right after Mom did," he said with a shrug. "One o'clock maybe?"

"They both left about the same time then?" Joanna asked Lucas.

"I think so," he said.

"Did she seem upset about anything?"

"No, everything was fine."

"Did she make any mention of where she was going?"

"Nope, she just left."

"When she still wasn't back when it was time to go to bed, weren't you worried about her? Shouldn't you have called your mother?"

"It's not my job to look after my sister," Lucas said indignantly. "We're the same age. I'm not her babysitter."

"Does Ruth have any good friends?"

"Only Jason Radner."

"I already talked to the Radners," Rebecca put in. "I did that first thing. I don't care for Jason much. He used to pal around with Junior."

Joanna's phone rang. She excused herself and walked away to take the call. "Hey, boss," Terry Gregovich said. "Spike and I are coming up empty here. The window screen is pushed open, all right, but if Ruth Nolan went out through that, she flew away without ever hitting the ground. Spike alerted a couple of times, but those trails led out to the street. I'm thinking maybe she got into a vehicle of some kind and rode away. Casey says to tell you that there are no visible prints of any kind on the window or frame. What do you want us to do now?"

"Keep going around the neighborhood in ever-widening circles," Joanna said.

"Will do," Terry replied.

Joanna ended the call as Marianne Maculyea drove into the lot. Her aging seafoam VW Bug was followed by a caravan of several vehicles bearing what Rebecca had jeeringly referred to as the "goody-goody church ladies." Joanna hoped the arrival of the refreshments and most especially Marianne would do something to improve Rebecca's agitated state of mind.

A few minutes later, Ernie Carpenter and Jaime Carbajal showed up as well. Knowing how late she and Deb had been out the night before, Joanna had directed Larry Kendrick to leave Detective Howell off the list for the early morning callout. Joanna pointed Ernie and Jaime in Chief Bernard's direction, telling them that, for now, the chief's orders and her orders were one and the same.

Joanna followed Ernie and Jaime over to the command post. Once the dectectives were given their separate assignments and had left, Joanna took a moment to notify Chief Bernard that the K-9 search had yielded zero results.

"Not zero exactly," Alvin replied. "If Ruth left in a vehicle, either under her own power or under duress, we have a whole other problem. In that scenario, a street-by-street search on foot is probably useless. I'm issuing an Amber Alert. I've already gathered what's needed to post it, but I've been holding back, thinking she'd turn up."

"Send it," Joanna advised. Minutes later the Amber Alert sounded on her phone.

Joanna spent the next half hour greeting deputies arriving from far-flung corners of the county and helping map out search areas. She also let people know that, under the circumstances, the 9:00 AM joint briefing had been postponed until further notice.

When Joanna's phone rang at ten to eight, the words "Guy Machett, office," appeared on her screen. She hoped that meant the call was from George Winfield, but when she answered, Madge Livingston was on the line.

"A woman just showed up here at the office," Madge said in her distinctively low-throated voice. "Says her name is Liza Machett, and she's looking for her brother. Doc Winfield isn't here yet, and I don't want to be the one who has to tell her what's happened."

"Don't," Joanna said. "I'll handle it. I'll be right there."

Chapter 28

It took less than five minutes for Joanna to arrive at the former mortuary that had been repurposed and turned into the medical examiner's office and morgue. When Joanna entered the reception area, Madge Livingston's desk was deserted. The room's only occupant, seated in a visitor's chair, was a young woman wearing jeans, a tank top, and a bright blue scarf wrapped around a recently shaven head.

"Ms. Machett?" Joanna asked.

The woman looked up uncertainly. "Yes," she said. "I'm Liza Machett. Who are you?"

There was no way to sugarcoat what was coming. "I'm Sheriff Joanna Brady, and I'm afraid I have some very bad news for you. Your brother is dead."

"Dead?" Liza repeated.

"Murdered," Joanna answered. "He was killed in his home on Friday night—tortured and murdered by at least two assailants. We've been doing our best to locate you and let you know."

Liza's face paled, but she didn't cry. Maybe she was too shocked for tears. "This is my fault, isn't it? Whoever did it is looking for the money I found in my mother's house. I thought it was hers, I swear, and I was using it to fix up her place so we could sell it. If I had known the money belonged to someone else, I would have returned it. Now the people who are after the money are chasing me, and they've killed everyone who has tried to help me—Candy, my landlady, Jonathan Thurgard, Guy, and maybe even some of the people from the Underground Railroad."

"The what?" Joanna asked.

"It doesn't matter."

It did matter, but Joanna let the remark slide because she had focused in on something else in Liza's previous statement.

"We know about Candy Small and Olivia Dexter," Joanna said, "but who's Jonathan Thurgard—a friend of yours?"

"Not a friend, not even an acquaintance," Liza answered. "He worked with my father, years ago. I had never seen him or even met him until last week when he showed up at my mother's funeral. He told me I needed to be careful because the guys my dad used to work for when he drove a bread truck were the kind of people who never forgot and never forgave. It must have been true. Somebody's been after me ever since, killing everyone who gets near me."

"Tell me about Jonathan Thurgard," Joanna insisted. "Is he from Great Barrington?"

"No, he's from Stockbridge, a town a few miles north of there."

"When did he die, and how do you know about it?"

"I don't know exactly when. I only know about it because someone told me—the woman who answered the phone at his house. I was looking online for information about the Olivia Dexter investigation and stumbled across what had happened to Candy.

"Jonathan Thurgard was the first person who told me about the bread trucks, but Candy knew about them, too. Candy was the one who said I was in danger and insisted that I leave town. With Candy dead, I thought maybe Mr. Thurgard could clue me in on what was going on, but when I called, I learned he was dead, too—supposedly the victim of a hit-and-run. I don't believe it. The same people who murdered Candy must have murdered Jonathan. Now Guy is dead, too, and it's all my fault."

At last the tears came. For obvious reasons the reception area at the M.E.'s office was fully stocked with boxes of tissues. Joanna passed one of those to the sobbing woman and then excused herself. Ducking outside, she pulled out her phone and dialed Deb Howell's number.

"Where are you?" Joanna asked when the detective answered.

"Still at home, getting ready to go in for the briefing. Why?"

"The briefing's been canceled because Ruth Nolan has gone missing. Where I really need you is here at the M.E.'s office. Liza Machett just showed up, looking for her brother. She's a wreck right now, and I want you to take charge of her."

"Will do," Deb said. "I'm on my way."

"Wait, before you come here, I need something else. When you interviewed Lyle Morton yesterday, did he happen to give you his phone numbers?"

"I'm pretty sure he did. They're probably in the report. Why?"

"I need them," Joanna said. "If they're in the report, Tom Hadlock can locate them for me. He's been holding down the fort at the Justice Center while I've been all over hell and gone."

While Joanna waited for her chief deputy to locate the necessary information, she struggled with her conscience. Lyle Morton was still a protected witness, but he was also a lying protected witness who wasn't even willing to share information when it might help track down the people who had murdered his own son.

And then there was Liza Machett, a woman who had been told that her presumed father was dead and who had crossed most of the continent to see the man she believed to be her brother. Joanna's heart went out to Liza. Her family had betrayed her; her friends had been murdered; she herself had been targeted. In this web of evil, didn't Lyle Morton owe his daughter the truth?

When Lyle answered the phone a few minutes later, he sounded testy. "I've already had an early morning visit by a U.S. marshal. Now, to what do I owe the pleasure?"

"This isn't a social call," Joanna said brusquely. "Consider it an official notification. Liza Machett just turned up at Guy's office looking for her brother. I have every intention of telling her exactly what's happened and why. If you want to give her your side of the story, I suggest you put some clothes on and come straight to the Justice Center. She won't be there, but we'll know where she is."

"No," Lyle said. "You can't tell her. You can't!"

"I can, and I will," Joanna said determinedly. "Just watch me. You have been duly notified, but tell me one thing. Does the name Jonathan Thurgard mean anything to you?"

"He worked for the Millers," Lyle said after a pause. "Drove a bread truck just like I did. Why?"

"Mr. Thurgard reached out to Liza at her mother's funeral. Now he's dead, too, supposedly as a result of a hit-and-run. I haven't had a chance to check this out—Liza just told me about it—but considering the timing, she's probably right. The people who killed Thurgard are most likely the same ones who are after you. Isn't it about time you came clean?"

"I'm coming to Bisbee," he said.

"Do that," Joanna said, "but once I tell Liza what I know about you, I wouldn't expect a very cordial reception. By the way, there's one more thing I should warn you about."

"What?"

"I believe the woman who thinks she's your daughter is dealing with some kind of cancer. Her head has been shaved fairly recently. She wears a scarf. When you talk to her, you might want to take that into consideration."

Joanna hung up without waiting to see if Lyle had anything more to say. She started to go back inside the M.E.'s office but changed her mind and dialed Amos Franklin's number instead. Her call went straight to his answering machine, so she left a curt message. "Sheriff

Brady here. Liza Machett just turned up here in Bisbee. She's safe. She came looking for her brother and had no idea he was dead until we told her. She thinks there may be another victim who's tied into all this—a guy named Jonathan Thurgard. He's from somewhere near you, a town called Stockbridge. Thurgard came to Selma's funeral claiming to be a friend of Liza's father. While there, he warned Liza to be careful of some of her father's former associates. You may want to check this out."

Hanging up, Joanna walked back into the building only to discover that George Winfield had arrived in her absence. Liza's storm of tears had abated. George was sitting next to the distraught woman, quietly conversing with her. Madge, acting with uncharacteristic kindness, was in the process of delivering a cup of coffee. All three of them looked at Joanna expectantly when she came back inside.

Joanna went straight to Liza. "I've just been speaking on the phone with a man named Lyle Morton who may or may not be your father."

"My father is dead," Liza said at once.

"No, he's not," Joanna insisted. "He lives near here. I believe the people who murdered your brother and your friends—the same ones who targeted you—are really after your father. They must have thought you could lead them to him."

"How could I?" Liza asked in dismay. "As far as I knew, he ran off with another woman when I was a baby. My mother told me he died years ago."

"Anson Machett did leave with another woman, but he's definitely not dead," Joanna told her. "I'm not sure what happened to the girlfriend, but your father has spent most of the last three decades hidden from view in the witness protection program."

"Witness protection?" Liza echoed faintly.

"Your father worked for the mob back in Boston and stole money from them. The sudden appearance of your mother's money must have caused them to see him as a renewed threat, because they've been moving heaven and earth to find him ever since."

"This is unbelievable," Liza declared. "Why didn't anybody ever tell me the truth about him?"

"I'm not sure anybody, including your mother, knew the truth. Financial records show that your father and Guy probably reconnected while Guy was in medical school, maybe even while he was in college. The two of them have been in contact ever since. Your father seems to be fairly well off. He may have given Guy some financial help in getting through school."

"If he helped Guy, why didn't he help me?"

Joanna hesitated. Liza's mother and brother were both dead. She had lost her home, her job, and her friends.

Now Joanna was about to take away the one thing the poor woman had left—the man she had always thought to be her father. Having suffered all those losses, Joanna believed Liza deserved the truth. What was it the scripture said? "The truth shall set you free."

"Anson didn't take you with him because he didn't believe you were his child," Joanna said carefully. "He claimed your mother had slept with someone else and had pretended you were his in order to trick him into marrying her."

Joanna said the words and left them there. When Deb Howell opened the door and walked into the reception room, the lingering silence was deafening.

"This is Detective Howell," Joanna added, leading Deb forward. "Do you have your own vehicle?"

Liza nodded numbly.

"You've had a series of terrible shocks. If you think you're up to driving, you can follow Detective Howell. If you'd rather she drove, that's fine. I'd like you to go out to the Justice Center for an official interview. And since Detective Howell was in attendance when I spoke to Mr. Morton last night, she'll be able to fill you in on the details. Is that okay?"

Liza nodded again. She and Deb were gathering up to leave when Joanna's phone rang. Once again she went outside to answer. "Sheriff Brady."

"Calvin Lee from the crime lab. I pulled one of those all-nighters," he said, "and I'm happy to tell you, we've got a match. The DNA on the cigarette belongs to the mother of whoever left the human DNA on your injured kitty. I'm confused, though. I could have sworn you said your suspect was a fourteen-year-old girl. The DNA definitely belongs to a boy. We haven't gotten around to checking out the clothing for either victim. The clothing problem has been assigned to another criminalist. I can tell you that someone is working on it, but it's not yet completed."

Joanna drew a sharp breath. He had given her what she needed, but with one unexpected twist—their suspect was the cigarette smoker's son? Lucas? Unbelievable!

"Great," Joanna said. "Thank you."

"One more thing, about that cat. What's her name again?"

Joanna had to think for a minute. "Star."

"How's she doing?"

Joanna wanted nothing more than to get off the phone, but Calvin had gone to the mat for her. "Okay, I think," Joanna answered.

"Well, my wife said to tell you that if she ends up needing a new home, you know who to call."

"I will," Joanna said quickly. "Thank you so much, but right now I've gotta go."

Fumbling her phone back into her pocket, she sprinted to her SUV. Then, with lights flashing and siren blaring, she raced back down the canyon's narrow twisting main drag.

She didn't dare send out a radio message. The last time she had seen Lucas, he had been in the parking lot at St. Dominick's with his mother, supposedly involved in the search for his sister along with everyone else. If he was anywhere near one of the patrol cars, he might possibly overhear the transmission. Joanna didn't want to give him any advance warning that she was coming.

That didn't leave much else for her to do but drive, hope, and pray.

Chapter 29

Turning into the parking lot of St. Dominick's, Joanna stopped next to Father Rowan and rolled down the window. "Have you seen Lucas Nolan?"

The priest frowned. "I think I saw him heading up the hill just a few minutes ago, probably going back to the house. I can ask his mother if you like."

If there was going to be a confrontation with Lucas, the last thing Joanna needed was to have Rebecca in the middle of it.

"No," Joanna said quickly. "Don't bother. I'll find him."

Lucas was only fourteen but, Joanna suspected, an exceptionally dangerous fourteen. Since he was also a self-proclaimed weight lifter, Joanna wasn't prepared to take him on without backup. She glanced around the lot and caught sight of Detective Keller walking away from the command post.

"Hey, Matt," she called. "Can I borrow you for a minute?"

"Sure," he said, striding toward her. "What's up?"

"Lots," she said. "Get in."

He was barely inside with the door closed when Joanna slammed the gearshift into reverse and backed out of the lot onto the street. "What's the hurry?" he asked. "Where are we going?"

"To Rebecca Nolan's place. The crime lab just called me from Tucson," she said grimly. "They got a match from the human DNA left on our injured cat. It belongs to Lucas Nolan."

"Lucas? Holy crap!"

"That's what I say. Father Rowan told me that he saw Lucas going back up the hill a few minutes ago. Presumably he's headed for the house. We're going to go pick him up."

Since Lucas had left the parking lot, there was no further need to maintain radio silence. Joanna thumbed her radio. "Locate Detective Carbajal," she told Larry Kendrick. "Tell him we've got a DNA match from Star, the cat. Lucas Nolan is a suspect as far as the cat is concerned. He's currently a person of interest in the Dowdle homicide. Matt Keller and I are on our way to his mother's house right now. Since we believe Ruth to be in danger, we won't need a warrant to go inside at the moment, but we'll need one for later. Tell him I want one ASAP."

"How do you want to do this?" Matt asked once she finished.

"Is there a back door to their house?" Joanna asked.

"Yes," Matt said. "It leads out to the garage, which is behind the house. The entrance to the garage is from Curve Street, the next street over."

"Okay," Joanna said, pulling to a stop half a block away in front of Moe and Daisy Maxwell's house. "We'll walk from here. You go to the front door. I'll cover the back."

"What's your take?" Matt asked. "Is this kid going to be armed and dangerous?"

"I'm not sure about the armed part," she answered, "but he's sure as hell dangerous."

They had gotten out of the Yukon and were approaching the Nolans' place on foot when a vehicle, an older-model orange Mazda, charged out the driveway behind the house. It screeched to a skidding stop, then reversed direction and barreled directly toward them, spraying gravel in its wake. As Matt leaped out of the way, he grabbed Joanna by the arm and dragged her with him. Matt's viselike grip on her arm was the only thing that saved her from being run over. Had they been walking with weapons drawn, one or the other of them might well have been shot.

"Hey, that was him," Matt gasped, looking at the fast-receding vehicle. It took a few seconds for him and Joanna to untangle themselves and struggle to their feet. "Are you hurt?"

"No," Joanna said, brushing herself off. "I'm fine."

"Lucas is only fourteen. What's he doing driving?"

Joanna was already heading for the Yukon. "He must not have gotten the memo that he's too young to drive," she answered over her shoulder. "Come on. Let's stop him before he kills somebody."

Matt was a good foot taller than Joanna, and most of his height was in his very long legs. He sprinted past her. By the time she climbed into the Yukon, Matt was on the radio, alerting Dispatch to the situation and asking for roadblocks at either end of Tombstone Canyon. It was a good call. Both Joanna and Matt understood that if Lucas made it to the highway intersections at either end of town, he would be that much harder to catch.

Joanna fastened her seat belt, rammed the Yukon into drive, and then pulled a dazzling U-turn in a space barely large enough for the maneuver. By the time they made it down to the intersection with Tombstone Canyon Road, the Mazda was out of sight.

"Which way?" Matt asked. "Right or left?"

"Fleeing felons always turn right," Joanna answered, so she did too, racing downhill toward the town's main area of commerce, which, by this time on a Monday morning, would be fully stocked with innocent shoppers and pedestrians—people totally unaware that mortal danger was hurtling toward them.

"That's how come Terry and Spike couldn't pick up Ruth's trail," Joanna observed. "She didn't leave on foot. Lucas must have carried her out of the house and then driven away in the car."

Matt nodded. "Probably in the trunk."

With lights and siren fully engaged, they careened down Tombstone Canyon. Joanna slowed considerably as they rounded Castle Rock, a huge stack of jagged limestone cliffs that rose up abruptly from the canyon floor. And there, in a cloud of dust, they found where Lucas's Mazda had come to grief.

An inexperienced driver, he had tried to take the turn too fast and lost control. From the skid marks on the pavement, they saw where he had zigzagged out of his lane and into oncoming traffic. After bouncing off the sidewalk on the far side of the street, Lucas had overcorrected, recrossed the roadway, smashed through the barrier on the far side, and finally crashed nose down into a cement-lined drainage ditch that had once been a natural stream through the canyon. Most of the year the ditch was bone dry, but occasionally, after heavy rains, it carried flash-flood runoff and debris away from houses and businesses and down through the canyon.

Joanna slammed on the brakes and screeched to a halt. She and Matt leaped out of the Yukon. With weapons drawn they raced to where the Mazda had crashed through a flimsy barrier—a guardrail made of two-inch pipe—that had never been intended to hold back a speeding vehicle. Already a crowd of twenty or so curious onlookers had emerged from the hotel on the far side of the ditch. They stood on the building's Victorian-era verandah, watching the action.

"Lucas," Joanna shouted. "We know you're in there. Come out with your hands up."

Other than clouds of steam billowing up from the shattered radiator, there was no sign of movement inside the vehicle. Matt used one of the supports on the barrier to lower himself into the ditch, dropping to a crouched landing the last three or four feet. Joanna watched anxiously as he approached the wrecked vehicle. After peering inside, he stood up and shook his head. "Nothing here but an exploded airbag," he told her.

Joanna turned to the audience of curiosity seekers. "Did anyone see where the driver went?"

The people on the porch shook their heads in unison.

"What now?" Matt called.

Joanna thought quickly. It's easier to run down-hill than up, and that's the way Lucas was going originally—downhill. The kid was far shorter than Matt Keller, and Joanna knew that even Matt wouldn't be able to exit the ditch without assistance. She had no idea how many tributaries might lead into the concrete-sided ditch or if they would be accessible or not as the waterway went underground beneath the businesses on Main Street. It seemed likely that the only spot where Lucas would be able to scramble up and out would be just beyond the main downtown area. There a steeply graded opening, locally known as "the subway," allowed access into the underground passage. It also allowed runoff from Brewery Gulch to enter the buried storm drain.

"You follow him downstream," Joanna directed. "I'll come upstream from the subway. With any luck, we'll meet up in the middle and cut him off."

"I'll need a flashlight," Matt shouted, "and so will you. Do you have an extra?"

One of the men on the verandah, a guy Joanna rec-ognized as the hotel manager, must have overheard the question. "Hold on," he shouted. "There's one in the office. I'll be right back."

They listened to the sounds of a dozen sirens echoing off the canyon walls as emergency vehicles converged on the scene. While Matt waited for a flashlight, Joanna jumped into the Yukon and headed down the street, grabbing the radio as she went. "Where's Jaime?" she barked.

Detective Carbajal had grown up in Old Bisbee and had spent his childhood exploring the neighborhood's every nook and cranny.

"He's on his way uptown to meet with the judge. There's a daylong conference of some kind at the Copper Queen Hotel." Larry said after a moment. "What do you need?"

"Our suspect just bailed out of his wrecked car and fled down the drainage ditch where it goes underground above Main Street. Matt's following him downstream. I'm going in through the subway so I can come upstream. We're going to try to catch him in a squeeze play. Have Jaime meet me at the subway."

"Got it," Larry said.

In Bisbee, the subway was a concrete-lined, truck-sized access hole, located at the far end of Main Street in the middle of a small plaza with lanes of traffic moving on either side. A chain fastened to several posts provided the only barrier. A chain-link fence might have been a more effective deterrent for keeping people out, but it would also have caused a dangerous backup when floodwater debris from up above roared down Brewery Gulch.

Turning on her flashers, Joanna parked next to the fence and looked around. Jaime wasn't there yet, but she couldn't afford to wait. Bailing out of the Yukon, she sat down at the top of the steep incline and slid into the ditch. Only a few steps from where she landed, the pavement closed over her head. Instinctively, her hand sought her holstered Glock, but after a moment's consideration, she didn't draw it. With sheer rock walls on either side, she didn't want to risk being injured by a ricocheting bullet.

Only a yard or two from the entrance she needed help from her flashlight to pick her way through the jungle of trash and fallen boulders that littered the surface. Rusty metal hulks—the remains of discarded stoves and dishwashers and refrigerators—had ridden some long-ago flood this far downstream and no farther. As Joanna eased past each piece of wreckage, she was painfully aware of how much cover those items offered her quarry and how little protection they gave her.

It was difficult to judge distances, but she suspected she had gone barely a hundred yards when she heard noisy footsteps pounding behind her. "Wait up, boss," Jaime shouted. "I'm coming."

She huddled behind a piece of something that turned out to be an old car engine of some kind and waited as a pinprick of light gradually blossomed into the welcome company of a handheld flashlight.

"Any sign of him?" Jaime gasped when he caught up with her.

Putting her finger to her lips, Joanna shook her head. Then, gesturing, she motioned for Jaime to take the far side of the tunnel while she took the near one. They moved forward in cautious tandem with their muffled flashlights aimed at the floor. Now and then they paused to listen for the sounds of footsteps approaching from the opposite direction.

Joanna estimated the tunnel's length to be half a mile or so. If Lucas was coming at a dead run, it wouldn't take long for him to cover the distance—longer if he hadn't had the foresight to bring along his own flashlight. A minute or so later, they heard him, blundering toward them in the dark. Without any discussion, Jaime and Joanna doused their lights completely and sought shelter. Joanna hid behind a rocky outcropping in the tunnel while Jaime ducked behind the unidentifiable remains of a rusted-out car that had come to rest several yards behind where Joanna was hiding.

She stood in the impenetrable darkness with her heart pounding in her chest. Lucas would pass her position first. That would mean she would have the first opportunity to tackle him. He was young and had not yet reached his full growth, but with a history of weight lifting, he might be far stronger than he looked. Based on that, Joanna knew she needed to take him by surprise and come after him with overwhelming force.

From the way he was scrabbling along, occasionally crying out in pain and cursing as he slammed into some unexpected obstacle, Joanna realized they were in luck. Lucas really was running blind. He had been in the dark far longer than she and Jaime had, especially since they had just extinguished their flashlights. That meant his eyes would be better adjusted and his vision would be marginally better than theirs would be. But if Lucas was more comfortable in the dark, that gave Joanna a chance to turn light into a weapon.

With that in mind, she tightened her grip on the business end of the new Mag-Tac LED flashlight Butch had given her for Christmas. Fingering the device in the dark, she located the switch that would activate the strobe light function. For someone who had grown accustomed to moving in utter darkness, she hoped the flashing strobe would be both blinding and disorienting. The problem was, it might disorient her as well. She hoped that Jaime, farther away from the light, would be somewhat less affected. He was Joanna's second line of defense.

Lucas was much closer now, running headlong in her direction. She heard his breath coming in ragged gulps. She waited until she was sure he was almost on her. Even then, she counted to three before she pushed the switch on the strobe and stepped away from the sheltering rock wall. He came bearing down on her, dancing in awkward jerks like some devil made incarnate before stumbling to a sudden stop. That was the moment when Joanna switched on the full beam of the powerful flashlight, shining it directly into his eyes. Blinded, he took a single swing at her, but he didn't come close to connecting.

That one missed blow provided all the incentive Joanna needed. Brandishing the heavy flashlight like a club, she swung it through the air and grunted in satisfaction as her very first well-aimed blow connected with Lucas in a dull, bone-breaking thud. He tumbled to the ground like a crumpled rag doll.

"Great work, boss!" Jaime exclaimed, coming out of hiding and aiming his own flashlight at their fallen quarry. "You nailed him."

"Keep an eye on him," Joanna ordered. "I need to check something."

When Joanna knelt down beside Lucas, she shined the light on his face at the stream of blood flowing from the cut her flashlight had left on his cheekbone. He was still wearing the same blue track suit that she had seen him wearing on several earlier occasions. It was far worse for wear now—torn, tattered, and stained with a layer of reddish dust. Reaching for the sleeve, she pulled it up, baring Lucas's forearm. The web-scape of scratches marring the pale skin were exactly what she had expected to find. The wounds appeared to come in several layers with the older ones scabbed over while some of the newer ones were still draining. When Joanna pulled up the second sleeve, the damage on that arm mirrored what she had seen on the first.

She shoved him hard in the ribs. The blow wasn't hard enough to do any damage, but it was enough to rouse him. Lucas groaned. His eyes blinked open.

"Where is she, you worthless punk?" Joanna demanded, shouting the words into his face. "Where's Ruth? What have you done to your sister?"

By then two flashlights were trained full on his face. Lucas squinted up at Joanna through the moving beams of light. "I'm not talking to anybody," he said with a sneer. "I don't have to."

Joanna realized then that it hadn't been just an illusion cast by the flickering strobe light that had made Lucas Nolan look like a devil. He really was.

Afraid she might be tempted to hit him again, harder this time, Joanna stepped away. "Cuff him, Jaime," she ordered.

From far up the tunnel, they heard the pounding sound of another set of approaching footsteps. "It's okay, Matt," Joanna called into the darkness. "We've got him in custody."

By the time Matt arrived, Jaime had Lucas in restraints and on his feet. The look of pure hatred Lucas aimed in Joanna's direction was meant to make her squirm with fear. It served only to make her mad as hell.

"Let's read this piece of garbage his rights and get him out of here. Then we need to figure out what the hell he's done to his sister."

Chapter 30

B y the time they made it back to the subway, a crowd had gathered on the plaza. As officers and medics converged on the scene, so did everyone else. Sliding down the concrete bank to get into the ditch had been easy. Getting back up and out was not. A fire department crew equipped with ropes appeared on the scene.

Using a rope and pulling herself hand over hand, Joanna was the first to emerge. Then two firefighters along with Matt Keller and Jaime Carbajal formed a human fire brigade and passed Lucas up to the surface. As soon as he appeared, handcuffed and with blood streaming down his cheek and onto his filthy track suit, his mother managed to slip through the perimeter of officers.

"What have you done to him?" Rebecca screeched, her voice echoing off the canyon walls. "What have you done to my boy?"

Joanna planted herself in Rebecca's path and barred the way. "Your son is under arrest," she announced. "At the moment we'll be charging him with two counts of assault with a deadly weapon, driving without a license, and reckless driving. I expect additional charges will be forthcoming."

"He's only a boy. You can't do this to him," Rebecca objected. "You can't!"

"This is a police matter," Joanna insisted. "Please step back."

As Matt and Jaime came up out of the hole, Rebecca made one further attempt to push past Joanna and reach her son. Joanna stiff-armed her.

"I told you to move back, Mrs. Nolan," Joanna warned. "If you don't, you'll be placed under arrest right along with Lucas and charged with interfering with a police officer."

Matt placed a firm hand on Rebecca's shoulder and steered the still-protesting woman away from the action. Meanwhile Alvin Bernard turned to Joanna. "What assault?" he asked.

"Matt and I were approaching Lucas's house when he tried to run us down with a vehicle. If Matt hadn't jumped for his life and pulled me along with him, we'd both be dead meat by now. We'll hold him on those charges for now, but what you really need to know is there are scratches all over his arms. I sent the crime lab a sample of Rebecca's DNA. Her profile came back as the mother of the male human whose DNA was found on our wounded cat."

Alvin's jaw dropped. "I thought we were looking at Ruth for all this," he said.

"Believe me," Joanna said. "So did I."

"So is Ruth in on it or is she another victim?"

"Good question. It could be she's an accomplice, but I doubt it. It's more likely that she's another victim, too, and we need to find her. I asked Lucas what he had done with his sister. He refused to answer."

Joanna paused before continuing. "What's happening to the wrecked Mazda?"

"I believe a tow truck is on the scene. Why?"

"Have Fred Harding go over that wrecked car with a fine-tooth comb. I have a feeling that's how Lucas smuggled Ruth out of the house—in his mother's car. Jaime was on his way to get a search warrant on the house before I pulled him into the tunnel. Judge Moore is involved in some kind of meeting at the Copper Queen. I'll have Ernie take charge of the search warrant paperwork and handle that. Once Judge Moore signs off, Ernie and Matt can execute the warrant. I'd like to have Casey Ledford in on that as well. She's great for fingerprints, but she's also good at crime scene investigation."

"I take it you think Lucas attacked his sister in their house?"

"I'd bet money on it," Joanna said.

It took time to sort out the logistics. The medics examined Lucas's bleeding jawline and pronounced that, although he would most likely have "a helluva headache," a trip to the ER wasn't necessary. Instead, the boy was hustled into a Bisbee PD patrol car and driven off to police headquarters, accompanied by Jaime Carbajal. Since Matt's vehicle was still parked outside Rebecca Nolan's house up the canyon, Ernie took Matt with him while Joanna summoned Casey.

Vehicles and people dispersed. At last Joanna's car was the only one still there, parked haphazardly next to the subway with the flashers on the light bar still blinking. She was about to leave when Moe Maxwell approached. She hadn't noticed him in the crowd, but when she saw him, she was saddened to see how haggard and lost he looked.

"Someone said you arrested Lucas Nolan. Did he do it?" Moe asked. "Is he the one who murdered Junior?"

This was still an active investigation. Moe was a grieving relative. Even so, Joanna had to be circumspect in her response. "Maybe," she said. "Matt and Ernie are on their way to Lucas's house to execute a search warrant."

"Tell them to look for a rabbit's foot," Moe said.

"What rabbit's foot?"

"Doc Winfield returned Junior's personal effects to us last night, and that's the only thing that's missing— Junior's lucky rabbit's foot. He had it in his pocket when he first came to live with us. He always carried it in his pants pocket during the day and in his pajama pocket at night."

"Thank you for that, Moe," Joanna said, climbing into the Yukon. "If anything comes of this, we'll let you know."

As she turned the key in the ignition she found herself uttering an unlikely prayer. "Please, God, let Lucas Nolan be stupid enough to keep trophies."

She was driving around Lavender Pit when Butch called. Not wanting to mention that someone had deliberately tried to run her down, Joanna tried to put him off. "I'm pretty busy right now," she said.

"I'm sure you are," he agreed, "but I thought I should let you know that I've just skimmed through some of the later stuff in Ruth Nolan's blog. It's unusual in that the earliest stuff is what shows on the welcome page and right after. The first entries are all sweetness and light, but along the way, it morphs into something much darker. You need to read from the back to find the most recent stuff, and that's downright ugly. She refers to the newer material as a collection of 'short stories.' Reading between the lines, you can tell it's coming from someone raised in a totally dysfunctional family. Plenty of physical violence. The father is depicted as a religious lout. The mother sleeps around. And the brother is drawn as a sweet-faced kid who would as soon knife you in the back as look at you. There are plenty of hints that both the kids may have been subjected to sexual abuse."

Joanna was aghast. "That's all in the blog?" she asked.

"That and more," Butch answered grimly. "This is Dear Diary with a really ugly twist. The difference between the first posts and the most recent ones is glaring. I think there must have been some kind of adult oversight when the posting first started. The later entries have little or no adult editorial input, and no adult savvy, either. As I said, the newer, darker posts take some navigating to find. Even so, they garner a lot of attention—four thousand or so readers per entry. From the names on the comments, I'd say there are a lot of kids out there paying attention to Roxie's Place."

Joanna knew the statistics. Most of the kids who run afoul of law enforcement had some sort of sexual abuse lurking in their backgrounds. As Joanna pulled into the lot and parked in a visitors' slot next to Chief Bernard's aging sedan, she asked, "Was there anything in the most recent posts about what's been going on with her this past week?"

"Nothing that jumped out at me. Why?"

"We believe Lucas Nolan may be responsible for his sister's disappearance. We've just taken him into custody. I'm on my way to talk to him right now. Is there anything in the posts that refers to problems between the brother and the sister?"

"Not that I noticed," Butch said, "but if you like, I can go back through the entries again. If I see something, I'll call."

"Thanks."

Inside the reception area at Bisbee PD, a clerk buzzed Joanna through a locked door and into the back of the building. She made her way to the booking area, where a solidly built matron was processing Lucas. Already clothed in an orange jumpsuit, he deposited his other clothing on the counter. When the matron reached for it, Joanna intervened.

"Please use gloves for that," she insisted. "It's possible that shirt contains important DNA evidence. I want all of Mr. Nolan's clothing placed in evidence bags, and I want the scratches and bite marks on his arms—all of them—swabbed for possible evidence as well—one swab and one bag per scratch."

The matron glanced at the complex road map of scrapes and scratches covering Lucas's forearms, then she gave Joanna a scathing look. "Are you kidding? All of these? Do you have any idea how long that will take?"

Joanna shrugged. "I don't care how long it takes," she replied. "I've got all day, and so does he."

"You're not going to find anything," Lucas boasted.

"I'm a cop," she cautioned. "Are you sure you want to talk to me?"

"It doesn't matter," Lucas said. "I'm a kid. What are you going to do to me? Send me to jail? Big deal. At least there they'll give me three meals a day and I won't have to cook them myself."

"Look," Joanna said. "The prosecutor will be here before long. He's the one who decides what the charges will be. If you tell me where to find your sister, I might be able to persuade him to give you a better deal."

"Screw you," Lucas jeered at her as the matron lined him up for his mug shot. "If you're so interested in Ruth, find her your own damned self."

Alvin emerged from his office and beckoned to Joanna. He led her inside and closed the door before he spoke. "I just spoke to Fred, my CSI. He got to the scene of the accident in time to take a look at Rebecca's sedan before the tow truck pulled it out of the ditch. He found a single strand of purple hair in the trunk of the vehicle and something else, too. A patch of something that appears to be vomit. He cut that part of the rug out. Our lab is a joke. I told him to take the hair and the piece of contaminated carpeting out to your CSI people at the Justice Center."

Joanna nodded.

"Of course, you understand that you, Jaime, and Matt will all need to be interviewed about what went on in the tunnel."

"Yes, I do," Joanna said determinedly, "but not right now, not until after we find Ruth Nolan."

Turning her back on Alvin, she left him standing in his office and went back to booking, where the matron was taking Lucas's prints. As Joanna entered the room, she took her phone from her pocket, switched it to record, and set it down on the counter. Lucas was staring at Joanna. The presence of her phone didn't seem to faze him.

"Be sure to collect a DNA swab from his cheek, too," Joanna reminded the matron as she returned Lucas's hard-edged gaze.

"Your sister told me about you," she added, lying through her teeth. "She told me that you like to torture animals in your spare time. You know, burn them, cut them, shred their ears—that sort of thing. Is that true, or is she making things up?"

"My sister's a liar," Lucas said venomously.

"In her blog, she claims she's been molested."

"I already told you. Ruth's always been a liar."

"You're saying she hasn't been molested?"

"I didn't know she put it in her blog. She pretended our dad molested her so we could leave Gallup with our mom. She hated it there."

"I thought you told me yesterday that she was fine with Gallup—that you were the one who hated it there."

"I guess I was mistaken."

"Either that or you were lying. Or are you lying now?"

Lucas pursed his lips and didn't answer. The matron had swabbed his cheek and was starting to work on his arms.

"You don't like your sister very much, do you?"

Again there was no reply.

"So here's the deal," Joanna said. "You're sitting here charged with a couple of felonies. Right now there's a chance you'll be tried as a juvenile and get off with being locked up until you turn eighteen. I understand that you despise your sister. I get that, but I doubt you'd want to hurt her. Help us out here, Lucas. Tell us where she is."

"What happens if I don't?"

"If your sister dies, all bets are off. Chances are you'll get tried as an adult and be sentenced to twenty years or so. Tell me about Junior Dowdle."

The sudden change of direction seemed to catch Lucas off guard. "What about him?"

"Did he like your sister too much, maybe?" Joanna asked. "Did he have a crush on her? Were you jealous of him?"

"Junior was stupid," Lucas said. "Dumb. Why would I be jealous of him? You think that's what happened? I killed him because I was jealous of him? That's the funniest thing I've ever heard."

Lucas started to laugh then, a laughter that was utterly devoid of humor. When the hollow cackle ended, he glared at Joanna in sneering insolence.

"You've got nothing," he declared. "Nothing at all. I'm not telling you a thing."

Joanna knew that she had pushed him as far as she could. He had already been read his rights. This wasn't an official interrogation, but if he called for a lawyer, it would all be over, and she wouldn't be able to continue the conversation. Wanting to prevent that, Joanna walked away. Using a back entrance, she let herself out into the parking lot. Once inside the Yukon, she locked the doors and then sat there with her eyes closed, taking deep breaths and trying to think.

She had understood what was behind the little bastard's last self-satisfied ugly grin. He knew exactly where Ruth was, and he wouldn't tell, no matter what. Joanna suspected that, in all probability, Ruth was already dead, but what if she wasn't? What if there was a chance that she had been injured but was still clinging to life? It was almost noon. If she'd already been gone for most of a day, that meant time was running out.

Chief Bernard had told Joanna that Fred Harding had found a single strand of purple hair in the trunk of Rebecca's wrecked Mazda. A strand of hair in the passenger compartment of the car meant nothing, but in the trunk? People didn't climb into trunks of cars of their own volition. Ruth had been in the trunk of her mother's car because she had been placed there by someone else. It wasn't hard to imagine that she had been unconscious at the time.

All right, Joanna told herself, trying to marshal her thoughts. Lucas put Ruth in the trunk. Then what? He took her someplace and dumped her, but where? He had been at the house, seemingly alone, in the late afternoon on Sunday when Joanna had gone there to talk to him. And he had been home again when his mother came home. He wouldn't have wanted to risk letting Rebecca know that he had taken her Mazda for an unauthorized joy ride. That meant the dumping ground would have to be somewhere fairly close by, someplace Lucas was familiar with, someplace no one was likely to go looking.

And then, as suddenly as if a light had been switched on, Joanna knew. Or at least she thought she knew. The cave where they had found Junior, the one with the glory hole just inside. Lucas knew all about it. It was close by. As long as no one realized Lucas was involved in what had happened to Junior and Star, no one would think to look there. Thanks to Calvin Lee, Joanna knew better.

As soon as that series of thoughts surfaced in her brain, Joanna's fingers sought the ignition key. She swung the Yukon out onto the roadway and merged into the traffic circle. She resisted the urge to turn on the lights. If she was right, she'd arrive at the Dowdle crime scene much sooner if she didn't wait around to summon additional personnel. And if she was wrong? No one would ever know, and Ruth Nolan, wherever she was, would be no worse off than she had been before.

Joanna drove up Highway 80 behind the main business district, pulled an illegal U-turn in a no-passing zone, and parked on the shoulder of the road near where the collection of emergency vehicles had clustered the day they had retrieved Junior Dowdle's body. After turning on both her overhead lights and her emergency flashers, Joanna grabbed her Maglite, jumped out of the vehicle, and scrambled up the wash. That second clump of scrub oak seemed impossibly far away. She clipped her all-important flashlight to her belt so it wouldn't hamper her as she climbed. By the time she reached the shade of the oak grove, she was out of breath; she had a stitch in her side, and her lungs ached with effort, but she was there.

Wanting to help her eyes adjust to the coming change of light, Joanna closed one of them as she made her way through the trees. She was relieved to see that as yet no one had made any effort to repair the damage done during the removal of Junior's body. The iron bars that had been cut away from the mouth of the tunnel still leaned crookedly against the rocky cliff, looking like a pair of wrecked doors that had been knocked off their supporting hinges.

Cautiously, Joanna stepped through the opening and switched on the light. The powerful beam illuminated the whole place, rendering her precaution of closing one eye unnecessary. She moved forward carefully, listening for any sound that would betray the presence of any other being, human or otherwise. She used the powerful beam of light to explore every chink and soaring crevice of the limestone cavern. A few steps from the abyss, she paused. "Ruth," she called. "Ruth Nolan, are you in here?"

For a long moment, all she heard was the hammering of her own heart, but then there was something else—a strange humming noise that was hardly human. She eased her way over to the edge of the drop and aimed the beam of the flashlight down into the hole. At first she wasn't sure what she was seeing. Netting of some kind seemed to have been strung from one side of the hole to the other. Caught in the middle of the net, dangling over the bottom of the hole like some kind of huge landed fish, was a silver figure of some kind.

"Ruth, is that you?"

In answer the figure struggled to move. As Joanna's vision improved, she realized that the silver came from a layer of duct tape that bound the girl's legs together and held her arms imprisoned at her sides. A separate strand of tape formed the gag that covered her mouth.

"Stop!" Joanna ordered. "Do not move! I don't know what's holding the netting in place. If you wiggle around, you might dislodge it. Stay where you are. I'm going out to call for help. My cell phone doesn't have service in here."

Another unintelligible pleading sound came from the bound girl. Joanna didn't need to hear the words to know what she was saying.

"I won't leave you. I promise. I'll be right back."

Joanna had to go only as far as the cave's entrance before she had enough bars to make the call.

"Nine one one, what are you reporting?"

"Sheriff Brady here," she said. "Contact the Bisbee Fire Department. I've found Ruth Nolan. She's trapped in some netting inside the glory hole at the same location where we found Junior Dowdle's body last week. Tell them to hurry. I don't know how strong the netting is or how well it's secured."

Ending the call, she went back into the cave and peered over the edge once more. "I'm back, Ruth," Joanna assured the girl. "I've called the fire department. They've got a team on the way to get you out of there."

Joanna knew that without the unexplained presence of that netting Ruth would have been dead.

The girl made another faint whimpering noise. This time Joanna couldn't guess what was being said, so she answered with what she knew. "Your brother is under arrest," she said. "We believe Lucas is responsible for what happened to Junior Dowdle and also what happened to you."

Twelve feet beneath the rim of the hole, Ruth nodded desperately. Turning the light away from the girl, Joanna studied the netting. It had been fashioned in such a way that anyone falling into the hole would be guided away from landing on the hard ledge ten feet below the surface. Instead, Ruth had slid past that unharmed and now dangled in the void above the remaining twenty-foot drop. Joanna could see where metal eyebolts of some kind had been drilled into the rock surface. After that, carabiners had been used to secure the netting to the bolts. It was an ingenious arrangement that had taken skill, effort, and time.

"Are you hurt?" Joanna asked.

Ruth shook her head. That could have meant either no, she wasn't hurt, or no, she didn't know. In Joanna's estimation, either answer was acceptable.

A thousand questions roiled through Joanna's head. Had Lucas carried her here or had he forced Ruth to walk on her own? If so, had she known what was coming—that he intended to shove her over the edge? Maybe he had simply rolled her into the hole. He must have been so confident of the outcome that he hadn't bothered to stick around long enough to watch her fall. Had he seen the netting, he most certainly would have attempted to cut it down.

Beyond the cave's entrance, Joanna heard a faint wail—the welcome siren from an approaching emergency vehicle.

"They're coming now," Joanna said reassuringly. "They have to climb up from the highway, but they'll be here soon."

She went to the entrance of the cave to meet them and was not in the least surprised that Adam Wilson was the first to arrive.

"Is she alive?" he asked.

Joanna nodded. "Did you do the netting?"

He bit his lip and then shrugged. "I figured it would take the powers that be forever to get around to putting the bars back up and doing it properly. I was afraid some little kid would fall in accidentally in the meantime, so I decided to do something about it. My grandfather always says it's better to beg forgiveness than to ask permission," he added with a self-deprecating grin.

"Well, it worked," Joanna told him. "It worked like gangbusters." Standing on tiptoes, she managed to plant a kiss on the tip of Adam's chin because that was as far as she could reach. "Thank you," she added. "Thank you so much."

"So how about moving out of the way so we can get her out of here?"

He didn't have to say it twice.

Chapter 31

Adam and his crew had come prepared to effect a rescue. They had brought along ropes and gaff hooks, which they used to raise the netting far enough to lift the girl out of it. After Adam kicked Joanna out of the area, it took less than ten minutes before Ruth was removed from the cave and her restraints loosened. Because she was suffering from both hypothermia and dehydration, they stuck a normal saline drip in her arm and wrapped her in warming blankets before placing her in a Stokes basket for the trip down the mountain.

As the loaded ambulance set off for the hospital, Joanna's Yukon followed close behind. At the ER entrance, she made use of her badge and uniform to follow the gurney all the way to the curtained cubicle where they stashed Ruth. Seated at the girl's bedside, she waited while a nurse took the required series of readings. When the nurse left, Ruth turned to Joanna. "How did you find me?"

"Lucky guess," Joanna said. "Can you tell me what happened?"

"I think Lucas tried to kill me," Ruth said. Tears came to her eyes. "Mom left right after I finished your interview. As soon as she was gone, Lucas lit into me. He accused me of ratting him out to you. Why would he think that? Rat him out about what? I tried to tell him I didn't—that I didn't know anything to tell, but he didn't believe me. He gave me a glass of chocolate milk and made me drink all of it even though it tasted funny—bitter, like it was spoiled or something."

"Made you?" Joanna asked.

"Lucas hits me sometimes, if I don't do what he says," Ruth answered quietly. "He told me if I didn't drink it, I'd be sorry."

"You mean he beats you?"

Ruth nodded. "And he would have done it again, so I did what he said, and then I fell asleep. When I woke up, I was sick to my stomach. I was also locked in the trunk of a car—Mom's car, I guess. I fell back asleep. When I woke up again, he was taping my mouth shut."

"You believe Lucas drugged you?" Joanna asked.

Ruth shrugged. "I think so," she said. "He probably used one of Mom's pills—like the one she gave me the other day when I had the cramps. That's what it felt like anyway. When I woke up again, he was carrying me up the hill. My legs were taped. He had me over his shoulder the way firemen carry people out of burning buildings. Then he rolled me into that hole—the same hole Junior was in. I thought I was gonna die. Instead, I landed on something soft, like a hammock. I was there for a long time. It was cold. I was freezing to death, hungry, and thirsty. And then there you were."

Joanna's phone rang. Casey Ledford's name appeared in the window. "Excuse me a minute," she said. "I need to take this." She went back out through the double doors and stood under the outside portico.

"What's up?" Joanna asked. "Did you find anything?"

"You're not going to believe it," he said. "Not in a million years."

"What?"

"They both have trophy cases."

"What do you mean both?"

"Ruth and Lucas," Casey answered excitedly. "We found loose boards in the floor under the beds in both Lucas's room and in Ruth's, too. The stash in Lucas's room included a baseball bat, a cigarette lighter, razor blades, a half-used pack of smokes, three dog collars—including one for a dog named Roxie—and a pink ribbon, too. Sound familiar? Didn't the owners say that Star was wearing a pink ribbon when she disappeared?"

"Yes, they did," Joanna answered.

"Oh," Casey continued. "And a mostly used roll of duct tape."

"What about Ruth's room?" Joanna asked.

"That's where we found the rabbit's foot. It's hard to tell one rabbit's foot from another, but I'm guessing it's Junior's. We also found a Timex watch. It's engraved on the back: 'Happy Birthday, Billy.' No idea who Billy is. Or was."

It didn't matter, not right then. What mattered was that both of them were involved—two evil twins, not one good and one bad. Joanna didn't bother going back into the ER. With the phone still clutched in her hand, Joanna raced for the Yukon. She punched Alvin's number before she turned the key.

"Has Lucas asked for an attorney?"

"Not to my knowledge. Why?"

"Put him in an interview room alone and let him sit there. I'll be there in three minutes. Sooner if I can make it."

"Without a parent with him? Why? What's going on?"

"You ever hear of John E. Reid?"

"Of course," Alvin said. "He's the guy who wrote the book on modern police interrogation. Why?"

"Because I'm on my way to try my hand at a little direct confrontation."

"Okay," Alvin said. "Lucas will be waiting. Do you want someone in the interview room with you?"

"Nope, I'll handle this one solo."

Lucas looked up curiously when Joanna entered the interview room. Then, feigning disinterest, he looked away.

"You'll never guess where I've just been," Joanna said. "At the Copper Queen Hospital—the ER—talking to Ruth." She watched how he responded to the news and was relieved to see the telltale bobbing of the Adam's apple in his scrawny little throat.

"Aren't you going to ask if she's okay?" Joanna continued. "Nah, I guess not, but that's all right. What's interesting is what she's doing right now. She's writing out a confession, Lucas, about how she helped you murder Junior Dowdle."

Lucas's eyes shot up in surprise. "No way!" he said. "I didn't kill him."

"Oh? That's not what Ruth says. And we gave her a great deal. I told her if she testifies against you, she'll probably walk. She says you planned it all in advance.

Premeditation means it's likely that you'll be tried as an adult. If you're lucky, you'll get second-degree homicide rather than first, which means you'll get out of prison when you're a few years short of forty. Think about it. You'll be older than your mom."

"I didn't do it," Lucas insisted. "I already told you. Ruth's a liar. She did it and she's trying to put the blame on me."

"Did what?"

"Pushed Junior over the edge. She told him there was a kitten that was stuck in a hole up on the mountain. He fell for it. Came right out through the window, just like that. He wasn't very good at climbing, and at first he didn't want to go in the hole, but then we told him to listen for the kitten. When he heard it crying, he went right under the bars. Then, once he got inside, he was scared of the dark. He stopped just inside the door and wouldn't go any farther. That's when Ruth sort of helped him along."

"She pushed him?"

"Yeah," Lucas said. "Sort of. She kind of shoved him with the end of a baseball bat."

"Who's Billy?"

Once again, Lucas's surprise was apparent. "How do you know about Billy?" he asked.

"We found your sister's trophies. They included Billy's watch. Who is he?"

"Billy Rojas. Just a kid in Gallup," Lucas said with a shrug. "He was sort of like Junior, only worse. He was in a wheelchair. He thought Ruth was his friend. When we invited him on a picnic with us, he was glad to go because no one ever invited him to do anything. It had rained. The washes were running. His chair went off the edge, and that was it. He drowned. The cops said it was an accident."

Filled with rage, Joanna gripped the edge of the table hard enough that her knuckles turned white. For a moment she said nothing for fear she might simply explode. She had walked into the room carrying a blue-lined notebook and a pen. Forcing herself to be calm about it, she pushed the two items across the table.

Lucas looked at them and frowned. "What are these for?" he asked.

"They're for you to write down what you just told me," she said. "Write it down and sign it."

"Why should I?"

"Because the first one to confess always gets a better deal."

"But you just told me Ruth had already confessed."

"Yes, I did," Joanna said. "I guess I lied."

When Joanna buzzed to be allowed out of the interview room, Alvin Bernard was waiting outside. "I already called Matt Keller," he said. "He's on his way to the hospital right now. And I checked with the ER.

They've admitted Ruth overnight for observation. We'll make the arrest there, and I'll post a guard outside her room."

"If you need any help with staffing, call me," Joanna said. "I'm sure I can spare a deputy or two overnight."

They arrived at the hospital in a multivehicle entourage that looked more like a parade than any kind of police activity. Matt Keller and Ernie Carpenter covered the outside exits in case someone was stupid enough to try making a run for it.

When they found Ruth's room, Rebecca was sitting next to the bed, looking out at the dull red tailings dump that rose up outside the window, blocking everything else from view. When Joanna entered, Rebecca frowned and stood up.

"What are you doing here?" Rebecca demanded. "This is a hospital room. Ruth's been through a terrible ordeal. She's supposed to be resting."

Ruth was lying on the bed with her purple hair fanned out across the pillow. She smiled brightly at Joanna. "It's okay, Mom. I told you. Sheriff Brady is the one who found me. If it weren't for her, I might be dead."

Joanna didn't smile back. "I've just been to see your brother," she said curtly. "When I left him he was writing out a full confession, explaining exactly how you lured Junior out of his room on the pretext of rescuing a kitten and then how you pushed him over the edge of the cliff with a baseball bat. Ruth Nolan, you're under arrest for the murder of Junior Dowdle."

Without a word, Alvin Bernard produced a pair of handcuffs. He slipped one on Ruth's thin wrist and fastened the other to the metal railing on her hospital bed.

"This can't be happening," Rebecca hissed. "It's impossible. You're crazy. My kids are good kids. They would never do such a thing!"

"Lucas is lying," Ruth insisted desperately. "Lucas always does that—he does bad stuff and tries to put the blame on me."

Joanna studied her, remembering the purple-haired sweet-faced girl who had sat in the backseat of Joanna's Yukon the day before, supposedly doing an interview of the local sheriff for her innocent-sounding blog. The old story of a serial killer inserting herself into an investigation was such a cliché that Joanna almost wanted to puke.

"No such luck, sweetheart," Joanna said. "This time the blame's all on you."

Chapter 32

As soon as Joanna left the hospital, the shakes hit her. It was all she could do to start the SUV and put it in gear. When her cell phone rang, it took four crows of the rooster to wrestle the damned thing out of her pocket.

"Where are you?" Kristin asked.

"Just leaving the hospital. I'm going over to the restaurant to tell Moe and Daisy what's happened. I want them to hear it from me first. Then I'm coming back to the office. What's happening there?"

"Tom Hadlock is putting together a press conference. He's planning on holding it here since we have more parking than Bisbee PD does. A lot has happened this afternoon. If you have a minute, Tom would like you to give him a briefing."

"Okay," Joanna said.

"And there are some people here to see you. Liza Machett is in the break room, and Roger Stephens just went out back to have a smoke."

"Roger Stephens of the U.S. Marshals Service? What's he doing here?"

"I asked him that, but he wouldn't tell me. He said it was confidential."

"Figures," Joanna said. "He'll have to wait. I'll talk to him when I get there, but right now I've got something important for you to do. It's time to celebrate, and we're having a party. I want you to order a dozen pizzas and put them in the break room. There isn't a single person in the department who hasn't put in extra time and effort this week. Besides, I haven't eaten since breakfast, and I'm starving."

Talking to Moe and Daisy was tough. Joanna gave them the news in Daisy's little office just off the kitchen. They were relieved, of course, and Joanna had to refrain from telling them that this was barely the beginning. Signed confessions or not, it would be months or even years from now before Lucas and Ruth Nolan would be held accountable for their crimes. For Moe and Daisy there would be no closure and no way to put the terrible wrong done to their beloved Junior right.

When Joanna arrived at the Justice Center forty-five minutes later, she wasn't at all surprised to see two enormous black Cadillac Escalades idling in the no-parking zone directly in front of the sheriff department's front entrance. The passenger windows were tinted to the point that it was impossible to see if anyone was inside. A guy in a dark suit and tie stood leaning casually against the driver's door of one vehicle. A woman in a similarly dark pantsuit leaned against the tailgate of the second one.

Grumbling under her breath, Joanna drove around back only to find a man she assumed to be Roger Stephens, also dressed in a suit and tie, leaning against the building directly in front of her reserved covered parking place. A shiny pair of snakeskin boots peeked out from beneath the hem of his trousers. The sidewalk around his feet was littered with cigarette butts.

"The smoking area is around to the side of the building," she said pointedly. "Away from the doors."

"There's no shade over there," he objected.

That was true, and it was also deliberate. No shade meant less smoking.

"What do you want?"

"I have a name for you," he said. "Richard Ransom."

"Who's he?"

"A former FBI agent from Boston, Massachusetts, who's now three small steps down from the secretary of the Treasury. Seems as though, back in the early eighties, Ransom was the only one of the guys involved in the Miller mess who was considered to be squeaky clean. Turns out, that's only because no one ever came forward to rat him out. He was also on Anson Machett's payoff delivery route.

"Funniest thing, when Anson was coming into witness protection, he never blew the whistle on Richard. There isn't one mention of him in Anson's file. Shortly after Lyle came into the program, someone began putting the bite on Mr. Ransom, and he's been paying the toll ever since. He sent money to a numbered account in the Cayman Islands without ever realizing that Anson Machett was the guy on the receiving end."

"So Lyle's been living in witness protection and making money by blackmailing people?"

"By blackmailing one person only," Stephens said. "At least as far as we know right now. Lyle faked the books and laundered his ill-gotten gains by using the blackmail money to make improvements and pay salaries at the Whetstone Retreat. When Cesar Flores's report about those old bills showed up, it was passed on to Ransom as a routine report. He looked at the evidence, figured out that Anson was probably the blackmailer, and started calling in favors, trying to get a line on where he was."

Stephens paused, took one last drag on his smoke, and then tossed the butt on the ground. "How am I doing so far?"

Joanna stopped and stared at Agent Stephens. "Fine about everything but the smoking," she said. "How the hell did you put this together so fast?"

"I didn't. It turns out Ransom was already under investigation. The FBI—the new FBI—was already working a program on him in a very hush-hush fashion. As soon as I started asking questions about this overnight, it rattled their chains, and they fell all over themselves trying to help me. They had a lot of the pieces, including contacts with various known hit men. They had put most of it together, but they were waiting for the final piece to fall into place before taking Ransom down. You provided that missing piece—Lyle Morton."

"Where is he?"

"He's under guard and in one of the cars you saw parked out front," Stephens said. "People don't get to stay in witness protection if we find out they're conducting criminal enterprises. We'll be flying him back to D.C. tonight."

"What about my murder charges?"

"We've located what we believe are the two hit men who were used here. They were placed under arrest in Tucson earlier this afternoon. You'll get them as the doers for your homicide."

"If somebody in the FBI knew this was going down, why didn't they stop it before Guy Machett was murdered?"

"Sorry," Stephens said, shaking his head regretfully. "I can't answer for the FBI."

"What about bringing Ransom here to face conspiracy and homicide charges?"

Stephens grinned at her. "Not gonna happen," he said. "You'll have to take a number and get in line."

"What are you doing here, then?"

"Lyle says his daughter is here—Liza. He wanted to come here to say good-bye. We're not wheels up for another three hours. I figured what the hell? If she wants to see him, why not?"

"Does she want to see him?"

"Beats me. None of your people would talk to me or let me see her. I believe the words your detective used were 'I can't possibly divulge that information.' Was she by any chance listening in on our conversation last night?"

"It was Detective Howell's phone," Joanna told him. "It's possible we were on speaker at the time."

Joanna let herself into her office with Agent Stephens on her six. "Wait here," she said, pointing at one of the captain's chairs. "I'll see if she wants to talk to you or to Anson Machett."

Joanna left him there, then detoured into the bullpen, where she found Deb at her desk, pounding away on a keyboard.

"I heard about Lucas and Ruth," Deb said. "Great job!"

"Where's Liza Machett?"

"In the break room."

"Lyle Morton is outside."

"I know," Deb said. "The marshals have him in custody."

"Does she want to talk to him?"

Deb shrugged her shoulders. "Beats me. Ask her."

Joanna started away, then she stopped. "Before I do, what kind of cancer does she have?"

"None," Deb said. "As in not any. The bald head and the scarf are part of her disguise."

"Disguise?"

"Somebody put her in touch with a group of people, mostly long-haul truckers, I believe, who help victims of domestic violence escape their abusers. Shaving her head and wearing a scarf was an added bit of camouflage. Nobody stares at cancer patients. It's rude."

"Okay then," Joanna said.

She made her way to the break room. Liza Machett, no longer wearing her scarf, was sitting on the frayed sofa, staring up at a flat-screen TV set where Judge Judy was busy declaiming her decision and blasting the two losers who had each accused the other of skipping out on a lease agreement. She looked up as Joanna entered.

"I already know he's outside," Liza said quietly. "I know he wants to talk to me. The hell with him. He already told you that he thought I wasn't his, and the feeling's mutual. I have no idea who my father is, but it sure as hell isn't him!"

Joanna was impressed. Liza may have lost almost everything and everybody, but she hadn't lost herself. Maybe it was true—the truth had set her free.

"Okay," Joanna said. "I'll go tell him."

She reversed course.

"Wait," Liza called after her. "What about the money? Do I have to give it back?"

"Not as far as I'm concerned," Joanna said. "I have it on good authority that the guy who was looking for you and the money is about to be taken into custody."

"All right," Liza said. "Good."

"Do you know where you're staying tonight?" Joanna asked. "There's a lot to talk over."

"Deb . . . Detective Howell said I should stay at the Copper Queen, but I didn't know if I could—if I'd still have money."

"You have money," Joanna assured her. "Not to worry. Sleep as late as you want. We all have a funeral to attend in the morning. We'll talk in the afternoon."

Joanna went back to her office. Roger Stephens was sitting in the chair where she'd left him, dozing. He started awake when she walked into the room.

"Liza's not interested in saying good-bye. She says to tell Anson Machett to go to hell."

"Fair enough," Stephens said, rising to his feet. "Can't say I blame her."

Chapter 33

By eight thirty the next morning, Joanna was in her office. Dressed in her formal uniform, she was trying to sort through the masses of resulting paperwork when Kristin knocked on her door. "There's someone out here to see you," she said. "Reverend Derek Nolan."

Joanna looked up from her desk. She was a long way from geared up to face down an accused child molester, but if he was here, it was time. "Send him in," she said, rising. "Ask Detective Carbajal to join us."

She suspected that if Jaime didn't like someone messing with kittens, he would go ballistic over someone who abused children.

The man who entered Joanna's office was tall and thin, and he looked a bit timid. "I'm sorry to disturb you, Sheriff Brady," he said. "I understand you're due to go to a funeral. If this is a bad time . . ."

"No, it's fine," she said. "Have a seat. I've asked one of my detectives to sit in on our chat."

Derek nodded and eased himself onto one of the visitors' chairs. "That's fine. I wanted to know if it would be possible to see my children. The hospital said that Ruth was being kept under a police guard and wasn't allowed visitors. I believe Lucas is here—in your jail."

Joanna returned to her seat and faced Derek. "The charges lodged against your son are very serious, Mr. Nolan. I thought about transferring him to the juvenile detention center, but the victim, Junior Dowdle, was very well liked here in town. Feelings are running high. I thought Lucas would be more secure here than there, at least until his arraignment. He is, of course, being kept segregated from the adult jail population."

Derek nodded again. "I understand," he said. "Will I be able to see him?"

Joanna remembered the material that Butch had unearthed in Ruth's blog—entries that indicated that both twins had most likely been subjected to sexual abuse. She was considering how to play this when Jaime tapped on the door and let himself into the room.

"This is Detective Carbajal," Joanna said, "and this is Reverend Nolan." The two men shook hands briefly.

"Will my daughter be brought here, too, when she's released from the hospital?" Derek asked.

"Most likely," Joanna said.

Joanna looked from Jaime to Derek. The man may have abused his children, but it hadn't happened here in Cochise County. If he was brought up on charges in the future, it wouldn't be her case. That meant she had nothing to lose.

"Ruth claims you abused her," Joanna said simply. "She says you molested both her and her brother."

"I'm not surprised," Derek said, nodding quietly. "I expected this. It's not the first time she's made that accusation."

"You're saying it's not true?"

"Categorically. If you'd like me to take a polygraph test, I'll be glad to. Name the time and the place."

"Why would she say such a thing if it weren't true?"

Derek Nolan sighed. "Because my daughter is evil," he said. "Utterly evil. Both my children are."

"This sounds suspiciously like an abuser attempting to push the blame off on his victims."

Derek pursed his lips. "Rebecca and I met and started dating in high school. She was a year older than I was. She went off to college a year ahead of me and went completely wild—drinking, drugs, you name it, she did it, so we broke up. A couple of years later, someone told me she'd gone through treatment and cleaned up her act. Eventually we got back together, married, and had the twins. A few years later, I was working as an accountant in Dallas when I realized that what I really wanted to do was be a minister. We moved to Missouri and I started going to seminary. That's when she fell off the wagon."

"A relapse?" Joanna asked.

"Big-time," Derek said. "And not just drinking and drugs, either. I found out she was screwing around behind my back. I started to divorce her. She begged me to take her back, so I gave her another chance. I thought when I got my first assignment and we moved away from the friends who were such a bad influence on her that things would get better. They didn't."

"Geographical cures hardly ever work," Jaime observed.

Derek nodded. "And it got worse and worse. She came into some money—a small inheritance from her grandmother—and she was off and running again. She didn't care how it looked or how it would affect me or the kids. Finally, she gave me no choice. I divorced her.

"Then one day last spring, she came into my office at the church and told me that she and her boyfriend were moving to Bisbee, Arizona. The boyfriend was bad news, a sometime silversmith with a drug habit.

I told her she couldn't—that we had joint custody of the kids and that she couldn't take them out of state without my written permission, which I wasn't going to give. That night, I found this under my pillow."

He reached into the pocket of his sports jacket, pulled out a worn envelope, and handed it over. Looking at it, Joanna saw the word "Daddy" scrawled in pencil.

"Open it," Derek urged. "Read it."

Joanna opened the envelope and extracted a piece of lined notebook paper. "If you don't let us go to Arizona, I'll go to the cops and tell them you molested me and tortured Lucas. Let us go or else."

The note was unsigned. Joanna looked back at Derek when she finished reading it. "This is Ruth's handwriting?"

Derek nodded. Two tears leaked out from under his eyelids and ran down his cheeks. He brushed them away with his sleeve. "I never touched her, I swear," he said. "Not once. Not ever. And I never hurt Lucas, either. The next day, I tried to talk to her about it. Ruth looked at me with those icy blue eyes of hers and said, 'They'll believe me, Daddy. They'll never believe you.'

"That's when I realized how truly wicked she was, but I also knew she was right. I wouldn't even have to be found guilty in a court of law. Just being accused of such a thing would mean that I'd lose my job and my life. They'd never give me another church. So I signed the permission document and they left to come here."

Joanna studied his face. There was no tell—only anguish. And this was the same story Lucas had told—that Ruth lied when she didn't get her way.

"Tell me about Billy Rojas," she said quietly.

"Billy? He was one of the kids from church. A sad case—wheelchair bound, not much of a family life. I was proud when Ruth and Lucas took him under their wing, but then he died. The three of them were out in the desert behind our house. There was a flash flood. The bank gave way and Billy drowned."

"Your children are killers, Reverend Nolan," Joanna said. "They keep trophies. We found the probable murder weapon in the Dowdle case hidden under the floorboards in Lucas's room and we found the victim's rabbit's foot hidden under the floorboards in Ruth's room. We found other things there as well, including a watch that I believe belonged to Billy Rojas."

For a moment Joanna gazed at Derek's shock-stricken eyes across the expanse of desk. "They had Billy's watch?" he asked numbly.

Joanna nodded.

"You're saying they're responsible for Billy's death, too?"

"Yes."

"Oh, my God," Derek breathed, shaking his head and almost sliding off the chair in grief. "I'm sorry," he murmured over and over. "So sorry for everything. I thought I had done a better job of raising them than that."

He didn't attempt to say that his children couldn't possibly have done what she said. He didn't have to. Joanna could see that he knew they had and he believed everything she had just told him.

Eventually, Derek lurched to his feet. "May I see Lucas now?" he asked.

Joanna nodded. Glancing at her watch, she picked up the phone and dialed Pamela Reyes, her new jail commander. "Reverend Derek Nolan is here to see his son, Lucas," she said. "I'll ask Kristin to take him over to the jail. Detective Carbajal and I have a funeral to attend."

By eleven o'clock that morning, St. Dominick's was filled to capacity, standing room only. Since Butch was one of the pallbearers, Joanna wasn't able to sit with him. Instead, she sat with Denny squirming beside her, trying to quell her frayed nerves. Joanna hadn't found out about Moe and Daisy's request until she finally got home late on Monday night. They had called the house earlier that evening to ask if Jenny would consider singing a solo at Junior's funeral. The song they wanted her to sing was his all-time favorite, "Jesus Loves Me."

Joanna hadn't admitted to anyone what Jason Radner had told her about that very song being the one Ruth Nolan had sometimes sung outside Junior's window. For all Joanna knew, she might well have used that very song as a tool to lure the poor man to his death. Joanna's reason for keeping silent was simple—she didn't want to betray Jason Radner's confidence, and she wouldn't unless a trial made it absolutely necessary. At the moment, Arlee Jones, the county prosecutor, was lobbying for plea agreements.

When it came time in the service for Jenny to step up beside Junior's flower-draped casket, Joanna held her breath. After a moment's pause, Jenny raised a hand-held mic to her lips and then, with incredible poise, began to sing a cappella. As Jenny's sweet soprano voice drifted through the church, filling it with the words of that beloved children's song, it was too much for her mother. An uncontrollable sob welled up in Joanna's throat. She tried her best to stifle it, but she didn't succeed completely. As tears rolled unchecked down her cheeks, Denny reached up and patted her face.

"It'll be okay, Mommy," he whispered in her ear. "Please don't cry."

About the Author

J. A. Jance is the *New York Times* bestselling author of the J. P. Beaumont series, the Joanna Brady series, the Ali Reynolds series, and four interrelated thrillers about the Walker family, as well as a volume of poetry. Born in South Dakota and brought up in Bisbee, Arizona, Jance lives with her husband in Seattle, Washington, and Tucson, Arizona.

HARPER LUXE

THE NEW LUXURY IN READING

We hope you enjoyed reading
our new, comfortable print size and found it
an experience you would like to repeat.

Well – you're in luck!

HarperLuxe offers the finest in fiction and
nonfiction books in this same larger print size and
paperback format. Light and easy to read, HarperLuxe
paperbacks are for book lovers who want to see
what they are reading without the strain.

For a full listing of titles and
new releases to come, please visit our website:

www.HarperLuxe.com